THE DOCTOR

The Pure One quivered.
He knew what she was.
her patient, Agnes Shultz, she had created her. He had seen the doctor in her office that day, and he'd watched the people going in and out. As some sat innocently in the waiting room, the doctor turned the others into victims. Then she came out for the next one and he could see the blood on her teeth. And on the necks of the poor innocents that came out he could see the red fang marks she'd left.

But they had to wait. He had to get the Vampire Queen first . . .

BLOOD WORK

*A terrifying novel of psychological suspense
by Fay Zachary,
author of* Fertility Rights

"Fay Zachary manages to find and explore another dimension of 'vampirism' . . . Her characters 'feed' off each other in such a way that they are all too familiar to us, perhaps reminding us mostly of what our mirrors reveal. She has introduced unique kinks into ways of dealing with death and with love . . ."
—JESSE SLATTERY,
author of *The Juliet Effect*

BLOOD WORK

FAY ZACHARY

B
BERKLEY BOOKS, NEW YORK

If you purchased this book without a cover, you should be aware that this book is stolen property. It was reported as "unsold and destroyed" to the publisher, and neither the author nor the publisher has received any payment for this "stripped book."

BLOOD WORK

A Berkley Book / published by arrangement with
the author

PRINTING HISTORY
Berkley edition / January 1994

All rights reserved.
Copyright © 1994 by Fay Zachary.
Cover illustration by Joanie Schwarz.
This book may not be reproduced in whole or in part,
by mimeograph or any other means, without permission.
For information address: The Berkley Publishing Group,
200 Madison Avenue, New York, New York 10016.

ISBN: 0-425-14047-4

BERKLEY®
Berkley Books are published by
The Berkley Publishing Group, 200 Madison Avenue,
New York, New York 10016.
BERKLEY and the "B" design are trademarks of
Berkley Publishing Corporation.

PRINTED IN THE UNITED STATES OF AMERICA

10 9 8 7 6 5 4 3 2

DEDICATION

In memory of my father, Harry Bortz,
who taught me the joy of imagining.

ACKNOWLEDGMENTS

My heartfelt thanks to the following:

Norine Dresser, for writing *American Vampires,* the book that inspired this story.

John L. Myers, for writing his novel and critiquing mine.

Gary L. Hoff, M.D., for his heart-stopping medical knowledge.

Lee Goodwin, auto maven, for all his expertise on vans and driving.

Bill Clede, Tony Mandile, and Earl Shelsby, for taking me by computer on a turkey hunt and teaching me how to shoot.

Eleanor Lyon Duke, for taking me on a genealogical adventure.

James A. Zachary (no relation), for his description of a charming genealogist who might make a good amateur detective.

The sun shall be turned to darkness and the moon to blood . . .
—Joel 2:30

PROLOGUE

The Woman in 202 Window

Philadelphia—fall, 1985

Pain stirred in Ruth's belly. She woke, sat up in the semidarkness. The pain, chased by its accompanying nightmare, seemed to bang around the hospital room and flail against the large plate glass window before melting through it like a ghost. She gasped, holding her belly, unsure that the pain had been real.

After a moment, she sighed and lay back against the slightly raised head of the hospital bed and listened to the snoring of the woman in the bed by the door. The woman claimed she never slept. It was Ruth who didn't sleep. How could she? The snoring never ceased. The bed sheets could never be smoothed beneath Ruth's elbows. The reddened skin on her elbows could never be smoothed by the sweet-smelling, sticky lotion they gave her. And dead flakes of skin on her back where the nurse had slapped on some lotion and rubbed for ten seconds, had pilled like a worn sweater, felt crumbly, irritated her.

Earlier they had given her phenobarbital. It had finally taken the edge off her aggravation. She was not sure how long she had dozed before the pain stirred. Now, with that hateful snoring, the wrinkled sheets, she might as well have not slept at all. A terrible tension seized her. She muffled a tiny cry, fought it off, and tried to go back to sleep.

Suddenly, her belly seized up, cramped down. For a moment she was so wracked with pain that her jaw trapped her cries. Then she screamed. With a spray of gathered saliva, her cries split the air in room 202, and broke through her roommate's sleep. The roommate's echoing scream brought the night nurse running.

The nurse took in the scene with a glance that swept past the frightened woman in the bed by the door and clicked on Ruth. "What happened?" she said to Ruth; "What happened . . . ?" A quick swivel of her head to the roommate.

The roommate huddled the bedclothes around her shoulders and shook her head.

Ruth, her pale face slick with icy sweat, tried to speak, but couldn't. Pain, now a thrashing alligator, gripped her belly; she could only cry out again.

The nurse flicked on a blinding light and ran toward Ruth. She read where the pain was from Ruth's strained position, from where her hands clutched at her gown. She read the pain's severity in Ruth's working mouth and frightened eyes. "What happened?" she said again, and set to finding out for herself. Tearing the bedclothes off, freeing Ruth's gown from her fingers, pulling the gown up to Ruth's chest, she exposed the abdominal dressing.

No bright red blood. Just the usual brown tinges near the incision line and an iodine stain along one strip of adhesive tape. Three full days had passed since Ruth's gallbladder surgery. She'd been up on her own several times in the past two days. Today, she'd eaten most of her scrambled egg and toast supper, leaving only her vanilla pudding. After just a few spoonfuls, that had cloyed. She'd coifed her brown hair to prepare for visiting hours this evening when Lionel had come with their two teenage daughters. They had all laughed a lot together, then laughed with tears in their eyes, because laughing hurt her and they were moved because she was such a good sport.

Since having her surgery, she'd barely complained about anything except the stertorous nighttime racket in the next bed. A good patient.

"OK. Tell me what happened. Show me where it hurts." Taking no chances, the nurse pulled out her bandage scissors and cut away the outer gauze dressing. The inner dressing was barely colored with serum and spots of blood. She peeled that back, too. The five-inch incision looked good, its edges neatly pulled together with intradermal sutures and sealed with clear plastic tape. A tidy job—typical of Dr. Bob Ryan's handiwork.

Ruth's hands gestured globally over her abdomen. Her belly was tight, though not distended. The nurse did not need her stethoscope to hear its rumble.

"Have you moved your bowels since surgery?"

Ruth nodded. "A little." Then: "I was afraid to push."

The nurse nodded knowingly. "Well, gas after surgery can be pretty bad. That's probably what it is. But I'll get Dr. Sanders, the surgical resident. I'm sure she'll say the same thing, though."

"If it's gas, it's the worst gas I've ever had." The nurse's calm manner helped reassure her, and the pain seemed to ease slightly.

"But it's the first time you've ever had your gallbladder out," said the nurse, as she patted Ruth's hand. She smiled, then left the room, promising to return with Dr. Sanders.

Dr. Sanders came quickly, and she did say the same thing the nurse had. After glancing at Ruth's chart, she added, "I see you've had trouble sleeping, too." Then she turned to the nurse. "Did she get the phenobarbital Dr. Ryan ordered?"

"Yes."

"Well, maybe a second dose will help. How about it, Ruth?"

"If it'll take care of the pain."

"We'll give you a combination of phenobarb and belladonna. That should relax your gut and help get rid of the gas."

Ruth sighed. "Hurry, please."

Three hours later the pain seized Ruth again. Her jaws locked again, grinding and spewing saliva. She could manage only agonized grunts. Her body slipped from her control. White coated saviors—wheedling, exhorting—descended upon her room; she flailed against them; they milled around, resorted at last to their restraints and needles. She heard Dr. Sanders say, "Dr. Ryan says we can't take a chance. We'll have to take a look inside."

A few minutes later they wheeled her, strapped into her bed, to the green-gowned and masked ones in the operating room. They bent over her for the second time in three days. Smiles in their eyes, murmurs blowing softly beneath their masks, furrows knitting their brows to their caps, they filled her veins with dark peace.

With consciousness, pain came again, slightly subdued, less angry.

"There's nothing physically wrong in your abdomen. Nothing was bleeding inside. It was healing well from the gallbladder surgery. We took your appendix out, just in case, this time. And gave you a pint of blood to replace what you lost in the surgeries." Dr. Sanders, her young face as creased and lined and tired looking as her scrub gown, bent over her. "We'll run more tests. . . ."

"It's not all in my head." Hollow-voiced hope. Shame that her mind had caused them all such trouble.

Dr. Sanders patted Ruth's shoulder. "Of course not. It's very real to you." That was not a lie. She knew it was real *to Ruth*.

Ruth understood.

◆ ◆

Phillip Trapp, The Lordly One, glanced away from the spinning centrifuge. His eyes fell on the rack of vials at the rear of his lab bench. He focused on the flask at the far right end of the rack. With eyes that looked like ponds scummed with blue-green algae, he focused through his thick lenses. The urine specimen had begun to change.

He had left the beaker standing for twenty-four hours before he would throw the sample away. It was a habit he'd developed in the last few weeks after seeing the Halloween television interview of the doctor, about the rare disease, porphyria. The doctor had figured out the truth. Porphyria deformed people's mouths and teeth, and made them hate garlic. Porphyria made light hurt their eyes, so they came out only at night. And it made them hungry for blood, because only blood could cure their terrible pain. They would do anything to get blood. They would sink their fangs into innocent throats and suck the blood. That's what stained their teeth. They had to do what they did.

Couldn't help it. The pain would be awful if they didn't; they might even die. *And there was no cure!* The doctor said so.

Phillip knew there was a cure. A cure most doctors refused to use. He had learned it when he was a child, when he, The Lordly One, had cured one. Even then, he'd known they were sick in their blood. He'd never told anyone that, because they wouldn't believe him. Only a Pure One could have received the sign. Everyone else would need scientific proof.

Well, now they had it! They'd believe that the doctor knew what he was talking about. He was, after all, a scientist; on the television program he was even wearing his lab smock, which was like the one Phillip wore now, but was longer and crisper. And he was on a network news interview, not "Twilight Zone." And there was one of them there with him, too. While the doctor was talking, Phillip had his eyes on her. She began to change before his eyes. The others, even the doctor, didn't seem to notice. Her teeth, the doctor was saying, were beautiful and straight. He didn't seem to see that when she smiled, they began to grow. Her lips and gums curled back, making them seem larger still. Then she smiled at Phillip through the screen and he could see the saliva run from the corners of her mouth. She was hungry, hungry for blood. And the doctor didn't see. The doctor smiled back at her and leaned toward her and patted her hand, without even noticing the claws her fingers were becoming. The doctor wasn't pure enough to notice. He turned his vulnerable neck to speak to the television interviewer, and the vampire sank her fangs into his throat and drank and drank and drank. Then she sat back in her chair and looked human again, twenty-four years old, with beautiful straight teeth. What a fool the doctor was, after all, insisting there was no cure! Every disease had a cure, if one was willing to apply it.

Phillip was willing. And now that he knew how to find people with porphyria, the vampire disease, he would seek them out and cure them before anyone was the wiser. He had been given a sign! And he would be in the right place to find them—in a hospital diagnostic laboratory, where he worked as a technician. And he would be in the right place to cure them, too—in the hospital pathology laboratory, where he worked as a diener and helped clean up after autopsies. His presence in the morgue never had been questioned, and what he did with corpses never had been noticed.

So, in the diagnostic lab he had begun reserving patients' leftover urine specimens after ordered tests were done. Just small flasks, set at the back of his lab bench in a rack. With them he left a note asking the next shift of techs not to toss them out; then he could check them the next day. That would allow enough time.

When nothing had happened with any of them until now, he'd thrown the specimens away, and drawn a line through the name of the patient on his notepad. They had all been clean. That was to be expected. It might take months or years before one turned up. But whenever any of them did, he'd be ready to take care of them.

He stood still now for a moment, in thrall, as if his mind were whirling in the laboratory centrifuge, separating out and congealing the most important elements of his thoughts. His hard, bony hand trembled slightly as he reached for the flask, lifted it, twisted it so he could view it from every angle. He could see his thin smile reflected in the glass, his reflection bobbing with the port wine colored liquid. Below the liquid's surface, his face looked fuller, less pale than it was; above it his brow looked grotesquely narrow beneath his spiky crew cut. In reality his lower face and jaw were thin, his brow was wide and high. And it looked more so because his colorless hair was clipped short, almost shaved, at the sides, and the joints of his skull bones protruded and the veins showed through. He was nearly as grotesque as the reflection, but it was an effect more to his liking; people drew back when they saw him.

It was not the reflection, though, that brought a phlegmy sheen to his eyes, it was the liquid itself. He had not expected to find one so soon. He was not even ready yet. He had not thought out all the details. He had not even plated the steel.

◆ ◆

A fading of the pain, the discharge of her roommate, and a change to a sleeping pill that really worked, had combined to put Ruth in good spirits a few days later. Her second incision ached, and the first had begun to itch, but these seemed minor annoyances. She found her humor improved to the point that she laughed when, late in the evening after Lionel and the girls had left after visiting hours, Dr. Ryan handed her a psychiatrist's business card. "In case you want to discuss the trauma you've been through here—with two operations in less than a week."

"Or the pain that was 'in my head'?"

He patted her arm. "It was real. And the surgery cured it. As sometimes happens for reasons we can only guess at. But, well, you might get blue, you know. It won't hurt to talk to someone. Dr. Murphy's easy to talk to." He patted her arm again and left the room.

Lionel is easy to talk to, too, she thought, and smiled. *And he doesn't charge a hundred and fifty dollars an hour.*

A brief time later, the evening nurse brought Ruth her sleeping pill and talked to her while she smoothed the unsmoothable sheets. Ruth then watched television till she felt her eyes and head grow heavy. Too tired to lift the remote control from her lap to turn off the set, she began to doze. Someone came into the room, lowered the head of the bed, turned off the lights and the television, tiptoed out of the room, and closed the door.

Ruth sighed and welcomed the quiet darkness.

She slept without dreaming for a few hours, then woke to see a tall woman leaning over her. She sat up.

The nurse jumped back and threw her hands to her face. "Hssst! Lie back!"

Ruth complied, puzzled at the fear in the nurse's strange eyes.

"That's better," the nurse said, still standing back. "I'm sorry to bother you. It's time for a shot." The woman's eyes looked like opaque blue-white marbles behind rimless Coke-bottle glasses. A pair of crimson lips slashed across a pale, triangular face barely softened by long blond hair.

Ruth drew away to the far side of the bed. "Shot? Why?"

"A special test. Hssst! Turn on your side." She snapped her head impatiently at her.

"But Dr. Ryan didn't say . . ."

"Doctors are busy, you know. Now roll over on your side." The sharp whisper and another sharp motion of the head frightened Ruth into compliance.

She felt the cover slide from her buttocks. The woman's hair brushed her hip; a needle drove home, followed by a shocking plunge of liquid.

"That's all," said the nurse. "I'll be back when it's had a chance to work."

Ruth rolled onto her back. "Work how?"

But the nurse had left the room.

When she returned about a half-hour later, Ruth felt leaden and dull.

"Hssst! Now onto the cart. We're taking a little ride." Her reedy voice seemed to come from somewhere beyond her strange, translucent face, which was wavering.

Groggy, Ruth wanted to stay in bed.

"Don't fight me." The nurse quickly grasped Ruth's right arm and leg, and with frightening haste pulled her onto the cart sandwiched between the bed and her legs.

"Not fighting."

"I've made sure you can't."

"Can't." She let herself be dragged onto the gurney.

The nurse strapped her onto it with wide webbed belts across her chest, arms, and knees. "I want you to be perfectly still. It's nighttime. Your best time. I don't want you attacking other patients." Then she pulled a sheet up over Ruth's face. "Now it's dark. The way you like it."

Ruth didn't like it. It frightened her. So did the strange things the nurse was saying. She wanted to cry out, but now she was very dizzy and weak. She felt herself swimming between consciousness and wavy darkness as the gurney wheels whispered through the halls and twisted and bumped onto an elevator. The elevator doors slid shut, the cage went down and stopped with a bump; Ruth felt the gurney bounce off and glide into an acrid smelling corridor.

The nurse uncovered her face for a moment. She thrust a mask over Ruth's face. A nail polish remover smell stung Ruth's eyes and throat, making her cough. Dizzily she swirled off into unconsciousness.

A few moments later she woke up in a narrow, enclosed bunk. The straps no longer restrained her limbs, but she still could barely move them—for there was no room. A cold ceiling, cold walls, black darkness pressed in on her. She felt the thin frost of her breath seeping from her mouth and nostrils. Deep beneath the indifference imposed by the medicines, a pitiful moth of panic stirred. She breathed a little faster for a while, which did not help . . . for there was little air left to breathe. She quickly used it up and the panic moth's wings stopped beating moments before her heart did.

She did not know it, but the woman in 202 by the window was now the woman in Drawer Five C.

No one had seen her being put in there; no one saw her being removed an hour before dawn by the same person who'd left her in the morgue refrigerator long enough to suffocate.

Nobody ever saw Ruth Manyon Spencer alive again, though Dr. Bob Ryan, Ruth's surgeon, saw a morgue attendant wheeling a body toward a black van parked by the rear service door at the receiving entrance to the hospital. He hadn't paid much attention, as he'd seen the man many times before. Phillip, who liked to be noticed for his eye-shocking purity, made certain that no one would recognize him when he was carrying out his mission as A Lordly One—to permanently cure the vampire disease. This woman would never be seen again, would never return to destroy or infect those she had not already destroyed or infected—her husband, her children. He'd driven a handmade, silver-plated blade through her heart before he'd placed her in his van. Then he'd traveled north from Philadelphia to a forest he'd known since he was a child and stopped at a trail so familiar to him that he could have walked it blindfolded. He dragged her body in its black plastic bag along the trail. Then he buried it in the grave he had dug the day before and covered it with the earth, and disguised the spot with newly fallen leaves and branches. Casually, he returned to his van, drove back to Philadelphia on the Pennsylvania Turnpike's Northeast Extension, and returned to his three-story row house on Pine Street.

Adolph, his muscular rottweiler, met him with a hungry whine as he entered the back door off the alley.

"Oh, dear, I forgot your dinner," he said, kneeling and rubbing his hands briskly over the dog's broad black body. "You haven't had liver in two days. I must remember to bring you some tomorrow." Organ meats were Adolph's favorite. But Phillip had been so zealous to cure the vampire, that he hadn't even thought about feeding his dog.

To remedy that omission, he burrowed in the pantry. At the back of a dusty shelf he found the canned dog food he'd stocked there in case he ran out of fresh goodies he'd scavenged from autopsies in the postmortem lab. He was usually quite thorough about removing the human detritus that neither the pathologist nor the cadaver nor the mortician had further use for. Succulent morsels for Adolph abounded.

He opened the dog food can and dumped the contents into Adolph's bowl on the floor. Adolph's whole rear shook and his short-haired body quivered as he wolfed down the entire bowlful in a few powerful chomps, then followed it with a bowlful of water.

As Phillip watched his dog's pleasure with pleasure, he planned the next steps of his vampire curing mission. He would not wait for a new specimen of purple urine to chance by his lab bench. He would do a little genealogy searching and find Ruth Manyon Spencer's relatives, who would naturally carry the porphyria genes. He would track them down, one by one, and cure them, too.

He'd start with Ruth's Pennsylvania cousins. Soon they would all join her beneath the earth of the Delaware State Forest. And they would never rise again nor stand by a forest clearing in the moonlight with their lips curled back and their nostrils flared to catch the scent of an approaching camper.

CHAPTER ONE

Three years later—spring

Zack James might have been a moss-covered gnarl at the base of the giant oak. He'd stuck his back up against the tree before dawn and sat waiting for the turkey hens he'd scouted out yesterday to come down from their roosts about seventy-five yards away and begin their feeding. Swatting at gnats in yesterday afternoon's humidity, he'd gone over every inch of that clearing. He hadn't seen anything unusual to make him think today would be different from any other early spring hunting day. He'd either get his old gobbler or he wouldn't. He'd either keep his promise to Maryellen or he wouldn't. He hoped he would, of course. Something told him a successful hunt would put his life back on track.

And this morning had started off well. The fog had burned off quickly in a brighter than usual sun. The humidity had dropped, leaving the air crisp, almost free of whining insects. Now he sat, barely moving, his thumb resting just above the safety of his camo taped Remington 870, which he held tentatively on one knee, shell in the chamber, gun ready for him to bring the butt to his shoulder. His camouflaged outfit and gear were so convincing that a squirrel leaping down from a newly leafing branch just after sunrise landed on the thick-barked trunk just above his head and scrabbled down his shoulder and wriggled its sensitive whiskers at the dappled net concealing his neck and the two-day growth of black beard on his jaw. Startled, Zack nearly swallowed the mouth call he held tongued against his pallet.

Then he expelled a breath. "Yelp!" A false call. It could blow the whole hunt.

The squirrel jumped to the leaf-covered forest floor and scooted off, right toward the nearby clearing where he'd seen the old longbeard scratching for acorns with the hens yesterday.

Zack took the latex diaphragm from his mouth. "Shit!" he said, as much from the foul taste of his grime-crusted gloves as from worry that his premature call might alarm the crafty old spring gobbler he was after. That longbeard knew these northeastern Pennsylvania woods about as well as Zack did. This was his territory; those were his hens. And he knew Zack's tricks, too: the way Zack switched calls on him when he moved from one spot to another. His gobble had even seemed like a taunting laugh last year when he'd come toward Zack, then suddenly turned and took off after the hen Zack had tried to distract him from.

"I'll get you next fall, you tricky bastard!" Zack had vowed on admitting defeat that day. Frustrated, he'd shaken his gobble box then. Much to his surprise, a younger tom had taken up the challenge and come charging at him. He'd barely had time to raise his shotgun and swing the gun to the proper lead on the other bird's head. But he'd thumbed off the safety and brought him down. It was not the bird he'd been after, but he hadn't gone home empty-handed to Maryellen.

On the drive back to Glenside, a Phildelphia suburb, that night last year, he'd played with the thought of telling her that this was the bird he'd promised to bring her. She never would have known the difference, couldn't have told a wattle from a plucked wing. Game bird hunting was his thing, not hers. She never even cooked what he brought home. He and their thirteen-year-old daughter, Poke, did that together, just as Poke and he sometimes would hunt together. Anyway, he'd decided not to lie to Maryellen. Maybe he wouldn't say anything—let her assume what she wanted. Nah, he couldn't do that, either. When push came to shove, he couldn't deceive Maryellen. She knew that. Deep mutual trust bound them together, and the tiniest nick in the weave could start it unraveling. So he told her the truth and promised he'd bring the old gobbler home for Thanksgiving. There was no way to keep that promise now; but there was no way he was going to break its essence. No matter what some stupid squirrel did now, a year later.

He put the call between his lips again and tongued it back up against his palate. In a few moments he sat back, fixed, against the tree. His somewhat anemic false yelp had brought a few echoes from descending hens, who no doubt were more enticing to males than he was at the moment. Nothing, apparently, had been lost—except maybe to the squirrel, who'd be competing for acorns on turf the turkeys fast claimed.

So, to the squirrels and the turkeys, Zack once more passed for some gnarled upheaved oak roots. He felt like that, too. Maryellen's death, like a sudden, ruthless storm, had ripped his roots up out of the ground that had anchored him, and left him contorted, knotted, tense, hanging on by his fingernails. That was how he'd felt the last six months since she died. Shit! He came here to try to stop feeling that way, and the first things he sees around him remind him that's exactly how he feels, and probably always will. Do you ever get over it, watching the woman you loved and lived with for sixteen years get sick and waste away and die in front of your eyes in just a few months? My God, it all happened so fast! Last spring—the last time he sat against a tree—maybe this very tree—there weren't too many this old—calling the longbeard, watching for his head to pop up from behind a tangle of blackberry brambles about thirty yards away, he hadn't even dreamed it could be this way this year. Only a year—no, not quite a whole year—ago. *Goddamn it! Turn it off, will ya!*

Then he thought again, *Maybe getting that turkey will help me turn it off.* It might help Poke, now fourteen, turn it off, too. The two of them could stuff, roast, and baste it, then sit across from each other at the dining room table and dedicate the meal to Maryellen. Then they could pack up the leftovers in portions, and he could go down to Market Street, not far from his office, and give them to the homeless guys that slept near the subway entrances and over steam grates. Maryellen would approve of that. Yeah, public health nurse that she was, she'd love that. *Come on, Tom, you old bastard. You don't have to die in vain. This is your chance to give your life some meaning.*

From behind his cupped hands, he sounded a deliberate series of yelps. The birds were feeding less than seventy yards from him, a large flock of hens, more than enough to satisfy even this old gobbler, whose mind would be on breeding this time of year. But Zack heard not a single tantalizing cackle from the hens. He shifted the diaphragm in his mouth, worked it back into place, and gave forth with the most seductive mating call he could manage.

He heard the gobble; raised his gun to his shoulder. In the clearing beyond the brambles, the tom was headed his way. Zack eyed the gunsight, punched off the safety, cackled again.

A lusty gobble bellowed, and the bird rushed toward the brambles and flew up and over them. It was always amazing to Zack that such a heavy, awkward looking bird could accomplish such a graceful low flight.

It was the old fellow, all right, running right at him, white banded red tail fanned, beard streaming, that proud white head almost too intelligent looking and beautiful to shoot at.

But Zack pointed the gun at it and squeezed the trigger.

A startled tunnel of silence followed the crack of the shot through the woods, as small animals and birds froze a moment before fleeing. The gobbler hesitated, wobbled, ran back toward the brambles, and was caught in them, while its legs continued to pump. Its red-crowned head sagged on its broken neck. Red spots peppered the soft white feathers of its head and neck.

Zack felt the momentary sting of remorse that always accompanied the bringing down of an admired quarry who'd played him a challenging game. It was tough to see the spunk draining out of the tom, the puff going out of those rich, brown feathers. But the feeling dissipated quickly, like the sharp whiff of gunpowder from the chilly morning air; Zack was on his feet.

CLACK CLACK!

More birds scattered as he pumped his shotgun clear of shells, stuffed them and the spent one into his jacket ammo pockets, then strode to the fallen turkey. *A twenty-pounder at least!*

His camouflage net shoved back, he felt his tired face crease in a satisfied grin. A few minutes later, his quarry slung over his shoulder in his game bag, he realized he felt happy for the first time in a year. He hadn't gotten this bird for Maryellen—he'd gotten it for himself. Something inside him was beginning, finally, to heal.

A blue jay's raucous cries scolded him as he flagged his quarry bag with a blaze orange scarf and strode off across the clearing where the birds had been foraging. Suddenly he heard a flapping and a yelping. He turned toward the edge of the clearing. A turkey hen struggled against something that held her leg to the ground. She pulled up again and again, crying out pitifully each time some hidden shackle brought her back down.

"Aw—poor ladybird!"

Zack slid his game bag off his shoulder, set it and his shotgun down, and started toward the struggling turkey.

She screeched and jumped first toward him then away from him in her panic. Buff feathers clouded the air. Zack knew he couldn't get near her without risking his eyes. He circled her and backed into the woods, pulled his camouflage net down over his face again, and placed a fresh diaphragm in his mouth. While removing his jacket, he called softly to the hen with some reassuring yelps and clucks. After a few moments, as he moved in closer behind her, she seemed to have settled down. Maybe she was only exhausted: She seemed more listless and resigned than calm as he tossed his jacket over her head. She froze. He grasped her in a body hug and blindly worked to free her leg from whatever it was that was holding it.

At last his hand grasped what felt like a metal chain entangling the bird's leg. He wrestled with it for a moment, trying to untwist it from around her claw. Even through his gloves he could tell it was a heavy jewelry chain, not one easily broken, yet not meant to bind securely. He figured that it had been buried and that the hen had scratched part of it up while scratching for acorns and insects. It couldn't be terribly deep if it had been lost here recently; but maybe it had tangled on something just below the earth's surface. The hen hadn't been strong enough to pull it loose, but Zack should be able to.

He tugged at it. The earth gave slightly around it. *Sure is tangled on something.* He tugged again. The chain pulled out far enough that he was able to loosen it from around the hen's leg and pull it off over her claw. He set her down and released his hold on her, uncovered her head. She limped around for a second, then flew off.

"Go, Ladybird." He watched her awhile, then, curious, turned back to the chain. It was heavy, ropelike silver. Several inches were exposed, and it still held tight to the ground, indicating an impressive length as yet beneath the earth. He noted the soil was not as tightly packed as he would have expected, and he realized that it must have been fairly recently dug up and tamped down again.

"Jesus! Something must be buried here!" He got down on his knees now and began to clear away last fall's thick deposit of yellow leaves. The earth he uncovered had definitely been disturbed. He felt the blood surge into his face as he tugged away more leaves and debris. A few minutes later the shape of the repacked mound he had uncovered became clear. His fingers tingled, his mouth grew dry. He realized he still held the turkey call in his cheek. "Oh Jesus. It isn't just something; it's somebody!" He sat down on his haunches and spat the call into his palm. Shakily, he found the box in his jacket pocket and returned the call to it. He had to think! What should he do? What if that long silver chain was around somebody's neck? Should he dig down and see? Should he pull on the chain again?

Yes, pull on it. Something had to be on the other end of it. If it was small, it would probably pull out of the lightly packed dirt. If it was big and heavy, maybe his pulling would break the chain. He hadn't pulled it as hard as he could have.

Thick as it was, he could break it easily enough. Zack was strong and fit. He kept his barbells, exercise bench, and punching bag in his office at Squire Technical Publishers so his sedentary work at the computer wouldn't turn his 175 pounds to flab on his five-foot-nine frame. And also to keep his mind from clogging up on his sixteen-hour work days.

His hands were strong and broad. They could forget how gentle the rest of him was when someone reached out to shake them if he didn't consciously remind them. They were precise, too, and restrained, from working the computer keyboard and mouse to create graphic designs for Squire's publications. People would see his designs emerge on the computer screen, and they'd look from the screen to him, at his long, uneven black hair, at his eyes, which might change from green to brown within seconds for no particular reason, at the perpetual shadow of beard that lurked in the shallow hollow below his high Amerindian cheekbones. Then they'd look at his camo hunting vest over his red-and-black plaid shirt and again at the computer screen and the proofs coming off the image printer and they'd shake their heads. Zack knew they couldn't believe that someone who looked like him could turn out something that looked like art, that someone who kept his shotgun in the corner behind the door of his office, which was rendered lopsided and out of kilter by his gym equipment, could turn out such incredibly delicate and well-balanced designs on paper. And they wondered, too, how Squire's polished executives, in their blue, three-piece suits, white shirts, striped ties, and shiny black shoes could tolerate Zack and his office. But when people looked at the computer screen and the proofs and the samples of Zack's finished work in their brochures and books, they knew that Squire could never find anyone better than him to supervise design and layout. They called it supervising. Actually, it was creating the artwork and executing the design from start to finish and explaining it to the clients, then following it through the publishing process. He was their one-man art department, grossly underpaid at forty thousand dollars a year. So they humored him and looked aside from his idiosyncrasies.

Now, Zack bent and grasped the silver chain. Looping it over his gloved right hand, he tugged hard. It gave slightly; he tightened it around his hand and pulled harder. Beneath the ground, something gave. On his next tug, the chain slid out of the earth. It was a neck chain all right, caked with dirt, and with a pendant on the end. The pendant had snagged on a dirty piece of black plastic—probably torn from a trash bag.

He pulled the plastic free from the pendant. A cross, made of heavy silver like the chain. It looked custom-made, not the kind of jewelry someone would have thrown away. Lost, maybe. Buried by accident with some garbage. Zack stood up.

"Or buried on purpose!" Jesus. Some stuff from a heist, brought up here and buried for safekeeping till the heat was off. That would explain it. That's why it wasn't too deep. So the guy could come back here and get it easily enough. Had to be a woodsman of some kind. Hiker or someone familiar with this forest.

The guy would have had to mark the place somehow. He looked around at the ground, at the trees surrounding the clearing. No markings that he could see. Zack patted his jacket under his arm. He'd brought his 35 millimeter camera, even remembered to put in fresh film. There was more than one way to mark a spot you wanted to get back to. He opened his jacket, pulled out his camera, and took some shots of the clearing: the boulder right at the center; the spot where the chain came out, with the chain and the cross lying right next to it; the trees to the north and south of the clearing. He snapped a picture of the tree trunks, so he could count how many there were and how they compared in size. He shot one of the clearing from the east, so he could get an idea of all the permanent features from that approach. After each shot he wrote a note on the back of his forest topographical map, so later he could put the notes together with the pictures. He took a compass reading, and marked the approximate spot on his topo map. On his way back to the road, he would count off his paces. He would tie pieces of his scarf as temporary blazes to trees so he could lead a ranger back to dig up the cache.

He studied the ground again. *Bring him back for what?* Christ, Zack's imagination had run away with him. One silver chain with a cross on it didn't mean one damn thing. What if there was just a bag of trash underneath there? What if there was nothing at all? Someone had done a good job of burying a campfire or something. Put it a little deeper than usual. Maybe some slob-hunter, some jacklighter taking deer at night out of season, was in there poaching, knew there were patrols around, buried something he shouldn't have shot in the first place.

Zack couldn't just run to the ranger station and say, "Here, I found this religious jewelry, so there must be some more under there." Shit! It was enough he'd wasted nearly a whole roll of film. Well, he'd have to dig down for himself and see. Couldn't have been too deep. This was man's jewelry, on a chain about thirty inches long, but the chain had been looped, so it would have been maybe just over a foot deep altogether. He could reach it by loosening the earth with his hunting knife, and scraping it away with his hands.

He didn't have to go very deep before his scraping fingers unearthed more black plastic—a large piece, this time. As he pulled it, more earth gave way. He must have found the rest of the bag. By grasping a segment in both hands and moving it from side to side as he pulled, he slowly worked it and part of its contents out of the ground.

The plastic was heavy gauge, the kind the TV advertisers threw down the outside apartment stairs to show how tough it was, but something had started it tearing. When Zack set his feet tight against the ground and gave it a final tug, his whole weight leaning away from it, it pulled farther out of the ground, then tore, throwing him off balance.

He recovered his footing and moved forward to see what he had unearthed. A stench rose from the disturbed earth. Garbage, all right. No cache of jewelry here. He should have left well enough alone, taken his silver cross as a souvenir of the hunt—kind of like a medal received for getting the longbeard and freeing the turkey maiden in distress.

He shook his head. Why someone would bury his garbage instead of burning it in a campfire or taking it back in his RV was beyond him. Well, no sense letting it stink up the whole woods. He'd just put the earth back over it and . . .

"Oh, Jesus, God!"

He'd uncovered a head—a human head. Couldn't tell if it was a man or a woman because the underground crawlers had gotten to it and done a job on it. But whatever it was, it was lying there on its back and its jaw had dropped down as if it had let out a scream when it died and never had a chance to stop screaming. Shreds of the torn bag lay underneath it, and more black plastic covered what must be the rest of the body buried a little bit deeper than the head.

Zack backed away and gagged. He was sure he heard that scream tearing around the woods. He was sure that if he came here again, the scream would still be rising like a terrible wind out of that gaping mouth. And the smell—there was no way he could ever forget that smell.

He wasn't sure why he took out his camera again and took two pictures of the head before he covered the face with the torn plastic, moved some rocks over its corners to hold it in place, and started back to his Ram, counting his paces as he walked, talking to his gobbler as he made his way through the woods, trying to figure out why the world was such an idiotic place. The turkey didn't seem to have an answer. Probably no one did.

Two hours later, Zack went back into the woods with Forest Ranger Bill Clay, in the ranger's vehicle. They parked next to a Jeep Zack had not seen before, at the edge of the trail that led to the burial site. It was afternoon, and the forest's birds and animals had quieted, but the humid air zinged with pesky gnats.

A hunter in camouflage emerged from the trail just as they got down from the van. He stopped and lowered his game bag from his shoulder.

"I got him before one," the hunter said. "Just took my time coming out." He looked guiltily from Clay to Zack. Then he unwrapped the bird. "See, it's a gobbler."

Clay, a tall, thin, wiry man in his late thirties, glanced at the bird and nodded. "Know if any other hunters are in there?"

He shook his head.

"You ought to be wearing blaze orange on you somewhere. Some guys forget the time. You move and they shoot," Clay said.

"Yes, sir." He rewrapped his trophy.

Clay opened the tailgate of his vehicle and got his rifle and a pick. He handed the pick to Zack, then reached in and got a sharp-edged spade.

"Some problem back there?" asked the hunter.

"Not so long as no one's back there taking hens. You better get your vehicle on out of here."

The hunter nodded curtly and hurried into his Jeep and off toward the main road.

"OK, Zack. Where's our body?" He said it as if he still doubted there was one.

Zack led him into the woods and to the clearing. It was less than a half mile in, and took only about fifteen minutes to get there. Now that he knew where it was, he was surprised nobody else had stumbled on it. The cover he'd hurriedly thrown on it and pinned down with rocks seemed obvious.

Clay motioned him to remove the debris and plastic from the head, and stood back while Zack used the pick blade's edge to pull it off.

The stench filled the air. Some blowflies appeared out of nowhere and dove toward the hole. Both men stepped back. Then the ranger stepped forward, turned a shade resembling his khaki uniform, and gagged. "OK. Let's see what else is under there. Just dig around it where the ground seems already loose." He took his intercom phone from his belt and punched in a code. "Clay, here," he said to it. "We got a body, all right. Get the county boys up here to get evidence and get it back to the morgue."

Zack tested the earth around a body sized patch, and found where it crumbled fairly easily. He drew a line with the pick, and the two men began to dig off shallow layers of the earth, swatting at insects as they worked. Two flies landed on the cheek behind the gaping mouth and dipped their proboscises into the decaying flesh. They clung in spite of Zack's brisk swipes. He let them be. At least they'd stay off him.

Clay's spade scraped into the earth. "Anything besides dirt, stones, twigs and stuff," he said, "save and we'll get it to the lab for study."

"Stuff like the cross?"

"Anything you wouldn't expect to find underground."

"I wouldn't've expected to find this."

"Yeah. They're usually not buried. This must have been well planned."

Zack uncovered some feathers stuck to the plastic bag about a foot deep. "Hey! What about these?"

Clay put his spade down and knelt to examine the feathers.

"A tom's," said Zack.

"Maybe the killer was a turkey hunter," said Clay. "Maybe he shot another hunter by accident, and buried him in a hurry. There's a guy that disappeared out here last fall, never turned up. Leave the feathers there, where they're stuck." He stood up and went back to digging, breathing through his mouth with his nostrils pinched together.

Zack walked to the head of the body, where the plastic had ripped loose in his hands. A third fly had joined the feast and others circled and darted around Zack's head. "This bag is really heavy gauge. It's only torn in this one place. There's not a crack in it anywhere else we've uncovered it."

"You must have pulled pretty hard."

"That cross was stuck in it somehow."

"Hey, there's more feathers here," said Clay. "A whole bunch of them. Looks like the killer might have sprinkled them over the bag. Why the hell would someone do that?"

"If it was a hunting accident—that might explain it."

"Or, some sort of ritual murder. I hear they use dead animals and birds and stuff. Why not feathers?"

"That's probably it, if it wasn't a hunting accident. The cross would fit in with that, probably." He shook his head and went back to digging. He decided he wanted it to be a hunting accident. At least that would make the whole thing more human. More flies settled onto the corpse's head. He tried to ignore them, but their buzzing drove into his craw, stirring up the undigested remains of a donut he'd had with coffee at the ranger station. He wished he hadn't eaten. He could taste the greasy dough and the soured cream in his stomach. The body's stench rose from the ground, intermingled with the taste in his mouth. His head began to spin.

He kept digging, trying to throw off his rising nausea. But it rose into his throat. At last he dropped the pick, ran to the edge of the clearing, and vomited behind a tree.

They had the whole body in its bag uncovered about a half hour later, and stood around for another two hours until the county coroner's office took over. Clay drove Zack back to the rustic station near the forest entrance, sat him down at a steel desk in a cluttered, furniture-crowded bullpen off the receiving room, and took a long deposition and told him he might be contacted by other police or called in to testify if they ever found the killer and brought him to trial. "Can you leave us your film? The county guys'll develop it. Take a first look."

"I guess so. If I get the negatives back. Kind of like to have them." He wondered why he'd ever want to see them again. The thoughts of looking at that rotting head in the ground would only make him sick. He would stare into that mouldering face, smell the scream that rose from its gaping jaw, and ask himself, *Why?* Maybe that's why he wanted the pictures. There might be an answer in them somewhere.

"Sure. I'll see that you get them. I'll get them back when they're done with them and keep them locked up here till you come for them. Call me in a few days. Should have them back by then."

Zack opened his camera and removed the film. He'd used the last two shots up photographing the bag with the feathers all over it. Reluctantly, he handed Clay the roll.

Then the ranger looked at Zack and said, "It's already getting dark. You look shot. Better not start home now. That's a three or four hour drive back to Philly."

"My kid's expecting me. She's fourteen. Alone in the house."

"Well, call her. We'll put you up here for the night. Nothing fancy—just a cot in an office. But you can get a shower. There's a diner down the road we can eat at. Bring back a thermos of their super coffee, and you're set to get out of here at dawn. OK?"

Zack thought a moment. It probably would be better for Poke if she knew he was staying in one spot overnight than if she was up all night worrying about where he was. It was Friday night. She still might be able to call up a friend to sleep over.

He called and suggested she do that. The idea seemed to excite her.

"I'll call Christy," she said. "OK if I go over there if her mom asks?"

Her mom, Eve Carter, probably would. A dozen times in the last six months she'd taken Poke in on short notice when Zack had to be away overnight on business. As independent as Poke was, he still didn't like to leave her alone in the house overnight.

"Just leave me a note. See you sometime tomorrow."

He didn't see her till Sunday evening. For when Zack and Clay came back from dinner at 9 P.M., a buzzing crowd of officers filled the ranger station receiving room and bullpen.

"Well, Zack, you really opened a can of worms up there," said the station chief. "The county guys figure there are at least a few more bodies under that clearing. And judging from the look of things, they might have been there for years. You really ought to stick around for the weekend. See what we dig up."

Zack stuck around till Sunday afternoon; Poke was delighted to be able to stay with Christy for Sunday dinner, and doubly delighted—in a teenager's perverse way—to know that her father had found a real dead body in the woods. By Sunday morning the Philadelphia *Inquirer* had already run a photograph of him holding the silver cross, and the television news channels had broadcast films of the excavations, which had turned up three more corpses—and a skeleton. The skeleton had been wrapped in heavy sheets instead of a plastic body bag, and it had a plastic bracelet around its wrist. The bracelet read, "Ruth Manyon Spencer, W.F., B.D. 7-1-49, Room 202W, U.M.C." Like all of the other bodies except the one Zack had discovered, it had a handmade knife with a twelve-inch blade still wedged in the chest. No turkey feathers. No crosses. No other immediately apparent relationship, except, as police missing person's records soon showed, the dead—two women and three men of varying ages—had all disappeared without a trace over the past few years.

A week later

"Family!" Zack said to Bill Clay on Saturday, when he went back to the ranger station to pick up his film negatives. He'd been thinking that all week long; as he throttled his custom-built, bright-blue four-wheel drive Ram along slick, twisting roads and through thick curtains of fog and rain draping the Poconos, he'd said it aloud over and over to himself: *Family, family, family*. Hunting jacket dripping onto the rough wood floor, he stood in the rustic bullpen among the troopers' plain steel desks and watched Clay amble to the row of battered green file cabinets against the black wall. Zack added, "When a bunch of innocent people get killed for no reason anyone can tell and they all turn up buried together, you can bet on a family connection."

Clay, the only ranger in the bullpen that morning, opened the top drawer of one of the file cabinets and retrieved a large brown envelope. He motioned Zack to sit in the maple captain's chair by his desk and gave him the envelope. "What makes you so sure? They don't look much alike in their pictures." He grinned as he took from his desk drawer a sheaf of photographs of the decomposed bodies lying on a morgue table, and pushed them across the desk to Zack. The knives had been removed from what was left of their chests.

"Yeah," Zack said, looking at the pictures and grimacing. "I bet they sure smell a lot alike!"

Clay laughed and collected the pictures and returned them to the drawer. "Thought you might like a look. These aren't in your collection."

"Yeah, thanks. I can do without it. Pictures of them alive would be a lot more use. Of two or more of them together. Family pictures."

"Their survivors don't even know each other, Zack. Why're you so sure it's family?"

"I know about families, that's why. It's sort of a hobby with me, studying family roots. You want to solve mysteries, you go back to the roots."

Reaching to a tray on the corner of his desk for a thermos and two foam cups, Clay arched questioning brows Zack's way. At Zack's nod, he poured two cups and slid one across the desk. "Roots? Seems a little farfetched."

"Maybe not all the way to the roots. But if they don't know they're cousins and they are, then you got to go back a ways."

"Maybe they aren't cousins. Ever think of that?"

From the doorway leading out to the receiving room came the scrape of heavy footfalls. "Mine are cousins."

As Clay looked up, Zack turned and saw a tall man with a sandy complexion, bright turquoise eyes, and thick salmon-colored hair. His long, blue, brass-buttoned raincoat distinguished him as a city cop with rank.

Clay stood. "Can I help you?"

The man held out a broad, freckled hand. "Crosby. Philadelphia," he said. "Thought I'd check out the murder site. Hell of a day for it, but it's the only day I have this weekend."

"Oh, yessir, Lieutenant. I talked to you on the phone a few days ago. Can't pick our weather, can we?" He introduced the detective to Zack.

"You're right about them being cousins. How'd you figure it out?"

"A hunch," said Zack. "What'd you mean by, 'Mine are cousins'?"

"The two that came from my jurisdiction. The Spencer woman disappeared from UMC hospital in nineteen eighty-five. The retired editor must have been snatched from his town house in Northeast Philly four months ago. He lived alone in a ground-floor garden apartment. One day his neighbors saw him go in, and he never came out. At least not when someone was looking." He shoved the coffee tray aside and slid a broad hip onto the corner of Clay's desk.

"That was the one with the cross, Zack. The most recent."

"Yeah, the first and the most recent are mine. And they're cousins. The editor's ex-wife called me yesterday and said he and the Spencer woman were distantly related through her mother's side. Mother's maiden name was Rand. So your hobby's genealogy, eh?"

"It's more than a hobby," said Zack. "It's a passion. When I'm not working, I'm doing some kind of genealogy. Traced my roots back to the turn of the century, then lost them. My great-grandfather on Mom's side disappeared. Have to go out to Arizona again sometime, try to find out what happened to him. On vacations I go to places my grandparents lived. See if I can't dig up cousins. Love to find family skeletons. Black sheep and stuff. When I'm someplace looking for my own roots, I do it for my BBS friends, too."

Clay's brown brows rose again. He asked questions with his face instead of his mouth.

"Bulletin Board System," Crosby explained to him. "Computer network."

"Right," said Zack. "I belong to a genealogy BBS. We have conferences and post messages and stuff for each other. You want to know something about genealogy, you'll find it there."

"You can do record searches?" Crosby said.

"Hell," said Zack, warming to the discussion, "anyone can do record searches! That's not where the fun is. It's digging the stuff out of family letters and junk like that, then chasing down addresses, and hanging around where houses are or used to be and talking to some little old lady who might have been around when your cousin lived there. Hell, that's what genealogy's all about."

Crosby stood up. "Sounds like detective work to me." He turned to Clay. "Say, maybe Zack can take me back to the place where he found my bodies. Looks like you need to stick around here at your desk, and I'd kind of like to pick his brain a little."

Clay looked at Zack. "If it's OK with you, Zack," he said.

Zack wasn't eager for a walk in the rain through the woods, but having his brain picked about genealogy tingled his scalp, like having a woman run her hands through his hair. No woman had done that since Maryellen died; and he wouldn't be able to turn to another woman, even if he found one now. The only things he had been able to turn to in the last nine months were work and genealogy. Outside his computer network, most people thought the subject boring. They pictured him with his nose stuck up against a computer screen or his butt stuck to a chair in a dusty archive room somewhere.

But Crosby—a detective himself—saw Zack the detective, hanging around bars or street corners, ferreting out stories from living people who might know how somebody lived and died and could answer the question, "Why?"

"Sure!" Zack said. "I'll take you up in my Ram."

The two men slogged through the sodden mulch laid by the trees in fall and seasoned over winter by frost and thaw, snow, rain, and animal droppings, and mixed by scratching birds, rodents, and carrion insects. The forest floor steamed in the chilly air as it did its eternal work beneath their feet, using their feet to its own advantage. Small creatures and breezes tipped leaf cups above their heads, dousing them with suddenly freed rainwater. By the time they reached the excavated graves, Zack's shirt, jeans, and shoes were soaked through.

Five pools marked the spots where the bodies had been buried. Bits of debris floated on them, jetted this way and that by raindrops still falling on them.

"Where were ours?" asked Crosby.

Not just "mine" anymore, thought Zack. Crosby was including him as partial proprietor of this mystery. He saw Zack as another detective, with questions and answers Crosby himself might miss.

Zack showed him the sites where the editor and the Spencer woman had been buried.

"Wonder if there were any more," Crosby mused.

"Or will be," said Zack.

Crosby nodded. "That's what we got to worry about. So number one and number five are ours, and they're related. Number two was that single mom that managed an insurance office in Scranton. Vanished after getting a phone call at work that her kids were in danger. Three was the thirty-four-year-old guy from Pittsburgh. Office cleaner on the night shift. Never got to work one night. Four was the guy that evaporated from his parked pickup on a Harrisburg construction site." He sighed and shook his head. "Maybe Scranton is next on his list. Ought to see if ours have cousins in Scranton."

"Makes sense," said Zack.

"Can you get anything on that through your BBS?"

"I guess I can try. It's one way to go." Zack suddenly developed a tickle in his throat. He coughed.

"Want a cough drop?" said Crosby, digging into his raincoat pocket and pulling out a damp box. He opened the box and shook it. "All stuck together. Here, take them all."

Zack, between coughs and headshakes, thanked him and took it and loosened a lozenge from the clump with his finger and put it onto his tongue. He worked up as much saliva as he could, so the mentholated mint would melt and start to work on the tickle. After several swallows, it began to work at last.

"This weather isn't doing you any good," Crosby said. He

motioned with a wide sweep of his hand that the two should head back to the Ram.

By the time they arrived at the trail head, Zack had a headache and his throat was feeling raw. Any conversation brought on a minor coughing spell, so the two drove back to the ranger station in silence. After getting some aspirin from Clay, Zack drove home through the diminishing rain, arriving at his house feeling achy and exhausted. *Coming down with a cold,* he thought. *Shit, I don't have time for that!*

The next Thursday

"I still think they should've let you keep the cross, Pop. 'Specially since you're doing the police work for nothing." Poke loaded the last plate into the dishwasher and tossed too much detergent in after it.

As usual, he decided not to correct her for the waste of detergent the way Maryellen would have. "It's not for nothing, it's for fun. Besides, it might keep someone from being killed, and the department can't afford a professional genealogist."

She wiped the gold laminated counter and tabletops with a sponge, and hooked the pot holder to a peg beside the electric range before surveying the small, neat kitchen and its dining booth and finding them in order. "They could afford to give you the cross. It was free. And finders keepers."

"If no one claims it, I might get it, eventually. Not sure I even want it."

"The killer's sure not going to claim it."

"It maybe belongs to someone in that family."

"Wouldn't they have said so by now?"

He looked at her long black hair and green-to-brown eyes and thought how much better they looked on her than on him. There wasn't very much of Maryellen in her at all. In fact, Zack decided, she looked and acted too much like him for her own good. She'd rather load a shotgun than a dishwasher; she'd rather wear those faded, hole-in-the-knees jeans and tail-out plaid shirt and spend her Sundays at the shooting range with her father than at Willow Grove Mall with her friends. "Families that have something like that happen to them don't hardly want to talk much. Some are still claiming they're not related. I'll bet! Somewhere there are some records that'll tie them together."

She closed the dishwasher and started it up. They left the kitchen to get away from the noise. "Maybe. Well, everyone's sure talking about them!"

In the small, dark, oak paneled family room he sat down in his vinyl recliner and brought up the footrest and leaned back. From the table next to it, he took the box of cough drops. He'd been sucking one after another and his mouth was constantly puckered; but the cough had hung on and kept him awake half the night. After pushing a lozenge into his mouth, he said, "That's part of why they don't like to talk. Hell, Poke, five of them killed in the last few years, and all buried in the same part of the woods."

"You're famous, Pop. Everybody at school's talking about how you found the body. They think it's cool."

"I hope you didn't tell them I'm helping Lieutenant Crosby with the genealogy search. I told you that was a secret."

"Naw. Even if it wasn't a secret, I wouldn't tell them about your dumb genealogy, and the cops not paying you for doing it. They'd think you were a nerd. It's not like finding a body. That's what they think is so cool."

"It wasn't cool. It stank. They wouldn't think I was so great if they'd seen me vomit."

"You didn't say anything about vomiting. Gross!" She sat down at the family room desk and booted up the computer. Unlike most young teenage girls, she almost never watched TV. Since Maryellen's death, the large console always sat blank and dumb across the corner he faced from his recliner. Poke preferred the computer, and was almost as good at computer graphics as her father was, and she was better at games, especially word games, which she could play alone or with someone on the computer network. "Want to do Word Scrambler with me?"

"My eyes are boiled, Poke." Her real name was Jill. Poke was short for Pocahontas, a reference to her Native American blood. None of Zack's Scotch-Irish background had seeped in. Little of Maryellen's Irish or Eastern European Jewish halves had, except for her petite frame. He hoped none of Maryellen's leukemia-prone genes had. "Don't you have homework?"

"I did it before you got home. You didn't really barf, did you Pop?"

"I barfed. Hey, Poke, how 'bout if you let me use the computer to go to the genealogy BBS conference tonight?"

She pouted. "I thought your eyes were boiled."

"I meant my brain was. It's important, Poke, for the search. I posted a message on the board with everything I already know about the family. I told them I'd log into the conference tonight, so we could talk about it in real time."

"What do you know about them, Pop? It's less than a week since you went back for those pictures and came back with that awful cold."

"I went up to Harrisburg to get the Spencer kids' birth certificates. Their dad flat out refused to talk to me. Anyway, I found out the woman was born in Phoenix. I might take a trip there and poke around. Especially if I get something from the conference about any Rands out that way."

"Cheeze, Pop! When did you have time for Harrisburg? Phoenix! You're crazy! Your brain really is boiled, isn't it?"

"Enough of your mouth. Great-gramps was near Phoenix when he disappeared, you know. I thought you couldn't wait to go to college there. Besides, you gotta have respect for your old man."

"Well, you're just so worn out all the time. You're going to get sick again, if you're not already. Or you're going to pop yourself on the head again on that dumb exercise machine. You wouldn't've let go of that thing you were pulling if you weren't so tired all the time that—"

"The cable snapped and the lat bar let go. I didn't let go! You're getting me mad, Poke."

She pouted. "I can't help it."

"Yes you can. You can move over and give me the machine, so I can relax in my own house and see if I can find that killer."

"I don't see how your dumb genealogy can help find a killer. Why can't the police—why can't Lieutenant Crosby—?" Her mouth drew tight around the words and her eyes began to glitter. She turned away from him.

"Ah, now, Poke. Hey, I—Look, I shoudn't've hollered at you."

Her shoulders began to shake.

"Shit! Look. Don't you know it makes me feel dumb to get hit on the head with my own equipment? I wish you hadn't brought that up."

She turned back and looked at him with tears streaming down her face. "It makes you feel dumb, but it makes me feel scared, Pop. You almost didn't go to the doctor. When you got that lump on your skull, I was sure—sure you were gonna—"

"Oh, Jesus—"

"Pop, please don't make yourself sick. You're coughing all the time, and up all night long. You ought to see your face. Your eyes are sunk in your head. I get scared when I hear you and scared when I look at you. I—I honestly do." She began to cry harder.

He clenched and unclenched his hands, feeling helpless. Then he stepped forward and took her in his arms. She threw her arms around him and sobbed into his chest for a few minutes. He held her and ran his hands through her long black hair and squeezed thick bunched ropes of it. "Hey, Poke, shhh. I'm sorry."

She pulled her head back from his chest and looked up into his eyes. "I didn't mean to make you feel dumb, Pop."

"It's OK. I'm used to feeling dumb. You're right, I've been on a ragged edge for almost a year now. You know—" He still couldn't come right out and say, *"since your mother got sick and died."*—"But I'm starting to get hold of myself again. That turkey hunt—getting that longbeard—well, for a second I felt like my old self again. This other thing threw me off."

"I know. We had to freeze the turkey. We couldn't even eat it fresh."

"We'll make a feast of it one of these days. But, look. I really want to log onto the conference. I promise to go nitey right after, before my face falls into the keyboard." He hugged her and grinned lopsidedly down at her.

She grimaced through her tears. Then she grinned back at him and pulled her arms tightly around him again.

"Go on," he said gruffly. "Go up to your room and play with your Nintendo."

She looked up at him again and gave him a peck on his beard-gritted chin and ran to her room. He was sure she wasn't crying anymore.

Sighing, he turned his boiled eyes to the computer screen. He switched on the modem and hooked into the computer network, and then to the genealogy BBS. A block appeared on his screen, in it: *"Check Messages!"*

"How 'bout that!" he said aloud with a grin. *Someone must have something on the Rands!*

A keystroke took him into his message box where two messages on the subject Family Murders were listed. He opened the first. "Hi, Zack," it read. "No relation of mine, I hope <grin>. All my antecedents died in bed. Don't know who they were there with and who caught them, though." It was signed by Randy Rand.

"Joker!" said Zack. There were always a few of them hanging around the bulletin board.

He opened the next message: "Zack—your message intrigues me. I'll log onto the conference tonight. Room B. We can talk in private." Signed by Yolanda Smith. He'd never met her or exchanged messages with her before. He crossed his fingers. This could be one of those miracles of computer networking. Out of a half million people who belonged to this particular system, the one who has the answer to your question just happens to read your message.

He immediately stroked the keys that logged him into Room B. From the list of names that appeared in a window at the top of his screen he saw Yolanda Smith had arrived before him. Below the window, sentences wrote themselves out across the screen, preceded by the name or nickname of the person who'd typed them in on a computer in some other room in some other part of the country or world. The conference was more like a party, with two or three individuals directing messages to one another, while others "listened" in. To someone who never talked to others by computer conference, it would seem both meaningless and confusing, of possible joy only to computer nerds. To Zack, it was actually like being there —wherever *there* was, listening to people he knew as they shared opinions and chitchat. He could break into the conversation whenever he wanted and add his own opinions, or start a conversation with anyone there who didn't decide to ignore him.

As he entered Room B, his name was flashed on the computer screens of everyone present. A few messages to others flashed across his screen before.

> Yolanda Smith: Hi Zack. Glad you could make it. I think you'd be interested in reading a file of mine in the library.
>
> Zack James: Yolanda, is your file on the Rand family?

After a few more unconnected messages to and from others, Yolanda signaled Zack that she wanted to talk privately. Since no one else seemed to have anything to say about the murders, Zack saw no reason to remain in the conference. He keyed in a signal that tuned out the conference messages and left the screen open for Yolanda's messages only.

Yolanda typed in: "I don't know if it's connected to the Rand family. The actual file is about some family black sheep of mine, named Champus. This cousin of mine killed quite a few folks by driving knives through their hearts."

"That's not a unique way of killing people," Zack entered.

From Yolanda: "It's unusual to *leave* the knife there."

"Yeah—right."

"My file's in Library 10, about my cousin, Gus Champus. Called Champ.zip. Humongous thing. About 100k long, zipped up," she wrote.

That would be about a hundred single-spaced pages, typed up, thought Zack. It would be a challenge to read through; he wanted to be sure it was worth it. "Tell me more," he typed.

"Gus was active just after the Civil War."

"Confed?"

"Yes. Had a grudge against certain people on the wrong side. Yankees. Offed them with a 12-inch handmade bowie. Then left the blade in their chest as a mark."

"OK. That's interesting. But that was 120 years ago," Zack tapped out.

"Didn't end with him. The grudge was passed down to his son and grandson. They carried on the tradition," appeared on his screen.

"Got away with it?"

"Long enough to make new Gus Champuses."

Zack raised his brow and typed: "You mean there's a Gus Champus alive today?"

"Maybe. One was born, but I couldn't track him down. But one thing about your message pricked my ears up. You said this Rand woman's mother lived in Phoenix. That's where Champus IV was born. Champus III lived there for years. Had a bastard son. Kid's mother—a whore—was killed in AZ, and the kid just disappeared. I think Gus III might've killed her and raised him in secret."

Hmmm, said Zack to himself. "And taught him the family tradition?"

"Right!" came back quickly.

"Don't know. It's farfetched to think it's associated to the Rand thing."

"Would be. But another thing. These were grudge jobs. Some victims related way back. Gus II took out a couple of Crandalls. Gus III did in a few named Randall, kids or married to their kids. Dropped the C. Could be your victim's dad dropped the a-l-l."

This could be a real hot lead! "Could be."

"Download my file. I wrote it as my master's thesis three years ago. Thought I might go back to Phoenix one day and sniff around a little. Time went by and real life got in the way. Get back to me when you've read it. I can send more stuff if you want. I love murder mysteries. Always wanted to be a real detective."

"Me, too." He wished he could tell her that in this case he was a real detective. Some day he might, especially if the Champus file led him to the killer he was looking for. Right now, tired as he was, all he could tell her was good night.

After work the next evening, Zack captured the Champus file on his computer disk and started to scan it. The more than a hundred single-spaced pages were too much to read on the computer screen. Especially since he'd barely slept the night before and had worked for twelve hours that day, and he had a horrible headache, a throat that was scratchier than ever, and his eyes oozed grit and tears.

He started up his printer, a noisy, clacking piece of iron that dragged continuously connected fanfolded paper through on a tractor and dropped it directly onto the floor, as he didn't have a collecting rack. Ignoring the ear-shattering noise, he sat on the floor and began to read the pages without separating them. The words began to blur. He started to cough. At last, he gave up and let the printer to do its job.

He got some warm water and salt, and went into his bathroom to gargle at his sink in the double bowled vanity area just outside the master bathroom.

Looking up at the mirror, he saw Poke, in her long, red polka-dot flannel nightshirt, who had just come into the bedroom and stood by the foot of the messy queen-size bed.

"Pop?"

"Yeah?" He gargled a mouthful of salt water to try to soothe his throat.

"I don't know what sounds worse. You or that printer. How come you're still up? You promised you'd slow down."

"I got a lead on those murders. Just downloaded a file. Thought I could—" He was overtaken by a coughing spell that left him trembling.

"Daddy, why don't you call Dr. Broward?"

She hadn't called him Daddy since grade school. "I don't need a doctor for a lousy cold. I'm just tired and I have too much to do."

"You're sick. Your face looks like a crumpled paper bag. You've been hacking all night every night. How're you going to sleep? Call her."

"I'll call her tomorrow if I don't feel better. It's nothing. First I caught that cold and now my throat's a little dry, is all. From the furnace going on all night and blowing on me. You keep that thing too high, Poke. Now go back to bed and leave me alone. The printer'll be done in a few minutes, and I'll close down the computer."

"OK. But promise you'll call her, Daddy. Please?"

"Yeah, yeah. I will."

He didn't. He always put off calling Doc Liz Broward. She knew too much about how he'd suffered going through Maryellen's sickness and death. He'd even cried in her arms, along with Poke, the day Maryellen died. And it didn't make sense, his going to a woman doc, one whose pedigree stretched back to the Mayflower on both sides. Sure, she was nice, and warmer than that haughty nose would let you believe, and she knew Maryellen personally from Penn. And he liked her. But, if he went to a doctor at all, which he never did as long as he could put it off, he should make it some son of a dockworker who lived in Conshohocken, not someone who came from a huge house in Bryn Mawr and lived in a Society Hill apartment.

So he didn't call her until he was so sick he started making mistakes at work. He couldn't afford to do that. He had to get better fast, because the more he read the Champus file, the more he found to connect the Civil War murders to the Rand family. Yolanda Smith hadn't even told him that some of Gus's victims were buried in the woods, that Gus was a metalsmith who made his own knives as well as jewelry, and that Ruth was the first name of more than one of his female victims. So he had to go to Arizona to see if he could trace Gus Champus III's bastard son and get more background on Ruth Spencer to see if somewhere way back, there were Randalls and Crandalls in her family.

You better get me fixed up fast, Doc, he thought the next Wednesday as he parked his Ram in the fifth tier of the medical office building parking lot. *I got to get to Phoenix.*

CHAPTER TWO

The next Wednesday—Philadelphia

"Please help me! Doctor Broward—Oh God, please help me!" The short, plump woman burst past a blocking receptionist into Liz Broward's private office.

Agnes Shultz's tearful outburst stunned the thirty-eight-year-old family doctor. She knew Agnes bore physical suffering well; only an extraordinary blow could have shattered her shyness enough to make her fly through a crowded reception room and dash through the back office without signing in. In a glance, Liz took in her patient's agony: Fear or pain had widened the brown eyes; distressed, nibbled fingers had torn through the dark brown hair and shocked it into wild coils.

Consciously steadying her own eyes and voice, Liz told her receptionist, "Have Elsie take care of Zack James for me, Claire. I'll see him as soon as I can."

"Dr. Meredith could see him, Doctor, if—"

"No. Elsie can start with him. But I want to see him myself before he leaves."

Liz wanted to see Zack herself because she knew that his basic illness was grief, and she wanted to help him deal with it. Jim Meredith, her physician partner in the joint family practice, had never treated Zack or his wife, Maryellen. Elsie, their nurse practitioner partner had. She would know about Zack's embarrassment at having to come in a month ago because a steel bar from some exercise equipment had slammed his head when a cable snapped. He'd waited until a knot formed on his skull, then had come in, pale and hyperventilating. The superficial wound had been easier to treat than the embarrassment. The grief was even harder to treat. He hadn't been able to talk about it, or cry about it again, since breaking up in Liz's arms the day his wife died. The medical emergency that brought him here today couldn't be properly treated without knowing that.

"I'll tell Elsie, then," said the receptionist, looking helplessly at Agnes, who demanded Liz's undivided attention now. She left, pulling the door shut behind her.

"Here, sit down." Liz led the frantic woman to the gray leather chair beside her gray oak desk, then took her own seat. "Take a few deep breaths. It'll calm you down." The soft colors of Liz's private office—peach walls, aquamarine carpet, and gray woods—and its uncluttered furniture and walls, created a calming effect. She'd wanted it that way, and had wanted the warm, intimate aura its small size expressed.

Agnes gulped a few breaths. "Help me, please. Do something! You have to do something! You're the only one that can help!"

It was an exaggeration. Yes, two other doctors had failed to diagnose Agnes's painful, incurable illness. And Liz had diagnosed and treated it, so that Agnes suffered few flare-ups, and those she went through were shorter, more bearable. But the other doctors weren't negligent or incompetent. Agnes's ailment was extremely rare, and its symptoms easily confused with other, more common diseases. That was why the other doctors had misdiagnosed it, and why their treatments had seemed—temporarily—to cure it. The first had used exploratory surgery, which, though it uncovered nothing to explain Agnes's excruciating abdominal pain, made the pain clear up. The second had been treating her with a drug for a bladder infection, when her arms and legs suddenly ballooned painfully. He'd speedily withdrawn the drug and treated her with Benedryl. The symptoms had cleared entirely in a couple of weeks. But when neither doctor could make sense of a third bout of symptoms, they blamed hysteria for her condition, and sent her to a psychiatrist.

When Agnes had come to Liz instead, desperate to find the reason for her agony, Liz had pored over the woman's health records for a sensible link between the clearing up of the first two attacks and the onset of them and the third. At first, the hidden connections had eluded her, but she knew they were there, and she knew she could find them.

She did. Not while studying the records but as she sat at her kitchen table, sipping a glass of red wine while her dinner warmed in the microwave oven. Her eyes fell on the glass of ruby colored liquid and the whole picture fell into place in her mind. There was a connection between the surgery that relieved Agnes's symptoms and the sulpha drug that brought them on again. There was a relationship between her first attack and the one that had brought her to Liz: Agnes had gone on a low-calorie diet just a couple of weeks before both the first and the third episodes. Agnes had porphyria. A simple urinalysis proved it. After standing for a day, her urine turned purple, the color of the wine in Liz's glass.

Liz brought Agnes's illness quickly under control with injections of the blood factor hematin, then and during her infrequent relapses. As bad as the pain sometimes got, Agnes had never lost control of her emotions. She bore her torments gracefully, bravely. Yet now she sat here quivering and crying. Stunned and upset by her patient's frenzy, Liz tried to comfort her, but Agnes was inconsolable, barely able to speak.

"Agnes? Where's the pain? What happened?"

The woman shook her head in wide arcs. Her shoulders heaved, her plump hands, twisting a shredded tissue, worked a damp hollow into the skirt of her navy blue dress. The dank smell of sweat and tears rose from her sodden bodice and damp, knotted hair.

"No pain? What, Agnes? I can't help till you tell me what happened." Worried that her patient would launch a full-blown flare-up, Liz hid her concern beneath a practiced composure. She leaned forward in her chair, head tipped slightly to one side, calm violet eyes probing for Agnes's evasive ones. She creased her forehead; her tawny forelock fell into her eyes.

Finally, her patience worn thin, she blew her forelock back and brushed it into place with her hand. She resummoned her self-control, then stood up and went to Agnes. Tilting forward, she placed her hand gently on Agnes's shoulder.

Agnes steadied her eyes, looked up. She sucked some tears from her upper lip and shuddered.

Liz stooped so that her face was directly opposite Agnes's. She grasped her patient's shoulders.

Agnes sighed again, then shook her head again.

Liz released her grip and straightened. She was five-feet-nine inches tall, and stately. She knew she had inherited her father's patrician bearing and her mother's high-bridged nose, which made her look haughty. Aware that these features and her Broward family membership unnerved people, she wore her hair loose and soft and chose relaxed, homey clothing, like the lightweight blue wool chemise she wore now. She donned her lab coat and doctor's gear only in the hospital or examining room. "I can't help if I don't know what's hurting, Agnes."

"I know. I'm sorry, Dr. Broward."

"I want to help." She pulled some tissues from the box on her desk and handed them to Agnes, who took them and jammed the kneaded one into her skirt pocket.

Agnes blew her nose loudly and looked up at Liz again. Finally, she said, "Fred took the kids and left."

"Oh, Agnes! Why?"

"Because of—of—of it."

She meant the stigma of her porphyria and the sensational news stories about it. "But, I thought he understood about porphyria. He saw how well you were doing."

"It was the article in the paper two weeks ago."

"Article? Not another one!"

"In *The National People's Examiner*. At the supermarket checkout. That the vampire disease theory was true. He thinks I'm a bloodthirsty vampire. He thinks I'll bite the kids, and turn them into vampires, too."

"You know what a rag that is!"

"It was in the regular papers, too. Right before my first attack—he was never sure. Sometimes even I'm not sure—"

Liz's face flared. She turned so Agnes wouldn't see her emotion. *Damn yellow journalists! Why don't they check out untested theories in the first place! Just because it came from a scientist at a convention didn't mean it was true.* Turning back to Agnes, she said, "He knows the theory's full of holes.

There are no such things as vampires. That was in the paper, too. *Too late!* Where is he? I'll call him."

"It won't do any good. He took them to his mother's. She always believed in vampires. She said the theory proved it. She tried to keep Fred and the kids away when I first got sick. She's been working on him ever since. Now she's taken them somewhere. He wouldn't tell me where."

"That's kidnapping!"

"Fred said it was OK. He's their father."

"No one has the right to take your children without your permission. When did this happen?"

"Over a week ago. I kept hoping—"

"You're sure she's not just keeping them at her house?"

Agnes shook her head. "I went there. No one was there. Not even him. He might of gone with them. He wasn't at work all week, either. No one there knew where he went. He just didn't show up—" Her shoulders began to shake again.

Liz made a fist so tight her knuckles cracked. She grasped Agnes's shoulders again and pulled her to her feet and straightened her with a hard, firm shake. "Agnes! Stand up!"

The woman looked at her, jolted out of her tears.

Startled at her own rashness, Liz let go of her shoulders. "I'm sorry. You're a strong, brave woman. You've taken charge of your life and your illness till now. You can't let this throw you into relapse. And I won't let you give in to that woman's ignorance. You're not a vampire!"

After a brief silence, Liz continued, "I'll give you a mild tranquilizer to help you clam down. A lawyer can help get your children back. Do you know one?"

She nodded. "But I can't pay him. I just work part-time. I don't have any money saved up."

For a moment, Liz thought her father's law firm might help Agnes. No. Better not get her father or anyone in his practice— even her fiancé, Eric—involved with this kind of case, with someone like Agnes. Then she remembered a firm her nurse practitioner, Elsie, had learned about. "I know who you can go to," she said. "They handle these kinds of things. A women's law firm. They don't charge if you can't pay. And they have other services, too, to help till you're back on your feet."

Agnes's eyes widened and grew black. "I—I don't want—I know he'll bring them back."

"Because you want him to. And you don't want to make trouble by getting a lawyer. But you can't sit around hoping and waiting. He's serious, he's kidnapped your children, and you have to tell someone besides me—someone who can help. I can only give you tranquilizers and moral support. That's not enough. This law firm can help. They know what to do for you and your children, and they'll do it."

Agnes suddenly reached for Liz and embraced her. Liz hugged her in return, held her awhile, then patted her on the back as she broke the embrace. "All right, I have some samples of Librium. It will take the edge off your anxiety and shouldn't make you drowsy. But you have to act! Go to work every day, and get legal advice right away. The worst thing to do is nothing. You fought the porphyria. Fight this."

The heat from Agnes's face had dried the remaining tears. Her round face was red and shiny, but she looked determined despite it. "Thank you, Dr. Broward. I knew you could help me."

"I'm glad you came to me." Liz motioned her to take her seat, and returned to her desk. From a deep drawer of drug samples she drew a few packs of five-milligram Librium capsules. She gave Agnes instructions on taking them as she slid them across the desk. Agnes nodded and picked up the packets and looked confused. Of course she would be.

Liz took a prescription pad from her center drawer and wrote down the instructions she had just given Agnes. She tore off the slip. "Here. Just read this over at home." She stood up and walked to her patient again, and patted her hand as she placed the slip into it. "You'll do fine, Agnes. You know you will." With a gentle touch at the elbow, she urged her from the chair, then guided her out to the reception desk.

"Claire, look up the phone number for the Women Helping Women's Legal Services for Agnes. No charge for her today." She ran her hands over the front of her dress where Agnes's tears had dampened and darkened the light blue wool. "Oh, and has Zack been seen?"

"Exam Room One, Doctor Broward. Elsie checked him over and his chart's in the door pocket."

"Good. Call me if you need me, Agnes," she said as she turned toward the room.

◆ ◆

Zack James sat at the foot of the examining table in the bright, white tile and steel examining room, his eyes puffy and bloodshot, his firm-boned face a few days unshaven as usual. His long, black hair was trimmed this time, and combed back away from his broad forehead; still he looked somewhat like a forlorn adult waif in his makeshift outfit of hunting vest, plaid shirt, and jeans.

The outfit, the hair, and his ruddy face were clean and kempt despite his eccentric appearance. He always smelled of outdoor things, like pine or freshly cut grass, though she knew he spent most of his hours at a computer in a publishing house office. The aroma couldn't have come from aftershave—that would have faded long ago—and this man would never use cologne. It must have come from his soap or deodorant. For as sad and drippy-eyed and runny-nosed and feverish looking as he was, he exuded cleanliness.

She used to think that Maryellen had been—at least in part—responsible for Zack's good hygiene, which was so at odds with his sloppy, hodgepodge attire. Maryellen had been among Liz's first patients. The women had met at The University of Pennsylvania, where Liz went to medical school and Maryellen got her master's degree in public health nursing. They had both attended some interdisciplinary classes in family health, and they'd developed a strong mutual respect for each other.

If Maryellen had not been married to Zack, Liz doubted that he'd have been in her office. First of all, he would not have come to a woman physician; second, he would have disdained a practice run by a woman named Broward, with all of its Main Line connotations. She was glad he had come to her, and especially that he'd continued to come after Maryellen died. During the months of her dying, both they and their daughter,

Jill, had shared their fears and anguish with her. At Maryellen's death, Liz had shared their grief. She'd lost a friend, after all. In the nine months following, she'd tried to help Zack and Jill handle it. The girl seemed to be shouldering too large a share of responsibility for a fourteen year old. Zack simply buried his grief under a monument of overwork and a refusal to sleep or think. Now, she feared, it had forced itself on his weakened immune system.

She took her white lab coat from its hook behind the door and slipped it on. Looking first at him and then at her nurse practitioner's notes on his chart, she said, "You sure have it this time, don't you, Zack!"

He nodded and mumbled, "Mmm-hmm." The mumble was an octave lower than his usual baritone voice.

"I'm sorry an emergency kept me." She read the nurse's notes more carefully: Temperature 103.5, pulse 94, respiration 30, blood pressure 122/80. His eardrums showed no sign of swelling from fluid collected behind them; his nostrils and sinuses were congested; his pharnx was red and purulent. The nurse had taken a throat culture and left the chest exam for Liz. "Elsie say what she thought?"

"I'm sick. The culture would say what made me that way. Probably need an antibiotic. I should drink lots of fluids, take an expectorant for my cough, a decongestant to keep my ears from getting infected, and Tylenol to bring down the fever, turn on my humidifier, and go to bed."

Liz nodded. "Elsie's right on track. It says here you have a dry, hacking cough. Not bringing anything up."

"Right." His voice rumbled.

"No chest pain."

He shook his head as if he had already told all that to Elsie and wanted to get on with being cured.

"OK. Take your vest and shirt off. I'll have a listen to your heart and chest."

He unbuttoned and took off his multi-pocketed, variegated hunting vest and handed it to her. Its pockets were full, and its weight surprised her.

Then he handed her his red-and-black plaid flannel shirt. It was hot from being caught between the heavy vest and his feverish body. She hung the clothes on the clothes tree near the door and took her stethoscope from her lab coat pocket.

He jumped when she pressed the diaphragm against his broad, hairless chest over his heart. "I'm sorry. I know it feels cold. You'll warm it up in a hurry with that fever."

"Ummm. It's OK."

She ducked her head slightly, put the stethoscope earpieces into her ears, and listened to his heart, which was beating fast for a man with his large, muscular frame. That was to be expected with a fever, and the beat was even and firm and she heard no murmurs as she moved the diaphragm from point to point over the heart valves.

She straightened and asked him to turn on the table so his back faced her. With her scope against the right side of his back, she asked him to breathe in and out with his mouth open. As she moved the scope up and down, and from right to left over the lobes of his lungs, she heard the fine rales of a pneumonia. They were present in both lungs. She shook her head and then listened again. There was no doubt. She wouldn't need an X ray to confirm it.

She straightened. "OK. Swing your feet around and face me."

He did.

"Zack," she said, "when did this start?"

"Don't know. Five, six days ago, maybe."

"Well, it's about time you got yourself in here. Frankly, I don't know how you managed to drag yourself in. You've got double pneumonia. You should be in a hospital."

"What? I'm not sick enough to go to a hospital."

She knew he was thinking of Maryellen. To his mind, only people as sick as Maryellen had been toward the end went to hospitals these days, or people needing the radical kinds of treatment that she'd had. Or people needing surgery.

"It's just that you should get complete rest. And plenty of fluids. And someone to check you regularly and make sure you get your antibiotics on time. You can't have that at home."

"I'm not going to a hospital. I'm not that sick. And I'm big enough to take my own medicine on time."

"In the middle of the night?" She sighed. "I didn't think

you'd agree. Look, I'm going to give you a shot of penicillin and enough samples to get you through the next few days. I hope you're stocked up on groceries at home. Can Jill take off some time from school to get you up at night for the medicine and make you meals and do laundry and so on, so you don't have to get up except to go to the bathroom?"

"My God! You talk like I'm some sort of basket case!"

"You're a sick man, Zack. You need rest and someone to get you your meals at least. If Jill can't take off school, or you can't hire someone to come in and help, then you have to go to the hospital. I won't let you leave this office till you say it's one or the other."

"Hey, you can't hold me here."

"No, damn it, I can't! Or, I probably could. It wouldn't take much physically to hold you. I'm surprised you're able to sit up on your own. I'm not exactly comfortable about the thought of you driving yourself home through rush hour. Damn it, Zack! Use your head."

"That lat bar knocked something loose in there. I can't use it."

"Well maybe you need it to hit you again to knock it back into place." She smiled ironically and shook her head. "Zack—" she said warningly.

He looked at her through bloodshot eyes. They were not so glazed that they didn't flash quickly from green to brown in the few seconds he stared at her. "OK. Get me the shot. I'll get Poke to take off school. Shit! I can't afford to miss work. How long do you think it'll take me to get better?"

"If we can knock the infection right out, you might only miss a week or so of work. Though you probably won't feel much like going in."

"I never feel like going in. I can't miss a week or so."

"You'll be lucky if that's all you miss." She went to her medicine cabinet and pulled out a vial of powdered penicillin, which she mixed with a syringeful of sterile water. She shook the aqueous solution thoroughly, and then withdrew it into the syringe. "Lie facedown and slide your jeans below your buns. I want this to go deep."

He complied and didn't complain. When he had tugged his

pants up and sat up, he said, "I can't miss even a week. I've got to go to Arizona in just a couple of weeks, and I have to take off then. Its too much time in a row."

"Maybe you can change your vacation plans. Your health's what's important right now. Besides, you may not be feeling well enough, even in two weeks, to enjoy a vacation. It's going to take five or six before you're yourself." After cutting the needle off at the shank, she toed open the trash can and tossed the broken syringe into it with a clatter. She lifted her foot; the cover clanged shut.

"It's not a vacation."

She wished it were. It would've been a sign he was working his way out of mourning. "Well, if it's work, then you won't be taking off more time."

"It's something else. And I can't put off going. I have to track something down as quick as possible."

"Track something down?"

"Yeah. I got a lead on what happened to the ones that were killed."

"Oh. Yes, I read about those bodies you found. That must have been grisly." Another shock that he hadn't needed at this time in his life. Why did everything seem to happen to people just when they were most vulnerable? No wonder he'd caught pneumonia.

"It stank. The whole thing stinks, but we're beginning to get somehwere."

"We? Who's we?"

"Lieutenant Crosby and me."

"A police lieutenant? You're working with the police? I thought you worked for a publisher. As an artist."

"I'm a genealogist, too."

"How does that help the police?"

"There's a family connection. I'm helping trace it down." He looked at her earnestly and said, "Look, don't breathe it to anyone. Poke's the only one besides Crosby that knows. If the press gets this, it'll blow our investigation out of the water."

"I'll hold it as privileged information. I'm your doctor." Her mind flashed to Agnes Shultz for a moment. "You're right about the press. Well, I hope you listen to doctor's orders so you can get well enough to do your detective work. So you're a genealogist. I'm surprised."

"What's so surprising?"

She looked at his uneven features, at what her father would call his bastard appearance. He surely would have been a cast-off, a by-the-way cutting from a well-pruned family tree that he couldn't possibly trace. "Well, frankly, I never thought much of genealogy. It turns me off."

"How come?" Zack got down from the table and took his shirt and vest from the coat tree.

Liz couldn't believe the energy he seemed to have, and the animation his face and voice had taken on since he'd begun to speak of his detective work.

"I don't like the way people use it."

He put on his shirt. "What's wrong with how people use it?"

"They use it to exclude."

His mouth fell open as he stood with one arm partly through his hunting vest armhole. "What!"

"I said, genealogists use it to ex—"

"I heard what you said," his voice rumbled forth. "And you, dear person, are full of shit!"

Her face grew hot.

He looked at her a moment and added, "Real genealogists use it to include." He finished donning his vest.

"That hasn't been my experience with the ones I know."

"You mean with the Browards and the Stanfords."

Drawing a quick breath, she turned and began to fumble in her medicine drawer for some Tylenol samples. She found a foil packet and handed it to him. "How did you know my mother's a Stanford?"

He took the packet and tore it open. "It's not hard to find out stuff like that. And you're right, your parents and their families do use genealogy to exclude. Except they don't use real genealogy. They use family history, put it all together in a book, and that's what people get to believe. Actually, they usually tell the truth—as far as it goes."

She drew a paper cupful of water from the sink tap and handed it to him. Her hand trembled slightly. "How do you know it's the truth? And how far it goes?"

"Well, I read about your family. And it's too clean. Too straight. No black sheep or skeletons." He palmed the two white pills into his mouth and washed them down. That set off a brief coughing spell, which he quelled with another few cups of water, half of which spilled down his chin.

He sat down on her steel swivel stool. His face was red, and he slumped a little and breathed heavily in and out several times.

She stared at him. She knew anger leapt from her eyes, and was appalled that she couldn't hide it. "I'll get you a cab. You have to get home to bed."

"I'll drive myself home."

"No. You absolutely will not!" Her voice sounded unusually shrill. She picked up the wall phone and asked Claire to phone for a cab for him.

When she hung up, he said, "How'll I get my van home?"

"It's safe in the building garage. I'll clear it with security to leave it for a week."

"A week!"

"If you feel up to it, you can come in and get it in a couple of days. But you probably won't feel up to it."

"Shit!"

"Why don't you lie down on the table and rest till the cab comes? I'll get you a pillow."

He slumped a moment, then nodded and shuffled slowly over to the table. She brought a small paper cased pillow, and he laid his head on it.

"I'll call some prescriptions in for you. What drugstore do you use?"

He told her. "They don't deliver. I'll send Poke to get them."

"Good. Now check your temperature every four hours. If it goes higher or doesn't come down in the next day or so, call me right away. I'll give you an instruction sheet."

He nodded, and his hair scratched against the paper pillowcase. He looked defeated.

Her anger eased. "Be sure to follow it exactly. Any questions?"

"No."

"Fine. I'll have Claire come get you when the cab comes." She turned and started to the door.

He rose on one elbow. "Tell me something, Doc."

She tensed. "What?"

"Aren't you even curious?"

She swallowed, trying to moisten her throat to keep her voice from cracking. "About what?"

"About your family history, and how far it goes and what it excludes and why. It's all there, bound in leather on a shelf in your church genealogy library."

"No. I'm really not the least interested. What may have been excluded doesn't affect me in the least. But I am curious about one thing, and that's why you're so interested in my family that you'd bother to go to my church's library. You certainly don't belong to my church and I don't think it's any of your business."

"Why not? You know a lot about my family history. Especially you know all about Maryellen's. You came right out and asked, and wrote it all down on that fat record. I got a right to know where my doc comes from and how it makes her feel about patients like me."

She flinched. "The family history in your record is vital to the care I give you. I don't see how—"

"I'll put it to you this way, dear person. Don't you think a family doc like you would be an even better family doc than you already are if she knew as much as there was to know about her own family and where she came from?"

Her face flared again. "I know all I need to know about where I came from."

"And if she knew about the ones who came from the same place but got excluded from the history?"

"Be sure to follow those instructions to the letter." She pulled open the door and left.

"Didn't you hear your dad, Liz?" said Eric Storrey, her fiancé.

She sat next to him in the large, formal dining room of her parents' rambling colonial Bryn Mawr home. The oval dining table with its fine white linen cloth could have seated fourteen, and often did when her parents entertained business associates.

Now there were just the four of them sitting on the Regency chairs with the red silk seat cushions: Her father in the armchair at the head, to Liz's left; her mother in the low-backed side chair at the foot, to Eric's right; and Liz and Eric side by side in high-backed chairs on one long side, balanced by the empty chairs across from them. Behind the chairs she could see it all in the huge, gilt-framed mirror above the antique sideboard: Eric in his hunter green shaker sweater, his brow knit above his unusual olive eyes; her mother, Grace Broward, who at fifty-eight looked more like forty-five in her peach silk blouse and matching pants, despite never having had a face-lift or coloring her graying hair; her father, Paul Broward, also much younger looking than his sixty-two years due to his tall, lean build and the tension in his large frame and jaws, which kept his muscles from sagging. His eyes were bright blue—made brighter when he wore blue, as he did tonight—and as young (or as old) as they'd ever been. Liz shut her eyes as they fell on her own reflection, and she noted the tension in her face. She stared at the shell pink ovals of her left fingernails, and the back of her long, slim hand.

Eric jostled her elbow, almost making her spill her coffee on his sweater sleeve.

She set the bone china cup in its saucer, noting that she'd let the coffee get cold while the others had finished theirs. She hadn't touched her rhubarb pie, made especially for her by her mother.

She always had Wednesday evening dinner here with Eric and her parents, and usually she looked forward to it. Evening meals the rest of the week were either rushed or lonely. During rushed ones she didn't have time to think; during the lonely ones, too many unbidden thoughts rushed at her. Thoughts about the direction her life had taken, regrets that it hadn't taken another, or several others, as less encumbered women's lives often took. She, who once seemed to have the whole world to choose from, actually had little choice left. She had run out of time at thirty-eight, and so had made a choice she'd sworn she never would: She was engaged to marry a suitable man from a suitable family. Her upcoming marriage had not been arranged, so much as programmed, as her parents' marriage had not been arranged in the traditional sense, but programmed by their families, both Main Line Philadelphians, both Episcopalians.

Liz's parents were well-matched products of their generation and society. They knew and loved each other and had realistic expectations of each other, of their marriage and its place in history and society, and of the value of social selection. Her mother had some unspoken reservations about the way these matters were handled. She went her own way when it didn't count, and had encouraged Liz to go hers when it did; but she discreetly supported her husband's values for his sake and for Liz's. Family ties were important. Important enough to *manage*. Important enough to endure what you couldn't change.

Grace Ellen Stanford Broward couldn't change her husband. He'd forever be what he was: a powerful lawyer whose skills brought pleasure to the powerful and pain to the weak; a bigot, lacking Archie Bunker's charm, who would try to destroy any unworthy who might try to woo Liz, his sole heir. He saw his prejudice as concern for good breeding. Liz saw it as social Darwinism. She rebelled against it when she could. She vowed that her own self-esteem would never rest on her parents' names, and that as much as she loved them both, she'd defy any scheme they might design to position her for the "right" marriage.

But she'd learned that the die patterning her future had been cut generations ago, not only by her family, but by a whole social system. As radically as society had changed, the changes didn't run deep, especially for women. Their social mobility—upward or downward—still depended on men's ambitions and class prejudices. The upper class existed, had bred her and had claimed her in spite of herself, because middle-class men, too, knew it existed. So they rejected her before she could reject them. She scared off men of even her own class because she was tall for a woman, imposing, a doctor. The Broward name and fortune put off most others, except for gold diggers and gigolos. Most men she liked in medical school and during her internship and residency had never approached her, had avoided her approaches, had seemed cowed in her presence.

She enjoyed sex, longed to have children, and time was

running out. She could have done worse than Eric Storrey, a kind, intelligent, open-minded man who joined Paul Broward's firm and had risen to junior partner because, whatever his name, he was a damn good lawyer. He was forty, nearly six feet tall, with thick brown hair and a handsome, square face with a cleft chin. Her father might have seen him as a good match for his daughter, and surely her mother could picture a grandson with his handsome features and possibly with eyes that turned from Eric's green to Liz's violet. But that had nothing to do with why Liz was attracted to Eric. She knew he loved her and would have wanted to marry her even if her parents had disapproved. If they hadn't approved, she might have fallen in love with him and agreed to marry him long before she had.

Now, she jumped as he jogged her elbow, and she saw that her father was frowning at her from the head of the table.

"Liz," her mother said, from the foot. "I've never seen you so distracted. Is something bothering you?"

"No. Nothing important."

"You mean not important to us." Her mother nodded and smiled at her own wisdom. Grace knew and knew that she knew. That's what gave her power in the family.

Liz smiled at her mother, admiring her. The two women understood each other. Liz consciously modeled herself after her mother in everything from her choice of clothes to her attitude. She silently thanked her mother for teaching her to love an often disagreeable father.

"As long as you're thinking it here and you're not going to listen to us," said her father, "you might let us in on it." His distinctive back-tooth lisp made "us" sound like "ush." He smiled at Liz.

She was never sure of what her father's smiles meant. Nobody ever was. That was his intention.

"I'm sorry, Dad," she said. "What were you saying before?"

"I've forgotten. That really was unimportant. Small talk, mostly, I think. I probably asked you how your day went. I'd monopolized the whole meal talking about mine. I do hope you heard at least something."

She hadn't heard a word.

"That's exactly what you asked her," said Eric. "How her

day went. Looks like she gave us the answer. Not too well, eh Liz?" He put his hand on her arm and bent his head around to look into her eyes.

She reached up and touched his cheek. He looked worried.

"I was thinking about a patient. It's not really dinner table talk." She never talked shop with her family, and seldom did with Eric. Being with them helped keep her emotionally demanding work in its place. She could change from work clothes, put on comfortable pants and a shirt in her favorite color, blue, and relax while the cook served grilled salmon and asparagus, two foods she loved but never cooked for herself.

"What kind of patient?" asked her father.

"Just—someone with something incurable." True, and more acceptable than the whole truth about Agnes. And less likely to stir up her father than if she'd added, *Someone rude and arrogant who told me I was full of shit.*

"Well, you can't cure them all, dear," said her mother. "Take heart."

"I know. I don't expect to. Let's change the subject."

"He doesn't have AIDS, does he, Liz?" Paul Broward grimaced as he lisped it.

"Dad, please. I don't want to talk about it." Then she added, to redeem herself in his eyes, something that for some reason mattered to her tonight, "My patient doesn't have AIDS."

"If he did, I wouldn't want to hear about it."

"Believe me, you wouldn't!"

"If you'd followed my judgment, you'd be in a specialty instead of the kind of practice where riffraff come in off the street with their dirty diseases. You'd be in Brian Horner's City Line Avenue plastic surgery practice where you could choose your patients, and you wouldn't have a nurse for one of your partners." He turned to Eric. "You ought to talk sense to her, Eric. If she doesn't catch AIDS, someday she's going to catch a lawsuit for having a nurse practice medicine under our name."

"I'll know where to go for a lawyer!" retorted Liz, "and it's my name, too. I can do what I want with it. Besides, Elsie's perfectly competent. Can we drop this now? I thought we'd dropped it long ago."

"Paul," said Grace, "I thought so, too. Don't let your father get to you, Liz. He just feels his power over you slipping away with your wedding only a month off."

Liz looked at her mother, whose eyebrows were lifted mockingly. Then she laughed. "Oh. I wondered what'd brought it on."

He saw Eric look from her to her mother and grin. He had gotten to know them and how they managed Paul. He'd learned from them how to defuse Paul's prejudices with playful irony while leaving his dignity intact. That had served him well as a junior law partner. It would serve him well as a family member, too.

He took Liz's hand and gently squeezed it. Maybe, she thought as she returned the loving pressure, it makes sense to marry someone who understands how people like my parents think, especially when that someone is very, very good in bed.

Liz always looked forward to Wednesday nights in bed with Eric, in the same way she looked forward to a meal of her favorite foods with him and her parents. Both experiences brought solid physical pleasure and spiritual satisfaction— deep, memorable, lasting. She once regretted never having had a passionate love affair, then she decided that either she wasn't very passionate about sex, or that this deep, slow growing to love someone was what passion really meant. It eluded most people in their excitement. They went from infatuation to infatuation and missed it, while she got right to the heart of it from the beginning with Eric. So, she anticipated her nights with him with warm arousal but not with insatiable, relentless, stirring hunger.

He squeezed her hand again. "Well, why don't we leave your folks to their plans for our wedding? The time is getting close."

She caught her breath and felt her face grow hot. The pressure of his hand felt suddenly electric. She grasped it tightly. "Yes." *She wanted to go with him now.*

"She hasn't touched her pie. Liz—?" said her mother. She frowned.

"I guess the pressure of the wedding is getting to me, too. I'm so busy I almost forgot. I love your pie, Mother. You know that. Can you pack it for me?"

"Well, I've made a whole one for you, as usual. But, yes, I'll wrap this slice, too. Are you getting the wedding jitters, Liz?"

Liz laughed. That was it! Suddenly being reminded of how close her wedding was—on the same day Zack James had been so unabashedly familiar with her. Calling her "dear person"! Telling her she was full of shit! That on top of dealing with Agnes Shultz and the usual press of patients needing her total attention and skill. Her nerves had been frayed. No wonder they seemed to stand on end and cry out when Eric touched her. No wonder her hand suddenly grasped the spongy knit sleeve of his sweater. No wonder she wanted to get out of here and jump into bed with him and get him inside of her, so he could do something about the appalling flames licking her very womb. "I guess so. I thought I'd be immune."

"I hope not. You'd miss half the fun! All right, I'll wrap your dessert."

◆ ◆

"I love you when you've got wedding jitters," said Eric, rolling off her and onto his back.

She'd been insatiable; he had been ardent and skillful as usual. But instead of being fulfilled and drowsy after lovemaking, she was overexerted, overexhausted, paradoxically soured while aching for more. Something inside her needed touching, and he hadn't reached it; but he seemed not to know this. In fact, he seemed to think that he'd never touched that something before, and that this time he had. *How differently men and women look at sexual pleasure,* she thought. *Well, things will certainly get back to normal and settle down after the wedding.*

She rolled onto him, teasing him by grinding her sticky belly against his, and kissed him. "I think I'm jittered out."

"Me, too, damn you."

She rolled off him, sat up on the edge of the bed, and reached for her nightgown at the foot. While putting it on, she found her slippers with her feet.

"You aren't getting up, are you? Aren't you going to hold me?"

"I'm afraid of what would happen if I did."

"Believe me. It's not going to happen. It couldn't!"

"Then I'm afraid of it not happening." She rose and started to the bedroom door.

He sat up. "You need to talk, don't you?" He got out of bed and pulled on his pajama bottoms. Then he followed her through her apartment to the living room, which overlooked the city and a stretch of the Delaware River unobstructed by oil storage tanks. She opened the draperies so the light filtering up six stories from below and a gibbous moon reflected from the river softly misted the apartment, bringing the spare Scandinavian furniture to muted life.

Her apartment made clear the differences between her and her parents. She preferred the clean elegance of simplicity over the gilded elegance of wealth. Besides, it fit in better with the way of life she liked and the busy life she lived. The sofa and chairs' creamy beige leather upholstery needed little care. The rich rosewoods of the trim and the tables were smooth and warm to the touch and the eye, though sometimes they embarrassed her as being anti-environmental. She hadn't known when she'd bought them that the woods were from endangered forests.

As she turned from the window, she saw the wood's burnished glow in the filtered light. It reminded her of her discomfort, of the feeling of being wrong and unthinking as only the rich could be.

Eric had sat down on the sofa. Again he said, "You need to talk, don't you?" He was, as ever, understanding and considerate of her needs, without her having to voice them.

Generally, she liked this. Not tonight. Everything about tonight seemed different. His closeness in this dim, quiet room, where she'd come to be alone with her thoughts, irritated her. His concern felt more like probing; his apparent ability to see right into her mind felt threatening, intrusive.

Though, for God's sake, there was nothing there for him to intrude on. Certainly no secrets she wanted to keep from him.

"Something's bothering you."

"No. I—for some reason I just feel overwrought."

"That patient that's dying."

She laughed and sat down across from him in the upholstered chair and put her feet up on the ottoman. "She isn't dying. It's bad, terrible in fact, but not fatal. But I've seen lots of terrible things. And, I've had patients that died before."

"Yes. About eight or nine months ago you had that woman who died of leukemia. That's about the only time you seemed to want to talk about it. You were shaken for weeks. You don't shake up easily, Liz."

She gripped the arms of her chair. "She wasn't just a patient. She was a nurse I took classes with. A friend. I saw her whole family suffer—"

"It hit you pretty hard."

Yes, it had hit her hard. She hadn't just watched them suffer. She'd suffered with Maryellen. She'd suffered with Zack and Jill. Though as the family's primary physician she wasn't in charge of the cancer treatment itself, she'd remained as involved as possible in Maryellen's care. By the time the incredibly virulent cancer had killed her patient, Liz had found herself almost a family member. She'd mourned with them. She had held them in her arms and they'd wept on her shoulder.

"Oh, God!"

"What's wrong?"

She shook her head.

Dear person! To them—to him—she would be a dear person, indeed! She stood up and walked to the large plate glass window and stared down into the lights. *And was he a dear person to her? Could that be? Few experiences were as intimate—as bonding—as shared grief. It could have made him dear to her, precious to her. So precious that she couldn't stand his criticism of her, his thinking she was full of shit. So precious that his audacity had stirred her anger.*

But *passion? No, no! That couldn't be! She couldn't be feeling that about Zack. Eric had stirred that. Thoughts of a lifetime with him, of children with him, had stirred that. Suddenly she realized that in a month they'd be married, and she hadn't given it much thought before, of what it would mean to her life. It was that. It had to be that!*

Or could it be that Zack had told her that she had been wrong all these years, that she had been rejecting him and men like him by not caring about her past and where she came from?

They had not been rejecting her at all, only her image of them as belonging to some lesser people. There were cousins out there, he'd told her, who came from the same place she had but were excluded by her family. If she didn't care about them, how could she be a good doctor for people like Zack? How could she care about Zack?

But she did care about Zack. More than she ever had cared about any other man. More than she ever had allowed herself to believe she could, until now.

She grasped the edge of the thick cotton window drape.

"Oh, dear God!" she whispered.

CHAPTER THREE

The following Sunday

Over the phone his voice sounded falsly pitched: too thin, too reedy. *Disguised!* Agnes thought. Still, he brought the first word of Fred—the first message from him. "When did you talk to him? Where did he go with them?" she asked.

"We'll negotiate the answers to those questions," he said.

Her eyes darted around the room, lighting on this piece of furniture and that—an end table, a rocking chair with a needlepoint cushion, a cluttered maple bookcase. They had all grown strange and dusty in the nearly three weeks that Fred had been gone. As if they belonged to someone else, or to a life gone before, one she knew of but couldn't recall.

"You'll have to talk to my lawyers. They said—"

"Hssst! You've charged him with abduction. He won't deal with lawyers. You've forced him into hiding. You'll talk to him through me or no one. Think about it. I'll call back later."

"No, wait! Don't hang up! I didn't want to charge him. I just wanted them to find him. They wouldn't look unless I charged him."

"Hssst! Yess. And defamed him in the newspapers. If it hadn't been in the papers, I wouldn't be calling. That was your big mistake."

"I didn't know it would—"

"Hssst! Well, now you must negotiate with me, or you'll never see your children again."

"Oh, God!"

"Maybe you should cry out to Satan. He's what made you what you are."

Her already coiled stomach quaked. Yes, that had been in the papers, too. His reason for leaving. Her disease: "Porphyria Victim's Husband Believes Doctor's Theory, Takes Children." And then they said, a few paragraphs down, that the theory had been scientifically disproven, but that nonscientific doubters, enamoured of folklore, still clung to its romantic appeal: *"For as horrifying as these monsters are to many, they still are basically symbols of sexuality. In fact, at least one modern science fiction writer has cashed in on the sexuality of vampire figures through her erotic portrayals of them in her best-selling novels."*

"Please! I'm not a—"

"Shut up! I can't stand pleading. If you want to see your children, you'll negotiate with me. Today. Not tomorrow. When and where I tell you. Those are the terms. And tell no one I've called you."

She would tell someone. At least she would try to reach Dr. Broward.

"I—I won't. I don't even know your name."

"I don't have one."

"Are you—coming here?"

"No. You're coming here. On the train. Walk to the station. Don't take your car. You don't have to worry. I live in a nice part of town, on Pine Street near Rittenhouse Square and the hospital." He told her the number.

Agnes knew that as long as she went during the day she'd probably be safe in that neighborhood of row houses where many young professional people lived because they liked to be near city amenities—the theaters, the shopping, and Rittenhouse Square itself. Maybe this man was a successful lawyer. Maybe he was a private detective. She could understand why Fred might hire someone like that to negotiate with her. Maybe he'd agree to bring the children back if she withdrew the charges against him. Maybe—she didn't quite know what could be negotiated in this. And this man's voice was so sinister and frightening. But what choice did she have? It was Sunday. The Women Helping Women hot line was just for real emergencies, like someone wanting to kill you, or you wanting to kill yourself. This was upsetting, but not an emergency like that. It was already noon, and she would have to catch the next train if she wanted to be sure to come back before it started getting dark.

"All right. I'll catch the next train. I should get there about 1:30."

"If anyone's out in the street, just walk by. I'll be watching from a window. When the coast is clear, I'll open the front door and leave it open. At your first chance, come straight in without knocking."

"But no one there knows me."

"Hssst! They know me! My business and clients are private. That's how I like it. Listen to me! No lawyers! No neighbors! I don't want anyone to see you coming here. Understand?" He gave her no time to answer. The phone clicked in her ear.

She understood, but she had to call Dr. Broward.

The doctor's answering service asked if it was an emergency. It wasn't a medical emergency. What could a doctor do?

"Sort of," she said. "I have to talk to her before I leave. About a lawyer that called me."

"What's your name and number? I'll page her at the hospital."

"The hospital? I shouldn't bother her there."

"No problem. She's just making rounds. I'll have her call as soon as she can get away."

"I hope it's before I leave."

"It should be within fifteen minutes or so. Is that soon enough?"

"I'll wait as long as I can."

Dr. Broward couldn't leave the patient she was with for twenty-five minutes, and by the time she dialed Agnes's number, Agnes had caught a train at the Noble Station. The telephone rang and rang and rang, for Dr. Broward was concerned about Agnes. The answering service operator had said the woman sounded distraught, even frightened. She said something about talking to her lawyer. Liz felt partly responsible for the mess in the papers the past few days; she had, after all, suggested Agnes take legal action. She should have guessed that an investigation into such a kidnapping would lead to publicity, not only about the kidnapping itself, but about Agnes's porphyria. She hung up and redialed the number. The phone line buzzed and buzzed and buzzed. Still no answer. "Damn it!" She hung up again.

Agnes passed by the three-story row house and saw the man in an upstairs window. He dropped the curtain as she glanced up at him. Across the street, an old man stooped over his cane and inched forward. A woman a few steps ahead of him cast a mean glance across the street at Agnes. The woman pouted and then stopped with a sigh that was almost a grunt and waited, fists dug into her hips, until the old man caught up.

Quickly Agnes turned her head and continued past the whole row of houses, glancing back over her shoulder at the old couple until they turned the corner. The street now empty, she returned to the house and saw that the door was open. She hurried up cement steps and passed through the door into a dark hallway. There, she stood and looked first up a flight of unlighted stairs, then through a peeling door frame to her right, where some daylight filtering through a dusty window revealed the massive hulks of some old-fashioned living room furniture.

As the stairway was darker than the room, and as she had to go somewhere beside outside (where she longed to be) if she wanted to get her children back, she gathered up what bone remained in her legs, and stepped into the living room.

No one was there. Maybe he was in the large room that lay toward the rear of the house on the other side of an arch through which she could see part of a dining suite. The light in that room, too, seemed swallowed up by dark, heavy furniture. If there were sounds in these rooms, other than those of her own breathing and a buzz that had developed in her head, they, too, had been swallowed by the darkness. She did not want to go forward. She knew that the man who lived here in this awful dark could not possibly help her get back her children. She knew that she must have been lured into a trap, and the only way out was through the front door. Turning toward the blazing light from the open door, she cried out and ran.

The door slammed the moment she reached the entry hall. She'd heard not a creak, seen not a flicker of movement before it shattered the silence, cut off the light. Yet in its burning afterimage on the wall now revealed, she saw him. He moved, and the lower part of him seemed to separate and come toward her, clanking, flashing what looked like a serrated knife.

"Easy, Adolph!"

He reined in the dog, whose teeth remained bared.

She stepped back, then froze.

"Don't let Adolph frighten you. He's trained to protect me. But he won't attack till I tell him."

Trembling, she could neither speak nor be still. A trickle of sound ran from her lips.

He pulled a key from his shirt pocket and turned toward the outside door.

She heard the metallic clack of the dead bolt.

"Living room, Adolph," he said, and shook the leash. His voice changed to a bark when he spoke to the dog. As if he and it spoke a common language.

The rottweiler led the way; Agnes did not follow them. Once in the living room, the man moved to the massive sofa and turned toward her. He stood where the filtered light from the window revealed his face. "We'll talk in here," he said.

Awestruck by his pallor, his gigantic frame, his huge, bony hands and head, she stared into his eyes. They looked like blue tinged oysters, or something that someone sick had coughed up.

"Oh!" she said. *So that's the reason for the dog and the darkness; he's blind!* There was hope. She could escape if he planned to hurt her. If he didn't see her sneaking out, he wouldn't tell his dog to attack. *Unless he would hear her. She'd been told that blind people have sharp ears.*

He seemed to know her fears, her revulsion, which he would have seen in her eyes if he could see. His mouth curled. "Hssst! Well, come in and sit down. You do want to see your children again, don't you?"

She looked from him to the dog, which strained at the leash and growled when her eyes met his.

"Adolph! Quiet! You're frightening our guest."

The rottweiler swallowed his growl, but his flexible, purplish lips quivered over readied incisors.

The man put his hand on his dog's head. "Sit! Or I'll get the training strap!"

Whining, the dog dropped to his haunches.

Agnes trembled.

"You see, he does what I tell him. He won't attack anyone or anything, even when he's very hungry, unless I tell him to." He sat down on the sofa and pointed to the chair across from it.

Agnes hesitated; then, seeing no choice, she crossed in a wide arc around the sofa, the man, and the dog. She sat. The deep upholstered chair sighed as her body sank into it. The maroon mohair was worn away and shiny where the back of her head struck the chair back. Her fingers gripped arms frayed by years of such grips. Her fingernails dug into twine once covered by welting. She could not let go.

"That's better. Now we can talk about your husband and children."

"Where are they? Please. I'll do anything he wants if he brings them back. I'll drop the charges. I'll—"

"Will you get cured?"

"Please! He's wrong about that!"

He smiled. "That's what you'd like to think. Or rather, you'd like us to think. It suits your purpose. But it's not a secret anymore. We can defend ourselves against you. As your husband decided to."

Her fingers twisted the welting cord. Overcome by helplessness, she tried to swallow but couldn't. Every duct and mucous membrane in her body had suddenly become parched. Her eyes widened with fear and pain. Why had she come here? He wasn't negotiating with her; he was torturing her. And Fred had sent him. At last she was able to whisper, "What do you—want from me?"

The man rose. He towered over her; his short-cropped hair seemed to bristle. The dog began to rise, but his master shoved him down again. "Not yet, Adolph." Adolph sat, keeping his eyes on Agnes, who positioned herself to rise at a run.

"We want a complete cure."

"But there isn't any. Just treatment. My doctor's treating me for it."

"Your doctor's wrong. There's a cure. He just hesitates to take such drastic steps. He's afraid."

"She'd cure me. Dr. Broward could cure me, if she could. Fred knows that. If there was a cure, she'd have told us."

Raising his eyebrows, he said, "Maybe I should call your doctor and tell her that she can cure you if she's willing to take the risk." His voice sounded almost friendly.

At his reasonableness, Agnes felt another surge of hope. She stood up. "Yes! Talk to her. I'm sure if there's something she doesn't know about porphyria, she'll try it."

Adolph's haunches quivered.

"Sit!"

In spite of his barking tone, Agnes wasn't sure if he was talking to the dog or to her. She lowered herself back into the chair. The dog remained tense; so did she.

"No. She wouldn't listen. Besides, traditional doctors have an oath not to use this cure. But my oath's just the opposite. I've vowed not only to cure you, but everyone else who has it, if I can find them."

Was he saying he was some kind of doctor? "But—how?"

He smiled. "It's a widely known cure. It's been known for hundreds of years—since before they named it porphyria to throw people off the track."

She knew why they named it porphyria: it made your urine turn purple, like port wine, and porphyria meant purple things in the blood. She kept forgetting exactly what the purple things were called.

"But it didn't fool me. I know what it is. I know the cure. Adolph!" he shook the leash. "Upstairs!"

The dog stood and started toward the entry hall. Holding the leash, the master followed. Agnes sat clinging to the chair, until the man said, "Tell Agnes to come with us," and pulled on the leash again.

The dog turned and bared his teeth at her again.

She rose, trembling, to her feet.

"In front of me," he said.

She walked toward him, taking deep breaths, as Dr. Broward

had taught her, to calm herself down. She placed herself in front of him, inadvertently touching his arm.

"Don't touch me!" He stepped back, so that the dog's leash tightened up and brushed against her legs. She almost tripped over it.

"There's no room between me and the dog."

"He won't let you go in front of him. Between us. If you want to be cured and meet your husband's demands, you'll stay between us. *But don't touch me—don't turn your head toward me or I'll turn Adolph's head toward you!"*

She drew a long, shuddering breath.

"All right, Adolph. Go up."

The dog went up the stairs, Agnes struggling to adapt her gait so that she would bump neither him nor his master, whose breath burned the back of her neck. They reached a landing, then turned down a hall with closed doors on either side. The light coming from a window at the end of the hall weakly illuminated the worn flowered runner beneath her feet. Agnes nearly stumbled over a bulge in the runner but caught her footing with a gasp.

Not so the man behind her. He tripped and, in trying to regain his balance, spun against a closed door and struck his head against the brass knob.

The dog roared and turned with a lunge at Agnes. His teeth sank into her right wrist. She felt it snap.

"Adolph! No! Away from her!"

Whining, the dog implored its kneeling master with its eyes while its teeth remained fixed in her wrist.

"Let go! Away!" He stood up and touched his head where it had struck the doorknob. Then he examined the blood on his fingertips.

Adolph dropped her wrist. She caught it in her left hand, and sank to the floor in shock.

The dog ran to its master and sniffed his bloody fingers and licked them.

"All right, boy. It's not her fault." Then he turned toward Agnes and kicked her leg. "Good thing it wasn't, or I wouldn't have stopped him. Get up." He kicked her again, harder.

She couldn't figure out how to get up without using both

hands. But, as his leg swung toward her again, she said, "I'm trying. Please!"

He stopped his leg in mid-kick and set it on the floor. With her uninjured hand, she grabbed for the pants leg of his brown work trousers and tried to pull herself up with it.

He pulled it away. "I told you not to touch me!"

She fell forward onto her broken wrist and cried out.

"Get up without touching me. Get up on your feet!"

She crawled to the door and used her good hand to grasp the frame molding to pull herself up. She avoided touching the knob, which was sticky with his blood.

"Lick the knob!" he said.

She looked at him, suddenly understanding. "No, I—"

"Lick it! I want to watch." His eyes were fixed on hers.

"You can see me. I thought you were blind. I thought that was why you had the dog." Then she looked at the curtained window at the end of the hall. It was the one he'd watched from for her. He'd dropped the curtain when she'd looked up. *Why hadn't she realized that?*

"I knew you'd think so. Most people do when they see my eyes without my glasses." He reached into his pocket and pulled out a pair of Coke bottle spectacles and hooked them over his ears and nose. His eyes lost their form altogether. "My vision is weak, but adequate. I can see quite clearly now. So can Adolph. So I suggest you lick the doorknob. Lick it clean, so that not a drop is left."

She stood, unable to obey.

"Tell her to lick it, Adolph."

"No! No, I will." She mentally turned off her taste buds and licked the knob quickly. Still, the metallic taste nauseated her.

"Clean. I still see some blood. Run your tongue all around it. Pretend it's your lover's neck." He grinned lewdly at her.

A bare moment's hesitation—then she licked it. Yes. She did what he wanted. Maybe he'd just brought her up here for sex. She'd be smart to obey him, not try to fight him. If she forced herself to think clearly, if she pretended to like it, things might work out right and she could get the dead bolt key from his pocket. Eventually both he and his dog would have to sleep. When they did, she'd sneak down the stairs and run out. The thought of a way out, another glimmer of hope, strengthened her. She ran her tongue around the knob, back and forth, running across the top and down around its neck. Her tongue in its dryness dragged on the sticky, carved brass. When she saw him lean over and leer at her, she took another sweeping lick, then ran her tongue over her lips and forced herself to smile at him.

"That made you feel better," he said. "It made her feel better, Adolph. We knew it would." He picked up the leash and shook it, and motioned Agnes to fall into place between man and dog. "Attic!"

The dog barked excitedly and started to scamper up the stairs. His master slowed him down so they could get there with no further accidents. Agnes, her left hand supporting her right, struggled to adjust her pace again, to keep herself safely between them, touching neither. The man's voice and manner had softened toward her since she'd licked the doorknob. He was obviously some sort of pervert who wanted to make her do certain things to stimulate him. Her wrist had begun to throb; still, she felt much more confident, now that she knew what he wanted. And she'd give him all that he wanted. She'd lick anything he wanted her to if she could get at the key in his pocket. Anything in the attic; anything on him, anything on the dog, no matter how sickening it was.

He switched on a light as he followed her and the dog into the attic, a large room full of unfamiliar equipment.

"This is my hobby room," he said, with obvious pride.

"What's your hobby?" Because the room was well lit, it seemed less sinister than the rest of the house. A long, wooden workbench stood at its center. A cabinet with drawers stood against a far wall next to a closed door. On a rack attached to the worktable were coils of metal wire, a butane torch, a soldering iron.

He told Adolph to sit, and he leashed him to the table leg. For the first time, the dog relaxed onto his stomach and placed his broad muzzle on crossed paws.

A chance! Maybe she could hit him over the head with something and get the key while the dog was leashed to the table! She looked around for something to help her escape. Her eyes lighted on a soldering iron. That might work.

He picked it up and moved it to a shelf high out of her reach. "I make things out of metal," he told her. "Jewelry. Certain useful implements. Tableware, for example, of gold and silver. Come over here and see how I do it. I'm working on something for you, and I want you to watch the final step."

"Something for me?" She was frightened, suspicious, but tried to sound pleased. She walked to him and stood next to him. She saw on the table a knife with a long steel blade. It glinted when he picked it up. She stepped back.

He laughed. "I'm not going to kill you with it. It will be a gift you can use. But it's not finished yet. I want you to finish it yourself."

"How can I finish it? I don't know anything about making knives."

"You don't have to. I'll show you what to do. The manufacturers have made it so easy." He reached for a small brown bottle on the rack and poured its contents into a shallow tray. Then he handed her the knife, handle first.

Shocked by the cold brass of the handle and the pain in her right wrist when she had to let it go, she nearly dropped the knife. Had she not had to use her left hand, she might have been able to gather up the nerve to stab him. But he was too big and strong. He would crush her. She needed something large and heavy. She needed to have him turn his back.

The knife was as useless to her as her broken wrist. He knew it. She held it and leaned against the dark wooden workbench.

"It's easy," he said again. "You simply rub that liquid over the blade. And that will plate it with silver. Then it will be ready. Something extra for you for agreeing to be cured—a silver-plated knife to take home."

"Home?"

"You want to go home, don't you?"

"Yes. But—"

"You didn't think I planned to keep you here?"

"You seemed to want—I don't know."

"You're here to negotiate. I set out the terms—your husband's terms—that if you want your children back you have to agree to be cured. I'll cure you when your gift is finished. After that, you'll be home to stay."

She knew there wasn't a cure. If there were, Dr. Broward would know. But he seemed to believe he'd found one. If all he wanted was to use it on her, she'd let him believe it was working. Then he would let her go home, away from the ugly dog, away from his ugly eyes. It would be over! "That's all you want? To finish the knife and to cure me?"

"That's all."

"Is it a pill?"

"No. A treatment. A single treatment that yields a permanent cure. You'll never come back again. That'll end it. Now and forever. Now, the knife. Dip it in the fluid. You can drop the whole thing in. It won't hurt if the handle's plated, too."

She set the knife into the shallow pan, and, at his instructions turned it over several times. When she removed it, both the knife and her fingers were coated with silver. She set the knife on the table and asked, "Will it hurt? The cure?"

"A little. But after that, your porphyria will never hurt you again. That's worth a little pain, isn't it?"

"I guess so. What next with the knife?"

He handed her a blackened cloth. "Rub it with this, till the coating sticks tight and no more is coming off. So it's even all over."

She rubbed at the top side, but the knife kept slipping beneath her hand.

"I'll hold it for you." He took another piece of cloth and held the handle while she polished the blade till it glowed with the soft light of silver. He looked at her and smiled as she stroked the knife. "You enjoy it?"

She hesitated. "It looks nicer."

He took the blade from her, and turned the handle toward her, and gestured at her to repeat the process on the handle.

"Lovely!" He said when it was done. "I'll gift wrap it for you." He wrapped it in a case and tied it with a silver ribbon and handed it to her with a short bow.

Then he wasn't planning to use the knife in the cure. The pain would come from something else. "Thank you," she said.

She gripped the case tightly, then slipped it under her broken wrist to support it.

"Now, to undress to get ready for the cure."

She didn't want those leering eyes watching her undress. If she had to have some kind of awful sex with him, she would; but till the moment it happened, she wanted to be out of his sight.

"That door next to the cabinet. It's a bathroom. You can go in there for privacy. I'm sorry I don't have one of those paper gowns for you to wear. But you can cover yourself with the shower curtain till we get things going."

Her mouth fell open with surprise.

"What did you think I was going to do? Rape you?"

"I—"

"I'd have to touch you to rape you. Hssst!"

It was the first time he'd made that sound since coming up to the attic. It stirred her fears again. But he'd done everything as he'd said so far: kept the dog off of her; given her the gift wrapped knife. He must not have intended to rape her. He must believe he had a real cure for her. Probably he'd convinced Fred that he did. Maybe Fred would pay him a lot of money if he thought he'd cured her. Or maybe he planned to extort money from her for getting her children back. It seemed so strange and implausible; but Fred's stealing the children, his believing the terrible theory about porphyria was implausible, too. Fred's mother was a little weird. She believed in vampires and black magic and witches. This man might be someone she knew.

"Hssst! Don't stand there staring at me. Go into the bathroom and undress. Then get into the bathtub and pull the shower curtain around you and call me."

She looked at the package in her hand.

"Take it with you. I'll open the door for you, so you don't have to put it down till you're in there. You can even hide it after I close the door."

Yes, he'd done everything he'd said. He did mean to try some cure on her. It would be over soon, and she could get her aching wrist splinted and go home. Never have to come back. "All right." She walked to the door, he opened it, and turned on a yellow bulbed light, and closed the door behind her.

The tiny room, tiled in cracked white octagonal tiles that looked about ninety years old, held an old toilet with rust stains ringing the bowl; a chipped washbowl; a footed tub with its porcelain grooved through to the metal with wear. A ring of tubing supported both shower head and shower curtain. A single towel, stained black, hung from a metal rod next to the sink.

She put down the case on the sink, and pulled her good arm from one sleeve of her blue dress, which she suddenly realized was sweat damp and torn. She then pulled the dress over her head and, trying to avoid further pain, slowly worked the dress off over her broken wrist. She tried not to cry out, but couldn't stop herself. The pain was nauseating, and she sank down into the toilet's broken seat and sat for a while till the nausea passed.

"I'm getting impatient!" he called through the door.

"I'm sorry. My wrist—"

"Oh, yes. Well, call me when you're ready. I'm all ready out here."

"Yes." She removed her slip, then slid her bra off her arms and pulled it, still hooked at the back, over her head. Last, she took off her shoes and panty hose. She tried to hang everything on the single towel rod, but things kept slipping off to the bare floor. Giving up, she left everything there. She didn't want him to think she was slovenly, but she couldn't help it. He hadn't wanted to touch her, but he had kicked her, and he could do the same with her clothes if they got in his way.

At last, she got into the tub and pulled the plastic curtain around her. The rings scraped on the tubing.

"Ah! Ready at last!"

Right at the door! Listening! Waiting—

The knob turned and the door flew open. He stood there, leash in hand. He smiled, then stepped back. "There she is, Adolph! Get her!"

She heard the curtain crackle as she tried to pull it tighter around her.

The rottweiler hurled himself at the curtain, ripped it away.

"The throat! The way she does it."

He believes it! Her cry of "No!" was broken by the dog's vicious roar.

The dog brought her down, and her neck struck the tub rim. The fury of the attack doubled the weight that hammered her down, and broke her neck. A blessing, because she felt no pain as his teeth sliced through her carotid artery, and the broken bones of her wrist cracked apart and burst through the skin.

"Off, Adolph. Enough! It's my turn."

The dog raised his bloody muzzle, licked his lips, then whined.

"Let's not make a mess we can't clean up. We want to keep as much of the blood in the tub as we can. You'll get your share in time. You know I only want one little piece."

Adolph jumped out of the tub.

"Stay in here. Don't get those bloody footprints in the workshop. They'll never come out of the floor planks." He pulled on a pair of latex gloves.

The dog sat.

Phillip took the knife case from the sink, unwrapped and opened it, then took out the gleaming knife. He stepped toward the tub. "She's in an almost perfect position, boy. Her head's hanging back and her chest is stuck out and those big fat boobs are hanging out of the way. I can slice down right between them and get it. The way we do in autopsies." He'd made the blade scalpel sharp, and he sliced down the center of her chest, made a slice to each side below her breasts, then pulled the muscle, fat, and fascia aside and free of the bones.

The dog whined at the cracking of sternum and ribs; then let out a short bark.

Phillip's mouth filled with saliva when he saw the uncovered heart. He touched it. It quivered. He began to sweat. *She lives! But not for long! He would see to it!* He flicked the knife and cut the aorta free. The heart fluttered and lost its blood. He cut loose the other vessels and lifted the heart from her chest. He took it to the dog.

"Just sniff! Don't eat this. It's for me. You can have the liver and kidneys as soon as I open her abdomen. Then we'll cut up the rest and I'll put it in the freezer for you. I don't know why

I didn't think of this with the others. It makes disposal so much easier. That hunter never would have found them in your stomach! Hah!"

He set the heart in the washbowl and let water run over it to wash out all the blood while he opened and exenterated the body in the tub and washed the organs before putting them on the floor for Adolph.

"You're a good boy to wait so long. But she'll provide you for a long time. And I haven't even had time to track down her family bloodline."

The dog fed furiously. Phillip would have liked to watch him, but he didn't have time. *He had to take care of the heart. It flopped in the sink under the stream of running water, still alive, still potent. He could see her already coalescing around it, her upper lip contracting away from the new incisors that were already beginning to form. In the tub, her legs jerked, and started to find themselves. They would rise in a moment, climb over the rim of the tub, dragging her gaping carcass across the room to throw upon him, swallow him up, and retrieve the heart from his hand.*

He ran the water over the knife and over his hands, then turned it off. The purplish organ played dead. He knew it wasn't; he wouldn't be fooled, for he could hear it beating, hear her laughing behind him. He thrust the knife through it then lifted it, his trophy, on the blade and laughed. "We got her Adolph. And this one will go in the freezer where no one will find her and set her free. No hunters! No doctors! Not anyone!"

In the tub, her legs and arms had stopped jerking. The new teeth loosened from the gaping jaws and one by one fell from her mouth.

The dog licked his chops and barked.

CHAPTER FOUR

Meanwhile . . .

Zack hadn't known how sick he was because the worst part of his sickness was the tiredness, the fatigue, the utter exhaustion; and Zack had long ago forgotten how it felt not to be unremittingly weary. He had forgotten how to stop fighting the weariness, how to give in to it, to turn his mind and body off for a while. Turning his body off seemed to turn his mind on to things he didn't want to think about: things like Maryellen's sickness, things like her being gone forever, that couldn't really be true, because they didn't make sense. They hurt his heart and his soul to the core. He knew the only way to kill the pain was to hurt so much physically, in every muscle, in every bone, in every nerve, that you didn't have to go inside and look at that other pain. You could stand the shattering headaches because they conveniently shattered your ability to think beyond them. You could stand the tormented muscles, the wearied bones— you could challenge and best them, get done what you had to in spite of them.

But the sickness had done him in, made him give in to his body, left him unable to do anything except sleep fevered, demon-filled sleeps. The illness drugged him and altered his mind, so that suddenly he had no choice. He realized that he could die from a sickness that had so much power over him, and he realized he didn't want to die. Saying he could keep himself from dying by denying he was sick wouldn't work now, and denying that Maryellen wasn't coming back wouldn't work anymore, either. He'd gotten an inkling of the relief facing her death could bring when he'd brought down the gobbler and felt that old heat surge to his groin. But the insight had fled in the wake of his uncovering those bodies, and with Crosby's request for help, which had suddenly presented him with something new outside of himself to throw himself into for a while.

Late this afternoon he had sunk into a sucking pit of bad dreams. He knew they were dreams; still, he couldn't throw them off. He could see a disk of light far away at the mouth of the well he'd stumbled into. His fingers grubbed through slime to win fleeting grasps on a substrate that liquefied at his touch and oiled his skin. Though he seemed not to advance through any effort of his own, the aperture above him grew closer, the bottom of the pit farther away, but more threatening. The floor's surface began to boil up the closer he got to the top, and the roiling noise it made from below reverberated up the well as its walls closed in on him like congested mucous membranes.

His head emerged from the pit into a draft of cool air. The pit was a living creature in the throes of deciding whether to disgorge or swallow him.

Suddenly he saw Maryellen, dressed in buff feathers, running into the forest.

"Stop, dear person!" he cried.

She answered, "Yelp! Yelp!" and tripped. Her leg became entangled in a vine. She fluttered and yelped piteously.

"Poor ladybird!" He broke free of the pit and ran toward her. The vines that entangled her came alive, snapped at his arms as he struggled to turn her loose. He wrenched them fiercely from around her leg. They made a strange popping sound as she broke free and flew off through the trees, away from him.

"Go, Ladybird!" And she was gone. He tried to fly after her, but he could not flap his wings. The vines grew tighter and tighter.

"Pop! Hey, Pop. You OK?"

He woke, entangled in sweat-soaked bedclothes. "Wha—?"

"What are you fighting with, Pop? Cheeze, you're all tangled up."

"Dreaming. Terrible dream." He stirred and turned and

twisted until he'd freed himself from the sheets. The room was lit by a single lamp on the fruitwood dresser, and the clock radio on the matching nightstand was hidden behind a water pitcher and glass. "Time is it, Poke?"

"Seven. You were sleeping so hard before, I figured you needed it more than supper. But it's past time for the penicillin. I had to wake you. Boy, you look terrible." She poured him a glass of water and handed it to him with the pill.

He palmed the pill into his mouth and sucked the warmish water from the glass. "Feel like I look terrible." His mouth felt pasty and he figured he must smell pretty bad, too.

She placed her palm on his forehead. "You feel cool, Pop."

"I think I sweated the fever."

She sighed and smiled. "Wow!"

"What kind of wow?"

"Dr. Broward called a while ago. Wanted to know how you were and if the fever was going down. I told her it was almost normal this morning and went up to a little under a hundred this afternoon. She said the antibiotic must be working. You're cool, Pop. Wow!"

"She called, huh? On a Sunday?" He sat up on the edge of the bed and rubbed his beard with his hand. He stood up. He didn't feel as top heavy as before, and the room looked more normal. For the last few days the path from the bed to the vanity alcove had seemed long and forbidding. His tall chest of drawers on the bedroom wall between the alcove and the bed had somehow been hard to reach and grasp for support. Now he felt no need for support to go to the bathroom.

"Yep. She said that in case you were feeling well enough to come in tomorrow to pick up the Ram, to stop in her office and she'll check to see if the pneumonia's dissolving. Pop, you don't really have pneumonia, do you? You said it was just a real bad cold."

He knit his brow and rubbed his face again. "She shouldn't've told you that! Shit!"

Poke's reddened face curled up in dismay. Her wide-set eyes drew closer together. "Why didn't you tell me, Pop? You should'a."

"She shouldn't'a. It was none of her business to worry you."

He walked across the bedroom to the vanity area and drew a paper cupful of water from the tap. He looked at himself in the mirror. God, he looked like hell, his usually shiny long black hair dull and oily, his beard beyond what even he could stand, his eyes puffed and caked with sleep crumbs. "Yech!"

He shuffled into the bathroom and shut the door and clunked the toilet seat up against the tank. A dark yellow broth of concentrated urine tinkled with little vigor into the bowl; its stench made him gag. He began to cough and to bring up whole lungfuls of choking phlegm. Afterward, he felt a little better. He shook his head and flushed the toxic humors down the toilet.

Poke was still in the bedroom when he came out and washed his hands. She was staring at him. "Daddy—" She put her fists up to her face and started to cry. She had just started calling him Pop again, after calling him Daddy for days.

"Hey! What's the matter now?"

"I don't want you to die, Daddy." She had rolled herself into a small quivering ball and was hugging herself ferociously.

He shuffled over to her and put his hand on her head. "I'm not going to die, Poke. Honestly. I'm getting better. You said yourself I feel cool."

"You were making such awful noises. You scared me." She uncurled herself and looked up at him. "Your voice sounds even worse. It sounded like you were coughing up your guts in there."

"I think that means I'm getting better. The bad stuff's coming out. It's loosened up, and that's why I rumble so much when I talk." He'd had enough chest colds in his life to know this.

"Do you think the pneumonia's dissolving?"

"I think so."

She sighed and smiled up at him with tears hanging onto her eyelashes. "You should'a told me, Pop. Dr. Broward told us about how sick Mom was."

"Well, she told Mom and me what she thought it was. But it was a long time before we took you to her office so she could tell you."

"Didn't you think I was big enough?"

"We didn't want it to be true. We kept hoping the specialist was wrong and waiting for it to go away. When the treatment didn't help and we knew it wouldn't go away, we told you. Mom wanted Dr. Broward to be there. She was her friend. She helped."

"It was true!"

He hesitated a second. Then, "Yes, Poke. Momma died," he said.

"I won't let you die, Pop! Not you, too!"

"I'm not going to. I'm getting better."

"I'm going to the doctor with you tomorrow. I want Dr. Broward to tell me you're really getting better."

"No, you're not. I'm better enough to go in myself. You're going back to school. You missed too much already. I can take care of myself."

She pulled away from him and looked hard at him. "You will go see the doctor, though."

"Yes. I promise."

"And you'll tell her to call me and tell me the pneumonia's really dissolving."

He hesitated a moment. "OK. If it'll help. I guess Mom would think that's OK."

"I think it's cool she called you at home on a Sunday."

"I think so, too, Poke," he said.

"I think Momma would think so, too."

Monday morning

He got out of the taxi at the curb, then took the parking garage elevator up to the fifth level and checked to make sure his van was still where he'd parked it five days earlier; after finding it there, he crossed the concrete tier to the orange door that led into the medical office building. The steel door's aquamarine other side told his eye what his ear knew immediately. The portal separated the hard sounds of engines' echoed screeches from the whispered whirs of air-conditioning and the carpet-silenced footfalls in the office wing. Outside, like the grease on the cement floors, rude angry reality lay, waiting for him to slip up; inside a few steps down the hall, lay compassion and the touch of Liz Broward's healing hands.

Just outside Dr. Broward's office, a bony woman over six feet tall with a heavily made up face and a maid's white uniform and thick lenses was pushing a small cart of cleaning equipment, and appeared about to enter the office. Alerted by Zack's cough, she turned as he approached, hesitated a moment, then pushed the cart down the hallway toward the women's room. Fumbling with massive hands in a large carpet handbag, she looked up and down the corridor. Then she withdrew a key and opened the door and whooshed in, leaving the cart in the hall. The rest room door closed behind her.

Zack pushed open the doctor's office door.

"Oh, Mr. James! You sure look different today!" said the receptionist. "The doctor's with another patient, but she's almost done."

A few minutes later, in the bright white examining room, as Zack sat on the paper-covered table with a thermometer in his mouth, Dr. Broward echoed the receptionist's exclamation: "Well, you sure look different, Zack! A world of difference." Relief crossed her face. She grinned.

The thermometer beeped. He took it out of his mouth and read it. "Normal," he said as he handed it to her. "I shaved."

Nodding at the thermometer, she said, "So I see."

"I hate to shave."

"I've noticed. Well, let's get that shirt off and see what's going on in your chest."

He hadn't put his hunting vest on this morning. Still, he felt weighted down and tired, something he hadn't noticed until after he rose from the waiting room chair and started into the back office. Taking off the shirt seemed to need all his effort. He tried to do it briskly.

"Pneumonia's a bitch," she said as he handed the plaid shirt to her. "It's going to take awhile." She motioned him to turn on the table.

He wished she didn't know how weak he felt, that she didn't always figure out how he was feeling. At the same time, her empathy always moved him. He nodded and turned his back.

Quickly she skipped the stethoscope over his back. "Looks

like we broke it up," she said, as she pressed his shoulder, signaling him to turn to face her again. "The rest is up to you. Take it easy for a while, and keep on taking the penicillin till it's gone."

"That's all?" He wanted to stay awhile.

She eyed him quizzically. "Well, keep taking the cough medicine. The expectorant will keep your chest loose, and the antitussive will ease the throat tickle."

"You don't need me to come back?"

"If you want to—well, yes, of course I'd like to check you in another week. No need to come in before, unless you have a relapse or something."

"OK. I'll come back Friday."

"Monday will be a week."

"I might go to Phoenix on Monday."

She glanced at him disapprovingly. "You ought to wait, you know. See how you feel."

"Look how good I feel today."

She sighed. "All right. Just make an appointment on your way out."

"Poke wants you to call and say the pneumonia dissolved and I'm OK."

"Jill?" She smiled and gently corrected him. "She means resolved. Of course. I'll be glad to. She's worried about you?"

"Yeah. You know. After—after what happened with Maryellen."

Her eyebrow lifted slightly; then she nodded. After a moment she let out a small sigh. "I miss Maryellen," she said.

"Me, too. I still can't believe she's gone."

"It's hard—"

Enough! He didn't want to talk about it anymore. Still, now that he'd engaged her, he didn't want to leave. "You're not still mad at me?" he said, breaking in.

"What?" She stiffened. He'd caught her off guard.

"About saying you were full of shit. I didn't mean it like it sounded."

She took her stethoscope from around her neck and shoved it into her lab coat pocket, managing to get only the rubber tubing into the pocket. The earpieces and diaphragm hung out, and the scope slipped out and clattered to the floor. She bent, picked it up, then stood up, red-faced. "I realized you weren't at your best."

"Anyway, I'm sorry. I usually don't say things like that to women."

"Yes, well—"

"Especially to women like you. You know—doctors?"

"How does that make me different from other women?"

"Well, I wouldn't say it to men doctors, either."

"Or to anyone you thought was better than you." She ripped open a foil packet and pulled out an alcohol pad. After vigorously rubbing it over the stethoscope earpieces and diaphragm, she shoved the instrument back into her pocket again, concentrating on getting the whole thing tucked in. Her face had turned purple.

"That's not what I meant. Shit!"

"You might want to make yourself more clear. Or keep your mouth shut altogether!"

His mouth opened. After a moment he said, "Yeah. I guess it's pretty big. My mother used to call me a bigmouthed shit—actually she said I was a bigmouthed, independent shit—typical Leo, if you know what that means."

"Your mother must be an astute judge of character. Now—"

"She doesn't use those kind of words, though. Like 'astute.'"

"What kind of words does she use? No, please don't tell me. I think I know."

He grinned. She wasn't moving toward the door, or making any other signs that she was dismissing him. She obviously didn't want to dismiss him.

He waited. After a long silence, she said, "You were right."

Now that surprised him. He caught his breath, and brought on a coughing spell that didn't end until he'd cleared a bolus from his chest. Weak again, and embarrassed at spitting up the phlegm in front of her, he shook his head.

She waited until he'd composed himself. Then, as if nothing had happened, she said, "I was full of shit."

"No. I mean—"

"I've been thinking about it. I should know more about my

family. Even if I don't owe it to my patients, I owe it to myself and my kids. You know I'm getting married."

He knew it. He'd read it in the papers, and it had bothered him. It had sent him, burning with disappointment at her defection from his world, to her church library. But why was she telling him now? What was she telling him now? "Right. In a few weeks."

"Yes, that's right," she said, looking surprised. "Well, what you said made me think. Anyway, I'm certainly not mad at you. It made me think—" She sighed. "So, I'll see you Friday." She handed him his shirt and fingered at the buttons of her lab coat, seeming to have trouble undoing them. "And I'll call—Poke." She'd never used the nickname before.

He put his shirt on and stood close behind her as she hung her coat on the door hook. She smiled at him brightly as she opened the door and ushered him through. At the white laminated checkout counter she held the smile steady and instructed the receptionist to make his next appointment.

He was confirming the date and time when the huge maid he'd seen in the hallway pushed her way out of the back office past him and the doctor and passed quickly through the reception room and out the door.

Looking stunned, the doctor said, "Who was that? What was she doing back there?"

"I've never seen her before," said the receptionist. "She came in a few minutes ago and said she'd left something in the back when she was cleaning before office hours this morning."

"What did she leave?"

"She didn't say. Just that she couldn't go home till she got it, and she was tired from working all night. Sounded logical." The receptionist looked at her boss defensively.

Dr. Broward pushed past Zack into the reception room, just as the outer door swung closed. "She dropped something." She bent and picked up a sheet of paper. "It's from one of our records." Standing and turning to the receptionist she said, "Claire, how did she get into the record room? She's not supposed to clean in there."

"Oh, Doctor Broward, I'm sorry! I didn't think—" Claire looked around the aquamarine reception room at the two patients waiting there in peach chairs with magazines suddenly pulled up in front of their faces. Embarrassment flared on her face.

"That's obvious!" Liz Broward's composure had slipped.

Zack had never seen her lose her temper.

Claire looked as if she was about to cry. He felt embarrassed for her, wanted to pat her on the arm.

"This is from Agnes Schultz's file. She must have taken Agnes's file." Liz ran to the door and threw it open. Zack ran after her and followed her into the corridor, as if he could somehow help.

The woman's cleaning cart sat outside the women's room door, exactly as she had left it before. The doctor ran to the rest room and pushed on the door. "Locked! Damn it! Zack, go get the rest room key from Claire."

"She's not inside," said Zack.

"How do you know?"

"Well, I saw her go in there before. I thought it was strange. At least I do now. She unlocked the door, and I figured she went in there to clean, but now I remember she left the cart outside, right there. It hasn't been moved an inch. She didn't take any cleaning equipment with her, and she closed the door after her. If she went in to clean it, she would have left it open so everyone would know the place was being cleaned. At least that's the way they do it in our building. And, besides, she wouldn't lock herself in someplace if she ran off with your records. She'd get the hell out of the building."

"You're right!"

"Besides, she was standing outside your office when I came in. As if she was going in. But when she saw me, she changed her mind."

Liz gasped. She ran back to her office. "Zack, come with me."

He did. He followed as she ran past the receptionist's cubicle and into a narrow back room with open, color-coded horizontal files that lined three of four walls. The colored index system would please any decorator, but the open arrangement would make a security consultant shudder.

"Is my file in there?"

She glanced at him. "Right now it's in my office. But we keep this room locked at night. No one usually gets in except Claire, my partners, and me." She ran to a row of files and quickly pulled out a record folder. "It's Agnes's. It's empty. That woman took the whole file! Except for this insurance record page." She spread the folder open. "Zack, I'm scared. I have to call her lawyer."

He looked at the folder and then at her face. "Hey, I shouldn't be here. This stuff is private. Look—I'll—"

"Private! I only wish it were. Haven't you been reading the paper?"

"I haven't seen a paper in a week. I couldn't focus."

"It's been on TV, too."

"I haven't even listened to the radio. My head would bust open from the noise. I haven't even checked my e-mail or the computer bulletin board."

"Well, it's not private. Now not even her medical records are private."

"Look, Doc—dear person—I still don't think I should be in on this."

"But, Zack! You saw that woman twice. Not that anyone could forget her. That face! Those glasses! Still, you saw her sneaking around here before. I'm going to call the police. I want you to tell them what you saw. And Agnes's lawyers, too."

"How 'bout the cleaning service? Shouldn't you call them first?"

"Yes. Of course. You see, you're helping already."

"Yeah, I guess so."

"You're a natural detective. No wonder the police wanted your help. Look, I have some patients to see. There's a coffee shop down on the first floor, next to the pharmacy. Why don't you go get some coffee and juice or something. I'll have Claire call the cleaning service and the police. Then I'll finish up here and meet you in an hour or so."

"She doesn't work for the cleaning service," Liz Broward said an hour later when she sat across the bistro table from him in the small self-service coffee shop. "The cart doesn't even belong to them. They had someone here in twenty minutes, and all their stuff is in a basement room where their cleaning crew left it at four this morning."

"Not surprised," Zack said.

"I'm just confused. Something about that woman looked familiar. I was sure she worked for the cleaning service, that I've seen her somewhere, pushing a cart down a hall. But someone that looks like that would get your attention! Maybe it was someplace else. Come to think of it, I never even really saw a maid here before. Just the building maintenance man, when we had a plumbing emergency one day. He was short and black and wore brown coveralls. Not a white uniform with a smock."

"Why would someone go through all this just to get a patient's medical record?"

"I brought you this," she said, taking a rolled newspaper from under her arm. Yesterday's front section, he saw. She pointed to an article about Agnes Shultz and the rare disease she had.

He read the article through. "Her husband thinks she's a vampire?" He shook his head. "Weird! How can anyone believe those things?"

"It helps them make sense of evil and suffering."

"Who says suffering makes sense? People just suffer, that's all."

She reached across the small white tabletop and touched the back of his hand. "Maryellen isn't suffering anymore, Zack."

Disquieted by her touch, he pulled his hand from her. "Dying doesn't make sense, either."

She sat back. "I know. Even though everybody dies."

"Look," he said, "I know you're trying to help. But let's not talk about that."

"I'm sorry. I hadn't meant to."

"We're not sitting here because you're my doctor."

"No. You're right. I've called the police. They're on the way here to get our statements. I'm scared about this, Zack. Agnes called me yesterday while I was making rounds at the hospital. She told my answering service she was going to see her lawyer and wanted to talk to me first. I've been trying to call her since. No answer. Not even late last night."

"What about her lawyer?"

"I just talked to her. She didn't have an appointment with her yesterday."

"OK. But I still don't get it. This woman's husband runs off with the kids because he thinks she's a vampire. The woman calls you, and then isn't home when you call back—"

"Even in the middle of the night," she coached him.

"Then someone breaks into your files and steals her records. So what? The story's been in the newspaper. What could someone want with her records? If it was her husband trying to get a case together, his lawyer would subpoena the records."

Liz threw her hands up, then brought them down on the table. "I don't know, Zack. The only thing I do know is that my name was never mentioned in the stories. So far as I know, only her husband, and maybe his lawyer if he has one, knows I'm her doctor. Even her lawyer didn't know till I called. And Agnes Shultz seems to have disappeared. And so have her records. I'd bet my family name that the woman who took them knows where Agnes is."

"Hey, Doc, don't bet your family name on anything. You wouldn't want it dragged through the mud." He grinned at her.

She caught her breath, openmouthed. Then she said, "I'd still bet it. That's how sure I am." She looked out the coffee shop door. "I just saw a couple of policemen go by. They're probably on their way to my office. Come on, Zack. I want to talk to them before afternoon office hours start."

So, she was willing to bet her family name on a patient! A patient who, according to the article, came from a working-class home not much different from his own. She was dedicated and warm, this high-class doc from the right side of the Schuylkill River. She cared about her patients, regardless of class and station. She cared about Zack! Jesus! Why should she care about a self-educated computer graphics artist? Why should he care if she did or didn't? Maryellen! That was the reason! His wife had been her friend. His wife had loved Liz Broward. Now, he was beginning to love her. Oh, God! This can't be happening! Where could it ever go? He'd get over his pneumonia, then he'd find another doctor. That was all. That was the only reason he'd come here. She cared about his pneumonia. That was all—

She was halfway out the door when he finally stood up to follow her. The pneumonia had unquestionably slowed him down.

She turned to him again. "I almost forgot you're sick."

"Yeah? Well it looks like you're going to have to cure me in a hurry, Doc."

"We'll give it all the time it takes. There's really no hurry. Where you're concerned, I want to be sure of things."

What should I do, Maryellen? he thought as he followed Dr. Broward to the elevator and then to her office.

The police were waiting. Tall, salmon-haired Lieutenant Bill Crosby introduced himself to the doctor, then turned to Zack. "Well, Zack! What did you dig up today?"

"Just happened to be here, Lieutenant."

"Sure get around. You know the woman in Scranton turned out to be a cousin, too. We're on the right track. Probably the killer's related, too."

"I don't think so. I got a lead about a killer that used the same MO during the Civil War to off some possible ancestors of these folks."

"That was pretty long ago, Zack."

"Well, it didn't stop with that generation." Zack explained what he'd learned from Yolanda Smith. "The Spencer woman was born in Phoenix, you know. I'll be going there next week."

He saw Liz frown at him.

"You know it'll be on your own," Crosby said. Then, misinterpreting Liz's displeased glance, he said, "But, Doctor, this isn't solving your problem." Then he presented his black partner, Officer Cheney, who'd been standing uneasily beside him, looking puzzled. "Zack's our genealogist," he explained to Cheney.

After acknowledging the shorter man, Liz said, "Zack's been sick. I was thinking he shouldn't travel for a while." After leading them to her private office, she gestured to a pair of gray leather chairs against the wall. They each pulled one up beside her desk.

Crosby settled his muscular frame into a seat. "The Shultz connection caught my eye, Dr. Broward," he said. "These internecine kidnappings really take some weird turns. But this vampire thing tops them all."

"There is no vampire disease, Lieutenant! And there's no such thing as a vampire."

"I know. I mean it's weird that anyone would really believe their wife is a vampire. Well, no, that's not quite what I meant, either. I got involved once in a case where the guy not only got his kicks from his wife sucking his blood, he sold her services through one of those sex sheets. They had a whole routine, where they brought in groups, like in a séance. Everyone held hands in a circle while he made a knick in their fingers and she came in dressed like a vampire and sucked on them. Someone thought they were running a prostitution ring from their apartment and reported them. A couple of plainclothes officers attended a party, acting like they were husband and wife. They begged off when they saw the guy used the same razor blade on everyone without sterilizing in between. All we could do was send someone out to tell them about safe vampiring. How the hell do you stop people from practicing what they think is a religion? I mean, they aren't really hurting anybody but themselves."

"Sick!" said Zack.

Liz Broward shook her head. "The folklore is sort of like a bible. The vampire icon makes sense to people. They can wrap all their fears in a black cape, then isolate evil and kill it for a while, if they use the right kind of device. It keeps coming back, though, and needs them to keep up their rituals. So it is a kind of religion. That's why people fell for it when a scientist named Dolphin proposed a link with disease. Now doctors could control it with medicine. But porphyria isn't curable. Patients relapse. They literally need blood or hematin, a part of the blood. Their families are scared of them."

Crosby nodded. "Yeah, I read about that in a book by a college professor." He leaned forward in his chair. "So, you mentioned a cart outside the women's rest room. Officer Cheney'd like to get a look at it."

"Of course. It's still there in the hall."

The policemen exchanged glances, and Zack suddenly realized he hadn't seen it when he and Liz had come back upstairs. He saw the startled look on her face when she came to the same realization.

"The building service—" she said.

"We already checked with them. They didn't touch it."

"She must have come back! I never would have moved it. I told Claire not to touch it, either."

Crosby's eyebrows knit together at the center of his freckled forehead.

"My receptionist."

"Oh, yes. The blonde with the sandwich from McDonald's."

"Some days she doesn't even have time for that. None of us do. Lieutenant, the cart was still there when I went down to the coffee shop to get Zack. That woman might still be in this building."

"Fifteen stories give her lots of places to hide," Cheney said.

"A woman like that couldn't hide in this whole city for long," said Zack. "Not even in Philadelphia," he said to Crosby, who grinned and nodded.

"Describe her," said Crosby.

Zack did. Then he added, "You only have to check four stories."

The policemen looked puzzled.

"Yes!" said Liz. "He's right. Actually five. If she wanted to get her cart out of here, she'd have gone out through the parking lot. The top parking level's on this floor. Then there's a ground level, just below street. But I doubt she'd go there. Dead end."

And Liz had said he was a natural detective!

Cheney was on his feet. "Where's the door to parking?"

Rising, Zack said, "Follow me."

Liz stood up. "I'll alert security."

Crosby said, "Good idea, Doctor."

She was on the phone as Zack and Cheney left the office.

The gas and grease smell that smacked Zack in the chest as they pushed through the metal parking garage door sent him into another coughing spell. *Would this goddamn pneumonia never let go!* he thought. His eyes began to water, and he stood helpless while Cheney sprinted down the corkscrew driveway to the level below. He supported himself against the orange number four painted on the concrete block wall until the coughing stopped and he could catch his breath. As the rattle of his hacking left his ears, he heard the chatter and squeal of a starting engine. From the darkened far end of the parking level a black utility van appeared. If its side panels had been draped windows, it would have looked more like a hearse than a delivery van. Its driver sat high in the cockpit seat, androgynous looking, with clenched large teeth and thick heavy glasses that concentrated the light around the eyes like glowing UFO discs as the van moved under a bank of overhead lamps.

Zack leapt forward. "Hey! Stop!"

His voice echoed off the walls, but was drowned out by the rev of the vehicle's engine, and the van spiraled off toward a lower level.

"Shit!" Zack said. "Goddamn pneumonia! I'd've had her if I was my old self!"

Still, his own van was only a few steps away. He grabbed his keys from his jeans' pocket and dove at the door, connecting and turning the key in a single motion. Scrambling into the seat, he stepped on the clutch and cranked the ignition. It barely chugged, then died. He pumped the gas pedal and cranked the starter again. The engine chugged, almost caught, then died again.

"It's been standing almost a week! Shit!" He put it into reverse and floored the clutch with his left foot, while heel and toeing the brake and gas pedal at once with his right, as he turned the ignition key again. The engine started, ran for a moment, then stalled before he could release the brake. He could smell the odor of gasoline as he tried to start it again. "Oh, Jesus God Shit! I flooded it!"

He pulled the key from the lock and jumped down from the van, slammed the door. He could hear echoes of engines, and the squeals of tires from below.

"Cheney! Stop her!" he shouted. But his voice was just another amorphous rumble swallowed by others in the reverberating concrete helix. He ran down the ramps and past bright blue slits of sky, from level to level to level. At the street level, he met Cheney and a brown-uniformed white man with an intercom sputtering on his hip.

Zack puffed and choked back a cough. "Black Chevy utility van. She was in it. Didn't you see her?"

Cheney shook his head. "A couple of vans passed me. No woman, though."

"A black Chevy pulled out a few minutes ago," said the security guard. "Guy with a crew cut was driving. No passengers."

Zack said, "I saw her."

"Must've been someone else. The only woman that pulled out was one of our doctors," said the guard.

"But, I'd swear—"

"Easy to see things like they aren't in this place. The light's bad, and there's lots of shadows. Can you give me a complete description? I'll keep my eye out for her."

Zack repeated the description. Then he said, "Did the Chevy van driver have glasses on?"

"Only saw him from the back. Practically a skinhead. Never mistake him for a woman."

"Her hair was long and blond. Down to the shoulders. Maybe I was seeing things," said Zack on his way back up the elevator with Cheney. "I'm just getting over pneumonia."

"That'll do it. I only had it once, but I'll never forget it. Took me three months before I wasn't tired again. Never want to go through that again. Say, since that woman got away, and this has to do with that vampire thing, would you mind if an artist came here so we could get a composite of this maid?"

They got off the elevator on the fourth floor. "It's OK with me if it's OK with Doc Broward."

"Some class, that doctor," said the policeman. "I'd be scared to go to someone like her. With a name like Broward. Her old man runs the priciest law firm in Philadelphia. Doesn't like cops. Specially my color of cop. Wouldn't let us lick the mud off his shoes. If he ever got them muddy."

"She's nothing like that. My wife was a friend of hers. That's how I came to her. Never thought much of going to a woman doctor, myself. But she's good. Smartest doc I've ever been to."

"No kidding? Who'd've thought?"

Crosby was talking to Claire when the men returned to the office. "No luck, huh?" he asked.

Cheney quietly told him what happened. Zack collapsed in a waiting room chair across from the only other patient.

"Mr. James," said Claire, "you look pale. Would you like to lie down in back?"

"I'll be OK. Guess I overdid it."

A woman came out of the back office. Liz Broward stuck her head out the door and nodded to the man across from Zack. "Sorry we've kept you waiting, Charles. We got backed up this morning." She turned to Zack, "Come back in with me a minute, Zack."

When he'd come into her office, she said, "She got away, I take it."

"I thought I saw her. But it turned out to be some guy. The police want to send an artist here to do a composite drawing."

"Oh?" She picked up her phone. "Claire, is Lieutenant Crosby still there? Good. Send them both back. And get Charles into the examining room and tell him I'll see him in a few minutes."

When Crosby and Cheney came back, she asked, "What's this about a composite drawing?"

Cheney said, "If this has anything to do with the kidnapping, it might help find the husband and kids, too."

"Makes sense," she said, nodding. "When can the artist come? I have a full schedule today. My partners don't have office hours today."

"We could have him come this evening, if you don't mind staying late."

"No problem for me." She looked at Zack.

He was having trouble keeping his eyes open. His muscles ached, and fatigue had overcome him again.

Crosby looked at him with alarm. "How sick is this guy?"

"I'm OK. Just overdid it."

"He's getting over pneumonia. He really should go straight home. Zack, you'd better leave your van here again. You shouldn't drive. I shouldn't have put you through this."

"You didn't put me through it. I did what it looked like I hadda."

"We'll get you home, Zack. The doctor's right," said Crosby. "And knock off that trip to Phoenix for a while. It's enough I got you soaked to the skin in the woods. Wouldn't want to feel responsible for sending you to your deathbed."

Zack didn't have the strength to argue. "What about the picture?"

"It can wait till tomorrow. Right, Doctor?"

"He should rest tomorrow. Should stay home a couple more days."

She was conspiring with them against him.

"We don't want to wait too long to get the picture. It fades from your mind," said Crosby.

"Can your artist go to his house?"

"Sure. But it would help if he could see you both together. To work out discrepancies."

"That should be no problem. I can go to his house. It wouldn't hurt to have me check his condition again."

"How do you like that!" said Cheney. "A doctor that makes house calls, in this day and age!"

"Is that all right with you, Zack?" she asked.

His amazement overwhelmed his fatigue long enough for him to stare at her, openmouthed. She'd never made a house call for Maryellen, though lots of times she visited her in the hospital and hadn't sent a bill. "Yeah, I guess so," he said. He gave her the keys to the van. "Get the engine running for me will you, Doc? I wouldn't want that to die, too."

Poke's eyes widened when she saw Zack get out of the police car and shuffle up the walk to the front door, where she stood anxiously. He realized she must have been frantic when he was not there when she got home from school at three.

"Daddy!"

"It's OK, Poke. I'm just a little too weak to drive. Lieutenant Crosby drove me home."

"How come he made you work when you're still sick!"

He told her what happened. "He didn't make me work. It just happened and I was there."

She looked nonplussed. "Dr. Broward made you do all that?"

"She didn't make me, either. I happened to be there, that's all."

"I'm going to call her, Daddy. She should've called me by now. 'Specially since she kept you there so long."

"She's going to. She promised. Give her a chance. Don't bother her during office hours. She's busy."

"Not too busy to tell me about my own father." She ran through the small entry hall into the cluttered family room, then picked up the phone on the table next to the computer desk.

He followed her and stood by the vinyl sofa. "Poke!"

She turned her back to him and pushed the programmed button. A few seconds later she said, "This is Jill James. Dr. Broward said she'd call me about Daddy. Now he's here and he looks just as sick as ever."

"Shit! You're embarrassing me, Poke. She's probably seeing a patient. I'm sure not the only thing on her mind."

She covered the mouthpiece. "You should be. Momma was her friend. She'd call me right away if she cared—" Her hand fell away from the mouthpiece. "Dr. Broward, Daddy looks pretty sick. You promised to call, but you didn't."

"If you took after your mother instead of me, you'd be much better off, Poke!" he groused. Still, Liz Broward must have thought the call was important enough for her immediate attention.

Poke covered one ear and pressed the phone against the other, and nodded a few times. "You're sure he's getting better? You're not just telling me that 'cause I'm a kid?" She nodded again, then turned and smiled broadly at her father. "Sure. OK, Doctor. I promise. And thanks." She set the phone back in the cradle.

"You sure are a nervy kid. You got your Jewish grandfather's chutzpah."

"She said I wasn't just a kid. 'A young woman that cares about her father,' she said. I deserve a call, and she was sorry she waited so long."

"That's what she said?"

"And she said you're really much better, but you'd get tired real easy and I should make sure you don't do too much and she'll see you tomorrow night at about 7:30. That's when the artist will be here. What artist, Pop?"

He explained about the composite drawing, and why the artist was coming here instead of to the doctor's office.

"That's cool, Pop. She's coming here to make sure you're all right."

"Well, mostly she's coming for the picture."

"No, Pop. Mostly she's coming for you. And me. She likes us, Pop. We're special to her because of Momma."

After a moment's hesitation, he said, "You think Momma would think it's cool that she's coming?"

"I think maybe Momma sent her. She saw you were sick, and she sent her."

He looked at his daughter, who seemed suddenly to be surrounded by a mysterious, womanly glow that he'd seen only in one woman before—her mother. The room, for the first time in a year, reflected the glow, in the polished surfaces of the sofa and the chair's vinyl upholstery, in the blank dark television screen, in the dark oak wall panels across from the square front window.

He moved across the room from the sofa to his recliner, unable to take his eyes off Poke. She stood and watched him, her eyes brimming, her mouth slightly open in a smile.

Suddenly Zack sank into the recliner. He sat forward with his elbows on his knees and his face buried in his hands. The tears that he'd fought off for a year drowned his remaining defenses and flushed the pain from his bones. He sobbed so hard and for so long, that when the grief finally passed, he could barely get up and climb the stairs.

He knew Poke was standing at the foot of the stairway, watching him pull himself up by the banisters, child enough to be crying her own tears, woman enough to leave him to deal with his. There was some of her mother in her, after all.

Tuesday evening

Restored by fourteen hours of unbroken, nightmare-free sleep, Zack had the most comfortable day he could recall. While Poke was in school, he read the *Inquirer,* and looked for some news of the break-in at Liz's office. Nothing on that. Only an item about Agnes Shultz's apparent disappearance, with speculations that she might be off looking for her husband, whose whereabouts remained unknown.

Zack sighed and shook his head and set the paper aside. For the first time since he'd gotten sick, he booted up his computer and hooked up to the network. An electronic mail message from Yolanda Smith was one of many waiting in his mailbox. She gave him an old address for Gus Champus III's bastard son's mother: the whorehouse where she had worked. "The place was torn down and a shopping center was built where it used to be," Yolanda wrote. "Don't think you'll have much luck there. That's where I got stuck and gave up."

For a genealogist, she'd given up easily. But, she'd told him her interest was more academic than professional at the time. After all, she'd done the search for her master's thesis; when that was finished, so was the search. She had to make a living somehow, and genealogy wouldn't be likely to provide one. Anyway, she was excited about Zack's involvement in the murder mystery and had just mailed out some Champus family documents yesterday, according to her message. They should arrive in the next day or so. He nodded in pleasure at that. Now he knew exactly what he'd do when he'd go to Phoenix next week. And he was going to go, all right! No matter what Liz Broward said.

She arrived at his house (which Poke had insisted on straightening up after school) at exactly 7:30 P.M. The artist, a tired looking gray-haired man close to sixty, arrived soon after, with a set of pictures of facial features, hair styles, and body builds of women and men. Leaning over the computer desk, which he'd cleared of its usual clutter of equipment and paper, he and Liz studied the pictures, told the artist what to draw in where, changed things several times because the mouth was too big, or the eyes behind the thick spectacles looked too normal, or the hairline was too low or too high, or the face was too round or triangular where it was supposed to be square, and too square where it ought to be triangular. They did this for front face and profile views. It took over two hours before the composite picture looked right to both of them. As an artist himself, Zack was impressed with the results.

"But you'd get better ones with a good computer program," Zack said, when the artist had packed away his drawings and was about to leave.

"I think you need the human element. You've got to be a good interviewer, too. Computers can't think. They don't have human intuition."

"They do if you give it to them. Look, you have four separate sheets there, each from a different angle. That means you can't see all around, picture the perp in action."

Liz looked puzzled. "Perp means perpetrator," the artist said. She nodded.

"You don't need to see her in action. We put it on a sheet, anyway, and people will know if they've seen her from the written description."

"What about the cops?" Zack said.

"What about them?"

Liz nodded vigorously. "I see what he means. I've seen computer graphics. We use them in medicine a lot. Especially surgeons. You can get right inside the body, see organs and things from every angle. It helps when you see the whole thing in real life. The police wouldn't know her from before, but if they had her in motion on a computer screen from different angles, they might recognize her better on the street, or wherever they run into her."

"Yes," said the artist. I've seen those things. But there's nothing like a skilled interviewer with real human intuition to pull out those little details you could miss. I've been working with the police for twenty-five years. You pick up things a computer never would dream of."

Zack was about to argue with him, but Liz cast him a silencing glance. "You're absolutely right," she said. "In medicine and crime fighting, there's no getting around the human element."

The man's face showed relief. He shook their hands in the foyer as he left, and bowed to Liz, whose empathy he no doubt appreciated.

She picked up her tote bag from the long foyer table against the side wall and appeared about to leave immediately after the man.

"Scared about losing his job," said Zack. "So he doesn't realize how much better and faster he could do it."

"Remember, you and I grew up with computers, Zack. But they're still strange and scary to him. Lots of people still won't touch them."

"I wonder if there's a program the cops could use."

"You could ask Lieutenant Crosby. He'd probably want you to do it for free, like the genealogy." She grinned ironically. "But, you're not thinking of putting that poor man out of a job?"

"Shit, no! But it would be fun to develop one, even for free, if they don't already have them. I could show him how he could do even more. The guy's obviously a good artist. I could convince him—"

"Convinced against his will—of the same opinion, still."

"That's not true. If I do it right—"

"It's so. You just proved it."

He laughed. "OK, dear person. I guess I'm the one full of shit this time."

She grinned. Then she said, "Zack, why not go ahead and develop the program for fun? What've you got to lose?"

"Maybe I will," he said.

From the top of the stairs, Poke called, "Did the artist go?"

"Sure, c'mon down, Poke. Say good-bye to the doctor."

She ran down the stairs. "Did you check Pop's pneumonia, Doctor?"

"Well, no. But I don't have to do much more than listen to him talk, to see how much better he is."

"Feel better, too. Look at me, Poke. I didn't even take a nap today."

"Don't let him get cocky about it, Poke," said the doctor. "Make sure he keeps his Friday appointment." The she looked at Zack. "Oh," she said, "I almost forgot." She reached into her suit jacket pocket and pulled out his van keys. "I got it started fine. Even took it for a short spin around the block to recharge the battery." She handed him the keys.

"You drove that tank? In Philly traffic?"

"Sure. I love to drive things like that. Go up to the Poconos sometimes in my RV. Just to be alone. Camp in the Delaware State Forest. Hike a lot, too."

"Alone! A woman shouldn't be out there alone! That's where I found those bodies."

"Oh? And who did you go with?"

"No one. But—"

"Zack, I've been on my own a long time. I'm not foolhardy. My RV's stocked with plenty of food and emergency supplies. I carry an intercom when I'm hiking. I know how to read a compass and follow blaze marks. I know where the ranger stations are, and I let them know the trails I'm taking. I even know how to handle a shotgun, though hunting's not my thing."

"I'll teach you to hunt," Poke piped up. "I sometimes go with Pop."

"I don't think I could do it, Poke. I get too emotional over animals. But thanks."

"Pop brought a turkey home from his hunting trip. We froze it. We never shoot anything we can't eat. Someone killed all the turkeys in the supermarket. That doesn't bother you, does it?"

"No. It's not a moral issue with me. Just a personal aversion to taking any creature's life with my own hands."

"You kill bugs, don't you?"

"Only indoors, where they don't belong."

"Hey, Poke, stop bothering the doctor about those things."

"It doesn't bother me. I know how I feel, and I respect my own feelings. But I'm always open to debate. That's how I learn."

"When Pop's better, we can cook the turkey. And you can come for dinner."

Jesus, that kid— Zack tried to read the expression on Liz's face.

"I'd really enjoy that. But let's wait and see." Her face showed no emotion, but her body jerked slightly and she tightened her grip on her tote bag.

"Well," said Zack. "I guess you'd really like to get home, Doc. You've been running around all day."

"And you must need some rest by now, since you didn't take a nap." She reached for the doorknob and turned it. "So, see you Friday." She opened the door and left.

"She's cool, Pop. Do you think she'll come to dinner?"

"Probably not. She's getting married in a few weeks. You got to be careful, Poke. You're not supposed to ask your doctor to your house for dinner. They don't like to get friendly with patients."

"She was friends with Momma. That makes her friends with us."

"Not that kind of friend. You got to learn to think before you open your mouth. You'll get us all in trouble if you don't."

CHAPTER FIVE

Wednesday evening

Nobody but Liz's father, Paul Broward, could make her feel small—physically or emotionally. She saw him inside the oversize doorway of the Bryn Mawr estate, waiting for her. As she rounded the curving driveway that circled a centuries-old maple tree in front of the house and parked her gold Mercedes-Benz next to Eric's dark green Jaguar, she felt herself shrinking. He wouldn't have been standing there, tall as the white columns supporting the porch roof, filling the entire entryway, if he hadn't been furious. Her mother, Grace, would have cajoled him out of a moderate anger, sat him down in the maroon leather easy chair in the den, given him his Dewars and water, and pushed the ottoman under his feet. By the time Liz arrived, he would have forgotten whatever had upset him. Or he would have saved it to lay on her later when it wouldn't disturb everyone's dinner, and when, sated with her favorite foods, Liz would be more likely to accept or deflect his criticism with humor. Thus Grace controlled, avoided family conflagrations in a household where the heads often held opposing views and where both felt compelled to prevail over their daughter's heart and soul. By nature, Liz tended toward her mother's more generous heart, more accepting soul.

Now one of two conditions applied: either her mother agreed with her father's anger and decided she should allow him to loose it upon Liz; or the anger was so overwhelming that her mother had lost her power to defuse it. Either way, Liz reckoned, she'd have to defend herself. And she'd been defending herself from herself all week. Her feelings about Zack, her impotence against Agnes's suffering had whipsawed her defenses, left her reeling and quaking inside.

She might have been able to handle her anguish at Agnes's plight, and her concern over the theft of her records. She'd almost always been able to leave work concerns inside her office doors. But her emotions toward Zack stalked her at work and at home. They lay beside her in bed at night, invaded her dreams, woke with her in the morning, dwelt in her. Now he had become bound in the Agnes case with her, as if some will outside her own were throwing her in with him. Had he been sent to test her every life commitment, her every resolve—her loyalty to her family, to Eric, to herself?

She couldn't have brought him on herself. Liz Broward could not have these feelings toward anyone, let alone someone like Zack. Liz Broward was too self-controlled. She'd long ago wrested control of herself from her father, who kept her in private girls' schools through high school and carefully managed her social debut and contacts with men (he thought) till she graduated. But the girls she went to school with were not the girls her mother had gone to school with. Social conventions had begun to break down. The boys at weekend parties were often middle class. Some of them were Jews and Orientals. A few blacks attended from time to time with white girlfriends whose parents, had they known, would have ripped them immediately out of school.

Liz had her first sex with Jerry Rubin, a Jewish medical student from Penn the summer of her high school junior year. The romance lasted long enough to deflect her from the road her family had mapped for her. Her first openly defiant act against her father was her refusal to even apply to his alma mater, Harvard, but instead to enroll at Penn. He had sputtered for months, and vowed that he wouldn't finance her education, a vow he stood by when she disdained law for medicine. Though she had no trouble getting scholarships based on her academic record and competitions, she hated taking money that could have gone to needy students. Luckily, her mother rescued her honor. From her own fortune, Grace Broward contributed to every scholarship grantor double the amount Liz got from them. Paul never suspected his wife was supporting his daughter's maverick behavior. He believed she was simply providing tax write-offs against her income. So Grace, and her generous heart and accepting soul, subtly managed her daughter's growth toward independence.

Meanwhile, Liz lived in dormitories and cheap apartments using stipends and student loans for living expenses. She told none of her classmates she was practically as poor as they were during those years. They wouldn't have believed her. And she and they knew she was sole heir to an estate that could send a whole class of medical students through school. That truth set her and them apart.

Her father's anger at her defection had cooled by the time she graduated. He couldn't ignore her *summa cum laude* distinction. Her valedictory speech—in which she'd paid tribute to what she admired of her parents' values—brought him accolades. In her own perverse way, with Grace unseen in the background, she'd upheld the family name. That was all that mattered to Paul Broward—then and now.

She understood that. And she never deliberately besmirched his name or dishonored him. But name and family didn't shape her life. It was the people of that name she loved, not the name itself. And one of those people, her mother, had helped form her values and tastes. Those values—the acceptance of all kinds of people (including her father); the openness to all kinds of ideas (including her father's); the caring for others' feelings (especially her father's); the compassion for luckless, suffering people—let Liz accept someone like Zack.

But those tastes—for refinement; for neat grooming; for a modicum of delicate language, at least in professional settings; and against bravado; against macho displays and arrogant antics—would rule out her loving him. How could she possibly want to go to bed with him? How could she imagine his two-day-old beard scratching her cheek, his long hair brushing her neck as he'd bend to kiss her breasts? How could she dream of going out with a man who wouldn't wear a suit or tie, even to a fine restaurant? Did he ever eat at any place finer than McDonald's?

It was impossible! Besides, Eric was perfect for her. She

loved him. But she dreaded going to bed with him tonight. As she'd dreaded it over the weekend, when she'd managed to avoid lovemaking, avoid going with him to the ballet, by pleading overwork. "I hadn't remembered how soon the wedding's coming up. We'll be off to Greece before we know it, and the load'll fall on Elsie and Jim."

"I guess I should be tying up my loose ends, too," he'd said. "I've got some briefs to work on."

Tonight would be harder to handle. What could she tell him? *"I'm too tired." "I have a headache." Married people's excuses. Certainly she couldn't say "I'm having second thoughts. I'm in love with this mixed-breed that looks like he crawled out from under a steam grating. Well, actually, he's very clean. His outfit is really bizarre. No, actually, it's kind of charming. And his language—well, he's just very frank and blunt. A lot like Dad, when you think about it. And he's right! I was full of shit. Why didn't you ever tell me that, Eric? If you cared for me, you would have. If you saw into my heart the way he does—"*

She pulled on the hand brake and got out of the car, trying not to look at her father. She couldn't imagine why he'd be angry with her. Surely he hadn't seen into her heart. Her mother was good at those things; but her father? Never!

As nonchalantly as she could, she dropped her keys into her purse and smiled and waved at her father.

Paul pushed open the storm door and came toward her, glowering, as if to stress a message he thought she was too thick-skulled to get.

"I'm sorry I'm late," she tried. She wasn't late. It was only seven o'clock. After working overtime to catch up with yesterday's paperwork, she'd come straight from her office without changing her gray wool shirtwaist dress, to avoid the lateness Paul hated.

He said nothing, but recaptured the door as it swung closed, and held it open for her. His faced twitched, his jaw was set.

"Have I done something wrong?" she said as she entered the high-ceilinged foyer and stood in the glitter of the massive crystal chandelier, which his icy blue eyes reflected. She avoided touching him.

He slammed the door behind her. Her mother had come into the foyer and stood toward the rear where the wide stairway spiraled toward its magnificent zenith two stories above her.

Looking for someplace to run to?

"Mother—?"

Grace Broward's face, gray as her eyes and hair, said, "*I can't help you on this one.*" She seemed untypically lost in the full silk folds of her violet pantsuit.

Liz looked around. "Where's Eric?"

"I'm here, Liz." He appeared from the den off the foyer. His face and olive eyes looked grim, pained. His beige sweater hung limp, as if worn by a hanger, not a man's broad shoulders.

Now she grew angry. "What brought on this warm reception? What's going on?"

"Liz," said her mother, "your father's upset—" Then she shrugged and threw up her hands.

"That's obvious. Eric—?"

He shook his head.

"Are you 'upset,' too, Eric? For God's sake, have I killed someone? Won't somebody tell me—"

"Come into the den, Liz," her father ordered.

The den promised comfort not hinted at in the foyer. The sofa and chairs of aged, brass-studded maroon leather, the deep mahogany wall and ceiling panels and molding, the wall-to-wall floor-to-ceiling bookcase crammed full of books and family memorabilia all breathed warmth.

But her father still breathed cold fire. He gestured her to sit on the sofa, then stood over her, arms crossed.

Her mother stood across the room in front of the bookcase. Eric sat down next to her, but didn't touch her. She looked from one to the other.

Then Eric reached to the end table beside him and picked up a folded newspaper. He tossed it onto her lap.

Its slap against her legs startled her.

Her father continued staring down at her.

She opened the paper—this morning's, which she hadn't had time to read—and glanced down at a boxed-off front-page story headlined: "*Vampire Case Woman Missing; Medical*

Records Stolen." The composite drawing of the maid appeared next to the article.

She gasped and read through the article, appalled at the misleading headline. The article details were accurate enough. So was the quotation from her that there was no such thing as a vampire disease and that vampires themselves were pure folklore. That hardly mollified her. People read headlines, not details. Once again, sensationalism had won out over cautious journalism, even in the non-tabloid press.

"I should've known they'd do something like that!" she said with disgust.

"I've always known you'd do something like that!" echoed her father. He tore the paper from her hand and flung it to the red-carpeted floor.

She caught her breath. "Like what?"

"Like exposing us to ridicule."

"Ridicule? How? I didn't ask to have my office broken into."

Her mother sat down across the room from her and shook her head, then looked away.

"You didn't have to let it get into the newspaper, Liz," Eric said.

Aghast, she sat back. "What are you saying! That I shouldn't have reported a theft?"

"Not exactly," said Eric.

"My office—my patient's privacy—was violated!"

"You handled it poorly," said her father. "You turned it into a circus. With you as the clown."

"I simply called in the police to investigate a theft."

"No money or valuables were stolen. No one was hurt. You could have just informed the police what happened and given them the burglar's description and asked them to treat it routinely. It wouldn't've made a ripple in the news. But, no!" Her father stuttered and turned from her for a moment. Then he turned and pinned her with his eyes. "No! You had to make a big case of it. You had to tie us all in with some ugly, low-class family's ignorant squabble over children."

Liz couldn't speak. She turned to look at Eric.

"It just looks bad, Liz. That's all. Why didn't you call us? We'd have handled it," he said.

"Handled it! What does that mean?"

"Kept it out of the papers. It's a routine office theft. Your name wouldn't have been mentioned in that dirty story."

"Is that all you care about? Children have been kidnapped, and their mother has disappeared, and all you can say is I should have kept my name—my father's name, which you plan to marry—out of it?"

"You should have kept out of it, period!" said her father. "It wasn't your medical responsibility. You diagnosed the woman's disease. Brava! You treated it. Brava again! You struck a blow against sickness and death and ignorance. You didn't have to publicly wallow in it."

Liz stood up. She looked at her mother.

"Paul," Grace Broward said. "That's not fair. Liz wasn't—"

"Wasn't what, Mother? How do you know what I was or wasn't doing? Why don't you stop trying to handle Dad? Why don't you ever tell him the truth? That he's an ignorant bigot and a bully!"

"Please, Liz. Don't say—"

"I'll say what I want. I'm thirty-eight. I won't let him control me."

Paul, white-faced, said in a tight voice, "A woman who can't control herself needs to be controlled."

"It's got nothing to do with control, Liz," said Eric, at last recovering some shoulders and rising and coming to stand between them. "There are just ways to do things. You're a doctor. You don't think like a lawyer. You don't know the consequences. This article probably isn't the end of it."

Liz clenched her fists and fought back tears. "It was, as far as I was concerned. If you hadn't all made me feel like a criminal—"

Her mother said, "Maybe your father overreacted, Liz. But you've no right to say what you did."

Eric grasped her shoulders. "Come on. Sit down. Let's put this in perspective."

She shook her head and shrugged off his grip.

Paul backed away. He turned and walked across the room to the bar and poured himself a drink.

"Let me get you a sherry, Liz," said her mother.

Liz nodded and walked to the window and pulled aside the heavy red velvet drapery and looked out the window. Wordlessly she took the amber drink that her mother had poured over ice as she liked it, and stood sipping it for several minutes as she watched the sky darken outside.

At last she dropped the drapery and turned. "I'm sorry, Dad. You know I'd never do anything to disparage our name. It means as much to me as it does to you."

"If you ever disgrace it, I'll never forgive you," he said.

"That article will just blow over, Paul," said Grace. "Why don't we go in and have dinner?"

"It won't just blow over. Eric's right. We haven't heard the end of it."

"What can possibly happen, Paul? Tomorrow they'll find something else to write about. Now, finish your drink. Let's all calm down—"

He turned on his wife, face twitching again. "Stop it, Grace! Stop handling me! Listen to me for a change! Stop deciding that whatever comes out of my mouth is automatically wrong!"

Grace grew pale. "No. I never—" Her eyes widened and turned toward Liz.

Paul's voice rose. "Yes you do! You've both been doing it for years. Isn't that right, Liz? If it's something I say, it's prejudice! If it's something you say, it's wise and wonderful!"

"That's not what I meant, Dad. We've all made mistakes. Mother loves you."

"How did you love me, Grace? By teaching her to disrespect me?"

"No! She taught me just the opposite. The disrespect I learned directly from you!" Liz strode past her father and banged down her unfinished drink on the bar. "I'm sorry, Mother. I'm going home."

"Paul!"

"Don't Paul me! I've had enough of it. Let her go. Good riddance!"

"Say anything you want about me, Dad. But don't you dare blame her. If anything, she made living with you and your hateful bigotry bearable. Without the grace she lent you, you'd be nothing but a nasty, spiteful old man!"

His mouth flew open.

Her mother burst into tears.

"Mother, I'm sorry!"

"Get out of here, Liz!"

"Yes. Yes." She ran toward the door.

"Wait, Liz!" Eric ran after her.

"Eric!" shouted her father. "Go with her and you don't need to show up at the office tomorrow."

Liz turned and saw Eric try to gain equilibrium. He took a ballet step toward her then stopped.

"I don't want you to go with me, Eric," she said, freeing him from an agonizing bind, as she freed herself from him.

He seemed to find his footing, poised perfectly between them. She turned and ran to her car.

She drove for an hour without choosing a direction, then found herself in the King of Prussia Mall. She drove through the multilevel parking lot, thinking she might get out of the car and lose herself in the mass of shoppers, maybe stop for a loaf of French bread. She could break chunks from it and eat them with a cup of gourmet coffee as she sat among noisy strangers in the tiny, open shop. But she knew she didn't want to be amoung strangers. She didn't want to be among people at all. Still, she felt terribly lonely, bereft. With one stroke, with some ill-chosen words that she hadn't meant to utter, but that said exactly what she'd meant, she'd cut herself off from her family, from Eric and, in a sense, from herself. For she had not meant to hurt her mother. And nothing she could do would ever erase the terrible pain she'd seen on her dear face tonight. It would lie forever between them.

After a few passes through the mall parking lot, she drove back toward Route 202, planning to pick up the Schuylkill Expressway and head home, but at the last minute, she took the Pennsylvania Turnpike toward the suburbs on Philadelphia's northeast. She had passed the Fort Washington Interchange when she finally realized where she was going; she was paying her tolls by the time she knew she had no intention of stopping herself from going there.

She pulled her car to the curb in front of the small, neat,

two-story frame house in Glenside. For a few moments she sat there with the engine running. It was not yet nine-thirty. The lights in the windows of the house's both stories were still on. She turned off the engine, got out, and walked up the driveway, then up a terraced flagstone walk to the front porch.

She knocked when she reached the door. The porch light went on. His face appeared at a window, then pulled away. He opened the door. He tightened the sash of his white terry cloth robe.

After a moment he said, "Come on in, Doc."

"I was visiting nearby—" She entered the tiny foyer and looked up at the stairs, where a hall light illuminated the landing.

"Nice of you to worry about me, but I'm OK. Got my van today. Thanks for charging it up." His voice had lost its rumble. He rubbed his chin self-consciously. He hadn't shaved since Monday.

"Then you're really feeling better. Good."

They stood for a while in the small entry hall. At last he said, "I was catching up on my computer mail."

"Then I've interrupted. I'll go."

"No. I do it off-line. I mean, I write the letters without being hooked up by modem to my network. After they're all written, I log on and send them, and pick up what's in my mailbox. Come on, I'll show you."

"You're sure—"

He closed the front door and took her arm. "Doc, I'm glad you came." He led her into the family room and between the brown vinyl sofa and recliner to the computer on its cluttered desk. He sat down and keyed in some words, then he looked up at her. "This isn't what you came for."

What did I come for? Is it written all over me? She tried to read his eyes.

He hit a few keys, and the computer screen went blank. He turned off the machine. "Let's talk." He went and sat in his recliner and motioned her to the sofa.

Dry-mouthed, she sat. After a few moments, she said, "Poke in bed?"

"Reading and listening to music."

She nodded.

"She's off for the night. Gave me my kiss already. Wouldn't've heard your knock under her headphones."

Yes, he knew why she had come!

Still he asked, "What's up?"

"I—I think I've lost my bearings."

He raised his eyebrows. "Think you can find them here?"

"I don't know. I've never really lost them before. At least I didn't think so. Maybe—maybe I never had any."

He stood up and walked to her and bent and grasped her shoulders and fixed her eyes with his. "You, dear person, have the best bearings in the world. You know exactly what you're doing."

"If I did before, I don't anymore. I've hurt my mother terribly. Someone who knows what she's doing wouldn't have done what I did tonight."

"We all hurt people we love. She'll forgive you."

"Maybe. I hope so. But, I'd never be here, Zack, if I knew exactly what I was doing. I don't belong here. I didn't plan to come." She let him hold her eyes and her shoulders until he relinquished his grip on them and went back to his chair.

"Well, you're here. Right or wrong."

She took a deep breath. After a while, she said, "I'm supposed to get married. I think that's what started all this. I don't want to marry Eric."

"Then don't."

"It's not that easy. I'm thirty-eight. I want to have children. The right way. Eric seemed like the right way."

"You're right. You've lost your bearings. Maybe you don't belong here."

The words struck her like sudden hail.

"I don't have time. Don't you see?"

"The way I see it, Doc, the only thing you don't have time for is a mistake."

"That's just it. I don't know what's a mistake and what's not anymore. It happened so suddenly."

His eyes latched onto hers again, and she felt her face burn.

"Yeah. It did." He didn't move, but his eyes continued to tug at her.

She could not move, could neither move nor speak.

"Liz—" he whispered at last, and broke the spell that froze them apart. He stood up and took a few steps toward her. "This is exactly where you belong."

"No!" She rose. "I'll go." Quickly, she crossed to the foyer. But his hand was on her shoulder. She turned.

"Please stay."

She caught her breath. *I'm taller!* she thought, incongruously. She shook her head. "I can't."

"I want you to stay, Liz."

"Poke—" She looked up the stairs again.

"She never comes down once she says good night to me. Even if she did, she'd want you to stay. She thinks of you as our friend." His hand drew her back into the family room.

"Friends don't betray—memories."

"You wouldn't be doing that. Those memories are safe. I finally put them where they belong. I'm free."

She sighed and nodded. She had seen it happening. "Are you sure?"

"If you are. If you know why you came here tonight."

She stepped back from him and kicked off her shoes. "You knew I was coming, didn't you? You weren't even surprised."

"I knew I wanted you to come."

"Yes. I knew you did, too. And I couldn't believe it."

"Yeah, a mixed-breed like me daring to want a classy Main Line doctor like you."

"But you know I'm full of shit."

He grinned, and reached for her hands and pulled her to him. "Yeah, that's what I like about you." Then he kicked off his slippers; and he and she stood on equal footing: eye to eye, nose to nose, mouth to mouth. "Be my true friend, Liz."

"Yes." She brought his hands to her face, then placed her fingers on his cheeks, and played his beard like a zither with her nails. "Music! I like that," she said, laughing. "It makes me buzzzzzz!"

Then she took a handful of his hair in each hand and wrapped the silky skeins around her hands, pulling his face closer to hers until their mouths almost touched.

His eyes, which had been brown a moment ago, turned green.

"Fascinating," she said. "What makes them do that? Your eyes?"

"Hey, dear person, you're pulling my hair."

"Does it hurt?"

"No. Just the right amount of tug. It's stimulating. Makes me buzzzz." He demonstrated by grasping and twisting her locks.

"More. Tighter," she said as she felt her scalp lift and tingle, as she pulled his hair tighter, and their mouths came together like friends. "More!"

Later, naked in the dark, their bodies welcomed each other like lovers.

She rose from the sofa in the predawn quiet and kissed his robe, which he'd rolled to make her a pillow. Then she rubbed her still naked body all over with the robe and its essence of him. Sighing, she crossed to him where he lay cupped in his recliner, and bent and gently kissed his forehead, his nose, his mouth. "Hush," she whispered as he opened his eyes. "I have to leave." She kissed him again, then bent to pick up her clothes from the floor where they'd fallen.

Only his eyes moved. They dwelt on her as she dressed, and followed her as she crossed the room to the foyer. They fixed on hers as she turned toward him one last time, and held her until a small "Oh!" escaped from her lips and she ran from his house to her car.

Her clothes, which she'd worn all day then fairly torn off and cast aside in her passion, were wrinkled and smelled of sex. The aroma filled her car, keeping her in a state of arousal as she drove through town to her apartment. He had spent only a small portion of his pent-up need on her, promising her more in the tears that rushed out with his coming. But they both knew the rest would have to wait. He had more healing to do, unshareable tears to cry yet. And she had unshareable agonies to live through, forgiveness to ask of her parents and Eric. She would have to wait until they could muster it, knowing that they might never be able to, knowing that she might never be able to forgive herself.

Still, she felt no guilt, no sense that she had betrayed any of them. They were caught with her in a trap of expectations laced with changing rules. She'd been fooled into a false sense of belonging—needing, as everyone needed, to fit into a describable niche. Sometimes she felt pushed into that niche by forces greater than herself, but that feeling was just part of the need, she realized now.

She activated the gate to her apartment garage and drove in, circling through the aisles to her slot. The concrete walls exuded an erotic riverfront dankness that made her shudder as she got out of her car and walked to the elevator. Inside the lift, she leaned against the wall and closed her eyes. She did not open them until the elevator stopped and the door slid open. Then she took a deep breath and hurried down the hallway to her apartment.

The light in the living room startled her; she'd entered the foyer expecting darkness. She stopped, shaken, inside her apartment door.

"Where have you been all night, Liz?" Eric stood under the living room archway, his sweater and face and hair rumpled. His hands worked restlessly at his sides.

She closed the door. "What are you doing here, Eric?"

"I came to be with you." He stepped toward her, his bloodshot eyes frightened, surveying her.

"I told you I didn't want you to come."

"Who have you been with?" His face was ashen, except for the dark hollows under his eyes. He had been there awake, all night.

"You shouldn't have let yourself in. This is my apartment."

"Tell me who you've been with."

"No. I told you not to come. If you came and I wasn't here, you shouldn't have let yourself in."

"I have a right, Liz—"

She sighed and put her handbag on the glass-topped foyer table. "I have to take a shower and get dressed for work. Please go, Eric."

"You can't just dismiss me that way. You owe me an explanation." His voice trembled as he said it.

"I know. But I can't give you one now. First I have to talk to my parents."

"What kind of woman are you? How can you be so calm!"

"I'm not. I'm quaking inside. My whole life has blown apart in the last week. I have to pull it all back together."

His face grew grim. "With or without me, Liz?"

Yes, she had to decide and to make her decision known. And she had no time for a mistake.

She could find no gentle words. Her talent for finding them had deserted her. "Please leave your key on the table when you leave, Eric," she said.

Then she walked past him. She could not look at him, could not bear to see the welt the slap of her words raised on his face. But better a cruel slap now than a million bitter barbs later when the mistake could not be undone. She heard the clank of his key on the glass foyer tabletop as she passed through the living room to the bedroom. The slam of the apartment door shattered the air. She cried out and ran into the bathroom. She stripped and turned on the shower, stepped in, and let the water run until it was as hot as she could stand it. Then she cried until the stinging water grew cold.

CHAPTER SIX

The Sun to Darkness

Thursday

Phillip quivered with anger at Dr. Broward. He knew what she was, she was Queen of the Vampires. She had not discovered and treated Agnes Shultz, she had created her. He had seen the doctor in her office that day, and he'd watched the people going in and out. As some sat innocently in the waiting room, the doctor turned others into victims. Then she came out for the next one and smiled and he could see the blood on her teeth. And on the necks of the poor innocents that came out he could see the red fang marks she'd left.

When Agnes had told Phillip the doctor's name, he had thought it was a sign that he was supposed to get the woman's medical records from her. *How lucky she was a family doctor!* he'd thought then. She'd have drawn out a whole family tree for him in those records, without even realizing what she was doing. He could track Agnes's bloodline through that. No genealogical searching like that he'd had to do on the Rands. He was right! Dr. Broward listed nine family members in Agnes's medical records—all living right here in Philadelphia. That didn't include her children and husband, who eventually would have to be caught and cured, along with the rest of Ruth Manyon Spencer's family.

But they must wait. He had to get to the Vampire Queen first. He could kill every one of her drones, but she'd create ten new ones for each of those in a single day. She was creating more this moment, and he hadn't even figured out a plan to get her. It would be revealed to him, though. There'd be another sign.

He'd always received the signs, since the day in the amusement park when he'd been shown he was special and had killed his first vampire.

He wasn't sure how old he'd been. Probably about five. He hadn't wanted to go to the park. The honky-tonk noises and sour smells made his stomach knot up. And his dad kept warning him about the black people that came there.

"Them niggers're everyplace, now they can't keep them out. Taking over the whole fucking place. Even the pool. Better stay away from there, El Beano. Bet they never saw no one whiter'n you. You'll scare the shit out of them and they'll grab you and toss you in the niggery pool water and turn you black like them, and you won't be an El Beano anymore."

That's what Phillip's dad had told him on the way to the park. His dad, a burly black-haired man with a red face and a beer permanently clenched in his fist, laughed the whole way there, while Phillip cried in the beat-up Nash's backseat. The park was Phillip's punishment for being a sissy, for running home crying when the kids teased him and called him El Beano.

"So let's make a man of our little El Beano. Let's give the niggers a look at him." Then he grabbed Phillip's arm and pulled him from the car.

Phillip wailed as his dad dragged him across the gravel parking lot and through the park gates. Every time a band of blacks went by, the old man yanked him toward them, then away. He guffawed and thrust out his chest. "Watch out nigger! This here's an El Beano. The fucking opposite of one of you niggers. Better not touch him." And the black people stared, but didn't say anything. "They better not try nothing. We got to let 'em in the park, but there's more of us here than them. But if they grab you when I'm not looking and turn you into a nigger, ain't nothing I can do about it. Your skin'll turn black, your hair'll get kinky and greasy with lint and stuff stuck in it. You'll get big white teeth with purple gums. No more El Beano!"

One black man brushed by, pulling by the elbow a woman with bright yellow hair and a light-skinned face.

"That one would make a good piece," his father said of the woman, as he jabbed Phillip's ribs.

"Go fuck yourself," his mother said.

His father tossed the rest of his beer down his throat and crushed the can in his hand before throwing it to the macadam walk and kicking it onto the grass. He laughed and splattered out some foam, and wiped his mouth with the back of his hand. "Bet that big black one's got something nice for between them ugly legs of yours."

"Yeah? Whatta you got? Some more little El Beanos?"

His father slapped his mother's face, then grabbed Phillip's shoulder. "I'll show you what I got when we get home."

"Sure, sure. I'll get out my magnifying glass." She ducked another whap.

Phillip let out a wail at the wrench to his shoulder, and his father whirled and brought his slapping hand around. "You want something to cry about, El Beano? I'll turn you over to some of them niggers."

Phillip sucked hard on the inside of his nostrils and cut off the tears.

"OK. Let's take him on some rides." His dad pushed Phillip's back against the painted wooden cartoon boy that stood at the beginning of the boardwalk leading to the Great Pippin roller coaster. The cartoon boy held a sign with a warning that kids too short for their heads to reach the top of his head couldn't go on the ride. Phillip was skinny and knobby, still in kindergarten, but his head was big and he was taller than most eight year olds. His dad pushed his belly in and showed the ride guard that Phillip passed the height test.

"OK. You can take him in," said the ride guard.

"Come on, El Beano. The guard says you go in. You got to listen to him. He's like a cop."

Phillip saw the bright metal cars with the apples painted on them rushing up and down the rails. He heard the screeches and chatters of the cars and the screams of the riders. He ran to his mother and grabbed at the front of her shorts.

She pushed him away. "Don't be a sissy. Your dad and me aren't sissies."

His father grabbed his arm and started to pull him along.

He tried not to cry, but couldn't stop himself.

"Shut up! All these people are looking at you. They're laughing."

A woman ahead of them turned and looked down at Phillip. She got a shocked look on her face.

His father laughed. "Should I feed him to that nigger over there if he keeps on crying?"

The woman looked at his father and shook her head; then she looked at Phillip again and blushed and turned away.

"You don't want us to feed you to a nigger, do you, El Beano?"

With a sudden whoosh, a coaster shrieked overhead, then circled into its final dip, which ended several yards away. As laughing crowds poured out onto the boardwalk, the ticket taker opened the entry gate, and Phillip's parents dragged him through. They tried to shove him into a space between them in a double seat. He was skinny enough to fit, but an attendant told them one of them would have to move to another car. Since all the cars were already filled with pairs, Phillip's mother got off and left him to ride with his father.

Holding him back with an arm, his father pulled the safety bar down, then pinned him against the side of the car with one massive thigh. With a jerk, the car began to move. It chugged a few feet and then went into a quick short dip that sent the blood roaring to Phillip's head. His father cackled as the train of cars jerked forward and began to climb.

Phillip closed his eyes and sat petrified. He knew he was still going up, and hoped he'd never stop going up no matter how long it took.

Then he felt his back go tight against the seat, and the air gushed against his face and chest, and pushed the breath out of him. Screams whipped about his ears, his father roared and howled.

They hit bottom, then rose again, and less than a breath later, fell again, and Phillip's stomach wrenched. He couldn't keep his eyes closed, and opening them and seeing the edge of the sky at the side of the car, and not being able to see the car, but only the park a thousand screams below, made his bones turn to water.

Now, as the roller coaster arrived at its apex, he reached for his father, whose leg a moment before had forcibly held him in place. He tried to hug him, and his father bellowed and pushed him away. "Don't be a fucking little faggot!"

Phillip withdrew. The cars rushed down again, up again, down again and then into the final turn and into the terminal. Suddenly it stopped.

Phillip tried to hold back his vomit till he got out of the car, but his stomach dipped one more time and he puked all over his father.

"You fucking little El Beano!" He grabbed his son's arm and pulled him through the terminal to his mother. "You take him! I fucking got to clean up."

"What do you expect me to do with him? Take him in the ladies' room?" She held him by one sleeve, grimacing as if she didn't want to touch or smell him.

His father, several long strides ahead of them, said, over his shoulder, "Where else would you take a faggot. The little bastard sits down to piss, don't he?" The man pulled way out ahead of them, quickly disappearing in the crowd.

His mother tugged on his sleeve. "Why'd you have to puke! You know we're both going to get it when we get home. Can't we go anywhere with you, you don't bring him down on us?" She pulled him toward the rest rooms housed in a brown wooden cabin down the walk from the swimming pool entrance. There was no one in front of the men's room, but several women and girls and a couple of young boys stood in line in front of the ladies' room.

The line inched forward in the stench-filled midday heat. Phillip had gotten hardly any puke on him, but he could taste it in his mouth and smell it in his sinuses, where a couple of curds had lodged. A woman came out of the ladies' room; another went in with two little girls; another woman came out; another women went in. Phillip's mother pulled him forward. He bumped into a woman ahead of him. She looked at him with disgust.

"He stinks," she said to his mother. "Why'n't you take him home and wash him." She turned without waiting for an answer.

The men's room door flew open, and Phillip's father burst

out, his soaking shirt in his fist, the front of his jeans drenched and sticking to his broad husky thighs, his face purple.

A couple of young black men passed him and went up the walk to the swimming pool.

He looked at them and then at his wife and son in the ladies' room line. He grinned maliciously and bolted toward his family. "Gimme the little El Beano faggot!" He said. "I know what to do with him."

Phillip tried to draw back, but his father grabbed him by both shoulders and picked him up and shook him.

"We're going where there's lots of niggers, El Beano. We'll let them wash you off in some nigger water."

The man carried his son, held off in front of him like a bag of garbage, to the swimming pool gate, amid the gasps—and some giggles—of the women. He bought a swimming pool locker key, and shoved through the line to the men's shower room. There, holding his hollering child in the crook of one elbow, he took off his own shoes and socks and rolled up his jeans legs to below his knees. He sloshed through a chlorine-smelling foot wash, and sped through the dressing room, and before anyone could stop him, he raced, fully clothed, through a shower gauntlet and into the pool area.

Phillip, too terrified to scream anymore, choked on his own saliva and mucus. He felt his father's pincering arm let go as the other hand grabbed his clothes at the waist. His breath pinched off by the tightening belt, he grew limp. Facedown as his father swung him over the concrete pool deck, he saw the man's hairy foot tops, his curling yellow toenails. The feet slapped a few times across the cement, then air surged into Phillip's lungs as his waist was uncinched, and he flew over the edge of the pool.

"Have a good swim in the nigger water, El Beano," his father cried as the water whacked Phillip's belly.

He swallowed a mouthful, and pain ripped through his sinuses. He heard a deafening roar before he passed out.

When he woke with a blinding headache, a black man was leaning over him. "He sure is the whitest white boy I ever saw," he said.

"Please!" Phillip cried. "Don't turn me into a nigger!"

Then his father came up behind the black man and said, "Well, look at that! He's still an El Beano after all. The whitest white boy, like you said."

Then he picked up his shivering son and set him on a green wooden bench outside Dracula's Castle to dry. "Your ma and me want to go on some more rides," he said.

Exhausted, Phillip fell asleep on the bench and didn't wake up until just before sunset. His parents came back after the sun went down, smelling of sweat, hot dogs, grease, and beer. He had awakened hungry, and would have liked to have a hot dog, too, but he could tell by the look on his father's face he wasn't going to get any dinner. Like being nearly drowned in a pool with all those black people, not getting supper was all part of his punishment for being an El Beano and a sissy and for puking on his dad.

"OK, El Beano, one more place to take you before we go home," said his father. "I'm gonna give you another chance to be a man. We're going into Dracula's Castle."

Draucla's Castle was close to the bench where Phillip had been sleeping. He'd watched people go in and out since he'd awakened, and at dusk a big flood light had come on outside and shone on some bats flying in and out of a tower. By daylight, he had barely seen the bats, and they looked like plain birds. But at night with the big light shining on them he saw what they really were, and it scared him. The light cast their circling shadows on the outside of the tower. Whenever someone crossed the drawbridge that spanned a moat and started into the fun house, one of the bats dove down at the person. Most of the people jumped and screamed, especially little kids and women.

His father dragged him toward the castle and shoved him past the ticket taker and up to the drawbridge, which stayed raised until ten or more people waited behind it. Phillip knew better than to cry. Nobody around him was crying, not even little kids. Most of those waiting were teenagers. When the bridge suddenly started down, they giggled and screamed. The bridge settled down with a creak, the people started across, pushing Phillip along with the crowd. A teenage boy started to shove one of the girls to the side of the drawbridge, as if to push her over the side into the moat. He couldn't have done that, for ten-foot-high steel mesh fences formed the bridge sides.

"No, Jerry!" screamed the girl.

"Aurgh! I'm Dracula! I'm going to drink your blood!" The boy shoved her against the fence and opened his mouth and pushed his mouth against her neck.

The girl screamed again.

The boy lifted his face from her neck. He opened his mouth wide and turned it so everyone could see him. He had grown long fangs that had blood dripping from them. The girl had blood all over her neck.

"Oh, Jerry!" cried one of the other teenage girls. "You're just too much."

"Aurgh! I'm Dracula. I'm going to drink everyone's blood." He began to chase the other girl, who ran screaming into the castle entryway. The girl whose blood he had already drunk was wiping off blood from her neck. "What a prick!" she said to another teenager. "We never should have brought him along. You know he does stuff like that. He's sick!"

The other boy lifted his hands and made crawling motions with his fingers in the air. "Vait till you zhtart growing fangs, my Draculette! You vill see how zhick old Jerr really is. Did I tell you about the night he drank my blood? Let me zhow you." He tipped back his head and pointed to a bright red mark on his neck.

She looked at the mark and laughed. "Yeah? Who gave you that hickey anyway? I know it wasn't Judy. She was with Jerry last night. That thing looks brand new. Wait'll I tell her."

He looked shocked. "Zhee was with Jerr? Augheee! Vait till I get him. I'll take care of him. Vith my handy little zhilver zhtake that I alvays carry vith me for killing vampires." He began to run through the castle door, swiping at the bat that descended at him from the tower. "Augheee! Verever you're hiding in there, Jerr, I'm going to get you. You bazhtard! Zhtay avay vrom my voman."

"They're both sick!" said the bitten girl.

"All men are sick pricks," said another. Then the two girls

joined hands as they ran beneath the diving bats and screamed their way into the castle.

Phillip, pushed by his father, went in afterward. The bat came down, but didn't bite at Phillip, because his father was taller and it swooped up just before it reached the man's head. His father laughed. "It ain't the ones out here you got to be scared of, El Beano. It's the ones inside. They'll make a man out of you. The only way you can keep them from sucking your blood is to kill them. Once they suck your blood, you won't be an El Beano no more. They're better'n niggers at turning El Beanos into themselves. You'll be a vampire. And your teeth will start to grow long like that kid's." He howled. "You see what he did to that girl? Better to be an El Beano vampire killer than one of them."

Phillip grabbed his father's waist. The man pushed him away into the dark castle. "Stop being a faggot! Ain't you learned anything?"

Phillip swallowed a whimper. His mother was right behind him, but it was too dark to see her. If he could see her, he knew she'd have a pouty scowl on her face for Phillip's bringing his dad down on both of them. So seeing her would do no good. He went where his father pushed him.

From ahead in the long dark corridor, he heard the teenagers scream. Then, from above, a large thing with flapping wings flew down and screeched. He turned and tried to run from it. His father twisted him back. The thing came almost to beside his face, screeched again, then flew away. Phillip now could hardly breathe. He thought he was going to pass out again. But his father's strong hands held him hard and pointed him forward, and pushed him relentlessly on.

He closed his eyes, and let his father push. Though he heard lots of rushing noises and screams and screeches, he didn't have to see. He knew his father would keep pushing him, and as long as he just kept walking, he'd somehow get through this ugly, dark castle.

On one side he heard clanking chains and something rattling. "Let me out! Let me out of this dungeon!" A shrill voice called. Then the voice screamed and something went, "Crack! Crack! Crack!"

His father laughed. "He's getting what you and your mom gonna get from me tonight if you don't kill the vampire." He pushed the boy forward. "His ass whipped off. Wish I had one of those cat-o'-nine-tails."

His mother said, "You kill the vampire for me, Phillip. Your daddy don't think you can do it. We got a bet."

In his mind, Phillip saw the boy called Jerry with the bleeding teeth in his mouth. The other boy said he was going to kill him. Maybe Phillip wouldn't have to if the other boy got there first. Maybe the other boy would get to him first with his zhilver zhtake. Phillip didn't know what that was, and he didn't have one. He hoped, as his father continued to push him forward, that the boy would have already killed the vampire before Phillip got there. Then he would see what a zhilver zhtake was.

Phillip screamed as something thin and wispy hit his face and clung to it. He began to flail at the stuff and tried to get away.

His father howled. "Hey! The spider's going to get you, El Beano! Run, boy, run."

Phillip opened his eyes and saw a huge spider coming at him over a web that had fallen over him. He tried to run forward and tripped. He scraped his knees on the floor. The web flew up and away from him. A woman behind him screamed. His father pulled him to his feet. "Tarantula almost got you," he said. He giggled. "Come on. We're almost to the vampire room now." He shoved Phillip forward with his knees.

Petrified, Phillip kept going where his father pushed him. He kept his eyes open, now. They'd grown used to the dark, and the corridor seemed a little lighter. Ahead, he saw a strange pink glow coming out of a cavelike door. Flashes of different colors came through the door and flickered against the corridor walls. Faces suddenly jumped at him. More flying things dove at him; they always missed by inches. Screams echoed all around him, boys', girls', women's, and an occasional man's. Louder than the screams was the strange, loud laughter coming from the room ahead.

"That's where Dracula is," his father said.

Jerry's name was Dracula.

"Dracula's the King of the Vampires. No one can kill him. He keeps coming back to life. Unless you put a silver stake through his heart. Come on, El Beano. Let's see if you're a vampire killer." He pushed him forward once again.

Phillip could not lift his feet, and his father got angry and lifted him and carried him the last few yards into the Dracula room. There was nothing in the room but flashing lights and a cemetery like the one not far from Phillip's house, except most of the gravestones were broken or tumbled over. All that Phillip knew about cemeteries was that dead people lived there under the gravestones or inside little granite houses that didn't have windows. He knew that the dead people sometimes came out at night and haunted houses they used to live in. His mother told him that when she wanted to keep him from going into the cemetery. Or to keep him from doing other bad things that might make the dead people come into his house.

He turned and looked at his mother now. Her thin face kept changing colors in the flashing lights.

"It's OK for you to go in this one," she said, as if she had heard him thinking.

He looked around the room and started forward toward the door at the other end.

Suddenly a hole opened up in the floor in front of him. He jumped back. Inside the hole was a large, funny-shaped black box. It was narrower at both ends than at a place above the middle where it angled out like elbows or wings. The cover was open just a crack, but as Phillip stared at it, it began to lift open on hinges, something like a toy chest. At first he thought it was opening by itself, then he saw that someone was inside it, pushing it open.

"It's Dracula," whispered his father. "He's coming back to life."

Dracula sat up in the box. He didn't look like Jerry, except for his long bloody fangs. His clothes were as black as the box. He had on a cape, which he wrapped around himself as he stood. When he began to laugh, Phillip recognized the strange laugh he'd heard coming through the door before. The laugh came not only from Dracula's bloody mouth, but from all the walls around him, from the ceiling, from the flashing lights that played over the broken gravestones. You couldn't get away from the laugh; you couldn't get away from Dracula.

"Someone pulled the stake from his heart," his father said, pointing to a bright red stain on the front of Dracula's white shirt. "There it is! On the floor next to the grave. You got to get it, El Beano. You got to put it back into his chest, or he'll suck your blood and turn you into a vampire."

Phillip looked to where his father pointed at the edge of the floor right before him, just in front of where the hole had opened up. Dracula was standing up all the way, now, laughing his awful laugh, coming toward Phillip, lifting one foot up and out of his grave.

Phillip was so full of fear that his fear grew too big to be fear anymore and turned into courage and strength. The silver stake, about as long as his father's shoes, which almost touched it, lay close enough for Phillip to reach. Dracula still had one foot in the grave, and his chest was now even with Phillip's nose. Phillip bent and picked up the stake and pulled it up hard and stuck it into the red spot on Dracula's shirt.

Dracula screamed. He staggered backward and fell back into his box, the box closed over him, except for one small crack, the floor closed over the hole and became a floor again.

"I told you he could do it," said Phillip's mother. "You don't think he can do anything. I always knew he could."

"Goddamn, he did it. You did it, El Beano. You're a vampire killer. Hey, you sure surprised me, today. The niggers couldn't turn you into a nigger, and Dracula couldn't turn you into a vampire. Let's go out and get your medal."

Phillip was breathless as his father dragged him out the door of the Dracula room to a small room where a funny looking old man sat at a table. "You kill the vampire?" the man asked Phillip.

Phillip nodded. "You sure it wasn't your old man? You look too skinny and little to do it yourself. But you sure as hell look scared out of your wits. Never saw anyone so ghost white in my life."

"He's an El Beano," said his dad. "A vampire killing El Beano. Give him the medal, old man."

And the old man rubbed Phillip's head and guffawed and

pinned a medal on his shirt. "Be proud of what you just did, boy. You killed him dead!" And for the first time in his life, Phillip felt proud and strong.

The feeling didn't last long, though. As Phillip and his parents left the Dracula Castle and started to walk toward the gravel parking lot to get the Nash, a bunch of teenagers ran laughing and screaming by them.

"Aurgh! I'm Dracula," cried the one they'd called Jerry. He laughed like the Dracula Phillip had killed had laughed. His fangs still dripped blood, and three of the girls he was chasing had blood on their necks.

Phillip cried out and looked up at his father. "He came back!"

"Shit!" said his dad. "It happens every time. You put the stake in, someone else comes by and pulls it out, and it starts all over again." His father roared with laughter. "One of these days, El Beano, you're going to kill a vampire and take him somewhere and bury him where nobody's going to find him. Then he won't be able to come back." Then his dad did something he'd never done before—he picked Phillip up and hugged him.

That was how Phillip received his first sign that he was a vampire killer, that he was so special that he couldn't be turned into a black man or a vampire, even by Dracula himself. It took him several years to learn what that meant, that he had been chosen to wipe out evil from the world however and wherever he could and that he would recognize evil by its bloody fangs and he would be able to drive a stake through its heart. His skin was a sign of his specialness. He read all he could about albinos as soon as he learned from a teacher that his father had been mispronouncing the word. She sent him to see the school nurse for "counseling" to help him "deal with being different."

The health teacher ran a class on "special" children, whose handicaps set them apart. He told the class that albinos were just like the rest of them, except they couldn't make pigment to color their skin and their hair.

Without pigment, Phillip was special. Born to be a vampire killer! Maybe he would even become a messiah. He knew what the sign would be for that. He'd read about it in the Bible. When the messiah came, the prophets had said, the sun would turn to darkness and the moon to blood.

He thought the sun was beginning to turn to darkness when his irises, which had once been transparent blue, developed a milky whiteness. They began to look more like marbles than irises. His doctor did not know why it happened, but said it might be a kind of protection for the eye chamber against the light. He'd never seen it before, but that was as good a guess as any. The light had hurt Phillip's eyes before the condition developed. Now it no longer did.

As more white moved into his irises, the sun grew darker still. He was sure he was the missiah, but he still had to be able to see. His doctor fitted him with heavy, thick glasses that gathered in enough light for him to see. And by the time Phillip was a teenager, the whites of his eyes stopped mixing with the irises. They were as white as irises could get and still function. He could see, even though the sun had turned to darkness. Now he'd be able to see when the moon turned to blood.

Phillip knew he was becoming not only pure, but holy. His father must have seen it, too, for suddenly the man changed his attitude toward his son. He began treating him like an equal and taking him along when he went hunting. He taught Phillip how to kill animals at night. His father had no use for regulations that told him when and how he could kill animals. Only sissies and faggots worried about hunting seasons and licenses. He'd kill animals whenever he wanted, and he loved the thrill of taking them out of season.

And he took Phillip with him to make even more of a man out of him. They'd go jacklighting together. Out of season, they'd drive up north into the Poconos, and go to the edge of the woods after dark and shine their headlights into them. The deer that they caught in the light just stood there, eyes wide. His father gave Phillip the gun and told him to shoot. At first the boy missed a lot, but the deer never moved, so he got lots of practice at aiming, and his father could still bring down the deer at the end. When he'd had a successful jacklighting, the man was full of good feeling for his son. He taught him how to clean the deer, to take out all of its organs and feed what humans didn't like to eat to their mangy dog, who loved things like kidneys and brains. It was a lesson Phillip carried into his work as a diener many years later in the hospital morgue.

They sometimes poached during the day, too. His father was very clever about it. They'd go into the forest one day and find a good spot to bury a carcass if they had to. "You got to watch out for rangers," the man explained, as they dug a hole in a spot not too far from the trail, then carefully camouflaged it by spreading a tarp and covering it with branches. They only had to bury a contraband deer one time. Phillip had run out ahead of his father, the way they'd planned. When he got to the place where they'd parked their car, he saw a forest ranger parking his vehicle.

Breathless with the thrill of danger, he ran back down the trail to warn his dad. Quickly, they dragged the deer to the hole they'd dug the day before. His dad pulled the camouflaged tarp from the hole, and they dumped the deer in and covered it with the tarp and branches, and temporarily ditched the shotgun.

"Nice day for a hike," said the ranger with a tip of his hat, when they passed him on the trail moments later.

"Not bad, El Beano," said his dad, with a hearty slap to his shoulder. "You gonna turn out to be a man, after all."

When the ranger had disappeared down the trail, his dad went back and got the shotgun. He gave it to Phillip to carry. "It's yours, El Beano. You earned it. You might have white eyes and hair, but you got a true-blue red heart in that skinny chest. You got pure heart. Pure as as the Lord hisself."

He was only thirteen the day his father gave him that validating sign that he was pure as the Lord. And he knew it was a sign, because of the number thirteen. Later he learned how significant it was, for it taught him a way to get rid of the bodies of the vampires, to assure they'd never come back. During the three years in which he killed the Rand vampires, he made many trips to the northeastern Pennsylvania woods, to the very spot where he and his father had buried the deer. The spot was emblazoned in his inner eye. He could find it in the dark, if he had to; for there his father had first recognized how much like the Lord he was. Forever afterward he'd treated him with great respect. He wished he could tell his father about his vampire killing mission. The old man would be proud of him. But part of the burden of Lordliness was that you could not share it. He'd taken the vow of secrecy. (It came to him one night in a dream in which he and Lordly Ones from around the world met in the forest around the buried deer and shared blood with one another and consecrated their common bonds. When he woke in the morning he'd found a cross-shaped spot of blood on his pillow as a sign that it had not been an ordinary dream.)

Not all signs he received were good signs. Lordly Ones had obstacles to overcome, as the Bible showed you. He was facing obstacles now; but that didn't surprise him. He'd received a sign a few months ago in the woods when he was burying the last of the Rand vampires.

As he had with the others, he'd dug the vampire's grave the afternoon before the day he would bury it. The ground was especially hard because of a recent hard freeze, so he couldn't dig as quickly as he usually had. He decided to dig a shallower grave, for the longer he remained there, the greater the likelihood was of a ranger coming on his van, and coming to look for him. The vampire lay in a chiller he'd specially rigged for transporting the bodies here. Early in the morning he would pull the corpse out in its black plastic bag and drag it to the hole for burial. He could not afford to be delayed by an inquisitive ranger, who'd use any excuse he could find to search the van for game taken out of season.

He'd gotten back just in time, for a ranger was entering the forest just as he was driving out to find a place to stay for the night. *His foreknowledge was another sign. It had saved him.*

That night he dreamed of the deer he had buried long ago. In the dream, the deer turned black and grew fangs and rose from his grave and began loping off into the forest. Then it turned and leapt toward Phillip's throat, and Phillip had wakened in a sweat. He should have known the dream was a sign that the grave was not secure, but he thought it was simply a reminder to take special care in driving the silver-plated knife blade through the vampire's heart.

He rose before dawn, determined to do that. He sheathed the knife at his hip and patted it to reassure himself. As an extra precaution, he took his handmade cross, which contained some of his messianic powers, from around his neck as he went to inspect the chiller. He placed it around the vampire's neck. He would not drive the knife home till the body lay in its grave, so the knife wouldn't be dislodged in its rough ride in the plastic bag over the root rutted forest floor. Such a mishap had almost occurred with Ruth Manyon Spencer. Phillip never repeated a mistake.

The sun had barely risen when Phillip reached the gravesite in the forest clearing. Quickly he uncovered the hole and brushed aside the leaves and branches he'd strewn on it the previous day. He pulled the plastic bag into the grave, then opened the head of the bag. For a moment he sat on his knees and grinned at the face of the corpse. He felt so pure, so wonderful! He snapped open his knife sheath and reached for the cross.

Suddenly he heard a raucous alarm and the flapping of heavy wings. From the tree above him a large turkey gobbler dove. The bird attacked him from behind, knocking him into the grave and slashing him across the face with a vicious claw.

Phillip's heart pounded wildly. His shoes slipped on the plastic as he struggled to his feet. He scrambled out of the grave.

Again, the turkey cried out and dove, driving Phillip into the brush. The bird ran back and forth across the clearing, at last flying at the corpse in the grave and tearing at the plastic bag.

"It's a vampire!" Phillip cried. "Leave it alone. It must not come back. It's evil!"

He pulled the knife from its sheath and ran toward the turkey, slashing, slashing. The knife found a home in the bird, which screamed and ran off with it. If the gash was eventually fatal, Phillip was never to know. With uncanny strength the bird flew off through the trees, the knife still embedded in it.

Frightened at the sign he had just been given, Phillip returned to the body. He had no knife to drive through the heart, but his dream last night had saved him. The silver cross around the vampire's neck would keep him from coming back. The Lordly One had done his job. The messiah in him was growing.

He hurriedly covered the body, spread the leaves and

branches over the freshly dug earth, and returned to his van. Someday he'd return to the spot with a new knife and get back his cross with his messianic powers. But meanwhile, he knew he'd have to be cautious.

The signs kept coming: *The Evil Ones, who always fought the Lordly Ones, wanted the vampires to come back. A hunter had discovered them, and now the knives had been pulled from their hearts, and the cross pulled from around one's neck. Their remains lay in a county morgue, waiting, waiting to reflesh themselves one night when the moon was full. They could only be stopped when the moon turned to blood.*

Phillip read that sign. He now wore a new handmade silver cross, which brought back his powers and gave him new wisdom. With that wisdom, he'd seen how to make sure Agnes Shultz would never reflesh herself. The knife would never be pulled from her heart. He would keep her heart with him for the rest of his life. Hers and those of her aunts and uncles and cousins and brother and all their children. No one would ever find them. He and Adolph would make sure of that.

But if he wanted the moon to turn to blood, first he must cure the Vampire Queen. First he must drive a knife through the heart of Dr. Broward. She must never be able to create another vampire of the innocents that came to her office. He would keep her staked heart with the others forever.

And the rest of her would not be wasted. Adolph would love to have the rest. Especially the kidneys and liver and brain. Organ meats were his favorite.

CHAPTER SEVEN

Thursday

"Hey, Pop," said Poke, "how come you're sleeping in the recliner?"

Zack sat up and glanced quickly at the sofa where Liz had fallen asleep after their lovemaking. His robe lay over the sofa's arm. He had rolled it up for her to use as a pillow. He was sure her scent still clung to it, as it did to him.

"Guess I didn't know how late it was." He pulled up the recliner's back and stood.

Poke said, "You sure were sound asleep. Didn't even hear me tiptoe through to the kitchen this morning. I made your coffee and put out the penicillin at your place."

"Jeez, how much more of that stuff do I have to take?"

"The coffee?" She grinned.

"You know what I mean, smart-ass."

Another grin. "Just till it's gone. There's enough to last till next Tuesday night."

"Yeah, that's right. OK, thanks. You've been a sweet little nurse and coffee maker. Now you're fired! I'm taking care of myself. Get off to school." He walked over to the sofa and picked up the robe and surreptitiously inhaled its aroma and smiled. He put it on.

"You're not going back to work yet, Pop, are you?"

"Not today. I might go in for just a little while tomorrow. The doc told me to take it easy for a while at first."

"OK. Just don't go in today. Not after sleeping all night half sitting up."

He hugged her. "It's the best sleep I've had in more than a year." Someday soon he might be able to tell her why. Or someday soon she might recognize Liz's scent and figure it out for herself. He wondered how a fourteen-year-old girl felt about her father's sex life. It was something he'd never thought about before. He'd never talked about sex at all to Poke. That had been Maryellen's job. He figured she'd been open about it and given her all the warnings she'd need growing up in a world where kids started having sex before they turned twelve.

My God! he thought. *I wonder if Poke—* He let go of her and looked at her. She'd done a lot of growing in the last year, and her mix of features from both sides of the family imbued her with an exotic beauty. Her shape combined the fullness inherited from his family with the petiteness contributed by Maryellen's. The males inhabiting the dangerous world she moved in suddenly loomed as ruthless predators in his mind.

"What's wrong, Pop?" she asked as she backed away from his hug.

He shook his head. "Nothing. I just realized how pretty you are. We got to sit down and talk one day."

She laughed. "Sure, Pop. Well, I got to run. See you later."

He swallowed hard and nodded.

She ran into the foyer and opened the outside door. A moment later she stepped back into the family room and said, "Don't worry, Pop. I can take care of myself." Then she dashed out, leaving him a little breathless.

A large brown package from Yolanda Smith arrived in the mail at eleven A.M. Zack had almost forgotten she'd promised to send him copies of the Gus Champus documents.

He grabbed a pair of shears and cut through the package seals.

"Yolanda! You sweetheart," he cried as he tore back the flaps and revealed the contents of the cardboard box. "This stuff is just what I need."

She'd sent, as he knew she would, the kinds of documents amateurs might overlook—not the deeds and courthouse records anyone could dig out with a little patience, but family letters and photographs, and lists of personal papers such as insurance policies and pensions applied for. He riffled through a sheaf of letter copies. Maybe in one of these was a name of someone still alive, maybe the whorehouse madam or a whore that worked there or someone besides Gus Champus III who'd patronized the place—someone who might know what happened to the bastard son.

Yolanda had made copies of photos, too. There was one of Champus III as a man of thirty, holding his infant son. And another of Kitty Gingrich, the boy's mother, with Champus and another couple. "Hmm," Zack said aloud, "I could make a computer program to figure out what they'd look like today. How 'bout that, Liz! Wait'll I show you what I can do with my magic box!"

Under the stacks of letters and photographs was a copy of Yolanda's research notes concerning Champus, and the dead end she'd reached when she'd gone to Phoenix and found that the whole block of houses that had included the whorehouse, a small private nursing home, a few private residences, including one belonging to a music and dance teacher, and a tiny Mexican chapel, had been torn down in the late seventies and replaced with a strip shopping center.

"Why did you give up there?" Zack exclaimed. "A place like that would be crawling with stories of the old place!" He shuffled the photos. "You even got all these pictures of what it was like." Someone had taken all these pictures, which showed the houses, the nursing home, the chapel. There, on the porch of the nursing home was an old man wrapped up in blankets and sitting in a rocking chair, and a Native American woman about twenty-five years old standing by the porch railing, and a small child sitting on the porch steps.

Zack took a deep breath. *Jesus! That kid is in a couple of pictures! That kid is Gus Champus IV!*

"Someone in these pictures is still alive," he said, as he went through them again. "If I can only get a name, something more! Maybe in the letters."

It took him several hours to go through the letters. Nothing definite there. There was only one way to learn more. He would have to go to Phoenix, go back to that old neighborhood. Yolanda had done at least some additional homework: she'd taken pictures of the shopping center and the surrounding houses. The old houses nearby had been there for decades. And in a picture of the shopping center, he could see a few generations of shoppers along the strip. One of those shoppers had to know what happened to Gus Champus III. An old guy who'd been to that whorehouse and now, blinded with syphilis, shuffled by the Taco Bell restaurant that stood in its place. A middle-aged Amerindian woman in a white nurse's aide uniform who might have had her first nursing experience caring for the old man in the nursing home rocking chair. Even that teenage couple, the guy hispanic, the girl angla, might have heard something about their neighborhood from someone who'd heard something from somebody else.

"Why the hell didn't you go up to those people and ask, Yolanda? It've been so easy to do three or four years ago when you took these pictures! If it'd been me—"

"Pop! Who're you talking to? What are all these papers you've got spread all over the family room?"

He jumped as the front door slammed to punctuate her question. "How come you're home so early, Poke?"

"Early? It's nearly four. I walked with Christy and we took the long way."

"Jeez. I got lost in this stuff."

She walked over and looked at the box and the scattered contents. "Genealogy junk." With an accusatory look, she said, "You didn't eat lunch, Pop. You didn't take your lunchtime medicine."

"I'll take it now. A couple hours won't make much difference."

"You said you could take care of yourself, Pop. That's why I didn't come straight home. You're doing the same thing as before."

"I'm not sick. So why shouldn't I? Look, Poke, this stuff is important. It's about those bodies. Or at least about someone that might have killed them. I'm going to Phoenix, Monday. I got to go. I'll ask Christy's mom if you can stay with them next week."

"You can't go on a trip. The doctor won't let you."

"She knows I'm going. At least she knows I've been thinking about it."

"And she's letting you?"

"Not letting me. She knows I make my own decisions about my life. Whether she thinks they're right or not."

"Well, it's stupid for you to go. You're still doing the kind of thing that made you sick in the first place. OK, you want to get sick again, no matter what the doctor says, it's up to you. I'll do what Momma did. I'll ignore your whining unless you take your own medicine."

She ran into the kitchen, and a few minutes later he heard the microwave oven beep and smelled pizza. The smell woke the appetite he'd ignored and lured him into the kitchen. She stood red-faced at the oven.

"Was that what Momma did?" he asked.

Pouting, she nodded. "I thought she was being mean, not caring about you when you were sick."

"Me, too. I used to get mad at her. When a guy's sick, he needs attention. And she was a nurse. All she could say when I'd whine is, 'Take your nasal spray.' Or, 'Did you take the Tylenol? There's a whole bottle full in the medicine cabinet.'"

"She wasn't being mean. You acted like a baby. You didn't want medicine, you wanted her to feel sorry for you. She told me men were all that way. Their mothers spoiled them when they got sick."

"What other neat things did she teach you?"

"You're mad at her, Pop."

Stunned, he started to deny it; then he said, "Yeah, a little, I guess."

She flashed him an unreadable look, then turned and took the plate of pizza out of the oven and carried it to the table. Setting it next to a medicine cup with a penicillin tablet in it, she said, "OK, this is the last time I play nurse. From now on I treat you just like she did. And I hate it when you get mad at her. You shouldn't. Not now!"

Friday

If he wanted to take off time from work next week, he had to tell his boss, Ted Squire, president of Squire Publications. That was why he shaved before going into work and wore a blue dress shirt without the tie and the only suit he owned, a ten-year-old wool blend gray flannel that Maryellen had insisted he buy for special occasions, and which he'd worn only twice—the second time being for her funeral.

He spent the morning going over some deadline matters: a large corporation's presentation for a state proposal that had to be in next week, the Ballet Company brochure to be used to raise survival funds for yet another tenuous year of programming, and a cookbook full of ads bought from a religious organization for their yearly fund-raising function.

"Thank God you made it in, Zack," said Ted, as he nodded over the completed artwork. "These are important clients." Ted, a neat, dark-haired man in his mid-thirties, revealed his anxieties through a twitch of his jaw and clicking sound in his throat. People who worked with him barely noticed these tics, unless they were nervous, too. Then they could measure the effects of their own words on him and dish out or withhold comments accordingly.

Zack saw Ted was more agitated than usual. The immaculate nails at the tips of his long fingers tattooed the papers on the desk. "I wasn't putting in twenty-hour workdays for nothing," Zack said.

"We appreciate your work, Zack." He pushed aside the illustrations, steadied his hands, and said, "So, you're feeling OK now, I hope." It was his first acknowledgment of Zack's illness. "You're looking pretty good."

"I have to take it easy, my doc says."

"Well, you better obey doctor's orders. We got to keep you well."

"Sure. So I can only stay another hour or so today."

"Well, just make sure you got time-sensitive stuff set up for next week. We fell a little behind, you know. Had to put some stuff out last week without your final look. It was OK, but we don't like to do that."

And they wouldn't do it long, either, Zack thought. Some other starving commercial artist was at the door waiting to take over the Squire art department the minute he turned his back. And this bastard would replace him in a minute if a single deadline was missed.

Still, he felt sorry for Ted, the Squire brother who seemed to take the business most seriously. The others disappeared when the work pressures built. "Well, maybe I could come in tomorrow and Sunday morning."

"Why do that? Rest up over the weekend. We'd like you to put in full time next week, if possible. Some big stuff coming up, and we could use some fresh designs."

"Jesus, Ted, I'm just getting over pneumonia." He coughed a couple of times to illustrate. This worked a small glob of mucus into a spot where it made his voice rumble a bit, giving the impression he hoped for. "I've got vacation time coming and I was hoping—"

"I sympathize with you, Zack. But next week's a really bad time. You've missed a week and a half already." His cheek sank, then heaved like a trampoline taking a bounce.

"But my doc says—"

Ted glanced at him sharply. Then he relaxed his features. "I've got it! Why don't you come in half days till the end of the month? You've got sick time left, and we can take it out of that instead of vacation. Then when things get slack, you can take your vacation. How's that?"

The bastard doesn't give a damn about me! Zack thought. *He knows there's no slack time. He knows I'm worth ten times the money he pays me. And he also knows no one else would pay it to me, either.* "Jesus, Ted. I was really counting on whole days off. For vacation, not being sick. I got other things I wanted to do next week. What if I come in all day tomorrow and Sunday?"

Ted leaned back and studied him. He looked down at the illustrations on his desk.

"I'll leave it up to you, Zack," he said after looking up at last. "I guess we've put a big load on you. It's one of the problems of small businesses like ours, made up mostly of family. There's no one to fill in with special talents like yours. We can't afford a dozen consultants. My dad started this out as a small printing company. The desktop publishing guys almost put us out of business. We got the minicomputer setup but didn't know shit about computers. Then you came to show us how to use the thing and gave us the demo on the graphics. Real design, you showed us. Not paint-by-number stuff." He shook his head, some of his awe at technology washing over onto people like Zack who could wield it.

Then he said, "I guess you need a vacation, and you deserve it. But it's a hell of a bad time for us."

Zack took a deep breath. Maybe he'd sold Ted short. They had put up with Zack's oddball antics, given him lots of time off. His health insurance was every bit as good as theirs. It had helped a lot with Maryellen. "Jesus, Ted, I hate to leave you in a lurch. Let me think about it. I could put off the trip awhile, if you'd let me work up this program on the minicomputer—"

"Sure, Zack. You can use if for anything you want. You know that." He reached across his desk for Zack's hand as he rose, confident he'd made a deal.

Zack stood up and grasped Ted's hand, and Ted slapped his shoulder. "You're the only one here that knows how to use that monster."

"They don't have to know how to use it. Their desktop computers are networked into it, and they just use them." He dropped Ted's hand. "Hey, I just thought of something!" He had thought of the home brew transportable computer he'd put together when he'd worked as a technician for a small technical firm. Unlike a laptop, it weighed about forty-five pounds; but also, unlike a laptop it had a high resolution monitor built in, so that the screen display was sharp and clear. He'd juiced it up with a few meg of memory, a graphics card, a 100 megabyte hard disk, everything but a color monitor. But he could code in color pixels, which would show up as shades of gray, and do as much with it as he could with his desktop at home. He had never taken it with him when he'd traveled, but he could: It would fit under the airliner seat.

"What's that?"

"Jesus! Why didn't I think of it before? I can take my trip and still work. I can hook up to the mini by phone. You can fax me orders, and I can run programs, even send graphics and tell the printer what to print. You can show the designs to the clients, then I'll talk to them by phone to answer questions."

Ted knit his brow. "That sounds scary. I don't know—"

"Shit, it's easy. I can show you. I'll set up the mini to host calls, then call in from home on my modem. I'll show you a sample of how it works."

"But if you call, anyone can. Our competitors—"

"No way, Ted. It'll be a one-man system. It won't pick up from anyone but me. No one will know the password. And just to make sure, I'll change the password once a month. You know what this can do for us, Ted? It can give us a leg up on the competition. I can draw up illustrations at home, late at night when they think I'm sleeping. In the morning, bingo! They're sitting in the print hopper ready for the client before I even get here. You can have him sold before lunch."

Rubbing his hands together and working his face excitedly, Ted said, "Wow!" His eyes glistened. "You're on, Zack." He shook his head, obviously once more awed by technology Zack had learned to take for granted. "Do whatever you have to do to get that thing working. Then send me a sample design tonight. I'll come in tomorrow morning, and if I like what I see, you take your vacation whenever you want."

"I'll convince you," said Zack with more certainty in his voice than in his heart.

Programming the computer to take calls on the phone line as well as through the office network took very little time. Squire had a phone line to dedicate to the system hookup. Zack tested it with a call from Ted on his own private line, using a dialed-in password. This impressed Ted all over again. So far, so good. Now Zack had to get home before Poke did. He didn't want to stir her up again about his not caring for himself. She obviously was angry about his going to Phoenix and her inability to control him. She'd also turned very sour when he'd admitted an old buried anger at her mother. One of those silly old angers that somehow lived beyond the grave, even if you didn't want it to. He wished it hadn't come up. He wished he could be as good a man as she wanted him to be. He had tried.

He'd been very good today, in fact, getting his breakfast, taking his medicine on time, taking out time for lunch—more pizza reheated in the office lounge microwave oven. Though he still felt a little weak on the drive home through a late April drizzle, he could remember times when he felt worse without being sick at all.

He arrived home at two-thirty and went directly to the Champus letters, hoping to get something more from them in the time left before he'd have to get to the all-night job of creating and sending a presentation through the wires to the office. But he fell asleep in the scatter of papers.

The smell of beef stew woke him up. Outside, clouds swallowed the daylight earlier than usual, making the room, with its single lit lamp shedding brightness on him alone, seem remarkably sheltering and warm. Another block of light framed in the kitchen doorway beckoned him to watch his daughter doing what she'd sworn she wouldn't—making sure his medicine was in the cup next to his place at the table.

He didn't talk about Phoenix through dinner, or tell her he'd already booked a round-trip ticket for a Monday morning flight. Sure, he'd better make certain about arrangements for her to stay with Christy for five days next week. But, after all, he hadn't closed the vacation deal with Ted, yet. He was confident that he would, of course. He'd sent designs and programs by modem to the network dozens of times and never failed. But why stir Poke up? She might feel much better tomorrow, when they could spend some time together and he could kind of sneak up to the idea. He'd promise her she could use the old transportable computer, which he'd stowed when Maryellen had gotten sick, and then forgotten about. She could use it to hook up to the network through her own telephone and play games, while he used the computer in the family room.

With these thoughts in his head, and after he'd insisted on doing the dishes and cleaning up the kitchen without Poke's help, he had booted up the family room computer and was about to switch on the modem, when the phone rang.

"It's Liz, Zack. Are you all right? You missed your appointment this morning."

"Uh—I guess I forgot it. Yeah, I'm fine. I went into work a few hours. Jesus, Liz. I'm sorry."

"It's all right. As long as you're all right."

"Well enough to convince my boss to give me next week off to go to Phoenix."

"I guess I can't stop you."

"No, dear person, you can't."

"Zack, can I come over?"

"To try to change my mind?"

"No. I just have to be with you."

"Sure, if you don't mind watching me work."

"I don't mind watching you do anything."

"It's something I have to finish tonight, even if it takes all night."

"I won't get in the way, I promise. But I have to come. Being with you, seeing you, will help me pull myself together."

"Sure," he said again. "Come on. Having you here will make the work easier. I want to show it to you, anyway."

After he hung up, he heard a sound in the foyer. Poke had come down the stairs. "Who's coming over?" she said.

"The doc."

"Dr. Broward?"

"Yeah. She wants to come over and watch me work."

"Not cause you're still sick? Just to watch you work?"

"Mmmmhmm."

"Pop—"

"She was here the other night, Poke."

"But that was with the artist."

"She came the next night, too. After you went to bed."

She looked at him, wide-eyed, then looked at the recliner and the sofa. "Oh, Pop!" Tears burst out along her lashes. She turned and ran upstairs.

CHAPTER EIGHT

Friday

Liz had slept well Thursday night, but only because her body had separated from her mind. In fact, that separation must have occurred during her cathartic morning shower, for she had almost no memory of Thursday. When she came to the office at 8:30 in the morning, Claire did not stop her at the reception cubicle and say, "Where were you yesterday, Dr. Broward?" Instead, she lifted her eyes from the schedule lying on her laminated white work counter and said, "It's not going to be as busy as yesterday." And, "The culture report on Charles Adams is on your desk. He called twice yesterday."

"Yes, I called in a prescription for him."

The words coming out of her mouth seemed to have bypassed her mind, and she looked up at a blank spot on the peach colored wall, wondering how she knew that. Then she shook her head and said, "I'll have to check the report to see if I gave him the right antibiotic. The Noroxin will probably knock out whatever he has. It's just so damn expensive. The lab report should have been in yesterday."

"They've been slow lately. We've had quite a few patients calling before we get a chance to call them."

"Yes. I'll have to check around for a new lab. They used to be reliable and cheap. Now they've gotten arrogant and expensive."

"Dr. Meredith said the same thing."

Jim had. So had Elsie. The three partners had talked together about it and done nothing. Always too busy, and the lab was in the same building. And the patients ended up paying more for medicines than they should. Liz pulled a prescription pad from a pigeonhole in Claire's well-organized work space, and held out her hand for a pen. Claire pushed one across the counter to her, and she picked it up and wrote a note to Jim to check out laboratories. He, too, had office hours today in the modern suite of offices and examining rooms they shared; still, they would be unlikely to have time to talk between patients. After putting the note in Jim's folder, she grabbed her own, went back through the narrow hallway to her office, and read the lab report that Claire had left next to some unfinished work from yesterday on her broad gray oak desk.

Yes, Charles's infection would have responded to tetracycline, a drug with a narrower range of effectiveness than the Noroxin she'd ordered for him, not wanting to risk his quick recovery for fifteen dollars or so. She cursed the lab under her breath, then spent the next forty minutes sitting on the edge of her gray leather swivel chair, going over records of patients she was scheduled to see.

Now she was fully aware of the feel of her office, the squareness of the room and the framed documents on the walls, of the hard oak furnishings. These things contrasted with the softness of the peach walls and aquamarine carpet and her own knit aquamarine suit. She was aware of sitting here now, and of the comfort that control of at least this small space always brought her. Had she been in control yesterday? She must have—she'd left some records to finish working on, but Claire said it had been busy. Liz looked at the records now.

They sparked her recall of emergency visits jammed in at lunchtime and late into the afternoon. She remembered now that she hadn't eaten lunch or dinner, but that she hadn't felt hungry all day, not even when she'd stopped that evening at the hospital snack bar on her way to see patients, and bought some sour coffee and a pack of cheese crackers to fill in her emptiness and take the edge off a headache.

She'd made three hospital calls, she remembered, all on patients Bob Ryan would be operating on in the morning. All had been well-prepared for their abdominal surgery, as Bob's patients usually were. She admired his skill and his caring attitude, which was why she never hesitated to refer patients to him.

Satisfied that she had done her part as family doctor in following through on her patients' care, Liz had gotten onto the elevator to leave the hospital. Sighing with relief that the workday was over, she'd pushed the button for the lobby. As the door began to slide closed, she'd jotted some notes that she'd later transcribe to her patients' office records. So she was not looking when the tall man with a lab coat and a cart of blood and urine collectors stopped the elevator door with his large bony hand and got on.

He had seen her, though, and quickly turned his back to her and kept it turned to her when she passed him and alighted in the lobby. He followed her off the lift and saw her turn past a group of visitors sitting in the deep, modern orange and blue chairs, and go out the tall double glass doors toward the parking lot. *It was the sign he had been waiting for. He would follow her, learn where she lived!* He pushed the cart to the round walnut information desk in the center of the massive lobby.

A pudgy pink and gray woman with a pink and gray volunteer's uniform sat smiling behind the desk.

"I'm not feeling well. Please call the lab," he told her. "Tell the technician I've left these specimens here. All labeled. She'll know what to do." He pointed to his cart. Then, without waiting for the woman to close her rounded mouth and respond, he took several long strides to the exit and reached it before Dr. Broward had gotten to her car. His van was at the opposite end of the lot from hers, but his long legs brought him to it before she'd even started her engine. By the time she'd finished writing notes to herself and backed the gold Mercedes-Benz out of her slot, his van was in the aisle behind it.

Then she looked at him behind her and waited a moment, as if to be sure he had stopped to let her back out. He stuck his hand out his window and waved her on.

She turned right when she exited the lot. A knot had formed in her stomach, contracting on Wednesday's memories. She swallowed it, only to have it spring up anew into her throat. "Damn!" she said. "God! What am I going to do?"

In her rearview mirror, small rainbows bounced across the headlights of the tall black van behind her, blurring them. She rubbed the back of her left hand across her eyes; still more tears came. She let them roll down over her cheeks; the heat from her face evaporated them as quickly as they fell.

Behind her, the van's headlights glared like owl eyes at the back of her neck. She wished the van would turn off, if for no other reason than that she didn't want anyone to see her crying. Liz Broward didn't cry. Liz Broward had not lost her bearings. She had had an argument with her parents. She had slept with her patient, and hadn't had the grace to remove the tawdry smell of sex from her body until after her fiancé had smelled it. She hadn't had the grace to lie to him about it. She'd thrown him out of her apartment as if he had betrayed her.

"Please, stop following me!" she said to the reflection of the van. *"Are you going to follow me around for the rest of my life?"*

Then, as if in response to her pleading, the van pulled off into another lane and started to pass her.

She took a deep breath and dug into her dress pocket for a tissue. Wiping her eyes and sniffing, she got control of her tears. She drove with the tissue held at her face for a few blocks, then blew her nose and stuffed the tissue into the trash bag on the floor between the seats.

By the time she reached her apartment, her tears had dried and she'd forgotten about the van, even forgotten about why she had been crying. She was tired—terribly tired. Finding her apartment parking garage key card, she slid it into the slot. The garage door rumbled open, then automatically clanked down behind her car as it passed through into the garage.

On the outside of the gray steel door, two bright round reflections shone for a few moments, then diffused and slid off the door. An engine purred for a few seconds, then growled a few times, and a black van made a few turns around the block before driving off into the darkness.

Now, the next morning, Liz, seeing the three records on her desk, recalled the notes on Bob Ryan's patients she'd scribbled on her pad last night. She transcribed the notes and jotted herself another note to go back and see the patients this evening. That done, she fell into the office routine: The patients were marched to her office or an examining room; she ran a tattoo from one room to another, grabbed charts from door pockets, slipped into and out of her long lab coat, dispensed handfuls of medicine samples from cabinets and drawers and scribbled prescriptions and orders on pads, diagnoses on charts, and codes for charges on long triplicate billing forms to be stamped by Claire with Liz's signature.

Once she passed Jim Meredith in the narrow hall on his way between patients. Her forty-year-old partner towered over her. She looked up at him. "Get my note?"

He grinned and wrinkled his freckled brow, so that his crooked red eyebrows disappeared into his crop of red hair. "Yep. Been thinking the same thing."

Holding fistfuls of paper aloft, they pirouetted around each other and resumed their respective morning tasks. It was only after morning hours were done that she realized Zack had not shown up for his appointment. She started back to her office to call him, when her receptionist stopped her in the hallway. "Dr. Broward, a woman's waiting in your office," Claire said.

"An emergency?"

Claire's blue eyes flickered away from Liz. "I guess so."

Liz frowned and knit her brow. Then, seeing Claire's obvious discomfort, Liz said, "All right. I'll see her." She approached the open door to her office and saw the gray-frosted honey hair from the back, and recognized the poised set of the shoulders and the expensive rose silk that clothed them.

She bit her lip, stepped in, and closed the door. She held the knob behind her for a moment.

The woman half stood and turned a little.

Liz swallowed. "Mother—" She let go of the doorknob but didn't move forward.

Grace rose all the way and faced her, gray eyes calm and composed. "I have to talk to you Liz. Can we go for lunch?"

"No. Sit down. I'd rather talk here. I'm glad you came." She gestured to her mother who sat again, then she took her own chair behind her desk. *My own chair on my own turf*, she thought. This was the place where she was always in control. Yet with her mother across the desk from her, she seemed to hold no authority at all. She tried to relax in her usual confident pose: back straight, violet eyes interested and calm, one hand in her lap and the other resting on her desk, but Grace's eyes on her wouldn't allow it. Grace's eyes—Grace herself—controlled everything. Everyone.

"Eric came to see me this morning," Grace said at last.

Liz felt her face grow taut. *He would go to Grace, of course.*

"He told me what happened Wednesday night. Or at least what he thinks happened before you came home and told him to leave your apartment."

Liz said nothing. She picked up a pen from her desk and began to rotate it between her hands. *Why must her mother always—almost always—be so unnervingly calm and beautiful? What gave her such unerring grace and dignity? And why did Liz lack those things in her presence?*

"What did happen, Liz?"

Liz played with the pen for a few moments, then put it down and looked into her mother's eyes, then away. "What did Eric say?"

"You spent the night with another man. Did you?" She leaned forward, clenched fist pressed against the desk.

Liz picked up her pen again and tapped it on the desk pad a few times. She looked at her mother's eyes again. This time her own didn't waver.

Grace took a deep breath and sat back. The corner of her lip quivered slightly, but her fist relaxed and she put her hand in her lap.

"What is it, Liz? A last fling before—"

"No. I'm in love with him."

"Not with Eric?"

"No. I never was with Eric. I thought I was once. Then when I realized I wasn't, I thought it didn't matter."

Grace stood up and turned away. "It doesn't matter, Liz."

"Are you saying you weren't in love with Dad?"

Turning to look at Liz again, she clutched the edge of the desk and leaned toward her. "No. I was in love with him. But that wasn't what mattered. What mattered was the things I didn't love about him that I learned to live with. To 'handle,' as you put it."

Liz's face grew hot. She reached for Grace's hand. "Mother, I'm sorry!"

Grace's hands slid across the desk and grasped Liz's. "Goddamn it Liz, to hell with being in love! You've undone a lifetime of love!"

"No, Mother!" Releasing her hands from Grace's, she stood. "Please don't say that!" Through a wash of blinding tears she saw her mother coming around the desk toward her. In a moment she was in Grace's embrace.

Her mother held her for a while, then ran her fingers through her hair over and over again. She, too, was weeping. "It's all right, Liz darling. Someday he'll figure it out, won't he? How I love him for all he is. How I've taught you to love him, too. In spite of those things we don't love. We've allowed him to be them, haven't we? Like I've allowed you to be what you are. Even risking you'd say things like you did."

"I'm sorry. I'm so sorry. Please forgive me." Liz clutched her mother for several moments, then released her. That she'd already been forgiven the unkindest, most damaging thing she'd ever done to anyone was clear.

The women stood, half turned away from each other. Grace rummaged deep in her leather handbag. Liz pulled a handful of tissues from the box on her desk and handed half to her mother, who nodded and thanked her.

Liz returned to her desk, sat, swiveled her chair so she looked out the large casement window. The outdoor light slanting through down-tilted blind slats singed her eyes. Closing her eyes, she turned her head. When she heard her mother settle into her chair, she opened them.

Grace smoothed her hair, and smiled. "I didn't come here for your apologies. But I'm glad to have them."

"I—"

With a curt headshake Grace, clearly in control again, said, "No. No more, Liz. That's done. Right now I don't want you to throw away your life. I think I see what's going on here. It might not look like a last fling to you, but that's what it is. You're thirty-eight, Liz. You were always more mature than most girls, and, well, I don't think you ever had an adolescence. Your contacts with boys in high school were limited. You never did fall in love before, did you?"

She couldn't help laughing. "I hate to tell you this, Mother, but I lost my virginity before I was sixteen."

"Yes. To Larry Rubin." Her brow lifted; her lips barely carved out a smile.

Liz's mouth fell open. "It—it was Jerry Rubin."

Ignoring the correction, Grace went on, "I'm not talking about sexual experiments. Or even your rebellion against your father when you followed your lover to school. Thank God you rebelled against him! I can just see you in that stuffy law practice. Or even in a City Line Avenue plastic surgery practice." She grimaced.

"What do you mean?"

"What you're feeling about this man now."

"How do you know what I'm feeling?"

"I can smell it on you, Liz," she whispered hoarsely, her nostrils quivering. "I've known it longer than you have. I thought it was Eric."

Her mouth drained of moisture, Liz stared at her mother.

"You're my daughter. My only child. You've been inside me, part of me. I've memorized you."

"How—"

"Never mind how. You'll either learn how or you won't. Besides, the how doesn't matter. What matters is that you still have a chance to go back to Eric. He loves you. He'll forgive you. And so will your father."

"Dad knows?"

"About this man? No. Eric could never tell him, and I wouldn't. But he'll forgive you for telling him the truth about himself."

"You want me to marry a man I'm not in love with to win my father's forgiveness? That's obscene! I can't believe you're saying it."

Grace shook her head. "Your father's forgiveness is irrelevant. You already have mine, and Eric can be convinced he was wrong about what happened Wednesday night. He wants to be convinced. I want you to give up the man you think you're in love with because he's wrong for you and you'll ruin your chance for a lifetime of love with a good, kind, compassionate man if you don't."

Liz stood up, clenched her fists, and pushed her knuckles against her desk's edge. This was one time she wouldn't cave in to her mother's superior wisdom. This time it was anything but wisdom. "You mean if I lie to Eric now and I keep on lying to him all my life about his offenses against me—the way you do with Dad—that I'll build a lifetime of love? That is, until my own daughter—if I'm lucky enough to have one—tears it all down with the truth! That's not what I call love."

Grace's face reddened and crumpled. "I never lied to your father. I gave him room to offend me and loved him in spite of it. So did you, till now. It worked. There's no perfect man, no perfect marriage, no perfect life. I love you, Liz—"

"I love you, too, Mother. That's why I'm not going to listen to you. That's why I'm going to forget what you just told me."

"No. Make up your own mind, but don't forget what I said. Whatever you do, however it turns out, I had to say it to you, and you had to listen." She gathered up her handbag and stood. Then she composed her face and walked unbent to her daughter's office door. There she stopped and turned and fixed Liz's eyes with her own.

"What shall I tell Eric?" she asked.

For a moment, Liz could say nothing. Then, "Whatever you think he should know," she said.

Grace smiled ever so slightly, nodded shortly, then left.

Liz grasped her desk and steadied herself. Her mother's shrewdness both appalled and frightened her. Grace had come here for only one reason: She was bargaining for time, knowing time—the two weeks still left before the wedding—was the only thing Liz still had on her side, as Grace saw her side.

Liz had wanted to erase that time. *Only indecision demanded time; decision demanded action. And, oh God! Liz wanted to act.*

And she would have acted, or let her past acts stand and speak for themselves. She'd meant what she'd done. She wasn't in love with Eric; she was in love with Zack; she didn't intend to turn back, to marry Eric.

Still, she owed the time to her mother, if only to prove she wasn't a willful adolescent in the throes of unreasoning passion. She wasn't, was she? Liz Broward knew what she was doing. She hadn't lost her bearings.

So, let her mother have her bargain. It was the least Liz could give her after the pain she'd caused. Besides, her decision was firm. It was, wasn't it?

Liz sat down at her desk and covered her face with her hands.

Two hours later she again bumped into Jim in the hallway. She grasped his arms. "Jim. I can't stay."

"That's OK, Liz. We'll talk about the lab business next week." He pulled his arms from her grasp.

She caught his arms again. "No—" She looked around and saw a patient being escorted to his office. "Please, Jim. Come to my office a second," she said, voice lowered.

He glanced at her, brow knit, then looked at his patient. He nodded at her, released one arm, and waved to his patient. "Be just a minute," he called to the man. "Sure, Liz."

She let go of his arm and turned quickly toward her office, across from his. "Close the door," she said as he followed her in. When he had, she nodded him to a chair and sat in her own.

"Something's the matter, Liz," he said, sitting forward in his chair.

"Yes. Can you take the rest of my patients today?"

He hesitated for less than a second. "Sure." He sat back in the chair and waited.

"Thank you."

"Tell me what's the matter, Liz." He looked at her earnestly.

"I don't want to keep you from—"

"My patients can wait. I don't think you can."

She turned her head away from him. "It's nothing I can tell you about. I'm upset. I can't work. I have to take time off to think. Can you and Elsie handle things next week?"

She heard him draw a sigh. "You don't have to ask us. Just take the time. Of course we can handle it." He stood up and strode around the desk and placed his long, thin hand on her shoulder.

After a moment she put her own hand on top of it. He tightened his grasp.

"I saw your mother leaving when I came back from lunch—?"

She heard the question in his voice and nodded. Then she looked up at him.

Letting go of her shoulder and straightening, he nodded, too. "Getting married's tough, kid. I've been through it. My bride and her parents—and mine—all survived." He grinned. "So did I, as you can see by the pictures of us and the twins on my desk."

"I'm not—I'm not worried about surviving." She managed a small tight smile. "Just about getting through the next couple of weeks. Through today."

"You'll make it, Liz. I've never known you not to make it." He reached for her arm and bent and kissed her cheek.

She captured his hand as he stood, and held it as she said, "Thank you, Jim. I love you."

"Sure," he said. "Name the woman that doesn't." He winked and kissed her again and left.

Though a few instructions to Claire and a short phone talk with Elsie put her office in good hands for the next week, she couldn't neglect the hospital rounds scheduled for the afternoon. Thank God there'd be no one admitted for surgery before Monday, if then. She could barely contain herself through visits with Bob Ryan's three patients. She'd neither phoned Zack nor heard from him.

She ran into Bob—a tall, heavy man nearing fifty-five with graying hair and shell-rimmed glasses—in one of their patients' rooms. He gave her a full report on their progress in the hospital cafeteria, where he insisted she join him and have a cup of coffee while he ate a late supper. "After all," he joked, "your patients are keeping me from Mary's great cooking." He made a face at the dish of spaghetti and wilted salad on the tray he set on the gray laminated cafeteria table. He grabbed a napkin and brushed some crumbs off the table.

She smiled, remembering the days of rushed hospital meals with rubbery gelatin cubes and dry ham and cheese sandwiches from a vending machine during her medical internship and residency. "I beg your most humble pardon," she said, placing her coffee mug down. She sat across from him.

"One problem with no smoking rules here, is where do you dump the cellophane cracker wrappers?" He shoved a discarded one aside. "Seriously, I appreciate the referrals, Liz. They're the most informed patients I get. You know what that means for their recovery."

"I can't take credit for their recovery, Bob. But thanks."

"Say, whatever happened with your patient whose records were stolen?"

"Far as I know, both she and they are still missing. My guess is she's somewhere searching for her husband and children. Her husband might have had someone steal the records."

"Vampire disease!" He shook his head.

"It's porphyria, Bob. Those patients suffer enough without being stigmatized."

"I've never had a patient with it. Guess it's out of my bailiwick. Not a surgical problem."

"God knows we all have plenty to keep up with in our specialties. Two doctors saw Agnes before she came to me. The first one operated on her. An exploratory. The second one referred her to a psychiatrist. But the woman knew she was physically sick."

He looked up from his salad and put his fork down. "Why the exploratory?"

"Abdominal pain—it's really severe. It can mimic a lot of things."

"Yeah. Can't rule out appendicitis without opening them up sometimes. Far as we've come with imaging." He turned and looked at the line of people entering the cafeteria at the far end of the room. "And lab tests," he said.

She followed the path his eyes had taken and saw he was looking at a tall, pale, white-smocked man with a crew cut. The man looked through thick glasses over the heads of diners, and his glance seemed to fall on her for a fleeting second before he quickly turned his head. She thought she'd seen him someplace before, but she couldn't recall just when or where.

She looked back at Bob. "Actually, you can find it in the urine. But you have to be looking for it, Bob."

"Port wine urine. Yeah, I remember about it. Never thought about using it as a rule-out test. But I've always found an organic reason for the pain the few times I've had to go in. What'd the surgeon find with her?"

"Nothing. He did take out a benign appendix. And she did get better. And, in a way, he sent her into remission. But he didn't know why. Thought she was one of those patients that psychologically needs surgery."

"That's another kind that's tough to rule out." He finished his spaghetti and sat back. "So, how did the surgery bring on the remission?"

"It wasn't the surgery. It was the blood transfusion she got during it."

"I'll be damned." He gave her an admiring grin. "And you figured it out."

She nodded and finished her coffee, glad she'd happened upon him. Recalling her moment of success in diagnosing Agnes had restored her confidence in her own instincts and intuition. She felt better than she had in two days.

"Well, I had a bit more to go on than the surgeon did. By the time she came to me, I knew what had brought on her attacks."

"I'm all ears."

"A low-calorie diet, a sulpha drug for a urinary infection, and some phenobarb for her nerves."

"All together?"

"No, on separate occasions." She set down her empty mug on his tray and looked at her watch. "Bob, it's been great talking to you. A nice break in one of those days, if you know what I mean. But I've got to make an important call."

He rose as she did. "Know what you mean. Thanks for the education, Liz. My patients thank you, too. I'll rule out porphyria before doing another exploratory."

She blew him an appreciative kiss as he started toward the tray dump near the exit and she headed for the phone kiosk outside the entryway. The light feeling her meeting with Bob had spawned dissolved in a wave of remorse as she dialed Zack's phone number. Tears filled her eyes again, and even if she had been looking behind her, she wouldn't have seen the disturbing features of the tall lab technician standing nearby and watching her finger tap out the numbers. The crowds partly obscured him; the noise of talk and the rattle of trays and dishes and coins forced her to cover her left ear so she could hear Zack with her right. Thus, partially deafened, she unconsciously raised her voice as she told him she wanted to come over. That made overhearing her quite easy.

After her first few muffled sentences, Phillip hardly had to strain to hear almost every word:

"Jack. Can I come over? I have to be with you." She wiped her eyes with the back of her hand, then covered her ear again.

She was sighing and looking relieved. "I don't mind watching you do anything."

She nodded, then wiped her eyes again. "I won't get in the way, I promise. But I have to come. Being with you, seeing you, will help me pull myself together."

So the signs were multiplying quickly. She was going someplace that might not be all locked up like her apartment. To Jack's house, wherever that might be. And again, he was there to follow her. She was stopping in the ladies' room near the cafeteria. That gave him time to take off his lab smock and get to his van before she would come to the parking lot.

He drove out of the lot and parked across the street from the hospital until he saw her gold car come out and turn left. *Another sign! He had foreknown which direction to face in!*

He waited until an oncoming car moved in behind her, then he pulled his van into the traffic. She was a slow, careful driver who never ran a light, so she was easy to follow, even from a distance, even at night in the drizzle that had started.

She turned north onto Broad Street. Probably going to Jenkintown or Abington. Maybe Jack was a doctor at the hospital there. He probably lived in one of those Tudor style mansions with trees around the place, on a big lot. If she went there often, if she stayed there long, he could get to her there. He never could in her apartment, and her office building presented too many impediments to a successful abduction. How lucky for him she'd had a bad day! How lucky she liked to watch Jack doing anything!

Phillip's mouth watered as he drove behind her up a rough, potholed section of Route 611. What did Jack do that she liked to watch? He had a feeling he'd like to watch it, too. Probably had something to do with sex. She said she'd keep out of his way. Maybe Jack had sex with one woman while another watched. Like his father used to do. Maybe afterward she sucked their blood. He'd seen what happened when the tears she'd been crying passed by the corners of her mouth. Her lips pulled back and the blood in her mouth mixed with the tears and began to run down her chin and drip to the floor.

She stopped for a red light. She was in the left lane, but she wouldn't turn off here if she was going to Abington. He'd make sure she didn't know he was following her: He pulled up to her right, and as the light changed, he went forward on Old York Road.

"Bitch!" She was trying to throw him off by turning left. Well, he wasn't going to lose her. He made a screeching right turn at the next block and gunned his engine. As the van tore forward ferociously, he took his foot off the gas and firmly pulled on the hand brake, and turned the front wheels sharply to the left. The van whipped into a 180 degree turn, which he cut off by releasing the hand brake. A bright flash of headlamps veered across his windshield. The van trembled and skidded on the wet street, and he barely missed striking an oncoming car that spun out of his way at the last moment. His wheels slid from one lane to another, then to the right and up over a curb and back to the right lane again. With a new burst of speed, he headed back to Old York, turned left, forcing more traffic to scatter and screech around him, and slalomed around cars ahead of him for the half block back to the light, which turned red a few seconds before he reached it.

Without stopping, he made a right turn, barely escaping being smashed in the back fender by a taxi. Ahead of him and several other cars, down the grade descending from the intersection, he saw her car, its wet gold iridescent finish gleaming as it passed measuredly under a streetlight.

A few blocks later she turned, much to his surprise, into a small residential street. When he reached it, he saw her turn again onto another block of small two-story framed houses.

The houses were neat and well maintained, but they were strictly working-class homes. He recognized the neighborhood as Glenside, and thought she might be taking a shortcut through to a more well-to-do section of town.

But no. She was pulling up in front of a yellow house, its small front yard slightly terraced, its driveway leading past the side of the yard to a one-car street-level garage.

Phillip pulled up to the curb at a house three doors up and across the street. He turned off his headlights and watched her get out of her car, and walk, umbrellaless, through the drizzle up the driveway to the front flagstone walk, then mount the porch and knock. Moments later a square of light opened, and silhouetted against it, she stood for a moment before stepping inside.

Then the door closed behind her. Phillip drove forward and parked the van across the street. He could see nothing through the lighted windows. He would have to move his van, park it on another street, then come back and get close to the house on foot. He could do that easily, for the nearest streetlight was half a block away at the corner, and the plants around the house were mature and thick. In his van were the black clothes he'd worn in the past to get close to the homes of his victims as often as he needed to. *Yes, this was a sign! This was the place he would abduct Dr. Broward from when the time came. And meanwhile, he'd take a look at what Jack did that she liked so much to watch.*

Poke let her into the foyer. As she set her tote bag on the table there, she could see Zack at the computer in the family room—a room crowded with furniture. She'd never really seen it before, as he had been all that had filled her eyes the last two times she'd been here. The brown vinyl recliner and matching tuxedo-style sofa filled the center of the room. A few steps away, against a dark brown paneled wall, stood the two-tiered computer worktable, bearing computer and printer, and piled with papers, some spilling over the edge and forming haphazard clumps on the floor. Next to the table, a smaller table held a telephone resting atop a stack of dog-eared telephone books. Slashing across the corner where the paneled wall joined a beige painted one, a large console television set with a cable box and rabbit ear antennae on top made space for itself in an otherwise too small room. Yet the room seemed ready to embrace any occupant and offer all diversions at once. Liz could picture Poke watching the television while Zack worked at his computer and Maryellen—What had Maryellen done here in the evenings? Worked on her public health nursing records? Read a book? Or composed poetry? Maybe she'd knitted or sewn. That didn't seem to fit. She may not have sat here with her family at all. Maybe she'd gone into the small living room on the other side of the foyer and sat in the more formal sofa there and listened under headphones to the stereo, shutting out the racket bouncing off the family room walls and windows. As Liz glanced into the living room, she noticed a deep bookcase piled with records and books, and decided that was more likely for the Maryellen she remembered—quiet, intense, private.

"Pop said you came here to watch him work."

Poke's voice took Liz by surprise; for a moment she'd been lost in her thoughts about this house and her place in it.

"Yes," she said after a second. "Do you mind?"

Poke shrugged. In indifference? No, Liz knew better than that. She could see the girl's wide-set eyes change from brown to green as Zack's did. Triggered by an emotional switch?

After a brief silence, Poke said, "Why do you want to watch him work?"

Zack turned from his computer. "Poke—"

"No, Zack," said Liz. "She's right to ask. OK if we go into the living room, Poke? We can talk there."

Poke's flushed face grew round and shiny, like a balloon growing taut from pressure building within. She seemed to plant her feet in the vinyl tiles of the entryway.

Liz stepped back to give her space.

At last she said, "OK. I guess so." She walked across the small room and lit a lamp next to the sofa. Then she sat in one of two blue upholstered easy chairs facing the sofa and stared at a place on the sofa across a glass-topped walnut coffee table.

Liz sat on the other chair and looked at Poke's profile.

For a moment, Zack appeared in the foyer. With a quick

glance, Liz sent him back to the family room. She wasn't sure if Poke had seen the interchange.

Then, "How come you want to watch Pop work?"

"I enjoy being with him."

"He said you came the other night." Poke suddenly turned her face toward Liz and shot her a challenging glance.

"Yes."

Poke blinked.

"You were in your room listening to music. He wasn't expecting me. I—hadn't planned to come."

"You shouldn't've. He wasn't sick. He didn't need you."

"Maybe I shouldn't have come. But I wasn't coming because he needed me. Just because I needed to be with him."

"Why?" The cry exploded from her in a burst of tears.

"I love him, Poke."

"He doesn't love you. You're his doctor is all. He's better. I made him take his medicine."

"I know. He needs you to help. He doesn't always do what's best for himself."

"You're not even a good enough doctor to make him take it. You're not even a good enough doctor to make him not go to Phoenix!"

"I can't make him do anything, Poke. I wouldn't."

Suddenly Poke got up and ran from the room. "I thought you were our friend!" she cried, as she reached the foyer. "I thought Momma sent you to make him better so he wouldn't die like her!"

Liz bolted up. "Poke!" She ran to the foyer.

"Go home! He's all right now! He doesn't need you anymore." She turned and ran up the stairs.

Zack ran in from the family room. "Jesus Christ! Poke!" He started up the stairs after his daughter.

"No, Zack! Not now. Leave her alone. I'm leaving."

He stopped and turned back to look at her. She ran up the stairs and grasped his arm and kissed him. "I'll be back. I promise. I love you."

Then she fled down the stairs and, grabbing her tote bag from the foyer table, ran out the door. As she crossed the wet lawn, her pump heels sank into the wet earth. She lost her balance and would have fallen down the terrace to the sidewalk had she not grabbed the branches of a thick spreading juniper bush and broken her fall. Barely feeling the short needles that stabbed her hand, she pulled herself up from her knees, then bent and took off her shoes and put them, mud and all, into her tote bag. She secured her bag and ran the rest of the way down the terrace in her stocking feet. The nylon slipped on the grass and she skidded and slammed against her car.

From behind her, a tall man in black rose out of the bushes and came toward her. She could see his distorted reflection in her car window.

She didn't turn, but called out to him, "No, Zack! She's not ready yet. I'll call you tomorrow."

Then she pulled out her keys and ran around her car to unlock the driver's door.

"We have to give her time, Zack," she said as she pulled her shoulder from his hand and pushed him away and slammed and locked the door. She couldn't look at him. If she saw him, she might make another mistake, ruin another lifetime of sacred love with some ill-timed words.

So, quickly, without turning her head, she started her engine and pulled the car forward into the dark, drizzly night, and left him standing there.

He knew she'd be back, of course. He hadn't expected to be able to take her tonight, anyway. *But wouldn't it have been nice? Wouldn't it have been a wonderful sign!*

CHAPTER NINE

Saturday

Zack grabbed up the family room phone on the first ring. The last two incoming calls had been hang-ups: the telephone had rung; he'd answered it on the second ring; a few seconds afterward, he'd heard a click. Puzzled, he'd waited until getting a dial tone. Sometimes computer-generated calls behaved that way, and annoying as they were, he always waited to hear the recorded sales pitch. He liked to be outraged by abuses of his beloved technology once in a while. It gave him the chance to mouth off at the abusers and to take pleasure imagining their faces when they'd listen to his filthy responses to their questions.

He shoved the phone to his ear and didn't say hello, just waited the way the crank, whoever he was, had made him wait before.

"Hello?"

He took a great breath at her voice. "Liz. Hey, I'm sorry. I've been getting deliberate hang-ups."

"Nothing obscene, I hope."

"Nope. Not even heavy breathing. I'm sorry about last night, too."

"No. There's nothing to be sorry about. How's Poke today?"

He picked up the phone cord and carried the set across the room to his recliner. "Sulking." He sat down and leaned back. "She hardly talked to me all morning. I wanted to take her out someplace, just her and me. Lots of things I wanted to talk to her about. She went out with her friend Christy instead."

"That's probably best, Zack."

"Anyway, I've decided to cancel my flight to Phoenix. She's mad at me, Liz. I'd better stick around."

She was silent a moment. Then she said, "If you cancel that trip, it shouldn't be because she's mad at you."

"You said I shouldn't go now, anyway."

"It's not the best thing for your health. But Poke's the issue now. You can't let her anger control your life."

"She'll think I don't care about how she feels."

"No she won't. She'll know you do. But she has to know her feelings aren't going to dictate how you live the rest of your life. The worst thing you can do—for both of you—is let a scared young girl manipulate you with tears and temper tantrums."

Sitting forward, he switched the phone to his other ear. "She manipulated you last night, Liz. I wanted you to stay, but you just hightailed it out of here and took off. Last night was when she deserved a real rap on the buns for mouthing off at you. I'd've given it to her, too, if you hadn't stopped me."

She sighed. "I'm glad you didn't. Zack, I was in her house, threatening to betray her mother. And herself. And she'd helped to set the whole thing up. I didn't have any right to stay."

He swallowed and felt a chill rising. "She can't keep you out. It's my house, too. Hey, you can't walk out on me, Liz, because of her."

"No, no! I'm not. We've just got to give her time. I told you that when you chased me to my car."

Bolting to his feet, he said, "What! I never chased you to your car!"

After a sucking sound and a second's silence, she said, "But I saw your reflection in my car. You touched me a second before I slammed the door."

"It couldn't've been me, Liz. I never even looked out after you left. I was too mad at Poke."

"Who could it've been? I was on your lawn. Someone ran after me and tried to stop me."

He thought for a minute, then said, "Wait a minute. It was raining. I bet you ran past those tall bushes and one of them touched you, and you thought it was me. You were pretty upset when you left."

She hesitated briefly. "Yes. I was. I also nearly fell on my way down the terrace. I could've brushed my own car door with my arm. Yes, that's it, I'm sure. And I guess I would have liked you to try and stop me—"

"I wanted to. Poke had me all torn apart. You, too. Shit! I should've come after you."

After a long, silent pause she said, "You didn't have to. We'll work things out with Poke. Meanwhile, don't let her stop you from your trip. You'll both be sorry if you do. When are you leaving? How long will you be away?"

"Monday, for five days."

"What time's your flight? What airline?"

"Seven-fifty-two A.M. on US Air."

"OK. I'll pick you up at six-thirty Monday morning. That'll get you there in plenty of time."

He swallowed. "Hey, I can get a limo. You don't have to—"

"No. I want to see you before you leave. And I don't think I should intrude on you and Poke this weekend. With me out of the way, you two might reach a truce."

"Ah, Liz, I want to see you, too. I'll be ready when you drive up."

He and Poke had reached a truce, if that's what you called just not talking about the things that you really wanted to talk about but couldn't. He kissed his daughter good-bye at the door at quarter after six as she held her duffle bag under one arm and her sleeping bag under the other. Then he waved at Eve Carter, Christy's mom, as she opened the minivan's rear door so Poke could heave in her gear.

Then, with a lump in his chest, he went around the house to make sure everything was secure. Upstairs he checked all the windows to make sure none had been left open. In Poke's room he saw her book bag lying partly open on the bed.

"Shit! She left her school stuff here."

He picked up Poke's phone and pushed the button programmed for Christy. After two rings, a machine picked up the other end of the line: "Hey, it's cool you called me on the phone; but you'll have to call back 'cause I'm not home. I know you think machine talking sucks; so this one doesn't take messages, yuk, yuk, yuk!" This was followed by a giggle and a beep.

"Talk about dumb kids!" He slammed down the phone. He had Eve Carter's number downstairs, and he'd call her about Poke's books when he got to the airport. By then she'd be back from the breakfast at McDonald's she'd promised to buy the kids for having to get up extra early this morning. Getting up early had been made even harder by the advent of Daylight Savings Time on Sunday. He could have picked a better time to go, he thought. Getting up at five had been rough for him, too. He left Poke's room and went downstairs.

There, he checked all the windows and the rear door off the kitchen. He set down the thermostat, then ran down into the basement and turned off the valves to the clothes washer water supply. He noticed how grimy the small window above the washer was. The corrugated well it was sunk in was filled with twigs and debris—a couple of plastic cups and a soft drink can—that had blown in or been washed in by the recent spring rains. He sometimes thought it would be better to have no basement windows at all than to have these stupid sunken things whose only vista was of the inside of a garbage can. Though once it had been more interesting when a family of ground toads had moved into the well and kept hopping up against the pane. Unfortunately for the toads, a neighbor's cat had discovered them, too. He ought to get a mesh cover for the well, but he kept on forgetting.

After a quick reconnoiter of the rest of the basement, he ran upstairs, pulled the plug on his computer and the TV, and got to the door and opened it just as Liz pulled up to the curb promptly at six-thirty.

He waved at her as she got out of her car, and heaved up his transportable computer in one hand and tossed his tattered clothing bag over his opposite shoulder, holding it in place with his chin while he deadbolted the front door.

She opened her car's back door. "Those should both fit in the backseat," she said.

He grunted and lifted them onto the seat and closed them in, then got into the front seat with her. She looked fresh and bright in a pair of lightweight blue jeans with a jeans jacket and a checkered cotton pastel blue and yellow blouse. He had on jeans, too, but instead of his usual hunting vest over heavy flannel, he had donned a beige cotton cardigan sweater over his plaid summer shirt. He had shaved, because he knew his mission required a clean-cut look. He would have to go up to strangers on the street and ask them questions about Yolanda's pictures, which were stuffed into a pocket of his clothing bag.

Liz leaned over and touched his cheek and kissed him gently before starting the car. "All ready?"

"All ready." Then he filled her in on the weekend's happenings as they drove beneath white dogwood festoons that arched over Wissahickon Drive. The hills still burst with blooms of azalea and rhododendron, most of which would be gone in the next couple of weeks. He told her about his deal with Squire to send work back by computer. He told her he had started developing the composite picture program, and that finishing it wouldn't take much time. "I'll show you how it works when I get back."

"Can't wait," she said.

He was glad she'd insisted on driving him in. The ride went much quicker than usual as they dipped under a network of overpasses and then crossed the bridge and entered the Schuylkill Expressway, headed for the airport.

In fact, he wished the trip would take longer, because looking at her haughty profile as she drove filled him with an aching joy that he hadn't felt for many, many months. Her soft, tawny hair reminded him of spun gold. His hand ached to reach up and touch it, to gently tug it till she had to turn those violet eyes toward him, then to tug it some more till her lips would have to touch his.

Going over the edge of the bridge with his lips pressed to hers would be a wonderful way to die, he thought. His eyes misted over at the thought, and he hardly saw the passing scenery along the road to the airport.

He barely noticed that she'd turned the car into a parking lot, and for a moment wasn't fully aware that she'd picked up a ticket at the automatic parking gate. She parked in a slot and said, "we'll take a shuttle to the US Air terminal."

He nodded and got out of the car and was about to reach in for his computer bag, when he saw her trunk lid had lifted and she was walking back to it. "Hey!" he said.

She reached into her trunk and pulled out a small leather-trimmed tweed suitcase and matching carry-on bag. She closed the trunk lid and smiled at him. "I'm going with you," she said.

"Jesus, Liz!"

"You don't mind?"

"Mind? I love it. But why the hell didn't you say something? I mean, this is one hell of a surprise."

"I didn't want you to have to deal with having to tell Poke we were going to be together this week."

The shuttle driver approached from the bus that was waiting by the lot entrance. "Take your bags?"

Liz gave him the suitcase and said she'd hold the carryon. Zack reached in and took his clothing bag out of the car. "I'll take the computer myself," he said. Then he watched as Liz locked her car.

At last he looked at her and said, "How the hell do you know so much about people? And what did I ever do to deserve you?"

She glanced at him enigmatically. "Let's get on the shuttle," she said. "We've got a plane to catch."

They had landed at Phoenix's Sky Harbor Airport at noon, Phoenix time, and were standing at the luggage carousel waiting for her bag to slide into view, before he remembered Poke's books.

"I'm sure she's discovered it herself by now," Liz said when he exclaimed at his forgetfulness. "She has a house key with her, doesn't she?" Her bag came down the stainless steel slide and she moved toward the carousel to grab it.

"Sure. And Eve Carter promised to stop in midweek to check on the house. Pick up newspapers and stuff from in front of the door."

She picked up both her bags. "Don't worry, then. Come on. I've ordered a rental car and reserved a room at a downtown hotel. The Hyatt Regency."

He flushed. He was sure the city hotel room would be nicer than the bare bones single he'd planned to stay in. All he'd wanted was a bed and a way to hook up his modem. The kind of place businessmen stayed, when they didn't want to have to pay for classy dining rooms that spun on the top of buildings or thick thirsty towels changed two times a day. He realized with a jolt that she was going to be paying for the room, and that it would have to reflect a life-style he could barely imagine. He didn't mind the thought of a woman paying for his hotel room. She could afford it. He didn't feel he had to call the shots about where they would stay or where they would go for dinner, or what kind of car they rode in or who drove it. Those things never had mattered to him. Maryellen had often made more money than he did before he got the job at Squire. Their vacations never took them to fancy resorts. They preferred camping. They never quibbled about whose money they used. In fact, if it hadn't been for her income, they never could have saved up the down payment for their house or afforded his custom-built Ram with its four-wheel drive. She'd given that to him for his birthday.

But he knew he fit into a custom RV, even if with its bright blue body and chrome trim and special built-in fridge and seats that folded down to make a bed, and seat backs with tables set into them, it looked a lot classier than him. In a downtown city hotel room he might look like a cheap cardboard picture from K Mart in an expensive frame from Tiffany.

Liz looked at him and smiled. "Come on, Zack. I didn't ask to come along, and I want us to be together, and I can't help wanting the kinds of things I'm used to. Besides, Phoenix is a casual city. All I took along in this suitcase is five days' worth of jeans, shirts, and underwear. Let the tie and shirt business crowd at lunch and dinner stare if they want to."

He grinned and nodded. "OK if I stare, too?" he asked.

Her lips parted slightly as her nostrils barely quivered. After swallowing, she whispered, "Don't you dare take your eyes off me for a second."

So that he wouldn't have to take his eyes off her, he walked a few steps behind her to the car rental counter, and then across a hot pavement to wait at a covered traffic island for the car rental company shuttle.

"Here on vacation?" the shuttle driver probed after they'd settled into the seat directly behind him.

"Not exactly," Zack offered, then said nothing more.

"Usually not this hot in April. Course it's almost May, isn't it? Anyhow, seems to get hotter earlier every year. Still it's a nice time for a vacation if you stay at one of the resorts. Lots to do for fun. Don't miss the Heard Museum. You like Indian stuff?"

"I love it," said Liz as she squeezed Zack's hand between their thighs. Her touch and the suggestive lilt of her voice sent heat rocketing through him.

"Be sure to go there while you're on your vacation."

"Right," said Zack.

The shuttle pulled into the rental agency parking lot. Zack tipped the driver as Liz went into the office. A few minutes later they were riding in a new 1988 Ford Taurus through the downtown Phoenix streets past the sweeping, modern buildings that made up the Civic Center. "It is hotter than I expected," Liz said. "I guess it'll make our work harder. Standing on a street corner somewhere showing people those pictures."

On the plane he'd explained what his plans were. Now as they drove west at two P.M., the sun already bored through the windshield and in spite of the air-conditioning, made him feel hot with a sweater on. "Guess I'll buy me a Stetson to keep the sun out of my eyes."

"Well, here's the hotel. We'll soon be out of the sun for the day," she said.

He loved the feel of the large gold and turquoise suite that overlooked the Civic Plaza. By pulling back the heavy turquoise drapes, he could see the people walking to and from the escalators that ran between the street below and the parklike expanse of the plaza. Some lingered beside the fountains and the tall fountain sculpture of the bird after which the city was named. He admired its graceful, abstract form and wondered for a moment if he could come up with something as beautiful and symbolic if he worked with metal and water instead of electronic bits of light and color.

As he stood there momentarily enraptured with the view, Liz came up behind him and circled his waist with her arms.

He sighed and captured one arm with his hand, then turned to face her. She'd taken off her jeans and blouse, and stood barefoot in white bikini-cut cotton briefs and a lacy bra. The light makeup she'd applied before picking him up that morning had worn off and she'd never reapplied it. For the first time, he realized that she never wore very much makeup, and didn't seem to care how long it lasted. Nor did she need it. Her skin held a tawny, natural glow, the perfect setting for those amethyst eyes. Framed within the soft darker gold of her hair, her face reminded him of a jewel set cameo he'd once seen a woman wearing on a silky cord around her neck. He knew that if he worked with gold and jewels instead of computer graphics, he might create beautiful jewelry, but never a piece of art as beautiful as she.

She kissed him on his mouth and lightly ran her tongue over his lips. He pulled her tightly to him, and pushed his bulging pelvis against hers.

"Hmmm," she murmured, then pushed him away with a laugh. "I'm going to take a shower."

"I need one, too." He began unbuttoning his shirt.

"No. I like the way you smell. Don't wash it off. You had a shower last time. I was the gamy one that night."

"No, dear person, I loved it." He recalled the tangy salt taste of her throat and the slight taste of wax in her ear.

"No. This time I want to be clean smelling and I want you to stink like a sweaty Indian." She grasped him and buried her nose in his neck. "Ah, that drives me crazy." She licked the crease of his neck. "You're so salty and delicious." Then she ducked from his grasp and ran to the bathroom.

"It's the Scotch-Irish part that sweats," he called after her as she closed the door.

He heard her laugh, and he heard the clack of the shower door closing and the swoosh of the running water. He imagined it running over her golden hair, and splashing her face with hungry kisses, and long tongues of it licking her neck and shoulders, swirling over and around her breasts, down the center of her, flicking in and out of her navel, fingers of it stroking her full, fleshy buttocks in the back, parting the tawny tangled triangle of hair in the front, traveling all over her as his fingers ached to do.

The water sounds stopped, but he still saw drops of it clinging to her, reluctant to yield her up to the towel she pulled from the rack as she stepped out of the shower stall. But now he gave up being water and became the towel as she touseled her hair in it, rubbed her face with it, stroked her neck and shoulders, grasped the ends of it and, reaching one hand over her head and the other behind a flank, rubbed it between her shoulder blades, dropped one end and grabbed it again, and stroked it to and fro across her back from shoulders to hips. He the towel now rubbed across her belly, flicking a drop of water that clung still to her navel. He the towel soaked up the beads of moisture from the hair between her legs, and avoided drawing away the slicker, thicker moisture in the cleft of her. He the towel was damp in her hands as she rubbed the last drops from her legs and dropped him at last in a loop around her feet and stepped out of him.

And stepped out of the bathroom door and looked at him, the man, the naked, yearning man.

He stood still, stared at her. She turned her body so that her shoulder touched the door frame, and arched her back slightly, lifting her breasts so the taut nipples seemed to quiver at him. She opened her lips and ran her tongue over them. Her eyes dipped to look frankly at his erection. Then she turned them on his face and said, "I want you to put your sweet Scotch-Irish–Indian cock inside me." And she came to him, and parted her thighs.

"You sure don't mince your words, Doc," he said as he entered her, standing.

Then she mounted his hips and wrapped her legs around him, and her lips against his mouth spilled out a torrent of explicit graphic prescriptions that he knew she hadn't picked up from any of her medical books. And he followed them to the letter, much to their mutual delight.

♦ ♦

Love's torpor lay thick upon them as the sky outside their window lost its evening flush.

The sun setting now behind unfamiliar brown mountains had set three hours earlier behind the tall, gray, pollution-shrouded skyline of Philadelphia. Once more the wail of sirens crisscrossed one another in the dark, mean streets. Once more Phillip's van left the meanest of those streets for the small, snug neighborhood in Glenside where Jack's house sat among the bushes on its small, snug lot.

Phillip knew the house and the neighborhood well by now. He had been here the past two nights, sometimes sitting in his van a few doors away to watch the man and the girl and their neighbors come and go; sometimes parking his van a few blocks away, then sneaking back and, in the cover of the thick shrubbery, going from window to window to see how the downstairs was arranged and what was going on there. The doctor had not come back, and the man and the girl were in and to bed early over the weekend. Jack must have gone few places during the day; for whenever Phillip had dialed the number he'd seen the doctor punch in on Friday, the man had answered the phone.

This morning Phillip had arrived before dawn, knowing he could only learn all that he had to about their activities by being here on a weekday morning. Then Jack would go to work, and he could follow him there to see what he did; and the girl would go to school, and he could follow her there and later see what time she got home. In a week or so he probably would know enough about their movements and how often the doctor visited, to plan on how he could abduct the doctor. His close encounter with her on Friday night had made him impatient. For he had had another sign about her after she'd escaped in her car. He'd run back up onto the terraced lawn to the place where she had slipped and removed her muddied shoes and slipped them into her bag. She had left a pattern of flattened grass, as children do on snow by lying down and rubbing their arms against the snow to make angels.

But she had not left a white angel in cold dead snow, she had left a black devil on living grass. Her knees had etched wings of bats. The heels of her shoes had incised the earth like fangs and sucked the mud out of it. Drops of mud on the bruised grass surrounding the holes encircled the wounds.

"Ahah!" he had cried at the sight. He'd run down the lawn onto the street and seen her car stopped at a stop sign beneath a streetlight at the corner. Though no cars were in the intersection, she'd remained stopped there. And through the wide rear window of her car he'd seen her turn her face in his direction. Her eyes glowed green in the yellow light. Her sneering mouth dripped mud. She lifted a shoe to her mouth and began to lick the mud from the heel. He hadn't seen anything more vile, more sickeningly erotic, since Agnes had licked his doorknob. But this was far more evil. Dr. Broward could suck life from the earth itself. She didn't need human blood to survive. And this meant only one thing: burying her in earth would do no good, even with a silvered blade in her heart. The moment the last shovelful had fallen into her grave, her casket would creak open, the dirt would begin to leak in and by midnight would fill it. Saliva would run from her mouth, as it was running now, and mix with the earth and turn it to bloodmud. And her snake tongue would writhe out, and insinuate itself into the mud, then ladle it into her mouth and the earth life would surge into her veins. At that thought, he'd flung his hands over his eyes and run back to the lawn and up the terrace, to look once more at the marks of evil she'd inscribed there. Yes! There was no mistake. He'd got closer, bent closer.

Then he'd cried out as the mud from the heel holes mixed with the collected drizzle dripping from the juniper branches she'd grasped and poisoned in her fall. He'd leapt backward as the rain mixed with the mud and the mudblood started slithering down the terrace toward his shoes. "Don't touch me!" he'd whispered hoarsely, as he'd turned and run through the soaking, sighing drizzle to his van. The sign was clear. He could not wait to kill her. This proved it beyond a doubt—she was no simple vampire, protecting other vampires with her potions. She was the high priestess of vampires, an ugly mutation that had gone from sucking the blood of humans to sucking the blood of Mother Earth, herself. Now nothing else, no one else could stop her. Only Phillip, the Lordly One. Only he had the way. There was no mud to suck on in Adolph's belly! There was no dark ooze for her impaled heart to wallow in, in Phillip's freezer!

At last, this morning, she had come again to the house in Glenside. A few minutes after the girl had come out with a sleeping bag and left in the Voyager with another girl and a woman, the Vampire Queen had driven up in her Mercedes-Benz, and Jack had come out of his house with luggage and gotten into her car. Then Jack had turned his neck up to her and she had sunk fangs into it and her mouth had come away from it with a bloody smile. Now Jack was a vampire, too, and his leering grin showed that he knew it.

Maybe Phillip could take them both! What a treat for Adolph lay in that husky carcass. The thick thighs and buttocks alone would provide meat for a week. The man-size organs promised juicy, filling delicacies for another. The two vampire hearts could be wrapped together and impaled on a single blade. Oh, how they would suffer, trapped perpetually frozen in their filthy vampire embrace, a hell of eternal hunger forever stirred by each other's nearness—a nearness neither could feed on!

He'd followed them to the airport and seen them leave together on the shuttle. No need to track them to the terminal. It was enough to know that they would be out of town for at least overnight. The house would be empty. He would return after dark and find a way to get inside.

Now he parked the van on a street a few blocks away where he'd never parked it before, and walked unhurriedly to Jack's house. As he'd expected, no porch light was on, and the light in the family room and an upstairs room didn't fool him. If Jack was like most people, he would set a timer to turn them on and off at night. The sound of music heard from outside the living room window made Phillip chortle. On the other nights he'd been there, no music had been playing at all. The living room had only been in use once—the twenty minutes or so when the doctor was there Friday night. On Saturday and Sunday nights, Jack had spent most of his time at the computer in the family room, and the girl went upstairs right after dinner. Her bedroom must be directly over the living room, for that was the room that was lit those nights until about eleven, which was usually the time Jack himself went upstairs. The music might fool some people into believing the house was occupied. It wouldn't fool Phillip.

On the weekend nights, Phillip had waited until father and daughter had gone to bed and no lights shone through the downstairs panes. Then he'd carefully made a close survey of possible ways to enter. The first-story windows were hardly impregnable. The only security devices on them were easily disabled locks and rods placed in the glide tracks to stop the windows from sliding open more than a few inches. But there was nothing to prevent him from jimmying loose the sliding pane and lifting it from the track.

Still, he preferred not to put himself in a position where a neighbor glancing down from a second-story window could see him climbing in. So he was delighted to find the basement had windows in sunken wells, and that the wells were not even protected with heavy mesh screens. With barely a tinkle of breaking glass, he made a hole through which he could get to the latch inside. And with barely a creak of the metal frame hinges, he forced the small, square window down. Through the well-hidden opening, he lowered himself onto the washing machine and from there into the basement.

His small flashlight lit the way up the basement stairs to the first floor. Once there, he quickly found his way through the kitchen, ducked through the family room so he couldn't be seen through the front window, and, with two steps through the foyer, easily reached the stairs. No need to linger on the first story. He'd seen just about everything he needed to from outside the window, knew where the telephone was, how the furnishings were arranged, so that he could find his way around them in the dark, which sooner or later he planned to do.

Now he ran upstairs and went through the three bedrooms and two bathrooms, saving the girl's room for last, for an idea had begun to form in his head since he'd witnessed the vampires kissing this morning. This entire family was infected and had to be done away with, and the girl, not the doctor, would be the easiest to abduct. With the girl under Phillip's control, he could do what he'd done with Agnes—lure the others into a trap, one at a time. What wonderful bait she would be! How Adolph would love it! One at a time he would crush their throats in his jaws, shake the life out of them, while the young, tender vampire bait looked on. And then, the bait herself, impervious to their vile blood, would act as diener under Phillip's direction, would wash their blood down the drain, would cleanse the organs and dress and butcher the meat. Phillip would show her how to wrap the loins, the ribs, the legs and arms for freezing, how to label and date the packages. Perhaps she would want a lock of hair as a keepsake. He would let her have it, of course. Or he would design a piece of jewelry made of bone, and give it to her. And then he would keep her around for his own and Adolph's entertainment. What fun it would be to taunt her until the dog's food supply ran low. Under Adolph's urging, she would plate for herself the blade destined to dwell in her heart. While Adolph snapped at her heels she would go to the freezer day after day, watching the meat store dwindle, till only two pieces remained, the hearts of her father and the doctor pinioned together—and then—!

As he thought these voluptous thoughts, he ran his hands over the clothes in the young girl's closet, and knelt on the closet floor to smell a pair of sneakers she'd left there. Then he looked under her bed and found a pair of panties, and smelled those. There was vampire smell on them. No mistake! She had been infected. He stood up and started going through the book bag that lay open on the hastily made bed.

"Poke?" A woman's voice rose from downstairs.

From about halfway down the stairs, she answered, "Yeah?"

Phillip gasped and he dropped the book he held onto the bed.

"It won't take long will it?"

"Nah. I'm just going to grab them and check my message machine. Couple of minutes."

Phillip dove under the bed. He pulled up his knees so his feet wouldn't protrude from under the foot. He heard her run into the room. He could smell her vampire breath. He held his own as she rummaged on the bed.

"Oh, shit!"

He heard more footsteps coming into the room.

"What's the matter?" said another girl's voice.

"Some problem, Poke?" said a woman's voice.

"The history paper!" said Poke.

"You know it's not due till Thursday," said the other girl.

"But you don't have a computer at your house, Christy. I started it on Pop's WordStar. Mrs. Carter, I have to stay and finish it. It won't take me very long."

The woman said, "Hmmm—This isn't a very good time, Poke. It's pretty late, and you girls have been up since before the sun. You could come back after school tomorrow."

"Not tomorrow. I've got gymnastics practice. We're competing with Willow Grove on Saturday."

"Well, would Wednesday be too late? You said it wouldn't take much time."

A brief hesitation and a sigh. "Yeah. I guess so. I'll come straight from school."

"Good!" said the woman. "I'm glad that's all taken care of. Let's go."

"Just a sec." She took a few steps. "Nah, no messages," she said.

"Well, you're sure to get some between now and Friday night when your dad gets home. OK, girls! Let's go."

Phillip could barely contain his joy until their footsteps tumbled off down the stairs and the front door slammed behind them. Then he crawled out from under the bed and stood at the corner of the window and watched as they bounded into the Voyager. As the minivan's headlights went on and the vehicle moved down the street, he held the girl's vampire redolent panties to his nose and breathed in the power it gave him. He stuffed them into his black jacket pocket and fondled them as he walked down the street to his van, dreaming of Wednesday afternoon and the excitement it promised him.

CHAPTER TEN

Tuesday morning—Phoenix

Zack parked the car outside the Taco Bell restaurant. It looked exactly the same as it had when Yolanda Smith had photographed the strip shopping center three years before. Not every business there looked the same. A pawn shop had replaced a small grocery store; the gas pumps in front of a Circle K had "Out of order" painted on their sides. No doubt due to vandalism: The hoses were gone, and the meters had been smashed, and the gas price on the sign above them was clearly out of line with the prices other stations displayed.

It's a good thing Liz wasn't with him, he thought. This neighborhood showed every sign of decay. Lawns of the post–World War II houses down the street and across were overgrown, filled with beer cans, plastic cups and bits and pieces of cars—even entire rusting cars. A trio of men, each a different color and age, leaned against the dirty window of the pawn shop and eyed Zack as he got out of the light blue rented Ford Taurus. Maybe he was dressed the wrong way after all. His current getup of neat jeans and cotton pullover striped shirt, and his clean-shaven face and neatly trimmed hair belied his toughness as fully as his usual rough getup belied his gentleness. *True self-expression totally eludes me, at least with what I wear*, he thought.

The look on his face and the flexing of his well-developed biceps and pectorals under the shirt were other matters. The three men's eyes suddenly absorbed themselves in avoiding his. The men shifted position, then turned and walked away as he approached the shop. Had Liz been along, the entire dynamics would have changed—he'd have had to abort the mission for the day. Thank goodness he'd insisted on her staying at the hotel. There she was phoning all the Rands, Randells, Crandells, Randals, and Crandalls in the greater Phoenix phone book, to see if any of them had a relative named Ruth, born thirty-nine years ago in Phoenix to a woman whose maiden name was Joan Rand.

"You'll be having all the fun!" Liz had complained over a coffee shop breakfast this morning.

"What's fun about hanging around street corners?"

"You never know what's going to happen. You know, Zack, I've never had a real adventure. My life's been so damned predictable and ordered. I'm not scared to go out and lurk around street corners and tap on strangers' shoulders. I've just never had the chance. Or the need."

"I didn't think you were scared." He'd hooded his eyes and directed them into his plate of scrambled eggs.

She'd set down her coffee and knit her brow at him. "But you're scared for me. You want to protect me."

That had brought his head up. He'd protested, "That's not it. You can take care of yourself." But inside his head he'd worried that she might be partly right. After thinking a moment, he'd decided that she wasn't. Maryellen often had gone into some of the worst neighborhoods of Philadelphia—places Zack was afraid to drive through—in her public health nursing work. He'd never tried to stop her, because she loved the work and wasn't afraid. Still, he'd worried sometimes. And if anything would have happened to her there, he'd have blamed himself for not stopping her.

"But I'd get in the way." Liz was studying his face.

He'd reached across the table for her hand. "You're never in the way, Liz. It's just not a two-person job. And the calls have to be made. They may be even more important than the street work. You don't know what's going to happen with them, either."

Now in the shopping center he saw, of course, that she would have been in the way, and not just with the mean looking vagrants that lurked on this strip. If he'd had to look at her face and body, to watch her stop an old man or old lady in front of the Circle K and smile as she showed them a photo, he'd have thought about last night and early this morning in bed with her. He'd have heard again her stunning gritty love words, and seen right through Gloria Vanderbilt's signature on her rump to the now familiar musky smelling flesh. His hands would ache to feel the pliant cheeks. And the old guy coming out of the pawn shop now would glance down at the front of his pants and see the involuntary twitch of the bulge there. If just thinking of her brought it on, her presence within reaching distance would ruin his concentration completely.

As it was, he had to wait until the stooped gray old man in an ancient tattered tuxedo passed him and had reached the sidewalk several yards away, before he could mentally talk his erection down, clear his throat, and follow the man. He caught up with him before he'd reached the corner.

"Excuse me, sir," Zack said.

Without answering, the man shuffled into the intersection and began to cross the street. Zack glanced at his tuba sized ears and realized his words could not possibly have made it through those twin cornucopias of carbuncles, dirty wax, and hair. He cleared his throat loudly, and got close to the man as he crossed.

"Sir?" he shouted.

The man turned his face to Zack. He fixed two red and rheumy eyes on him through dirty glasses. Those eyes and a red, bulbous nose gave his face its only color. Even the lumpy receded gums in his open mouth were colorless, though a few black teeth added contrast. So did the breath that rose from his mouth. It provided a vivid sensory impact exceedingly more unpleasant than his face. Zack didn't know what dregs of family treasure he'd left at the pawn shop, but he knew immediately that the proceeds would go into buying the cheapest wine available. If he could get it home past the mean trio, who had begun to follow them.

Zack took the man's elbow and gently helped him across the street. "Just want to ask you something," he said. "Show you some pictures. Let's get away from those bums." He was looking back over his shoulder at them, and reaching for the shoulder holster wallet under his shirt as he shouted the last. His wallet held only the pictures, and Zack carried a gun only when hunting, but the goons didn't know that, and evidently didn't want to risk his intentions.

The old man, having little choice, nodded and didn't try to escape Zack's hold. What, after all, would he have to lose except a momentary safe harbor? "What kind of pictures?" He stopped at the curb and looked down at it through his cloudy spectacles before stepping up on it with one foot and dragging the second foot up.

As soon as they both were safe on the sidewalk, Zack dropped the old man's elbow and reached into the wallet and extricated several photos. "This neighborhood and the folks that lived here maybe twenty-five, thirty years ago. Thought you might have lived here then. When there were houses and a church there instead of a shopping center."

The man stopped and looked up at him, his eyes suddenly alert and cunning. "Maybe," he said.

"Maybe?"

"Yep, maybe." He started walking again.

Zack stood for a moment, puzzled. The man had either lived here then or he hadn't. There couldn't have been a maybe about it. Striding forward again, he caught up to him again and said, "Maybe you lived here then? Or maybe you knew the people? Which?"

"Both."

"You knew them both, or maybe you knew one or the other?"

"Maybe and maybe not."

What was going on here? Zack had been back to old neighborhoods looking for his own relatives, and people he'd shown pictures to had either looked at them and shaken their heads, or they'd stared for a few minutes and looked puzzled and then shaken their heads, or they'd screwed up their faces and then suddenly burst into smiles, looked up, and said, "Hey! I knew that guy!" and then started with a long string of stories that they'd finished up over a cup of coffee or a beer.

But this guy hadn't even looked at the pictures and all he had to say was, "Maybe," before turning away and starting to walk

BLOOD WORK

again. And the old man knew something. He'd seen that sudden flash in his eyes, which hadn't looked capable of lighting up. They looked like the last light in them had flickered out long before this neighborhood got as bad as it was.

"You do live here now, don't you?" Zack asked.

"Maybe." The man turned and looked at him again, as if trying to make something clear. "Maybe I do and maybe I don't."

"Well then—"

The man was moving on. His step seemed somehow more vigorous. Suddenly Zack realized his step now had purpose! "Shit!" Of course he wasn't going to answer. Not until Zack had given him something. Bought him some wine or given him some money.

Zack reached into his pants pocket. *Some street detective he was! When you're looking for information about a whore that was murdered and about the bastard son of a serial murderer, you aren't going to get answers—not even "no"—unless you pay for them.* He pulled out a ten dollar bill and gave it to the old man. Let him buy his own wine.

After taking it and looking at it, the man said, "Live here now. Maybe lived here a long time." He kept on walking.

Zack gave him another ten.

"Lived here twenty-five, thirty years ago, too. Maybe I knew some of the people. Maybe I knew about the nursing home across the street, too."

Zack grinned. "I didn't say anything about a nursing home. Just a church."

"Yep, well, maybe there was a nursing home and maybe there wasn't. I'd have to think about it some more to be sure."

"OK. Think five dollars' worth more." Zack had less than twenty left.

"Yep, there was a nursing home there all right."

"Right next to a whorehouse."

"Never went in there myself. Don't believe in it. Guys got theirselves sick. Or worse."

"Any of those guys in my pictures?"

The old man stopped, then started to cross the lawn in front of an old prefab post–World War II house, the kind put up in droves for returning GIs in the forties. This one showed signs of a series of early upgrades followed by years of deterioration: A carport had slumped onto a broken cement driveway. A pathway bordered by chunks of old concrete led to a crumbling porch. Portions of wooden porch rail remained standing against a rusting metal glider, whose only purpose seemed to be to support it; the rest of the rail was gone, leaving only a few jagged post holes in the wooden floor. A few flat rocks resting in rotting, termite-eaten splinters served as steps up to the porch, where an old door provided a plank on which to enter the house, which itself looked surprisingly sturdy, though neglected. The door plank still had a knob on it. The old man picked his way through the obstacles to the front door and pushed it open. " My house," he said. "Lived here since getting out of the service."

Zack stood on the plank a foot or so from the entry. He wasn't sure whether the door had been left open as an invitation for him to enter; he wasn't sure if he wanted to enter if it had. A dank, sour smell poured through the doorway.

The man, who had disappeared into the bowels of the house (Zack couldn't imagine the interior as anything other than bowels and their fetid contents), now reappeared at the doorway. "You bringing them pictures in?"

"Sure," said Zack. He went in. He left the door open, because he couldn't bear to touch the doorknob; but the old man walked around him and closed it.

"Bring them pictures in the kitchen. The light works there." He walked through a hallway that ran between two rooms lit only by what sunlight could work its way through filth-encrusted windows. One room had some hulks of overstuffed furniture sitting on the vestiges of a rug. The other had a mattress on the floor with a few rags that might be blankets lying nearby.

Zack's skin crawled, and he tried to look straight ahead so he wouldn't have to imagine the old man sleeping there. He followed the man into a small, square room that contained an old refrigerator with its door hanging open, a small, square, chipped metal table and two chairs without backs. On the walls were doorless cupboards stuffed with junk in all imaginable categories—books, tin cans, broken bottles, combs, a ham bone, a shoe, a dirty cracked drinking glass—the whole lit by a single, naked yellow ceiling bulb. Zack saw no sign of anything edible in the entire kitchen. He wondered what the old man could have in the house that he might hock at the pawn shop. Then he recalled a sign on the shop door. "Checks cashed. No ID needed."

The man sat down on one chair and motioned Zack to the other. "Lessee the pictures."

Before sitting on the old wooden chair, Zack looked at the seat. It was grimy, but had no fresh dirt or sticky spots on it. He sat across from the man and held out the photos. The old guy grabbed them greedily in gnarled yellow hands that had nails growing in every-which-way except for one—the finger that would have had that one on it was cut off at the second joint.

For a few minutes, the man went through the pictures, one at a time, nodding slowly, shaking his head.

"Well?" Zack said.

"That's it, all right."

Zack waited as he went through the pictures again.

"Yep. That's it."

"The whorehouse?"

"Well, maybe I'm talking about the whorehouse and maybe I'm not."

Zack sighed. "OK. How much for the whole thing? Houses, people, everything."

"Hundred dollars."

Zack shot up. "Hell, I don't have a hundred dollars. I never carry that kind of money with me. Not even around my own neighborhood, and especially not to a place like where those goons hang out across the street."

The old man nodded. "Didn't think so. Don't carry it myself. Doug keeps my Social Security money for me in his safe. Better'n a bank. Anybody ever break in there'd get his head blown off."

"Doug?"

"Kid that owns the pawn shop. Give him my check every month. He gets me my hooch and sandwiches at lunch and dinner. Never have to carry a dime."

"Those goons know that?"

"Yep."

"What were they after you for, then?"

Reaching into his tuxedo vest, he pulled out a pint bottle of whiskey. He opened the top and took a swig, then held it out to Zack, who shook his head. "They don't like no one to have nothing. Don't care what it is, they try to get it. Sometimes they take my sandwiches, too. Try to go when they ain't there. Sometimes I make it, sometimes I don't."

Jesus! What a horrible way for an old guy to live! Zack swallowed hard and reached into his pocket and took out his last ten dollar bill. All he had left besides his credit cards and a checkbook was a few dollar bills and some change. "This is all I got. I need the rest in case I get stuck somewhere."

The man took the ten and said, "I know them all, except the old fella in the rocking chair. The kid's Gus. The one man and lady is Gus the Third and Kitty Gingrich. The other man is my brother and his whore friend."

"Your brother!"

"Yep. Want to see some more pictures?"

For the first time in years, Zack found himself speechless and stuttering. Things like this just didn't happen! Not to him, anyway. He'd expected to have to show the pictures to dozens of people, and would have been lucky if a single one knew anything at all about even one of the people in Yolanda's snapshots. That's what had always happened before when he'd tried to get information on family pictures of his own ancestors in Tennessee. "Sure," he finally said, trying to control his excitement.

The old man went to the refrigerator and pulled the door all the way open. The hinges were broken and the door sagged. He shoved some things around inside the refrigerator. "Think they're somewhere in here," he said. "Kind of a mess, though. Haven't looked at them since my wife died about six years ago and I stuck them in here."

"Take your time," said Zack. "Much time as you need."

After taking almost every box and sundry item from the fridge and setting them on the floor, the man finally said, "Yep. I knew they were here someplace. Box they're in has a lot of this orange and black stuff on it." He pulled the box out, and it disintegrated in his hands, throwing spores of mold and mildew into the air. The pictures, many of them stuck together, scattered all over the floor.

"Have to get a new box from Doug." He picked up a handful of pictures and tossed them onto the table. Then he and Zack together gathered up the rest and stacked them between them. Zack rescued his own shots from beneath the pile and stuffed them back in his wallet. He watched while the old man went through forty or fifty pictures.

The man kept shaking his head from side to side. He pulled out a few pictures and showed them to Zack. "Kitty, again. Right before she got killed. Here's one of the kid."

"He disappeared. You know what happened to him? You know if he's still alive?"

"Don't know for sure. He went off with my brother and his whore one day. Don't know if he's still alive."

"Jesus! Your brother would know, I bet."

"It's my brother I was talking about not knowing if he's still alive."

"Shit! You can find out through Social Security."

"Don't care much. Him and me never got along. I was glad when he left for California. Hope I never see him again."

Zack dropped the picture on the table. "Look, I'm going to level with you about why I came here. I came from Philadelphia. We just had a bunch of murders out there. The bodies all had knives through their hearts. That sound familiar to you?"

"Sounds like what Gus the Third got hanged for. And his father before him."

"Right! And if Gus the Fourth is still alive, he just might be carrying on the family tradition."

"Could be, I guess."

"Mister—Sorry, I don't even know your name."

"Chet."

"Chet, I've got to find out about your brother. Or somebody that knows about what happened to Gus the Fourth. But I need you to help. You've got to find out through Social Security where he is. I can tell you how to do it, but only a family member can start the trace for a missing person."

"Ain't missing, far as I'm concerned. Gone and good riddance, far as I'm concerned. Let sleeping dogs lie."

"But what if Gus Four is killing those people—"

"What if? Someone'll catch him like they did the others. Hang him."

Zack stood up. "But your brother might know if it's him. If he's even alive. Or someone that knew your brother. At least tell me his name."

"Same as mine."

Zack took a deep breath. "What's your last name, then. You never even said."

"None of your business. Might as well leave, now. I ain't gonna tell you no more." The man started pulling the stack of pictures in front of him into a single pile. He circled his arms around them and looked up at Zack, taunting him.

Reading him at last, Zack said, "OK, Chet. I'll tell you what I'm going to do. I'm going to go back to my hotel and get ahold of some cash. You think about things tonight. I'll come back tomorrow morning with a hundred dollars, like you asked. That be enough to get you to start a trace on your brother?"

"Maybe," the old man said.

Zack whooshed out an exasperated sigh and left the kitchen. After nudging the front door open with his foot, he turned back and shouted, "Think about it, Chet. I'll be back tomorrow morning." He could get the cash right now from an automatic teller machine. But let the old bastard get a little hungry. He'd use up the thirty-five dollars Zack had already given him in a hurry. Probably wouldn't last him through the day. Yeah, tomorrow the old guy would be hungry as hell, and he'd give Zack all the information he'd need to start an in-depth investigation on Gus Champus IV. *Jesus! Chet's brother might even have raised the kid for Gus Three!* he thought.

Now, Zack couldn't wait to get back to the Hyatt and tell Liz what he'd already dug up in just a few hours. If she'd thought he was a good detective before, wait till she heard about this! He wouldn't have to tell her that most of it was plain old dumb luck.

When he arrived at the hotel room at 2:30, he found a note by the phone:

Adventure strikes! I'm off to visit Carmella Rand, Ruth's cousin! Back by 6, unless it gets too interesting.

Love, Liz

Talk about dumb luck, he thought, with mixed excitement and disappointment. He'd wanted his news to make the big impression. *OK. So we happen to make a good team. Both smart enough to make the most of dumb luck. And lucky enough to look even smarter.*

Then he read her PS:

Don't take a shower! We'll eat in.

He laughed. "Not this time, Doc. The way I stink now would scare away a horny sewer rat." His pores, every inch of his clothing, had absorbed the stench of Chet's breath along with the breath of the rooms he lived in. A shower might remove it from his body and hair, but on the way home as he'd smelled it in the car, he'd considered burning his clothes and wondered how he'd get the smell out of the car. He'd left the windows open a crack when he'd parked. Once more aware of the wicked odor, he peeled off his clothes and put them in a large plastic bag the hotel supplied for laundry and double knotted the top. He stuck it in the corner of the closet, planning to forget it when he left.

Then he showered and shampooed with a whole bottle of the shampoo the hotel provided. His smell when he got out and dried reminded him of how Liz had smelled the night before when she'd come to him. Thinking of that as he donned the thick terry bathrobe with the Hyatt insignia on it, he hoped she'd be back much earlier than six.

She hadn't returned when he finished his bath.

Just as well, he thought. He'd completely forgotten his pledge to Ted Squire to put in at least a few hours work a day on business. In fact, this morning, after hooking his modem into the phone jack the Hyatt provided, he hadn't even booted up his machine to test it. He'd better do that now.

Within moments he had connected to the minicomputer at work and found a single fax message there. "Zack," it read, "had second thoughts about making you work on vacation so soon after being sick. Nothing here that can't wait till you get back. Relax and have a good time. You deserve it. Ted."

Tears leapt into Zack's eyes. *How the hell can so many good things be happening to me at once? During the horrible year after Maryellen got sick, I thought nothing good could happen again. Now there's Liz, and our luck in the Champus and Rand thing, and all at once Ted—a guy who never seemed to give a shit about anything—Jesus! Better cross my fingers! This can't last forever—*

He disconnected from the mini and shut off the modem. Still shaking his head at his luck, he loaded the composite picture program he'd been putting together. He was totally lost in his work on it when he felt Liz's arms around his waist.

As he turned, she kissed him loudly on the cheek and laughed. "Bastard! You took a shower!" Then without waiting for his mock apology, she laughed again and danced back away from him. "Oh Zack! What a wonderful adventure! Wait till I tell you what happened!" She ran to the bathroom. "Oh, but I really have to go!"

In all the times he'd seen her she had never seemed so young and girlish. Something had happened to the serious, often intense Liz Broward he'd known. Less than a week ago she'd come to him, bearings lost, trying to find her direction in his embrace. The right place at the right time, he thought—for both of them. All of them. Poke, too. Maybe she didn't appreciate it now, but she would. *Oh Liz, how I love you,* he thought as she came out of the bathroom, still laughing.

"What happened?" he asked, getting up from the chair by the computer and crossing to sit on one of the two king-size beds. "Don't keep me guessing."

"She's Ruth's cousin! Just about as old as Ruth would be now. They were friends. She told me how their families used to get together for Sunday dinners at each others' houses. Ruth's parents' house is still standing. And she has some pictures of everybody. She's going to make me copies and send them to me."

"Jesus! Did you see the pictures?"

She bounced down on the edge of the bed across from him

and grinned. "Yes. Of everyone but Ruth's father. She said everyone was afraid of him. He had some disfiguring disease that eventually killed him. Something he picked up in Africa, she thinks. She knows he came from there. Anyway, he was the one that took most of the pictures. And Carmella's going to send me some copies of letters, too. Maybe we'll find a connection to Champus there. She says she doesn't think there were any Randalls or such before. But I haven't called everyone in the book. Never even got through all the Rands." She took a deep breath and smiled with every inch of her face. "So, what do you think? Would I make a good genealogist?"

He reached over and ran one finger around her face, tracing the smile. "You'd make a good anything. I love you, Liz."

She caught his hand. "Oh, God, how I love you, Zack. To think of how close I came—"

"All I can think of is how close you came to me last night."

"Yes. Let's think about that." She tilted her trunk forward across the space between the beds and caught his face in her hands. Soon they were making love again, this time wordlessly. He fell asleep inside her and did not need to dream.

When he woke he saw her naked rump turned toward him, the hill of her hip bathed in a strange flickering amber aura. For a moment he thought it was confirmation of her ethereal purity, and he tried to touch the halo without touching her. As the radiance encircled his hand, he smiled, then let his fingers rest on her hip.

She turned slightly and caught his hand against her and silently stroked his fingers. He withdew his hand from hers and threw his arm over her waist. She grabbed it there and held it in the buffer zone equidistant from her most erogenous points. He tugged playfully at her hand, pretending to try to take possession of her delta of Venus below, or the hillocks of her breasts above.

"Mmmn, Zack, no."

"Why not? Don't you like it?"

"I love it." She kept his hand prisoner as she extricated herself from his arm and sat up. "What's that light flickering?"

"Your afterglow. That's why I thought you wanted more. Let go of my hand."

She caught it between both her hands now. "Not till you promise to be good."

"I am good."

She laughed. "Too damn good! Come on. Promise. Oh, Zack, that's not my afterglow. It's your computer. When did you turn it on? How long have I been sleeping?" She dropped his hand and got out of bed.

"We've both been sleeping a couple of hours. I was working on the computer when you came in. Remember?"

She grinned at him. "I've been keeping you from work."

"Right! But what's worse, you didn't even give me a chance to tell you what I did this morning while you were having tea with Carmella Rand."

"Tell me."

"OK. But not till you cover up that sweet body of yours so I can think straight."

"Better yet, I'll shower and get dressed for dinner. You can tell me in the dining room." Grabbing the robe he'd dropped on the floor between the beds, she ran into the bathroom and turned on the shower.

To force his focus away from further amorous musings, he dressed in clean beige slacks and a pullover brown and white shirt, donned clean socks and mesh tan court shoes, and sat down again in front of the computer. He ran a test on his composite picture program to see if he'd managed to get out the pesky bug that had been muddying the screen each time he'd tried to rotate a three-dimensional image. He saved the new code, then loaded the debugged program and typed up the commands.

After a series of keystrokes, he had the face of the record-stealing maid, as he recalled her, on the screen. Because his monitor was monochrome instead of color, he couldn't catch the effect of her garish makeup or the odd blond of her hair. But the features in high resolution were crisp and clear.

"That's eerie, Zack!" said Liz, as she came up and looked over his shoulder while rubbing her hair dry. "How do you do it?"

"Professional secret." He flicked the contrast knob on his monitor so the screen light went out. "Ready for dinner?"

She was fully dressed in another of those designer jeans outfits she seemed to have an unending store of. "Not till I dry my hair." She waved her blow drier in the air. "Tell me about today while I'm doing it." She plugged the drier into the outlet near the dressing table and flicked it on. As she brushed and blew the damp mass of tangles into smooth tawny waves and curves, he told her what had happened with Chet this morning. Her eyes grew wide and excited. She turned off the drier and set it on the dresser.

"What wonderful luck! We must be destined to find something. To do it together on our great adventure in Phoenix."

He felt oddly uneasy. "Why do you keep calling it an adventure, Liz?"

"Maybe it's everyday for you. Not for me. I've never done anything like this before." She didn't seem to have noticed his disquiet.

After a short pause he said, "When you call it an adventure, it makes me think you're—that it's some sort of fling you're here for."

She opened her mouth. Her eyes clouded for a moment. She turned her head.

"Liz?"

She snapped her face toward him again. "No! Don't say that."

"You're not sure, are you? You still have a couple of weeks to make up your mind. Meanwhile—an adventure."

"Zack, no! I'd never do that to you."

"No. You wouldn't. Not on purpose, anyway. Tell me something. Did you ever tell Eric you weren't going to marry him?"

"I took away his key to my apartment."

"You're not answering my question."

"I don't have to tell him. He knows it."

"Does he know you're here with me, having an adventure?"

"Nobody knows that. Not even my partners know where I am. I just had to leave Philadelphia—everyone, everything there. Nobody even knows I left." She walked to the bed that they'd hadn't loved in, and sat down on the edge and dropped the hand holding the hair brush into her lap. Then looking imploringly at him she said, "Zack. Please give me time. Like Poke, I need time to get all my feelings straight. I know I love you. I know I don't love Eric. All the rest—it has to fall into place. *Please give me time."*

Yes, time. Of course she needed time! He'd had it, hadn't he? Almost a year since she'd first held him weeping in her arms before he'd known that he'd loved her all those months and hadn't even realized it. And she had had to make the first move. And he'd had to lie weeping in her arms, then lie aching in her arms still another time before he could say out loud to her that he loved her, and still could not say out loud to her all the things he felt for her, and about how afraid he was of losing her and how he was afraid to have her. He could not be right for her. Not for a woman like her.

He walked to the bed. "Oh, God, Liz, I'm sorry." He sat next to her and took her brush from her hand, set it aside, and held her hand.

They sat for a while hand in hand, and she cried a little, not with any heaving or shaking, but just with tears working one at a time up from under her lower eyelids and rolling down her face. She let them roll over her chin, and a couple of them dripped onto his hand in her lap. And he felt kissed by them. At last she half sighed and said, "My hair's dry. Let's go have something light for dinner. It's already after ten back home."

After dinner with little talking, they went for a walk around the Civic Plaza in the balmy evening. He admired the phoenix fountain sculpture, and told her his thoughts about the differences between making art out of metal and water and of making it electronically with codes, keys, and light on a screen. That reminded them of the program on his computer in the hotel room.

"You blackened the screen so I couldn't see what you did," she said.

"I just wanted to tell you about more important things. Like Chet. I want you to see the program and how it works."

"Good! Let's go back. It's been refreshing, having time together without the air catching fire around us." Her lips curved in irony. "Guess we need that, too."

"Not too much of it. But now I know I love you even when

my temperature's normal. I liked just sitting and walking quietly."

"Temperature? You did finish the penicillin today, didn't you?"

"Hey, doc, what is this?"

"A rather extraordinary house call."

"Yeah, it sure has been. I took it. Now let's head back. It's my turn to be the professional consultant."

He grabbed her hand and squeezed it and they ran all the way back to the hotel, laughing like teenagers in love.

After a few minutes of fooling around in the room, they sat, still laughing, at the table. He turned the screen on again, and the picture was right where he'd left it. Again, she caught her breath. "It looks exactly like her, Zack."

"That's just from the front. Look what happens when I press a few function keys." He turned the woman's head around so that she could see it from several angles. Then he pressed another key so that it continued to revolve slowly in space.

"Brrr! She looks nearly alive. Even weirder in amber, though."

"Yep. Now suppose we change something. Let's give her a new hairdo or something so that if she happens to go to the beauty shop—"

"They'd never let her in!"

"OK, well, she does it herself at home."

She nodded.

"What should we do on her?"

"How about long bangs. Make them come down over her eyes."

"Just happen to have a pair of long bangs in the box." He keyed in a command to replace the long hair with short hair and bangs.

Liz leaned back in her chair and clapped her hands together. "Wonderful! I love it!"

"Gives her a whole new personality."

"Gives me a whole new set of shivers."

"Yeah," he said seriously. "She's not the kind of broad you'd like to run into in your back office."

"Or in the rest room."

"Or in a dark parking garage." He thought for a minute. "Say, let me try something else. I made up this package with her in it, but I threw in a whole bunch of features. Men's and women's, too. I got the perfect hairdo for her. The security guy at the lot said something. Here, let me show you." He did another hair replace command. The short hair and bangs disappeared, and a short crew cut replaced it.

After a second Liz asked, "Are you going to leave her bald like that?"

"No, Liz. She's not bald. Look closely. The guard in the garage said he saw a guy in a black van drive out. He said this guy had a crew cut so short he looked nearly like a skin—"

Liz jumped up. "Zack! Dear God! Rotate her. Turn her around!"

"Sure." He pressed the rotate command. The head turned slowly through several rotations, then back in the other direction, as he commanded.

Liz's eyes and mouth made a triangle of Os on her face. She stared at the turning head. Amber sparks flickered in her eyes, "Turn it again. Again."

At last she sat down with a tremulous sigh. "OK. You can hold it." She was shaking her head dazedly. Then, hollowly, she said, "Look at him, Zack. That's the person who took those records. He was wearing a wig and makeup. I know who he is. He works in the hospital. And he does drive a black van. I saw his car behind mine one night. In fact, I'm almost sure of it. But I was so distracted, I didn't see it until it flashed into my mind this moment."

Zack froze. "He was following you! Jesus, Liz!"

"No. I was backing out of my parking space in the hospital lot. He stopped to let me back out. Then he was behind me for a few blocks, but I don't think he was following me. Why would he?"

"Maybe he's crazy. He looks crazy."

"Yes he does. And maybe he is. Zack, I'd better fly home tomorrow. I have a terrible feeling that something pretty awful has happened to Agnes Shultz, and this man is behind it. The sooner we get a copy of your program to the police, the sooner they can pick up this man for questioning. I'll get his name and address from the hospital personnel records."

"Dear person, just make sure he isn't following you around. Don't let him know you suspect him. Be careful," he said.

"Dear Zack, you bet I'll be careful. It's not just myself I'm concerned for."

"You'd better let the police watch out for Agnes."

"I will. That's not who I'm concerned for, either. I think something more than clues in our investigation probably will come out of our adventure."

"What else?"

"Well, Zack, the timing was right and the exposure pretty intense. And if wanting something to happen so much you can almost taste it helps it happen—"

"What if two of us want it to happen so bad we can taste it?"

"Why don't we test that theory tonight? We can increase the exposure."

"You're the doctor, dear Doc," he said, as he turned the computer off.

CHAPTER ELEVEN

Wednesday morning—Zack

Zack's uneasiness about Liz's leaving without him changed first to excitement and then to a new kind of worry on the drive from Sky Harbor Airport to the western side of Phoenix. She was probably right in thinking that the weird-looking lab technician had not been following her; yet her best protection that he wouldn't harm her—or others—lay in getting the composite drawing program back to the police. They could view the picture on their own computers. Maybe, he thought, he could sell them on using the program. He didn't want to take their artist's job from him. Zack could teach him how to do computer graphics. Maybe Liz was right that the old guy would resist the whole idea. But if the program helped the police to solve this particular theft and Agnes Shultz's disappearance, that resistance might break down. Zack would teach the guy to be all the artist he could be. All because of what Liz had rightly termed their wonderful adventure.

Adventure! What a breathtaking thought! But scary, too. Life was so much more than a series of adventures. And adventures all came to an end in a letdown. Routine and the dull grinding problems of work and family took over. Sure, the memories of adventures helped ease the dullness. You could sit there and grin as the memories passed in front of your eyes like an exciting movie. But Liz's love for him seemed rooted in the adventure itself. Her love for him was her adventure, a break with her past that, maybe, had no future, *because of the past she was trying to escape.*

Wait! If what she said was true, there might be a future! Hadn't she said in so many words that she might get pregnant from the lovemaking of the past few days? Because she wanted it so bad she could taste it? She wanted to have a baby almost more than anything. She'd told him that, and that she wanted to have it the right way. Well, that must mean something! She wanted his baby so bad she could taste it. To have it the right way, as she seemed to see it, she'd have to get married—to him.

He wanted that, of course. He was crazy about her. And what a mother she'd make for his baby! And what a mother she'd make for Poke! He had never known a woman like her. Never dreamed of knowing one. Never imagined that such a woman could truly want his baby, want him. An adventure with him was one thing; marriage another. She knew that, didn't she? Yes, that was what bothered her. She could have his baby "the right way" without marrying Zack. She could marry Eric, couldn't she? In her class of people, no one would dare to ask why the kid looked more like some bastard Indian than like Liz's husband. If it would. There was plenty of Anglo-Saxon in Zack.

That was why she hadn't told Eric the wedding was off, wasn't it? Because she wasn't sure that she wanted to marry Zack; she was only sure she wanted an adventure with Zack, and a baby out of it, so someday she could look at it playing and see him in it and think of their wonderful adventure.

No! Liz wouldn't do that. Not Liz. All that she needed was time to get her thoughts together. Maybe it was better she'd left. It would give him time, too. And Poke. All of them needed time.

"You're out of your mind, Zack!" he said aloud to himself, as he pulled the Taurus into the strip and to a parking slot in front of the Taco Bell. "Liz loves you, man, and you're so sure it's impossible you're scared shitless!"

He punctuated the words with a hard pull on the hand brake, jolting the car to a thumping stop before putting it in parking gear. A burly man coming out of the Circle K wheeled toward the car, fists raised, as Zack, teeth still bared in self-outrage, got out and slammed the door. He considered assuring the man he was not mad at anyone but himself, but when the man backed off and walked away after eyeing him briefly, he decided that a mean look might be the best deterrent he could wield in this neighborhood. With a firmly implanted scowl, he walked across the street and turned toward Chet's house. The nasty trio was nowhere in sight today; still, the scowl might come in handy. With the hundred dollars in his wallet, he could use every weapon he had.

Nobody followed him, though. The street seemed calm, its decay somehow surreal in the brilliant morning sunlight. The burly man's truck had driven off in the opposite direction; no other traffic, foot or vehicle, passed him. Only a mangy brown dog limped along across the street, stopping occasionally to nose around a piece of promising looking garbage before licking it lackadaisically and moving on.

A few flies darted at Zack as he turned up the path toward Chet's porch. He hadn't seen a fly since arriving in Phoenix, not even in this stinking house. Possibly there were none in the house because Chet had no food around, and, therefore no collection of decomposing waste. Probably the streets had no flies because the hot low slung sun in this low humidity quickly dessicated animal feces and food litter. This kind of neighborhood in Philadelphia would buzz with hungry flies. Many times, he'd swatted his way through them in downtown Philadelphia and its different kind of squalor.

Suddenly, his stomach turned at thoughts of the body in the woods, the blowflies diving at it. He flapped his hands at the insects, and mounted the flat rocks to the door plank, and belched as he strode to the front door.

It was a few inches ajar, and the flies that he batted swirled around his head then spun through the opening. The horrible stench from inside seeped out. Zack backed off for a second before knocking on the door. He grunted, realizing the absurdity of such a civilized gesture. But still, he waited a moment before pushing the door open and calling, "Hey, Chet!"

No answer but the whine of a fly as it passed his ear.

He pushed the door farther and called again, loudly, recalling the man's hearing difficulty. When Chet still didn't answer, he began to step in. No, the guy was obviously not here. The house was silent. This was a home, and he had no more right to intrude here than in any other home. Chet could not have gone very far. He'd probably gone to the pawn shop. Zack would check for him there.

"You Doug?" Zack asked of a tall, dark-haired man about his own age behind a teller-like window at the pawnshop.

The man nodded and squinted at Zack. Zack could see that this shop was, as Chet had said, more secure than a bank. The musical instruments, guns, jewelry, and stereo equipment arrayed here could be clearly seen through the heavy glass display cases, but to get to them you needed either a key to the back of the cases or a complete burglar kit. Heavy chicken wire reinforced the glass. More wire secured each item. The alarm system was visibly attached to each item and at every point of possible entry. Of course, you could shoot your way in, but on seeing Doug's wary glance and position, Zack doubted you'd have a chance to draw the weapon, let alone escape, again as Chet had said, without getting your head blown off.

"Who's asking," Doug said, eyeing him head to toe.

"Zack James. I met Chet yesterday. Said he banks with you so he doesn't have to carry cash. You get him stuff to eat and drink."

"Yeah?" Doug shifted slightly and smoothed his thick black hair with a nervous hand.

"Looks like the old guy doesn't have too many friends around here. Goons always follow him?"

"Right. So I take care of him best I can. Do it for a dozen old people in the neighborhood. They don't have much else."

Zack nodded. He looked around the shop. "Place doesn't look like you'd find a Good Samaritan in it."

"That what you came for, Zack?" he said, his voice impatient. This man trusted no one, and wouldn't be sweet-talked.

"No. I'm impressed, though. Doesn't hurt to say. But I came because I'm looking for Chet."

"Probably home."

"Just there. He didn't answer the door. It was open a little, and I pushed it farther. Hollered, but he still didn't come. Don't like to push into people's places, so I thought I'd check with you, since you give him his food."

Doug knit his brow. "You sure he wasn't there?"

"I hollered, then listened. There wasn't a sound."

"He didn't come in this morning. Was wondering where he was. Only time he ever misses is when he's sick. I was going to check on him later."

"Think he might be sick? Maybe I'd better go in." Zack hesitated for a moment, thinking, then said, "On the other hand, maybe he went someplace else to buy something. I gave him some money yesterday. Figured he'd blow it at a liquor store or something."

Doug stiffened. His face seemed to catch fire. "For fucking Christ sake, what'd you give him money for!"

Shaken at the fury in the man's dark voice and eyes, Zack took a step backward. "He did me a favor. Look, I showed him some pictures. I'm looking for someone. He knew them. But he only told me things when I paid him."

"You fucking stupid idiot!"

"Look," said Zack, trying to swallow but finding his mouth suddenly too dry, "I knew he'd probably just buy more hootch. But, Jesus, he gets that from you anyway and—"

"Asshole!" He shook his fists and his head at the same time. "You know what you did? You got the old man killed is what you did!"

Stunned, Zack could not move or speak.

"You better get the hell over there in a hurry, asshole! Maybe he's not quite dead yet. I'm calling the rescue squad, but I hope you know how to give CPR. If there's still time for first aid."

Zack belched with fear and sick shame. He spun and ran from the shop. He flew across the street and down the block, sped across the yard, up the steps, across the plank, and shoved with both hands through the door. Greeted again by buzzing flies, he followed them through the hall to the kitchen. They were diving to the table where a spilled liquor bottle lay, then spinning up and circling the lightbulb, ricocheting from wall to wall and toward the floor. At least a dozen were darting around the head of the man in the tuxedo. Some had landed on his face and around the corners of his gaping mouth and nostrils and ears. They covered his eyelids, crawled on his neck in a feeding frenzy.

A bloody broken bottle lay above his head. Another lay shattered in a pool of liquid, also encrusted with flies. Torn photographs, scattered from one end of the kitchen to the other, lay soaking up more liquid or stuck to Chet's crumpled form.

Zack stopped in his tracks. *Oh, Jesus! Doug was right! Those three saw me give Chet the money. Jesus! I gave it to him right there on the street while they were following him. Oh, Christ, how could I have been so stupid! Oh Jesus, I'll never be able to forgive myself. If it wasn't for me, this old guy wouldn't have gotten killed!*

He took a step forward, for no good reason. Even if the guy still was alive, which seemed impossible since the flies were already dining on him, Zack could do nothing. He'd never learned CPR, though Maryellen had begged him to attend a free class. All he could do was to wait for the paramedics to come. And not wait in here. What good would it do to stay here and watch? It could not erase his stupid, unthinking act. Nothing could.

He turned and walked through the house to the front door. No sirens or lights signaled the approach of help. No need for them. Nothing would help Chet, and nothing could help Zack. Standing by the open door, he put up his hands to his face and began to sob.

He barely heard the sound of creaking floorboards in the hallway behind him. When he finally did, and realized that someone was coming, slowly, relentlessly toward him, he continued to sob; he didn't want the intruder to know that he was readying himself to whirl and strike. Zack may not have learned CPR, but he had learned how to box, and his fists could be deadly weapons, especially to a surprised assailant. *If nothing else, Chet, I'll get the lousy bastard that got you!* he thought.

The footsteps came closer, and along with them a horrible smell, so strong that it cut through all the other smells in the house. The movements were slow, but not deliberate and firm. Then he heard a moan and a curse.

He turned suddenly, then stepped back and almost fell backward out the front door. Grasping the door frame, he righted himself.

"Get the goddanged flies off me!" Chet was stooping a few feet away, looking like a bee keeper collecting a swarm. He waved his arms, batting himself about the head. The insects clung tenaciously. "Goddanged flies!"

For a moment, Zack couldn't move. In front of him the flyman weaved and swatted at himself, behind him someone was running across the plank.

"Rescue squad," a young man said. "Let me get by!"

Dizzily, Zack moved out of his way. "Not dead," he said.

"Good thing! No use resuscitating dead ones." The paramedic's attempt at humor trailed off as he looked at Chet. "Jesus! What the hell—"

"Goddang flies. Get 'em off me."

"What happened, mister?" The paramedic and another who'd joined him looked like they weren't quite sure what to do. "What happened?" he said now to Zack.

Zack had begun to figure it out. "He must've puked and fallen asleep in it."

"There's some blood on him. Did someone hit you?"

"Might've. They was mad I didn't have money left. Spilled a whole bottle. Broke one and came at me with it. Puked all over him and I think he dropped it. Didn't do it on purpose, but it worked."

Zack thought he saw the flies around Chet's mouth curve up in a kind of smile.

"Can't take a chance he's hurt," said the first paramedic.

"Got to get the flies off to see where the blood's coming from," said the other.

"How the hell do we do that?" his partner whispered. "We can't swat them right on his face."

Zack, who'd been wondering what Maryellen would have done in this kind of situation, had stopped thinking like a street detective and begun to think like a public health nurse. He closed off his nostrils and breathed through his mouth and leapt forward and began to tear off Chet's clothes. He flung off the vest, then the shirt, then hollered at Chet to sit on the floor and pulled off the old man's beltless and buttonless pants. He whipped the pants around Chet's face, and dislodged about half the flies that way. Some of them dove for the vomit soaked clothes, others buzzed off toward the kitchen where Zack was sure they'd be distracted for a while.

"OK, Chet, where's your tub? Time for a good hot bath."

"Hot bath!" said the paramedics in unison. "You're kidding. There's no water heater in this house."

"Cold, then," said Zack, chagrined. "You got a tub?"

Still brushing at his face, Chet said, "Never use it."

Zack turned to the paramedics. "Time he did. Let's carry him in."

They shrank back.

"OK, Chet, up on your feet." He bent to the unpleasant task of helping the old man up. "Which way?"

"Can walk by myself," said Chet, pushing him with surprising force and starting through the dark bedroom with the mattress on the floor.

Seeing him naked, Zack wondered how he could walk by himself. He was crooked and bent, and none of his joints seemed to work right. His skin lay loose on his skeleton; the buttocks hung limp on his hips like wet laundry, and flapped against pale, translucent thighs; a slug of a penis receded into his colorless flat scrotum as he walked.

After passing through the bedroom, Zack and the paramedics followed Chet through a door frame into a bathroom. Wood floor boards showed through a remnant of old linoleum, which covered only the area under the claw-footed tub and a sink that hung precariously from its exposed plumbing. A toilet with no seat leaked rusty water around its tank and base.

"God!" said Zack, "I thought you said you didn't use the tub."

"No use for taking a bath. Tap don't work." Most of the flies had left Chet's head, though a few still buzzed around it. "Might as well use if for something."

The something he used it for was to store a collection of old newspapers, clothes (or what was left of them that could be used for clothing), and various items such as those he kept in the refrigerator.

"You got a tap that does work?" Zack said, seeing the sink tap couldn't possibly deliver water.

"Kitchen."

One of the paramedics said, "Look, this guy's obviously OK. No reason to check him. I can see from here, all he's got is a little cut behind his jaw. You go ahead and take care of him." He signaled to his partner to leave, and they started out.

"Wait a minute!" Zack said. "You go in there and check him over right. How do you know that's all that's wrong?"

"Look, mister, there's someone out there that's a real emergency. This old souse'll be the same if we check him or don't. If he chokes on his puke instead of just sleeping in it, we might be able to help." The medic turned again.

Zack leapt at him and grabbed his shoulders. "Schmuck! You get in there and check him over. He's a human being. Treat him like one."

"Get your hands off me!"

"Check him out!" Zack turned him forcibly around to face the old man, who had sat down on the seatless toilet and was farting and pushing out liquid diarrhea. He shoved the man toward the hapless fellow.

"OK, OK." The paramedic made a cursory gloved-hand check of the man's head and body, then gingerly listened to his heart with a stethoscope. He tilted Chet forward on the toilet, and looked in with a grimace. "Can't do anything about that," he said. He stood up. "He'll live. We'll put in a report that he'll live." He looked around the room and shook his head. "All he needs is a good bath and something to wipe his ass on."

Chet mumbled something and got up and walked to the tub, tore off a piece of one of the newspapers and wiped around what looked like a very sore anus.

The medics snorted and walked out. The old man dropped the paper into the bowl and flushed the toilet. Zack couldn't believe his eyes and ears when it worked.

The tap in the kitchen worked, too, and Zack stopped up the sink with a piece of rubber he cut, using an old razor blade, from the sole of an old shoe. He had to fill and empty the sink several times and use several old rags as sponges to get off all the vomit from Chet. It took him a while to think of going over to the Circle K to buy some detergent that was mild enough to use to wash the old guy's hair. They didn't have any bar soap or shampoo. To finish the grooming job needed to make him less attractive to the flies, which still held residence in the kitchen, Zack used as many odds and ends from the refrigerator and bathtub as he could find. When a comb from the refrigerator broke, Zack used his own, and left it on a shelf for Chet.

After Chet himself was clean, Zack scrubbed up the kitchen floor, and picked up all the stinking clothes in the hallway and wiped the floor around where they'd lain. In a large plastic sack, also bought from the Circle K, he discarded the old tuxedo, the dirty rags, the torn photographs, and everything else he found that bore unremovable traces of vomit.

Chet sat in the kitchen chair, wearing a hodgepodge of clothes pulled from the bathtub, and watched Zack through freshly washed lenses, as he worked. He hummed as Zack killed as many flies as possible with rolled up newspapers.

Surveying his work as he finished, Zack took a deep breath. The house still stank, but the old man himself was probably cleaner than he'd been in years. He felt unexpectedly satisfied. He turned to Chet.

"Want me to go and get you something to eat from Doug?"

"Yep."

He nodded and went to the pawn shop. He explained to Doug what had happened. Doug shook his head.

"Gonna kill himself eventually. Nothing any of us can do anything about. Sorry I yelled at you before." He went to a back room out of Zack's sight and returned with a cold, plastic-wrapped sandwich and a Coke. "This'll keep him going for a while. He'll be in tomorrow for his hootch, and I guess I'll give it to him. Not much else to kill his pain."

"Like I said," Zack said, as he took the food through the teller window, "this is a strange place to find a Good Samaritan." Then he turned and walked back to Chet's house. Chet was still sitting by the kitchen table where he'd left him. He gave him the food.

The old man sniffed at the sandwich and set it down on the table. "You still want to know about Gus the Fourth?"

Zack had forgotten completely his original reason for coming here. He looked down at the man, surprised. "Yeah. You know where he might be?"

Chet cocked his head to one side and showed a gummy, black-toothed smile. "Maybe," he said. "And maybe not."

"Shit!" said Zack.

"My brother knows, though. He raised him."

"Your brother, right," he said, coolly.

"Want to know my brother's name?"

"Maybe. Maybe not."

The old man cackled, obviously pleased at Zack's joining his game. "Chet. Same as mine."

"You got the same name as your brother?"

"Sure. Don't you? Last name is Chet. First name's George. Lives in California. If he's still alive. Could find him through Social Security if you want."

Zack grinned. "I'll need your help."

Chet picked up his sandwich and took a bite. He held it out to Zack.

"No thanks. Not hungry." That was true enough. His appetite wouldn't be coming back in a hurry.

"Well, maybe I can help and maybe I can't. Let me think about it awhile," he said. "Come back tomorrow."

"You bet I will!"

He fully intended to follow through on that promise.

Wednesday afternoon, Philadelphia—Poke

Poke got out of the minivan in front of her house.

"OK, dear, be sure to be back before eight," said Eve Carter.

"OK."

"Don't forget your pizza," said Christy. She handed down the Pizza Hut box.

Poke grabbed it. "Thanks." Its redolence tweaked her appetite. Maybe she'd eat it before doing the rest of her history paper. It was already after four and she hadn't had her usual after-school snack at the Carters' house. Mrs. Carter had taken them on a quick shopping trip and to get the pizza instead of having them walk home on a day that threatened rain.

"Now, if it does rain, I'll come after you. But don't you dare wait till it's dark, either way."

"Sure," said Poke. Parents were all alike. Afraid to let you get wet. Afraid to let you walk in the dark. Pop was just the same. Thought that kids were too dumb to take care of themselves. Parents were the dumb ones. Look at Pop. Too dumb to go to a doctor till he nearly died. Then too dumb to take his own medicine. Then so dumb he had to go off on some stupid detective trip before he was even all better.

"And take those stray newspapers on the walk inside, so no one will know you're not home. And don't forget to water that plant in the kitchen."

"Right. OK, I'll see you later." More dumb stuff. So what if people knew she wasn't home! Besides, she was now, at least for a few hours. And who did Mrs. Carter think always watered the plant? OK, so she might not have thought of it today, but, big deal, she'd be home on Friday. It wouldn't die before then. Why did parents always have to remind you of everything when they were the ones that forgot to take their pills? She sighed and stepped up onto the curb and waved to Christy as she made a face about parents that her friend would understand.

Christy waved and made the face back. Poke laughed and ran onto the porch, unlocked the front door, and ran into the house, leaving the newspapers outside. She could get them later. Meanwhile, she was starving for the pizza.

In the kitchen, she tore the box open and pulled a slice stringily free from the rest of the pie. She closed her eyes and bit into the cheesy morsel. It had everything on it except mushrooms. She hated mushrooms; she loved jalapeño peppers, pepperoni, onions, ground meat, green peppers, and double cheese. She chortled at the pleasure of every bite, of every exciting, spicy swallow. She danced around the kitchen as she ate the pizza. Being in her own house for the first time in three days was fun. No one could tell her what to do. At Christy's house everybody, including Christy and her brother, told Poke what to do. Here she could eat as much pizza as she wanted with no one else's big eyes greedy for it, making her feel selfish for eating the whole thing.

Here, when she'd stuffed herself, she could open her mouth wide and press against her stomach with her hands and burp. She did that. Then she laughed and ran around the kitchen making loud burps, before getting herself a glass of water from the tap and drinking it, not just to relieve her thirst, but so she could burp some more.

After a few minutes of that, she decided to run upstairs to her bedroom and see if she had any messages on her answering machine. Of course there were none: everyone knew she was staying with Christy and had called her there; still, she was disappointed.

As she started back downstairs, she heard a thump from below. She stopped on the stairs for a second. Someone must have knocked on the door. She ran the rest of the way down and opened the door. No one was there; she noticed the newspapers on the walk and ran to get them. A little rain had begun to fall, and a wind had blown up. Maybe she'd have to call Christy's mother. Not because she didn't want to get wet, but because she didn't want her homework paper to get wet or blow away.

As she ran back onto the porch, the front door slammed closed. "Shit!" she said. "I left the key in the kitchen!" For a minute she was scared. Then she remembered that the combination dead bolt lock couldn't automatically lock you out. Her father had it installed on purpose that way and taught her to always lock the door and carry her key when she went out. That habit had become automatic.

Thank goodness! Still, she turned the knob slowly and took a relieved breath when the door opened normally. Having it slam on you felt scary. Especially when this door never slammed before like that. You really had to push it to slam it. Maybe the wind had slammed it. It wasn't that windy, though. And the wind was outside and the door opened inward and that seemed kind of weird.

Well, empty houses always seemed weird when you'd been away from them even for a couple of days. Poke wasn't quite sure why that was so. She knew why it felt that way after her mother died, and she and Pop had returned from a three-day stay with her maternal grandparents. That had felt weird because she knew her mother's ghost was in the house. Her mother's ghost still was there, but it was a loving, friendly ghost that made the house feel welcoming and did things like bring Dr. Broward to make Pop better. Maybe Momma was a little angry because Pop had slept with Dr. Broward. That was going too far. Pop shouldn't do things like that. You were supposed to wait longer if you really loved someone.

Don't worry, Momma. I'll make him wait longer. She's supposed to marry someone else, anyway.

Poke closed the door and went back to the kitchen to throw the newspapers in the trash can and take another slice of pizza before starting on her homework. As she bit into the cold pizza, she noticed something she hadn't seen before: the basement door was slightly ajar. A funny smell was coming from there. It reminded her of the way her coat smelled when it got wet. Sort of like an animal, maybe.

"*Eww!*" she cried and slammed the door. She suddenly remembered that a bunch of field mice had got into one of the houses down the street. They ate up a pile of laundry and the neighbors had had to move out to a motel for a few days so the house could be fumigated. She knew there was a basket of laundry next to the washer. Some of her good clothes! They'd all be eaten up! This house was really getting creepy. She'd better get her homework done and get out. She turned and went back to the table and looked at the last few slices of pizza. The mice must have smelled it and come upstairs. There were spots of pizza that looked like something had nibbled at it. "Eww!" She looked at the half-eaten slice in her hand and ran to the sink and threw it down the garbage disposer.

The garbage disposer growled loudly as it ground up that piece and the rest of the pie that she shoved in after it. After turning the switch off, she started toward the family room. She heard a noise that sounded like the grinder hadn't quite stopped. She went back to the sink and looked at it. Just to make sure it was all right, she turned the switch on and off a couple of times, letting the water run through for a little while. She shrugged her shoulders, and, at last, went into the family room and turned on the computer.

It didn't turn on! "Cheeze, this place is really weird!" She tried the switch a few more times. Nothing happened. With all the things that were happening today, this was the worst. That paper was a whole third of her history grade, and Mr. Murtaugh, her teacher, would not accept excuses. She'd always loved her father's computer because she could turn in such nice homework papers even though she could hardly type. Now she hated it. It had eaten up her homework and she couldn't get it back out. She started to cry and pace around the family room, trying to figure out a way to finish her paper without staying up all night and borrowing Christy's mother's old-fashioned IBM Selectric.

She cried very loud, knowing that no one could hear her, feeling that if she cried loud enough she could make the computer turn on. Suddenly she heard a sound quite different from the echoes of her cries. The sound startled her into silence. She froze. Someone was singing loudly in the living room.

"Cheeze!" It was the stereo. Pop always put it on a timer so it would go on when they were away from home. That was to make people think they were here and to keep them from breaking in. Pop had a whole routine about things like this: cancel the mail; cancel the daily paper; lock all the windows; turn off the water supply to the washer—he must have done that and then left the cellar door open—unplug the TV and the computer, in case of a storm—

"Cheeze! Am I dumb!"

She sighed, plugged in the computer, and finally got down to doing her homework. She was deeply engrossed in it fifteen minutes later when she realized with a start that someone was standing in the archway between the family room and kitchen. For a few moments she continued to stare at the screen; then she looked up and screamed.

The tall man stepped toward her. He held a huge, dark brown dog on a leash. The dog growled and took a step toward her. "No, Adolph! Stay!"

Poke screamed again.

The dog growled and shivered.

"Not now, Adolph! Don't be in such a hurry. We'll take her home with us. That will be fun, won't it?"

Adolph whined.

Poke started to get up from her chair, but her knees had melted. A cold sweat crept up her back.

"Don't try to run away. Adolph will stop you if you do. I won't let him touch you if you do exactly as I tell you."

Poke began to cry.

"Stop whining! It annoys me. I can't stand whining women!"

"Momma!" Poke cried.

"Momma? There's no one here. Don't try to trick me. I'm far more clever than you."

"My Momma died. You scared me. I wanted her."

"Poor orphan. How sad. Well, I won't hurt you. I promise there's nothing to be scared of *if you do exactly as I tell you—hsst!*

He sounded like a snake. She began to tremble.

"I will wait a few minutes for you to calm down and realize that you must simply do what I want to be safe from harm."

"What—what should I do?"

"Call your friend's house and tell her mother that your homework is taking longer than you thought, and that she shouldn't pick you up until about nine-thirty."

"But—"

"Adolph, she's hesitating. Do you suppose she doesn't know how hungry you are?"

Adolph growled and shivered again.

"He hasn't eaten all day. But, hungry as he is, he won't touch you unless I tell him to attack. Well?"

Poke turned and looked at the telephone. "What if she doesn't believe me?"

"Why shouldn't she believe you? You don't lie to her, do you?"

"No, but—"

"Then she'll believe you."

Poke wondered if Mrs. Carter had seen the look she had given Christy about how dumb parents were. That was a kind of lie.

"Are you going to call?"

Poke picked up the receiver. The Carter number was coded into the telephone's memory. She pushed the button. The sound of the tones of the number sounded like a scary nursery rhyme played on a music box. The ring of the phone at the other end sounded like Adolph's low growls.

"Hell-oh-oh?" It was Mrs. Carter's cheerful voice.

Poke swallowed.

"Hello?"

"Ahh, hi, Mrs. Carter. It's Poke."

"Oh, hi, dear. I was expecting you to call. Weather's pretty bad, isn't it? Ready to go?"

Adolph growled.

"No!"

"Oh? When do you think, then?"

"I—I guess it's taking longer than I thought. Probably won't be done before nine-thirty." She looked up at the tall man. He was the scariest-looking man she had ever seen.

He smiled and nodded and snapped the dog leash against his leg to still the restless angry animal.

"That late? Oh, my. Well, maybe I can come a little earlier and wait—"

"No! Please! Don't come earlier."

After a moment's silence, Mrs. Carter said, "Is everything all right, Poke?"

"Yes. I just can't work with people hanging around. It makes me nervous. I make too many mistakes typing. That's why I don't like to use your typewriter. It doesn't fix up mistakes like the computer."

"Oh. I'll have to break down and get one of those someday. All right, dear. I'll be there at nine-thirty."

"OK. Thanks. Oh and Mrs. Carter—"

The man stepped toward her, his face growing mean.

"Yes?"

"N-n-nothing. Just say hi to Christy."

She laughed. "Yes, it has been a whole two hours since you've seen each other. Bye, darling." She clicked off.

Poke set the phone down as fast as she could, given her trembling. "It's OK. She's not coming till nine-thirty."

"Very good." He pulled the dog's leash tight. "All right, Adolph. Sit down and be a good boy. We have about two hours to go before it's dark enough to take Poke to the van. Poke—what an odd name. Never heard one like it before."

"It's my nickname. My real name is Jill."

"Which would you rather we use? You're going to be with us awhile. At least until the doctor comes to get you. She will come to get you, you know. It's not you we want, Poke. It's the doctor."

"What doctor?"

"Dr. Broward, of course. She's a very evil woman. Would you like to know all about her?"

"Y-y-y—yes."

"Well, I'm going to tell you. But I'd rather wait until I get you safely out of here. When we get to my house, I'll tell you all about her and tell you how you can keep her from hurting your father."

Oh, Momma, you are *angry aren't you!* "How can I keep her from hurting Daddy?" she asked, and she began to cry.

Wednesday, Philadelphia, meanwhile—Liz

Liz did not get to her apartment until after five P.M., though her plane had left Phoenix before eight in the morning. The flight with a stop in Pittsburgh had taken six hours, and the time change from Mountain Standard to Eastern Daylight had cheated her of another three.

Not that she wanted another three hours to deal with. She was simply exhausted and wanted the peace and comfort only her own spacious and secure apartment could offer. For, as no one had known she had gone, now no one would know she was back. She could wait as long as she wanted before making or answering phone calls or responding to the messages on her answering machine.

She had even considered not running through the seven messages until tomorrow, when she would have had a decent night's sleep. Still, she was not even sure that not listening to them would help: once she knew they were there, she would have to see who left them. If she did, maybe one would nag at her, and maybe she would return that call and get it off her mind; if she didn't, then *all seven* would nag at her, each with its own uncertainty.

Better to get them then.

The first three were inconsequential, at least for the moment. Jim had called to say that the lab situation had been cleared up and he would give her the details whenever she came back. They were getting on fine without her, so don't worry.

That had been the least of her worries.

A friend from medical school had called while passing through town. Liz was sad to have missed him and his wife, but they would be back in the fall for a conference.

The third message had nothing more than, "It's me, Liz. I'll call back." She didn't recognize the voice.

Then, she picked up message number four, from her mother. "Liz, it's Tuesday night. I interpret your silence with only a week and a half until the wedding to mean you haven't decided not to go ahead with it. I'll consider your further silence to mean I should move ahead on our plans. Please call me by no later than Friday night if I'm wrong. Eric still loves you. So do I, dear."

Liz stopped the tape. "And what if I hadn't come home before Friday night?" How she wished she hadn't! Then things would be out of her hands. She'd have had to go through with the wedding then, wouldn't she? To prevent a disgrace on her family even greater than what she'd inflict by calling her mother right now and saying, "No, Mother, I'm not going through with it. I'm in love with Zack, and even if being in love doesn't matter, as you say—and you know, Mother, you know so very very many things I can only guess at—even if it doesn't matter, well not being in love does, at least I think it does, and I'm not in love with Eric."

She picked up the receiver. She would call her mother now, and bring an end to this ridiculous charade. Then she decided to wait. With a trembling hand she replaced the receiver in the cradle. It could wait until she'd at least picked up the other messages. Maybe her mother had called again since last night. She'd expect that Liz would call in from wherever she'd been the past few days and pick up her messages. But she might double-check. Grace wouldn't leave it to chance. Grace never left anything to chance.

Liz should have known that. When her mother had been in her office Friday, Liz had had her chance to take control of the situation herself. How easy it would have been then! When her mother had said, "What shall I tell Eric?" Liz should have, could have said, "Tell him the wedding is off." And Grace would have known she meant it. And that would have been that.

Why had she not let it be that? On Friday she had been sure. Not any longer!

She had left Phoenix and Zack this morning because she was no longer sure. The intensity of her passion frightened her. The excitement of being with him, of playing detective with him, of disappearing from home and telling no one, of throwing herself into intrigue and mystery, terrified her. Not because she had learned anything inherently terrifying in what either she or Zack had discovered. Even recognizing the hospital lab tech as the one who had broken into her office wasn't in itself frightening. It angered more than frightened her, for now she would alert the police, who could easily apprehend him. What appalled her was that she was running away—not from herself, not from her life, not from her family—she was running away from making up her mind about whether or not she wanted to run away. She'd known it last night. Worse, Zack was beginning to know it.

And still she could not face it. She could not call her mother yet. She still wanted something to happen, to take it out of her hands.

She wanted to be pregnant with Zack's child. And she might be about to be. She had told him the truth about the timing, about the exposure. His semen, which for the past few days had poured into her, would probably be rich with sperm. In preparation for marriage, she had not used oral contraceptives for the whole year. Her periods were regular, and she knew when she ovulated. She had lain with him inside her yesterday and again last night, so as not to allow a single drop of his semen to escape. She wanted to be pregnant so she would not have to make up her mind. If she was pregnant with Zack's child, she could not marry Eric next week. He would know, and it would destroy him.

But the wedding was not far enough away. She wouldn't know for sure that she was pregnant, at least would not know in time to have the pregnancy make up her mind. The timing was all wrong. She'd have to make up her own mind—but not until Friday afternoon. She still had till Friday afternoon.

There were three more messages. *Go through them. Maybe you'll find something in one of them that will take it off your shoulders, Liz.*

A call from a woman friend wanting to know how she was. "Haven't seen you for ages." *Haven't we invited Carole to the wedding?* she thought. Yes, she was sure Carole was on the list. Strange she would call just a week and a half before—

She hurriedly went on to the next message, a call from Bob Ryan: "Liz, tried to get you at your office. No one seems to know where you are. Something important came up. Please call me as soon as you can. At home if you want. Here's my home number."

"Oh God! One of my patients! I've never done that before, gone off and not told anyone how to reach me. I hope nothing happened to one of the patients he operated on. Better call back right away."

She replayed the message to write down his number, then sat down at her rosewood desk and called him.

"Liz! Jesus, I'm glad you got my message. Didn't mean to upset you. I realized later you might think something went wrong with one of your patients."

She sighed. "I did. But I never should have gone off without telling someone where to reach me."

"You looked awfully upset the other night in the cafeteria. I hope everything's all right." His concern comforted her, and she was glad to be focused for the moment on something outside herself.

"I've been going through a personal crisis. But I'm fine. What's on your mind?"

"It's what you told me the other night. About the symptoms of porphyria, and how exploratory surgery might seem to cure it because of transfusions. At the time I didn't think of it, but in surgery this morning I was doing a cholecystectomy, and I suddenly remembered something."

"What's that, Bob?"

"Three years ago I had a cholecystectomy patient. She did fine for a couple of days, except for trouble sleeping."

"Not unusual after surgery."

"No. Then suddenly one night she had terrible pain. At first the resident thought it was gas. Lots of excess peristalsis. Gave her something for that, and increased her sedation. Then not long afterward she starts screaming and writhing. We couldn't take a chance something hadn't come loose inside, so we opened her up again. Still nothing. We gave her blood because of the two surgeries in a few days. Her second recovery went fine."

"So, in retrospect you think it's porphyria? Could be. I'd be interested in looking at her if you want."

"You can't."

"Oh?"

"I'd bet it was porphyria, Liz. Not just because the transfusion cured her. There's more. I'd ordered phenobarb for sleep. Partly because she was a very nervous kind of lady."

"Bob! That was probably what brought on the attack. What happened with her then?"

"That's the reason I thought it was important to call you. She's dead, Liz. Her body was one of the ones that were dug up in the woods last month. She just up and disappeared from the hospital in the middle of the night."

Liz gripped the edge of the desk and sat bolt upright. "Ruth Manyon Spencer!"

"Yes. And, well, it sounds farfetched, but your patient with porphyria disappeared and I thought—"

"But you never diagnosed her. Nobody knew she had porphyria. So how could that—" She gasped.

"What's the matter, Liz?"

"Her father had a disfiguring disease. He lived in Africa. I wonder if it could have been South Africa. There's a genetic strain among South Africans. Bob, you must have run tests of all kinds. Urine tests before the second surgery."

"Well, I did. But not for porphyria, Liz. I never dreamed of it."

"The technician!"

"What technician?"

"Bob, you're right. You never ran a porphyria test on her. But somebody else could. He'd just have to let the urine rest till the porphyrins showed up."

"But why would anyone do that?"

"I don't know why, but I think I know who. And you're right. There is a connection between your patient and mine. And I'm afraid Agnes Shultz met the same fate as Ruth Manyon Spencer. And now I know why he stole Agnes's records, too."

"Why?"

"It's a matter of genealogy, Bob. He knows that porphyria can be genetic. He's looking for her relatives, and I've listed a slew in her record. The worst thing is, Agnes doesn't have the genetic strain. And neither did Ruth's cousins on her mother's side of the family. Those were the ones he killed and buried with knives in their hearts."

"He must be crazy. Burying people with knives in their hearts. Why in the hell—"

Liz let out a small cry. "He left them in their hearts! Of course! Bob, he was killing *vampires!* Dear God, the man thought he was killing vampires. He left them with a stake in their hearts so they wouldn't come back to life!"

"But nobody really believes that shit, Liz. It was just a clever theory by a well meaning scientist."

"Yes, but after the media blew it out of proportion, lots of innocent people believed it. Agnes Shultz's husband believed it enough to kidnap his children. And he's not even a madman. You don't have to live in Philadelphia very long to know there are lots of crazies out there. And one of them believes Dr. Dolphin's vampire disease theory. And he works in UMC. Bob, we have to stop him. Somehow we have to stop him before he kills somebody else."

CHAPTER TWELVE

Meanwhile, Phoenix—Zack

When he returned to the hotel room smelling even worse than he had the previous day, he was overwhelmed by its loneliness without Liz and by his own incongruous presence in this setting without her. He wasn't sure he should stay another two days in such expensive, voluptuous surroundings, yet he couldn't leave. The essence of her had permeated the bedclothes and closet and drawers. He would have to stay and breathe it in.

It's amazing how essences don't let go, he thought ironically as he stuffed still another outfit into the plastic laundry bag for disposal. This trip had been more expensive than he had expected. He had only two more sets of shirts and jeans with him, and one would be sacrificed tomorrow when he would go back to Chet's house again. Well, at least he hadn't had to give Chet the hundred dollars. And he probably wouldn't have to. The old man wanted him to come back again for only one reason: He wanted to lose some of his pain in the companionship of a human being who cared for him; he had to hang onto this unaccustomed currency for as long as possible.

How little of that currency is around, Zack thought. How few and how easy the sacrifices you have to make to exchange it! What were two sets of clothes? What was getting your hands in vomit compared to having someone's hands clean you up and clothe you, having someone say, "I'll be back to see you tomorrow"?

He took his shower, and all the bad smells went away, but the essence of the old man's need clung to him still. The experience of the day would never leave him. It had changed him too much.

Adventures like this always changed you, he thought as he dried himself and put on the Hyatt bathrobe. *They might end, and for a while you'd go around with a kink in your gut, wishing that they hadn't, but later you'd know you had to have them because you had to change or your life meant nothing.* How Maryellen had changed him! And his adventure with her had ended. How Poke had changed him! How Chet had changed him! And, oh, how Liz had changed him! And all of those adventures would end, sooner or later.

No, not with Liz! I'll keep that from ending somehow!

There was one way he could hold her, no matter what happened. He had a way of doing it. Even if she chose to leave him, he could call her back whenever he wanted to. He could see her day after day, watch her change through the years, view her from every angle, still and in motion.

He turned on his computer and loaded the composite drawing program he'd created and spent the next few hours re-creating her, putting together her profile, placing her eyes at just the right spot relative to her nose and hairline, designing a forelock that would fall forward over her brows when she'd become exasperated, making lips that smiled, half smiled, looked serious, parted slightly with desire, a tongue to flick out and run over them. He coded in color, though he couldn't see it on this computer. His home computer had an extensive palette; it would capture the amethyst eyes, the many golds of her hair, the tawny shade of her skin. Someday he'd go beyond her face and head, and draw in her body. He'd have to study that more, see it from different angles. The adventure would have to last at least a little bit longer for that. He knew now it couldn't last forever. That was impossible. But just a little longer—

The telephone rang. He looked up with a start and realized the sun had set. The clock on the nightstand between the beds said 9:06. He hadn't eaten since breakfast and wasn't hungry. No one but Liz and Eve Carter knew where he was staying. He'd called Eve late this afternoon on his daily check and knew things were fine. Poke had gone home to finish up some homework, and she'd tell her he'd called. And Poke wouldn't call back. She was a little angry at him still.

So it had to be Liz. She was the only one who'd call him after midnight. She probably wanted to tell him she'd arrived home safely and that she loved him and missed him.

He picked up the phone on the nightstand while keeping his eyes on her picture on the computer screen.

"Zack!" she said. Her voice sounded strained, frenetic.

"Are you OK?"

"Yes. But something's happened. Gus Champus isn't the killer. You can stay there if you want, but it might pay for you to come home."

He sank onto the bed. "How do you know he's not the killer?"

"Because I know who is and why. It's horrible, Zack. And mad!"

A stab of disappointment struck his breastbone. A wild-goose chase! Nothing had come out of this trip. His hunch, the essence of a good detective, was off base by 2500 miles! "Are you sure?"

"I wouldn't call you now if I weren't."

"This trip was a waste!"

He heard her draw a sharp breath. "No," she said after a moment, "if it weren't for the trip, we couldn't have put it together. If I hadn't been there to see that program, if you hadn't insisted I make those calls, we wouldn't have all the connections between Agnes Shultz and Ruth Manyon Spencer."

He knit his brow and rubbed his beard. "What connections? What does the program have to do with Ruth Manyon Spencer? What did those calls have to do with Agnes Shultz?"

"Everything, Zack. Both of them had porphyria. They were both killed—and I know now Agnes is dead—by a man who believed they were vampires."

Zack sat stunned, his left hand stopping in midstroke on his chin, his right tightly gripping the receiver. Only his eyes moved as Liz explained how she'd put together all the clues, including the silver cross and the knives left in the chests of all the victims.

"It had to be the lab technician, Zack. He's the only one who could be connected to both. Bob Ryan is going to check the microfiche at the hospital tomorrow to see who was on duty in the lab when Ruth's emergency urine specimen was taken. Meanwhile, I'll take the floppy disks to Crosby and tell him all I know. It would help if you were here, Zack. Can you leave tomorrow morning?"

He hesitated. Then he quickly explained what had happened with Chet. "I'd feel like hell not showing up, Liz. But I don't have to stay long. I'll check out of the hotel before I go to his house and get a flight out as soon after noon as I can."

After a moment's silence, she said, "I love you, Zack."

He looked at her face on the screen. "Oh, Liz, I love you so much. Do you know what I've been doing since I got back to this room? I've been making an image of you with my program to keep you here."

"Oh, Zack. I—"

"I can look at you. I'm looking at you now. I can turn your face from side to side. I can watch you smile or cry."

He thought he could hear her crying now.

"Liz, I can't stand being without you. Please don't marry that guy."

"Zack," she said. "Oh, Zack." Then after saying nothing for an endless time, she said, "Let me know what flight you're taking. I'll pick you up at the airport."

"Liz—"

"Yes?" she whispered.

"I'll call you first thing in the morning."

"I'll be here."

He hung up the phone. Then he returned to the computer and turned her face away from him, so he could see the back of her head. "Good night, Liz," he said before switching off the machine.

The gnawing in his stomach felt less like hunger than grief, but he knew from experience food would help. No longer able to stay in this room without her, he dressed and went downstairs to the hotel coffee shop where he ordered a hamburger and fries and a Coors. Though he ate and drank without tasting anything, the meal did take the edge off his emptiness. He paid the check and went out for another walk around the Civic Plaza. The evening was cooler than last evening, but it felt much warmer than Philadelphia. Tourists swarmed around the Plaza. From the snatches of conversation he heard, he figured most of them were conventioneers of one kind or another. They were all talking about business deals and today's speakers and how it was hotter here than they'd expected this time of year. He hadn't known what to expect, so it really didn't matter to him.

After another fifteen minutes he knew he couldn't find solace here, so he went back up to his room and turned on a TV movie. Since he seldom watched movies and had no idea from the title what it was about, he didn't realize it was a vampire movie until he'd watched quite a while. He switched to another channel, then from channel to channel, and after a while remembered why he seldom watched TV. He flicked it off, changed from his clothes into his pajamas, and lay down in the bed that didn't have Liz's smell in it. Maybe because of jet lag, which he hadn't allowed himself to give in to over the past few days, he fell into a deep sleep.

The telephone jarred him out of it. His hands fumbled over the nightstand, finally coordinating with his eyes when they focused on the blinking red telephone light. After first knocking the receiver to the floor, he got it in hand and to his ear at last.

"Zack? Zack, it's Eve. Something terrible's happened. Oh, Zack, I'm sorry! Please come home."

He bolted upright. "What! What are you talking about?"

"Oh, Zack. Poke's disappeared. We've been looking for her for hours. Somebody broke into your house through the basement. The police have been there. There was no sign she was hurt there or anything, but she called me earlier and sounded real upset. Told me she needed more time for her homework and insisted I shouldn't go pick her up before nine-thirty. The police think she's been abducted. But she must have walked out on her own. She took her key with her and—"

"Why did you wait so long to call! Jesus Christ! Poke! God!"

She sobbed into the phone. "I—I thought she might have just gone somewhere. Out for a walk in the rain. She liked to do that. And then, when the police came and found some traces of wet footprints, a dog's and a man's and what looked like hers leading away from the house, it looked like she might have gone for a walk with a neighbor. The police asked around about who had a dog, but nobody knew anything—"

Zack paced back and forth between the beds as far as the phone cord allowed, trying to make sense of what she said, trying to tell himself that this was some awful nightmare. "How could you let her out of your sight! How could you let her go out of the house in the dark? Why didn't Christy stay there with her?"

"Zack, I didn't! She—she—I'm sorry. I'm sure she's OK. She wouldn't have gone with someone she didn't know. Not without fighting. There's no sign of a fight—I, oh, Zack." She began to sob again.

"Jesus, Eve—I shouldn't've blamed you."

"Come straight home, Zack. Please. Maybe you can tell the police something. They'll find her, I know. She'll be all right."

He began to sob. After a few moments, he composed himself enough to begin to think things out. "I'll get a flight out as soon as I can."

"I'll pick you up at the airport."

"No. I can get someone else. I've got to call someone else right away. I'll call you when I get home. Good-bye, Eve."

He slammed down the phone and turned on the lamp and found Liz's phone number, thinking how strange it was he'd never called her before. It rang a few times before she answered, sleep in her voice.

He heard her gasp when he told her what had happened.

Her voice controlled and firm, she said, "I'll pick you up. Get the seven-twenty A.M. flight. The one you put me on. It'll get you here just after five. There's no use trying to fly out tonight. Not that you'll sleep. But you have to have time to get yourself together. First, call the airline. Then pack your things. Then have room service send up something to eat. Nothing stimulating. No alcohol. Warm milk and a turkey sandwich, something like that. It'll make you feel calmer, if that's possible. Then check out of the hotel. I've already signed a charge through Friday. Tomorrow morning, take the courtesy shuttle from the hotel to the airport. Just leave the car there. I'll call the rental company to pick it up. So the only thing you'll have to deal with is picking up your ticket at the airport."

"Liz—"

"Hush! Just take it one step at a time. When they start serving on the plane, get yourself something good and strong to drink, and hunker down for the flight. You'll change flights in Pittsburgh, but the gates are practically next door. I'll be waiting for you when you touch down in Philly."

"Dear person—"

"I love you, Zack. We'll find Poke and she'll be all right, I promise you. Whatever we have to do to get her back, we will.

Thursday evening, Philadelphia

He arrived at the gate, eyes red and swollen, face gray, crumpled and unshaven, uncharacteristically bent by the weight of his luggage. Liz took a deep breath before going to him and embracing him. He set down the computer and garment bag and held onto her. He smelled of tears, fatigue, and alcohol, a sour, needy smell. She would have to hold him up, she knew. Hold herself up, to hold him up.

"Come on," she said at last. "Let's go to the car." She picked up the garment bag.

He nodded and picked up the computer.

In the car she listened to his gratitude: He could not bear this without her; he could not have gotten this far; her words, her taking his hand and leading him step by step across the country, her being here made all the difference, made a man of him.

She did not tell him that he had made a woman of her. That was not what he needed now. He needed hope, and there was some to give him, a frightening, awful kind of hope, but hope. But she would not tell him until they got to his house. It would be too painful for him to bear for the forty whole minutes beside her. She would wait until he could act on the hope.

She had already begun to act on it since she'd come home from meeting Crosby at the precinct headquarters this morning and found the message on her machine. It was a simple, frightening message: "Dr. Broward, the girl is unharmed. I will release her only through you. She will leave only after you and I are left together for long enough to cure you of your evil disease, as I have cured your patient. It's a permanent cure, Doctor. What a shame you neglected to use it. But it's not too late. The girl will leave messages for her father. He must make the arrangements to get her back. Hssst!"

She had played it three times, and known its meaning better with every playing. And with every playing, she knew more of what she had to do. Her first call had been to Crosby. He'd agreed that with all the information she and Bob Ryan had gathered—the suspected killer's name and address; that he worked as a lab technician in both the diagnostic and pathology labs, sometimes as a diener and morgue attendant; that he'd signed off on Ruth Manyon Spencer's preoperative urine tests; that he might have had access to her the night she disappeared—the most important things they knew were that he was delusional, probably hallucinatory, and had a dog, probably vicious. They could not simply apprehend him. They could not afford to back him into a corner. They had to play for time, and they had to have a plan—a plan that would work on him *only because he was mad. A plan that would compel him to act upon his madness!*

"It might work," Bob Ryan had said when she had outlined her idea for him in his office. "He's certainly crazy enough to go for it. But, Liz, it's too damn risky. An overdose of either agent could kill you. The phenobarb in the Donnatal can make you stop breathing. The methacholine can throw you into cardiac arrest."

"Yes, I know that," she had said. "But Gary Hoffman will be ready when I get to the ER."

"He's good, the best cardiologist you could find. But even with that precaution, you're risking your life."

"Maybe."

After studying her from across his desk for a few moments, he'd shaken his head. "You're not risking your life for a patient, are you Liz? You're risking it for a lover."

She'd held his eyes with hers for a moment. "I'm doing it for myself, Bob."

He'd nodded briefly. "Does he know how risky it is for you?"

"I haven't told him the plan yet. He's on his way back right now. With that program we need to carry it out. He'll know it's risky for all of us; he won't know how risky it is for me. I'm counting on you not to tell him."

He'd risen and walked around his desk and bent and kissed her. "OK, I'll coordinate things with Brian Horner. Zack and he can meet in my office tomorrow morning and use my computer. I'll get the portable methacholine outfit from respiratory therapy right now. It should fit in your satchel. You have the Donnatal?"

She'd stood, then. "Yes. Plenty in my office."

"The timing has to be perfect, Liz."

"I know. As soon as you've set things up with the ER and pathology, let me know. I'll phone in from my office five minutes before taking the methacholine. It should take about fifteen minutes for Jim to get me to the hospital."

Bob furrowed his brow. "You're sure you shouldn't tell him what's going on?"

"I'm sure. He's got to be scared as hell, and look it."

"Even if you told him, he'd be scared as hell. I am."

"I will be, too. Scared it won't work. Scared that Poke—" She'd swallowed then and shaken her head. "Whatever happens to me, Bob, the rest of the plan has to go through. Promise me that. Promise me the rest of you will get that child back to her father, no matter what happens to me."

And he'd embraced her and nodded his head and promised.

Now, just two hours later, she drove her gold Mercedez-Benz up a quiet Glenside street and pulled into Zack's driveway. He was staring at his house as if he had never before seen it.

She stopped the car and put her hand on his. "Before we go in, I want to tell you something. Poke is all right. At least for now. She's been kidnapped for ransom. We know who has her and what we have to do to free her."

He stared at her. "You know? How? Why didn't you tell me till now?"

"I didn't tell you because I am the ransom."

"You—" He half shook his head.

"Yes. He must have followed me here. That night I ran out in the rain. He was after me, and he knew that he couldn't get away with coming back to my office, and that he couldn't get through security at my apartment."

He drew his hand out from under hers and stared uncomprehendingly at her. He drew away from her against the car door, but made no move to open it.

"He must have decided that this was the best place to get to me. He probably cased the house, observed your activities, saw us leave the house empty, then broke in and waited for the chance. Poke gave it to him Wednesday night."

He kept on staring at her, shaking his head, seeming somehow afraid of her, untrusting of her.

"It's me he's after, Zack. He left a message on my machine. He said Poke left one on yours. Come on. Let's go inside." She reached for his hand, saw him twitch it away from hers, and stopped in mid-gesture.

Stung to the quick, she pulled her hand back and drew a deep, tremulous breath. She'd known he'd be horrified, but hadn't expected he'd turn so much anger on her. By throwing herself into action, by working out the details of the plan to free Poke and foil Phillip Trapp with his own madness, she'd avoided being angry at herself for bringing this terror into his house. Now she must face the full brunt of it, encompassed and magnified in his. It was worse than her father's anger, worse than any anger she'd known. She whipped her head around to face her window, her face and eyes blistering with his and her aggregate fury.

After several moments she heard him draw a breath and open the car door and get out. He opened the rear door and took out his computer and garment bag, and started to his front door.

Catching her breath she got out of the car and followed him onto the porch. He unlocked his door, then shut it on her just as she was about to step in.

"No Zack, don't—"

The lock clicked as she reached for the knob. She shook the knob, then dropped her hand. She waited for several minutes, the time it took for her trembling to stop, then walked down the steps to the walk. She didn't hear the door open behind her; she did hear him say in a barely audible whisper, "I can't listen to it, Liz. Not unless you're here with me."

She turned and walked back up the stairs, then followed him through the door and into the family room. Without turning on the light, he walked to the telephone table and pressed the message button on his machine. Then he stepped back away from it, and the two of them listened as it plodded through eight long messages. Neither dared to skip through any of them; they needed the time to be ready, as if they could ever be ready, to hear message number nine with all of the hope and dread it would deliver.

"Daddy, I'm OK."

"Oh, Poke!" He threw his hands over his face. A line of the message was lost.

"—won't hurt me."

A growling sound, and the whine of a dog. In the background his voice, "Hssst! No, Adolph. Sit!"

"He won't let Adolph hurt me, either. He says I can come home if you bring Dr. Broward to him so she can get cured. She has a terrible disease. It makes her turn into a vampire, and he knows how to cure it. Please, Daddy, make Dr. Broward come. He'll let me go if she comes. And she'll get better, too. She won't drink blood anymore and make other people sick. He saw her sitting in her car just down the street from us drinking some blood."

The dog barked and growled.

Poke cried out, "Daddy!"

Then Phillip got on the phone. "Your daughter will be all right. She will call you back on Sunday morning and tell you where to bring Dr. Broward. Hssst!"

The next message began to play.

Zack turned to look at Liz. "What are we going to do?"

"Give him what he wants, Zack. Me. Only we won't wait until Sunday. And we won't go to his house."

"But he wants to kill you, doesn't he? He wants to put one of his knives through your heart."

"Yes. And we're going to give him every possible chance to try. And he's going to think he succeeded. Because of my love for you, Zack—and because of your love for me, and because of his madness, it will all be possible."

Then she took him by the hand and sat down on the sofa next to him and told him the plan, what he had to do, step by step, what she would be doing step by step.

His eyes widened when she told him what would happen after she'd be rushed to the emergency room.

"You won't have to watch any of that," she said, "but when it's over, you'll know that it worked because of you."

"Yes, I think I can help make it work." He shuddered. "I couldn't watch. I can't even stand to imagine it, Liz. Seeing—"

She reached over and placed one long graceful finger over his lips. "Try not to imagine it. Just imagine Poke running out of that house into your arms."

"Yes. Yes. Oh, God, it's got to work, Liz."

She stood up. "Right now you need some sleep. I've brought you something." She crossed to the telephone table where she'd set down her tote bag and pulled out a small vial of pills.

"Soma," she said, as she poured one into his hand. "A mild muscle relaxant. Take it with a glass of water. It'll help, and you should be alert in the morning when you're working with Brian Horner."

He stood up. "What will you be doing tomorrow, Liz?"

"Putting some last details in place. Going over the setup at the hospital. And maybe just praying." She turned herself half away from him. "And I have to call my mother."

"Will you stay here with me tonight? I don't want to be alone."

She turned toward him again and touched his face. "Neither do I. I need to stay with you, sleep with you, hold you all night."

♦ ♦

She lay beside him, touching his hand until it twitched to tell her that exhaustion combined with the Soma was carrying him off, finally, to sleep. Then she turned on her side facing toward him, let her arm fall across his waist, and allowed herself to fall asleep, too.

She woke about two in the morning to find her arm still around his waist; but he had turned on his side facing away from her, his knees drawn up in a semi-fetal position. Her hand had fallen on his penis, and it had grown hard. She realized that he, too, had awakened, and she tightened her hand on him.

He sighed and turned to her, and she lifted her leg over his hip and brought him into her. With her hands holding both sides of his face, his mouth pulled tightly against hers so that her cries had no place to go but into him, she loved him with a love so fierce it could leave no room for despair. She knew they might never lie together again, that this might be the love that challenged death to try and wrest her from him, him from her. The exquisite pain and pleasure of what might be her final act of love for him girded her soul. She would leave his bed in the morning ready to face what she must.

Of all the tasks she faced on Friday, the most difficult was her call to her mother. Rather than getting it over with the moment she arrived home to change her clothes in the morning, she put it off, first until after she'd spoken to Bob Ryan again, then until after talking to Crosby, then until after an emergency afternoon appointment with her lawyer regarding changes in her will.

At last, after a light supper and a heavy dose of sherry, she listened to her mother's message again, erased it, and, without sitting down, dialed the number.

Grace answered on the first ring. Clearly she had been waiting for the call.

"Liz! Where have you been? Nobody seems to know."

"Traveling, Mother. I had to get away."

"To think things out, I suppose."

"Yes." She sipped her second glass of sherry. One glass usually was enough to take the edge off of her anxiety. The first had hardly touched her.

"And? Have you thought them out?" Liz could picture her sitting at her French antique desk, running a perfectly manicured, red-tipped finger around the leather trimmed desk pad.

"Not perfectly. Mother, I'm ill. I—I have to ask you to postpone things."

She must have sat forward abruptly as Liz heard something brush against the phone mouthpiece. "Ill? Has all of this brought something on?"

"I'm not sure. That is, I don't think it has anything to do with anxiety. I'm having—certain symptoms."

"What kind of symptoms? What's the matter, Liz?"

She took a large draught of the amber liquid, gasping slightly at its bite into her esophagus. She coughed and excused herself for a moment while she swallowed down some saliva. Then she said in a hoarse voice, "I'm having tests done tomorrow. Gary Hoffman's doing them."

"The cardiologist! You're not having heart trouble."

Keeping the irony out of her voice she said, "It may be. The symptoms are ambiguous. But persistent over the last couple of weeks. Enough to keep me from work—"

"But you left town?"

"I didn't want to face the truth. Of what it might be. It's frightening, Mother."

"Oh, Liz, why didn't you say something! If I'd known I'd never have—"

"It's nothing you did. It's nothing anyone did. It just happened. Anyway, tomorrow I'll know more. After the tests."

"You'll call me right away."

"I promise you'll know as soon as it's over. But either way, I can't go through with things." Things—not the wedding—the closest she could get to the truth was "things." "Not now. You'll have to postpone." Postpone—not cancel. But not from indecision, this time; simply because to cancel might become unnecessary. "I'm sorry."

After a moment, Grace said, "I'll take care of it. Don't worry. Just get well, darling Liz. Please, baby, get well."

"It may just be something minor, Mother."

"Get well."

"Mother—"

"Yes?"

"Tell Eric I'm sorry. Tell Daddy I'm sorry. Mother, please forgive me, please tell Daddy to forgive me. No matter what."

"You know we all love you, Liz. Not to forgive you would be impossible."

"I love you, Mother. Good-bye."
"Good-bye, dear."

She hung up the phone, quickly, and finished the sherry in a single gulp. Now, whatever happened, Grace would be ready. Liz would be ready. If tomorrow was ready, let it come.

CHAPTER THIRTEEN

The Moon to Blood

Saturday, 8:30 A.M.

"Dr. Broward! You're back. Are you all right? You look—" said Claire as Liz hurried through the reception room and through the door leading to the back offices.

"I came in to pick something up. Is Dr. Meredith in yet?" She looked past Claire to the hallway. Jim's office door was closed.

"He's seeing a patient. We didn't know where you were. I gave your home number to a patient. I hope you don't m—"

So that was how Trapp had got her home number.

"If you're talking about Jill James, it's all right. She reached me."

The receptionist looked relieved. "I didn't want to—"

"Claire," said Liz, touched by the woman's devotion to duty, "I trust your judgment. You know when I have a special relationship with a family. Thank you for taking the intiative. It was a terribly important call." She placed her hand briefly on Claire's arm.

Claire's face relaxed. "Oh, then I'm so glad I did it. Will you be back to work Monday?"

After a pause Liz said, "I'm not sure, Claire." Then she started back to her office.

Jim's door opened as she passed. "Liz! I didn't expect you back," he said as he ushered a woman out and directed her to an examining room. As the woman disappeared inside, he looked at her worriedly. "You look exhausted, Liz. Vacation didn't help, eh?"

"If anything, it made me feel worse. I don't know. I've been under terrible stress, and it's taking a physical toll."

The freckles on his brow darkened and knit together. "It's not like you to react to stress that way. Are you sure there's nothing else wrong?"

"I—I hope not. But I'm feeling bad enough. I have to get something from my office, then I'm heading straight home to bed."

He took her arm and squeezed it. "Good. Oh, by the way, your mother called."

"When?"

"Thursday, I think. She was terribly concerned because you hadn't returned her call to your machine and nobody seemed to know where you were."

Taking a deep breath and swallowing, she said, "I didn't pick up my messages till I got home. I talked to her last night, though. She knows I'm back."

"Good. Well, you better get what you need and go home. I don't want to lose a perfectly good if somewhat stressed-out partner." He winked and went to the examining room and closed himself inside with his patient.

For a moment she could not move. Then she gathered up her resolve once more and went into her office and closed the door behind her. She didn't immediately let go of the knob, but leaned back against it to steady herself. Waves of fear rushed at her, buckling her legs, undermining her footing. For one stunning moment she felt faint; for another she felt impelled to turn and flee.

No, Liz! Do it! You have to go through with it!

She straightened her back and let go of the knob, and strode purposefully across the office and set her satchel on her desk. Holding onto the desk edge, she pulled out the drawer filled with medicine samples. She rummaged through it, looking for Donnatal elixir.

"Damn it!" Of course there was none. The only samples she had were tablets. They would never do. They wouldn't work quickly enough, even in her tense, empty stomach. There was elixir in the office, in two places: in the locked medicine cabinet in the lab room, and in the pediatric examining room.

To get it from the lab meant picking up the key from Claire's reception desk. The pediatric examining room was the better choice. She went there. The door was closed. The chart in the door pocket meant a patient was in there waiting for Jim. She realized suddenly that Jim had a full schedule of patients who would not be seen because of her. At least one of them was a child.

Poke is a child! She reminded herself. *Zack's child! Almost like my own. And I'm the one who put her in danger.*

She ran to Claire's fortunately empty cubicle and took the medicine key from her drawer. She hurried back to the lab room, also vacant, and unlocked the medicine cabinet. From the cabinet she extracted a bottle of green liquid, put it into her suit pocket, and relocked the door.

She then ran back into her office just as Claire, who served as nursing assistant on Saturdays, came out of an examining room door, a chart in her hand. Liz would have to get the key back to her drawer without calling attention to her trip to the cabinet. If Jim found out she'd been there, he might figure out her scheme and the whole operation could fall through. Perhaps she should have told him, and made him a conscious agent in the plan.

But, no. He never would have allowed her to take that risk. It had to be done this way.

Once more behind the closed door of her office, she went back to her desk and opened her satchel. When she saw the inhalation kit inside, fear overcame her again. She sat frozen, one hand reaching into her pocket for the Donnatal, the other poised above the inhaler with the methacholine in it.

Then she grasped both at once and put them in front of her on the desk. For a moment she stared at them. They looked so innocent: one a medicine mild enough at proper dosage to calm the bowels of children, the other in proper dosage a safe diagnostic tool to help uncover clinically inapparent asthma. Liz did not plan to take them in proper dosage. Either one in the dose she planned to take could kill her. But she did not plan to take only one, she planned to take both. If Dr. Gary Hoffman's theory was right, if the timing and the counterbalancing effect of the medicines were on target, she should make it to the hospital emergency room on time. But she had little room for error, *and no one had tested Gary's theory before her.*

She unscrewed the Donnatal bottle cap and measured four tablespoonfuls into a clear plastic drinking glass. Then she checked the inhaler valves and readied the small mask to be drawn over her mouth and nose.

All was in order. She grasped the telephone receiver and called the hospital emergency room triage desk.

"It's Liz Broward, Jennie," she told the nurse, the only one on the ER staff involved in their delicate plan. "You should be getting a call from Jim Meredith in less than ten minutes."

"Everything's ready, Liz. Gary's briefed the special cardiac team. The others don't know a thing. God bless you. We love you."

"Thank you, Jennie." She slowly lowered the receiver into the cradle.

After looking again at the paraphernalia on her desk, she rose and walked to her office window and slanted the blinds downward so she could see the street below. She realized she had never looked down at it before, and couldn't recall the last time she'd walked it. She always came into her office through the parking garage, which opened to the rear of the building, and she could barely remember what the front looked like.

My God! How little I've seen of the world. Even the parts closest to me.

Stunned by a craving to look at and remember at least this one small part, she turned and ran toward the door. She could make it down and back in five minutes. Yes! She promised herself she would just run down and back up.

But no! She stopped herself. Her hunger was a lust to escape, a ruse thrown up by fear in the face of her will to be brave. She'd allowed herself too much time already. She should have said she'd call two minutes before taking the Donnatal, not five. Or she should have poured it and checked the inhaler after making the call instead of before. That had been a mistake. It had given fear a chance to work on her.

It had also given her the chance to face it down. And now she did so. She walked slowly, deliberately back to her desk and sat down. There were two minutes more. Second by second she counted the first minute down.

Fear grabbed her again and shook her by the shoulders. *You don't have to do it, Liz, you can fake it! Who would know?* fear whispered to her. She had argued that out before, with Bob and Gary and Jennie and their fear. Yes, and with her own. But she knew she could not fake it. She had seen cardiac emergencies and would know immediately when they were real or fake. No, it had to be this way to convince Jim and the ER team who would be readied outside the entrance with their oxygen and IV kits the moment she showed up. *And to convince him!* She fought panic down once more.

Now only ten seconds remained. She lifted the clear plastic glass with its less than an inch of green liquid at the bottom. As if in a toast, she said, "OK, Gary Hoffman, we'll see if this thing's going to work." Quickly, she drank down the sweet, minty potion.

She knew if she waited she'd feel the soothing effects of the elixir's near tablespoonful of alcohol within minutes. That alone might make the next step easier; but she couldn't afford the luxury. She tossed the empty glass into her wastebasket, put the bottle of Donnatal into her satchel, and placed the small mask of the inhaler over her mouth and nose and quickly sucked in six deep inhalations of methacholine.

She'd barely shoved the inhaler back into her bag and snapped it shut when her chest tightened and her heart began to palpitate in a wild, erratic rhythm. Terrified by the stunning sensation, she pushed herself to her feet. Wheezing and sweating, she staggered to her office door. Her face felt about to burst. She scarcely could turn the knob, and nearly fell backward in pulling open the door.

"Claire!" She coughed and choked.

The woman came running toward her. "Dr. Broward—Liz *Oh, God, what's happening!*"

Liz clutched at her chest. "Heart—get Jim—" She slumped to the floor. *Head up. Don't lie down.* She fought to keep her head upright. She clawed to get near the wall so she could lean against it.

"Jim!" Claire shouted. "Liz just collapsed!" She ran to an

examining room and pushed open the door. "Liz! She's having a heart attack!"

Jim flew to Liz, took one look, and said, "Call the ER! Tell them I'm bringing her in and to have a cardiac team ready." He scooped her up in his arms and carried her through the door to the waiting room. A wide-eyed man held the front door open, and preceded them down the corridor to the parking garage door, which he also opened and held.

"God bless you, Doctor," the patient said.

Jim took no time to answer. He strode to his Lincoln, which was always parked just a few spaces from the door, coded in his lock combination, and opened the rear door. "OK, Liz. You're going to be OK."

She wheezed and clutched at her chest. She could barely catch her breath. Any moment she thought she'd lose consciousness. Not too soon. She'd never expected such agony, never dreamed of such terror.

He sat her, back propped against the door, legs along the seat, left shoulder against the back of the seat. He fastened a seat belt around her to hold her. "We'll be there in five or six minutes. Hold on, baby. Hold on, partner."

"Hurry."

He was in his seat before the word was out of her mouth, and soon she felt the rocking of the car as it spiraled down through the garage. The garage gate was open, and a security guard was clearing traffic so that Jim's car could get directly through into the street.

"Atta girl, Claire!" he said. "Always great in an emergency."

Liz had counted on that—had counted on both of them. During the brief moment she remained lucid, she prayed they'd forgive her for the anxiety she caused by dragging them into this. But she had to drag them—they would have stopped her if they had known. And she knew they would forgive her when they realized the stakes in her gamble with death: the life of a child she loved dearly.

She lost consciousness, regained it, lost it again, and once again regained it a second before Jim pulled the car up to the emergency room entrance. Through all the incredible suffering, she felt a stab of joy as the paramedical team converged on them and lifted her from the car onto a gurney, taped an oxygen tube onto her nose, and inserted an IV needle into the back of her hand, all the while wheeling her on whispering wheels through the hallway, and between curtained partitions to the section where Gary Hoffman stood ready to rescue her—if he could.

Phillip Trapp stood ready with his specimen tray as they rushed her in. They had called him in on his day off to cover a lab staff shortage. And then they'd called him to the ER to stand by to draw blood on an arriving cardiac patient as soon as they'd got her stabilized. And now he saw her and knew it was a sign! Dr. Broward had fallen into his hands. She lay gasping and clutching her chest behind the drawn curtain. He heard Dr. Hoffman call out, "She going into arrest!"

Her heart was sputtering! And Dr. Hoffman would have to shock it into life again, get the bee-beep, bee-beep, bee-beep on the monitor synchronized again.

Phillip smiled as he heard the order to defibrillate. In the space between the curtain and the floor, he could see the cardiac team's white clad legs dance around the pallet. He reveled at the rhythmic sounds of their motions as they drew around her, clapping the leads to her chest; his heart sang to the music of the hurried commands to send the electric surge through her chest again and again; he exulted as her body convulsed with a thud against her pallet each time the switch was thrown.

Thud! Rest—Thud! Rest—Thud—and then an agonized simultaneous deep breath by the team and a long—endless—electronic whine.

"Shall we try one more time, Gary?"

"No. Let her go. Goddamn it! We tried, Liz. Goddamn it to hell, we lost you!"

Someone switched off the cardiac monitor, silenced its cry.

One by one the team members came out from behind the curtain, their faces ashen and drawn. Dr. Hoffman remained behind, then came out, his lips grimly pursed. Phillip would not have recognized him if he had not known who he was. His dark hair, usually perfectly combed, looked as though he'd been trying to tear it out. He probably had, Phillip gloated to himself. His face was crumpled and gray. Phillip could barely keep his glee from showing. It was Phillip, not the doctor, who would soon have Dr. Broward's heart. His mind was racing, trying to come up with a plan to get it.

Dr. Hoffman looked up at him. His mouth flew open, as if he was flabbergasted at seeing Phillip. Then he said, "Forget the blood samples. She's dead." He walked halfway across the room, then suddenly turned toward Phillip again and came back. "Aren't you the technician that sometimes works in pathology?"

"Yes," said Phillip.

"They're short today. We'll need to do a post on Dr. Broward. After we notify her family, we'll call up to Diagnostic for you. Maybe you can help Dr. Morgan with the autopsy."

The doctor's words clamped around Phillip's chest and shocked his heart to pounding. He nodded, feigning sorrow, but joy thudded in his head.

The doctor walked out between the rows of curtained emergency bed cubicles. Phillip dawdled awhile, playing with his cart of sample tubes, hoping for the chance to look in at Dr. Broward when no one as watching. For some time, nurses and medics and patients came in and out every few seconds. Then the triage nurse, a tall, stately woman with blue-green eyes, appeared from the outer room, swept quickly by him, drew back the curtain, and entered Dr. Broward's cubicle.

"Oh, Holy Jesus Christ! Jesus! I can't believe my eyes. Liz Broward!" She raised her hand to her face, then tentatively touched the face of the corpse and drew back with a gasp.

Phillip stepped through the open curtain just as the nurse drew away. She backed into him, turned, and cried out. "You! What are you doing here!"

"I came to draw blood. I know her."

"Don't leer at her then!"

"I'm not leering. Just looking. They want me to help with the post."

"Cold! How can you be so cold?" She burst into tears and shoved past him.

He stared after her a second, trying to hide his pleasure at having shocked her. Then he looked at Dr. Broward's face—a face with no tawny glow, a face with the waxy film of death already settled on the high cheek bones and the haughty, arched bridge of the nose. The eyes had turned back into the head, stared perhaps into the skull. He reached over and closed them, and smiled.

She smiled back at him and he saw her teeth were already growing.

Phillip jumped back. He didn't need to see any more. He returned to the diagnostic lab and waited for a call from Pathology.

The call came at seven P.M., three hours after Phillip's regular shift was supposed to have ended. Earlier, he thought they might have forgotten to call him. Communications in hospitals often slipped, especially in cases like these where he'd been given the assignment informally while making his rounds.

The moment his shift was over, he'd gone down to the morgue to see what the holdup was. No one was there. He'd checked the census pad, and found that Dr. Broward was in drawer Five C. Chuckling, because he recalled that he had suffocated his first vampire there, he'd pulled the drawer open. The cold air had seeped out and created a breeze around him. Once more he had seen her face, now set and still, except for her mouth, which had parted when he'd looked at her, and showed its fangs. A toxic vapor had curled from between its lips. Sharply, he'd shoved the drawer to.

"Oh, yes, Trapp," a voice from behind him had said, "I'm running late."

He whirled and saw Dr. Morgan, the pathologist, in his heavy rubber apron.

"I've been doing tissue sections all day. Couldn't get to this post earlier. We're terribly short this weekend."

"Are you ready for her now, Doctor?"

"Actually, no. Neither logistically nor emotionally. I find it hard to face working on a colleague."

"I'm sorry."

"Nothing can be done about it. At any rate, I've a little more work to do. Gives me a chance to put off the inevitable." He'd smiled wryly. "Why don't you go up to Diagnostic for a little while. I'm sorry to keep you waiting. I know you're already putting in overtime."

"I don't mind. I want to help you."

"Well it shouldn't be long. I'll have you called when I'm about to start."

It seemed very long indeed. Her fangs were already growing. But Phillip was out of danger as long as she remained in the drawer, where the chill would retard both her movements and regeneration. The fact that she'd died of a heart attack was in his favor. The heart would have to heal completely before her full transformation could occur. Still, he was edgy and excited, and dove for the lab phone every time it rang. Then, at last—

When he arrived at the steel autopsy table, the pathologist already had her open and had removed and bisected the heart.

"You took long enough to get here, Trapp. I called for you forty-five minutes ago."

"But the call just came."

The man stared coldly at him. "I told you I dreaded doing this. Not only did I have no help, I had no one for moral support."

"I came as soon as they—"

"Of course! The asshole we have on the desk has been fouling things up all day. This has been one shitty day, Trapp. From start to finish." He took a large slash at the heart, and opened the left chamber, and ran his gloved thumb along the inner walls, inspecting as he went. "Here's the bastard, Trapp. A lousy infarction. What a shitty thing to happen."

"Yes, Doctor."

"I can't bear this. That's it. We know what took her. Why look for anything else. I'm not going into the cranium. If she had a stroke, too, so what? This puppy here was enough!" He set down his knife beside the bisected heart. "Take over, Trapp. Hose her out and sew her up and get her back into the drawer." He moved to the head of the table and looked down at Dr. Broward's face.

"You sure were a beauty, Liz." And he bent and kissed the forehead of the corpse.

Phillip started forward. "Don't! Watch out!"

Dr. Morgan stared at Phillip for a moment, then shook his head, tore off his gloves, tossed them down on the table. "Be sure to put the heart back in before you close her." He began to sob and then left.

How could the fool have kissed her! Couldn't he see that the mouth was opening again, and that two long fangs had begun to protrude?

Phillip's hands trembled as he pulled on a pair of latex gloves and grasped the heart, which was starting to beat, its two halves writhing toward each other, its severed valves flapping like bat wings. He would join them together, all right. He picked up the dissecting knife and pinioned the heart halves together. They fluttered a moment, then stopped.

That done, he looked at her face again. The mouth lost its courage; the fangs withdrew.

Now he had no time to lose. The knife had no silver on it and might be less effective. He had to get the heart back home. There he'd been keeping the girl busy, he thought with a malicious grin. She'd already plated one blade, and he'd told her that she must have a second done by the time he got home tonight. He would bring her a great surprise! She could impale Dr. Broward's heart with those small, delicate hands of hers.

"Ah, and I have a surprise for you, too, Adolph," he said as he removed the liver and set it next to the heart.

Then he washed away as much contaminated blood as possible, closed Dr. Broward's chest and abdomen, delighting in each stab he made with the needle—for he knew she felt pain even more now than when she was alive—and moved her at last to the pallet and from there back into drawer Five C. He put her heart and liver into a black plastic sack and went out the rear service exit to his van.

Meanwhile—Zack

At eight P.M. sharp, Zack, suspended in agony in his Ram behind the hospital, saw Trapp leave the building through the rear service exit. Zack had expected that; the man had long before moved his black van to a loading slot just outside the door, and the timing was just about right. What he hadn't expected was that the man was not pushing a gurney with a body on it through the dark shadows of late evening. He had only a small plastic sack, which he held at length from his body as he walked. He opened the van's tailgate and climbed in. Zack could not see what Trapp was doing, but he emerged a minute later without the package, closed the door, and went around to the front of the vehicle where he stood and stared up for a moment at the reddening sky.

A red sunset in Philadelphia was rare, worth watching. Phillip stared at where the glow was coming from, behind a row of tall buildings to the *east*. Yes! It was the *east* the glow came from, from the edge of a bright disk wheeling up over the buildings, climbing into the sky. The moon stained the whole sky red, for the moon had turned to blood.

Zack grasped the steering wheel and fought off the fury that flared in him. He could grab the bastard now and crush his voice box with a single choke hold. But Crosby and his goddamn rule book said that's not the way to do it. You had to prove the guy really had Poke before you could move on him. They knew he had her, they just hadn't been able to prove it, and the only way you could was to get into his house. To trick your way in just as they were doing. But it looked like things were going wrong already. Maybe Trapp hadn't fallen for the first part of Liz's plot.

Trapp started his engine and ran it for a few seconds, then the van backed out, turned, and slowly left the service lot.

As it disappeared around the corner, the woman he was expecting came running out of the service door, wearing black and carrying a large Woodward and Lothrop shopping bag. He opened a rear door and she climbed in quickly. She flashed him a grim smile and a short nod as she climbed in and sat.

"It's all right," she said in an oddly strained voice. "He didn't take the body, just the heart."

"You were right then, Liz," he said. He reached out to touch her hand. "And you made it all right. You are all right, aren't you?"

"As good as can be expected." She nodded. "Let's go."

He closed the door and jumped into the front seat and backed out of the slot, his eyes seeking hers in his rearview mirror. He needed to find the courage they usually held. They flashed an icy green fright instead—like emeralds instead of amethysts—as they caught the light from a yellowish spotlight mounted over the hospital door. *My God! What's she put herself through!*

"You're not all right, are you? What happened in there?"

"I don't feel very good. It's been harder than I thought."

He took his eyes off her and started the van forward. "Liz, I was so worried," he said, his concern for her momentarily distracting him from his rage at Trapp.

After a brief hesitation, she said, "Well, that part's over. He went for it. Now we have to bring this part off. That's not going to be easy. We found out from a neighbor of his that the dog is monstrously vicious. It tore another neighborhood dog apart."

"That bastard! That rotten bastard! Leaving Poke there with that dog! I wish you hadn't said it. Shit!"

"I'm sorry. I didn't think. But we have to be ready for the worst."

He turned his anger on himself. "Shit! You've been through a lot. You don't even sound like yourself. I shouldn't've hollered at you."

He heard her draw a breath. Then she said, "I don't feel like myself either. I wonder why I went along with this—"

He glanced at the mirror again. She was slumped, an uncharacteristic pout on her lips, her eyes glittering wildly as they passed beneath streetlights. He turned his eyes toward the street again and said, "You went along with it because of Poke. In fact, you didn't just go along, you planned the whole thing out."

"Of course. Look, we shouldn't be talking at all. It's not very far. I have to get ready." She leaned down and the shopping bag rattled. He could hear her removing its contents. "I hope I can do it right."

"I can help you with it. Did you practice?"

"Most of it. But it's not my usual getup."

"Hmmph, he thinks it is."

"I know. I saw his face when he leered at her."

He was stunned. *"Leered at her?"*

"The body on the autopsy table. We watched on the monitor.

The one they use for medical students and doctors to observe dissections."

"How can you watch that stuff?" He shuddered. "It's hard for me to imagine you doing some of the things that doctors have to do."

"My ER training helped. I do what I have to, I guess. That's what got me into this thing to begin with." She leaned forward. "Isn't this his street? Where's his van?"

"I cased the neighborhood this morning. There's an alley behind with garages. He probably went in the back way. You ready yet?"

"Drive around the block one time. I'm all but ready."

He had to drive around twice before she said, "OK."

He stopped the van and turned and looked at her. "Perfect!" he said. "I think your plan is going to work, Liz. We're going to trap that monster and get Poke back. I know it! Thank you, thank you my dear, dear person for doing all this for Poke and me."

"I'm doing it for Liz," she said. "I wouldn't do it for anyone else."

What a strange thing for her to do! Talk about herself as if she weren't there. As he turned now and looked into her glittering eyes, he was sorry he'd let her put herself through what she had. But, she, after all, had chosen it. It had worked so far, and Lieutenant Crosby and Cheney were sitting in a black unmarked car across the street, waiting for her and him to go up and knock on the door of the hovering town house with the light in the attic window. They had to get on with the rest of it. He'd make amends to Liz later. "OK," he said. "You go up and knock. I'll stand right off to the side of the door where he won't be able to see me."

He got out and opened the door for her; she got out, and without so much as squeezing his hand walked slowly and deliberately to the steps leading up to the stoop. She stopped for a moment and turned her frightened eyes on him, then quickly turned away from him and mounted the steps.

He mounted the stoop after her and then flattened his body against the house next to the door. He was frightened for her, frightened for Poke, and bristling with anger at Trapp. With every cell mobilized to take the man down, he nodded at her. "Knock!" he said. "And keep on knocking till you bring the door down if you have to."

But he knew it wasn't her knock that would draw Trapp to the door. To count on that was taking too much of a chance, and Liz had left nothing to chance in her wild, terrifying plan to free Zack's daughter, the worst of which was yet to come.

He saw her waver a moment before knocking three times on the door.

Poke wavered a moment before touching the heart on the metalworking table in front of her.

"Hssst! Do it, now! There's no time to wait. It must be the silvered blade!"

She'd plated it heavily today, because rubbing the blade had helped her stop crying and start thinking. She had thought about attacking the dog with it, but he was so large and fierce, she knew she would stand no chance. Phillip had promised Adolph would not attack her unless he ordered it, or the dog felt threatened, or she tried to escape. As long as she made no sudden moves, and stayed up here in the attic, she would be safe. There was nothing much to do here, except polish the blade. She had no appetite for the food he'd left her—some rancid cheese that even the dog turned away from when she offered it, thinking that food might bribe some friendship from him.

But now there was this, the heart on the table, two halves lopsidedly joined together by a razor-sharp knife. A vampire's heart, he had said. *Dr. Broward's heart.* She couldn't do it. She couldn't touch it.

But Adolph had growled and strained at his leash, and Phillip had relaxed his grip on it slightly.

She reached out and touched it. It felt rubbery, much like the heart of the deer she'd once helped her father clean and dress. A little smaller than that, and the deer heart had not been cut open and Poke had not felt the same way about touching it. She thought for a moment of the day she'd invited Dr. Broward to come hunting with her and Pop. She'd said she couldn't shoot an animal, not for any moral reasons, but just because she couldn't. And now Poke was touching her heart and would have to put a knife in it. A knife Poke herself had plated.

"Hssst! Pick up the knife, Jill."

"I'll take the other one out first."

"No! We can't take a chance. She may already be regenerating. Evil has so many ways—"

Adolph whined suddenly and turned and pulled toward the attic door.

"Stay!"

The dog growled and tugged at the leash, and whined again as his master would not give him rein.

"What is the matter with you!" Then he cocked his ear. "Someone knocking? Ignore it. They'll go away. They always do. You know that, Adolph. Hsst!"

Then he turned his attention to Poke again, who stood with the plated knife just above the heart. "Bring it straight down with all your strength. Aim for a spot that will slice through both sides so it doesn't split apart. It must remain together."

Poke felt vomit beginning to creep up inside her throat. She knew that Dr. Broward was already dead, since this was her heart. But she knew at the same time she was killing her again. Poke would always think she had killed her if she plunged this knife through her heart, because for a while she had hated her for sleeping with her father. Still, she lifted the knife higher, and held onto it with both cold, sweaty hands, and took a deep breath and closed her eyes.

Then a voice came from the heart on the table. "Answer the door!" it said.

Poke stood with the knife frozen between her hands.

"You made a mistake, Phillip," the heart said. "You've failed with the total cure. I'm in agony at the door. Answer it. I want to be cured. I did not choose this eternal damnation. It was thrust on me by Satan. And only you can cure me. But you've made a terrible slip."

"Aargh!" cried Phillip.

The dog strained at his leash as the knocks at the door grew more insistent and frantic.

"Dr. Broward!" cried Poke. Dr. Broward was speaking

through her heart! She dropped the knife, and it rattled from the table to the floor.

Phillip stiffened and the veins that brought color to his face seemed to drain and leave it whiter than ever.

"Pick it up! I knew the other wouldn't hold. Pick it up and drive it through her."

Poke fell to her knees and began to crawl under the table for the knife.

The heart kept talking, begging Phillip to come downstairs and let her in.

He cried out in an agonized voice, *"Never mind!"* He dove for the table and grabbed at the heart, but it slipped from his hands and fell to the floor, still talking, still begging.

It slid across the room and Adolph grabbed it in his teeth, and the dissecting knife came loose and the two sections separated.

"No, Adolph, you fool. It's her heart! It's for me!"

The dog whined, and the still talking piece of heart fell from his mouth.

Phillip dove for it and picked it up. He carefully grasped the section with the dissecting knife still in it. "Now!" he cried to Poke. "Give me the other knife."

She crawled from under the table with the silvered knife in one hand. Then she slid it across the floor to Phillip, who fell to his own knees, placed the heart on the floor, and grabbed the knife and impaled the heart with such force that the blade drove into the floorboards. Then he pulled out the dissecting knife and slid it away toward Poke.

"Please, come cure me," the heart pled on. "Help me. I want to die!"

He covered his face for a moment as Poke crawled toward him and the heart. He spun toward her just as her knee touched the handle of the dissecting knife.

"Aaugh! Get up!" he cried to her. Then, to Adolph, "Downstairs!"

In that moment his head was turned again, her hand clasped the steel knife handle and she stumbled to her feet. She knew this was some kind of trick. Someone had figured out a way to get her away from Phillip.

Suddenly he looked at her again, just as she hid her hands behind her. The look on his face had changed and he smiled. "She wants me to cure her. She probably thinks it will make me give you back to your father. But it's too late for that, you know. She's already bitten him. Already infected him. We won't release you until after we've cured him, too."

"No! Daddy!"

"But meanwhile you must watch while we cure Dr. Broward once and for all. Adolph is very hungry now. And he's taken down vampires before. In fact, he is still enjoying the last one. He gets everything but the heart, you know. The heart is for me. Come down!"

Poke looked at his crazy eyes, and then at the dog's crazy eyes, and then at the heart, which still spoke in Dr. Broward's voice from the floor. She wanted to cry out to the doctor that she would not let Adolph hurt her or her father, but she needed every ounce of strength and courage just to follow Adolph and Phillip down the stairs without letting Phillip see the knife in her hand. If Dr. Broward was at the door, then this was not her heart. And she'd come to save Poke. And she would help Poke stab the dog and get away. She cried, "OK!" And they all went downstairs to the front door.

Phillip opened it just as She was knocking again, and She nearly lost her balance. When She regained it, he saw Her and gasped. For a moment he wanted to back away, but he knew that Adolph would keep Her from touching him if She tried; so he opened the door wide.

She opened Her mouth and showed Her long fangs. Already there was blood on them. She must have feasted on innocents along the way. That was what had nourished Her, kept Her going as he'd stabbed away at Her heart. He had known all along She was more than an ordinary vampire, and it would take extravagant means to finish Her off. But he was startled at Her quick regeneration. Her face was exactly as he'd last seen it in the morgue, its waxy undeadness magnified by the terrifying blaze in Her eyes. Her undead fingers had clawed up and grown long, brilliant red nails. She lifted one to Her mouth now and sucked it. "Cure me!" She cried, "before I infect another soul. I can't help myself. Only you can cure me."

"Come in. The cure will take only moments." He backed away from the door and She stepped in.

Suddenly She lunged at him and knocked him backward. "Now, Adolph!" he shouted as he caught his balance and pushed her away.

Zack flew through the open door as the dog lunged for her. He caught the leaping animal's shoulder with his own. The blow deflected the huge dog only enough to miss her throat; but his claw slashed at her just below her ear, and ripped away part of her face. She screamed and grabbed her face in her hands.

"Daddy!" cried Poke. She began to run toward him.

"No! Poke! Stay back!"

"Get Jill, Adolph!"

The dog roared and leapt at Poke. She raised her hands and screamed as he flew at her. Zack could do nothing to deflect him, as the animal was between him and his daughter.

At that moment, Crosby and Cheney burst into the alcove. Zack heard the thud as the dog knocked Poke down, and he dove at the beast's massive shoulders. Blood was spurting out from beneath the enraged monster. Zack beat him on his muzzle, then tore open his jaws until he let go of Poke's arm, then, cried to Cheney to shoot the dog's rear legs.

Cheney's aim was true, and the dog howled and pulled away from Poke.

"The medics are right outside," said Cheney to Zack.

Zack bent forward over Poke, who was covered with blood and unconscious. He could tell her arm was broken, but couldn't tell where most of the blood was coming from. With tears running down his face, he moved the broken arm gently to rest on her chest, then lifted her.

He heard a clanking noise and looked down. A bloody dissection knife lay at his feet. It had fallen from her other hand. *Thank God she had taken after him!*

He carried her out to the medics.

They took her from him, and rushed her into the ambulance.

From inside he heard a pair of gunshots and a woman's scream. "Liz!" he cried. He had forgotten Liz, her face ripped away by the dog the moment before the beast had attacked Poke.

He ran back into the house. The dog lay dead and bleeding at Cheney's feet; Trapp lay bleeding at Crosby's feet, and Liz stood trembling against the wall, her hands covering her face—and not bleeding at all.

When he ran up to her and gasped, she uncovered her face. Half of it looked fine, but the other half fell loose and hung from her jaw. She looked up at him and reached one hand up to her face, and peeled the rest of it away.

"Dear God! You're not Liz!" he cried. "What went wrong? Who are you? What happened to her?"

She touched his face gently and said, "I'll go back with you to the hospital and you can see her."

CHAPTER FOURTEEN

Two hours later

He saw her in repose, so still, so silent that he was afraid to touch her. For a few moments he let his eyes dwell on her and drink in the shape of her face, the soft fall of her thick, tawny hair against the pillow, so that he could never forget her quiet dignity, and the gift of supreme courage she had given him.

"Oh, Liz," he said at last, and bent to kiss her closed eyes. "Why didn't you tell me? I'd never have to let you do it if I'd known."

Her eyelids moved at the touch of his lips. One hand reached for his. The other, with the IV attached, raised slightly. She barely opened her eyes. "Zack?"

"It's me, Liz."

She seemed to have trouble forming a smile, though her eyes opened almost completely. Her attempt at a grip slid off of his hand. "Poke?"

Picking up her hand and holding it to his lips, he said, "She's doing OK. We got her. Your idea worked."

She nodded against the pillow, then closed her eyes again.

After a moment he laid her hand down, squeezed it lightly, and left the room.

Jennie was standing in the door, still staring at Liz and shaking her head.

In the van on the way to the hospital, after they'd learned that the blood on Poke had come from the dog, she had told him her feelings about what had happened with Liz.

"The awful part was seeing her face on that body in the ER.

I never expected it would look so real—her face, I mean. I knew up here," she pointed to her head, "that it wasn't really Liz. But, God!" She shuddered and closed her eyes and clenched her hands in her lap.

Zack glanced at her as he drove. She looked nothing like Liz now that she'd peeled off the mask and wig. Her hair was lighter than Liz's, her nose shorter and straight, her cheekbones less pronounced. Her blue eyes were three shades lighter than Liz's and had a touch of green. Yet before, on the way to Trapp's house, he'd interpreted their icy glitter as fear. He'd been fooled by the handiwork of plastic surgeon Brian Horner who'd created the mask and its underpinnings from Zack's three-dimensional computer model of Liz. "Yeah," he said. "I can see how you'd feel."

"I knew they'd moved Liz to the next cubicle, and that the Donnatal had kicked in and stopped her heart spasms. I knew the whole defib routine had been faked, that the corpse was a woman who'd died in the ER a few hours before. But I wasn't prepared for that!

"Then, that monster came in and stared at her. His mouth was watering. He closed her eyes, and then jumped back as if he was afraid of her. I knew she was right, he was completely delusional. He didn't just think she was a vampire, he actually saw her starting to come back to life. I was so scared to death about facing him for the second part of the plan, but I knew Liz would never be able to do it. The phenobarb in the Donnatal was depressing her. Gary'd put her on a respirator for a few hours just in case and the IVs helped move it out of her system. But there was no way she'd be awake enough soon enough. So I just had to do it."

"She never told me it'd be so dangerous. She said one drug would counteract the other and she'd be fine and she'd see me in the van." He followed the ambulance into the emergency lot.

"We all knew it wouldn't be quite so easy. I was part of the plan from the beginning. Brian Horner made two masks. He tried one on me last night, and I looked in the mirror and it was eerie. But I laughed and thought how neat it would be to dress up in it and put in the fangs. I knew it would be scary, but after four years in ER, I don't scare easily. But that was before I saw him working on that corpse.

"I could tell he thought she was coming back to life by the way he kept looking at her face. When the pathologist kissed her forehead, he looked horrified and afraid and shouted at him to be careful. As soon as Dr. Morgan left, he grabbed the heart and impaled it on the dissecting knife—the one Poke stabbed the dog with." She looked at Zack as he drove into a parking space and pulled on the hand brake. "He cut out her liver before sewing her up. For the dog. He said it was a surprise for the dog."

Zack bit down nausea. "Thanks for not telling me that before."

"I was imagining all sorts of things, but I wouldn't tell you. Believe me, I was awfully relieved when I saw Poke standing there. At that minute I stopped caring what happened to me, as long as she was OK."

He leaned over and kissed her. "Thanks for making sure she would be. Let's go in. I want to be there when they take her to the OR."

It was only after Poke had come out of surgery, her forearm bone set and splinted in a cast, the small lacerations on her shoulder cleaned and bandaged, and he knew for certain she was otherwise physically unharmed, that he'd left her in the recovery room and gone to see Liz. Jennie had waited outside the door and now looked at him with wonder as he came out.

"I still can't get over it," she said. "I wonder if I ever will. How did you do that on your computer? How did you make her so perfect? It's as if you re-created her."

"You got it all backward, Jennie," he said, "She re-created me."

EPILOGUE

Six weeks later, in Liz Broward's office

Zack felt awkward being called in like this, but she hadn't wanted to come to his house just yet. She said Poke wasn't ready, considering what she'd been through. She especially wouldn't be ready for Liz, who was tied up in her mind with all the horror she'd been through.

And Zack knew Liz was right about that. That their love affair had been wounded deeply, though their love itself had strengthened and would outlast the wounds. She could not come into his house when Poke was there, and he could not leave Poke alone for the night. He'd stopped working late, and did many pieces at home on his computer, sending them by modem to the office. And he'd come to enjoy that routine.

He didn't enjoy communicating with Liz only by phone, though. As often as they spoke, speaking was never enough. He wanted to touch her, even if he couldn't sleep with her. But neither could take off time from work to meet for even a few hours during the day. Sometimes even their short phone conversations were interrupted, except for those he made late at night after Poke was asleep. And those made their mutual longing worse.

The previous day she phoned him at work and said, "Zack, tell Ted Squire you have to see your doctor tomorrow. Say she found something on a test that needs follow-up."

"I hope it's nothing serious," he said, mildly alarmed.

"Don't worry. It's self-limiting. But tell him I insist you come in without delay and I promise you won't miss any more work." Her voice had sounded almost playful, and he judged that her sole reason for calling him in was that it was the only way they could see each other. Few bosses could argue with a doctor's order; and a doctor could arrange for fairly complete privacy in her office.

"Sure, Doc," he said.

"First thing in the morning," she said.

He'd barely been able to sleep for excitement, but he found himself feeling awkward in her waiting room, and still more awkward as Claire called him back and left his chart on Liz's desk. One thing doctors didn't have control of was emergencies. One had relegated Zack into second place this morning, and that made him feel very out of place here. He was not only not sick, he had lied to his boss to get here. At least he thought he had lied. And he thought he wasn't sick. But the longer he sat and looked at his chart on her desk, the more he wondered if she'd sounded not serious to keep him from worrying about something he should be worried about.

He stood up and reached across the desk for his record and flipped through it to his most recent visit.

He heard the office door close softly.

"You won't find anything in there," she said, coming up behind him and snatching the record from him. "Even if you could figure out what all those arcane abbreviations mean." She put the chart down on her desk. The efficient doctor look on her face slid off.

"Dear God, how I've missed you, Zack!" she said. She stood still for a moment then lifted her hand.

He caught it and pulled her to him. "This was a mistake, Liz. How can I go back to work now?" He held her and did not dare kiss her.

"I had to see you. Even if only for a few minutes."

"Do you usually torture your patients?"

She laughed and ran her hand through his hair and rested her fingers for a moment on his face. "Only when they torture me." She kissed him briefly, then with obvious reluctance, pulled herself away. Sitting in her chair, she smoothed her hair and her soft deep blue knit dress.

He couldn't take his eyes off hers, till she dipped them away.

At last she said, "Sit down, Zack. I really do have something important to tell you."

He sat. "Real medical stuff?"

"Not exactly. Just sort of." She smiled an unreadable smile.

"What does that mean?"

"Well, we doctors like to get involved in things that are only tangentially medical. It makes us feel important to be in on some of life's greatest mysteries." Her smile broadened.

"Liz—"

"I'm pregnant," she said.

"Oh, Liz."

"You know I couldn't tell you on the phone. I thought I'd tell you where most doctors like to tell their pregnant patients. Only this time I'm telling the father first."

He wanted very much to swallow, but he couldn't. In fact, he couldn't move.

She came around her desk and sat on the corner and leaned forward and stroked his face. "I worried that taking those overdoses would keep it from taking. But the embryo must have been on its way, not yet attached to my uterus. A day longer, a day sooner, and things would probably have been different."

"I'm so happy, Liz." He grabbed her hand and kissed it, kissed her wrist, kissed her all the way up the arm, then stood and hugged her as hard as he dared, knowing what was inside her.

"I am, too. I love you, Zack."

"When are we going to get married? We have to get married."

She released her hold on him. "That'll have to wait for a while."

"Wait! For what?"

"Partly for Poke. She's going to need a lot more counseling before I move into her house."

"Partly—?"

"Partly because I'm not sure I want to be married."

"Not sure!"

She looked at him and then turned away for just a moment. When she turned back he saw her face reflected the pain in his.

"I love you," she said. "More than that, I'm wildly in love with you. Physically I want you so much I sometimes can't bear it. That's part of why I'm not sure. But I'm not naive enough to think that not getting married will make that last longer. Either way it's not going to last forever."

"You're talking crazy!" He pressed his fists against her desk.

"Maybe. I feel a little crazy. But all of this, what happened, has made me realize that I was never sure I wanted to get married. I wanted a baby. When I realized how much I loved you, I wanted your baby. I will always love you and your baby—and Poke, too—very, very much. Whether or not we do get married."

He did not doubt her love for him and Poke. She'd risked her life for them. That truth, and the held-out possibility in that "whether or not," kept him whole in this moment that threatened to tear him apart. He sat down, head pounding, wanting to cry.

She came to him and stooped and gathered his face in her hands. "Zack, I'm sorry. I didn't mean it to be this way. I'm a proper lady from a very proper family that looks very much askance at women who have babies out of wedlock. The decision wasn't easy for me." She kissed him full on the mouth and stood up. She walked to her window and looked out, then turned toward him again and laughed ironically.

"I'll probably be the first black sheep in the Stanford and Broward families."

He stood and looked hard at her, at those amethyst eyes that twinkled through her tears and his, at that wonderful patrician nose, the golden-hued skin stretched to just the right tension over the high cheekbones, at the graceful, long fingers and perfectly oval, perfectly manicured nails. He had wanted to re-create her beauty, to keep it for himself, and he almost had. And looking at her body and knowing what grew inside it, he thought, *Maybe not almost, maybe our baby is a girl.*

He walked over to her and touched her waist, then touched her chin and tilted it back. "You, dear person, are full of shit! You still don't know anything about your family. If you did, you'd realize you've probably got dozens of black sheep cousins out there that never made it into the family histories in your church."

She laughed. "You really think so, Zack?"

"Damn right. And now that they're going to be my kid's cousins, too, I'm going to find out who they are and where they lived and everything I can about them."

"Oh, Zack! Can I help you do that?"

"It might mean some travel. Lots of black sheep went west back in the Civil War days. And I know my great-grandfolks lived in Arizona. So we'd have to go back there. Yeah, you can come along if you want."

"You're damned right I want to. Won't it be fun, Zack! Won't it be a wonderful adventure!"

Oh, yes! he thought. *Oh yes!*

Any time lived with Liz Broward anywhere in the world would be a wonderful adventure indeed!

Chilling National Bestsellers by
New York Times *Bestselling Author*

ROBIN COOK

__HARMFUL INTENT 0-425-12546-7/$5.99
When an innocent doctor is charged with malpractice and harmful intent, he follows the deadly trail of the real murderer in a desperate attempt to prove his innocence.

__VITAL SIGNS 0-425-13176-9/$5.99
Dr. Marissa Blumenthal's dream of becoming pregnant has turned into an obsession. A successful pediatrician, she will try any scientific method available to conceive. Until the horrible secrets of an urban clinic erupt in a nightmare of staggering proportions.

__BLINDSIGHT 0-425-13619-1/$5.99
Under a haunting aura of suspense, forensic pathologist Dr. Laurie Montgomery discovers a darkly corrupt scheme of murder, high-level cover-ups, and inescapable fear.

Look for *Terminal*
A Berkley paperback coming in February 1994

Payable in U.S. funds. No cash orders accepted. Postage & handling: $1.75 for one book, 75¢ for each additional. Maximum postage $5.50. Prices, postage and handling charges may change without notice. Visa, Amex, MasterCard call 1-800-788-6262, ext. 1, refer to ad # 433

Or, check above books and send this order form to:	Bill my: ☐ Visa ☐ MasterCard ☐ Amex (expires)
The Berkley Publishing Group 390 Murray Hill Pkwy., Dept. B East Rutherford, NJ 07073	Card#_____ ($15 minimum) Signature_____
Please allow 6 weeks for delivery.	Or enclosed is my: ☐ check ☐ money order
Name_____	Book Total $_____
Address_____	Postage & Handling $_____
City_____	Applicable Sales Tax $_____ (NY, NJ, CA, GST Can.)
State/ZIP_____	Total Amount Due $_____